Susan R. Sloan is a former attorney who lives on an island in Puget Sound. This is her fourth novel. Visit her website at www.sloanbooks.com.

Also by Susan R. Sloan

Guilt by Association
An Isolated Incident
Act of God

Susan R. Sloan

BEHIND CLOSED DOORS

A *Time Warner* Paperback

First published in the United States in 2003 by Warner Books
First published in Great Britain in 2004 by Time Warner Books
This edition published by Time Warner Paperbacks in 2005

A CIP catalogue record for this book
is available from the British Library.

ISBN 0 7515 3562 1

Typeset by Palimpsest Book Production Limited,
Polmont, Stirlingshire
Printed and bound in Great Britain by
Clays Ltd, St Ives plc

Time Warner Paperbacks
An imprint of
Time Warner Book Group UK
Brettenham House
Lancaster Place
London WC2E 7EN

www.twbg.co.uk

For Ron Montana . . .
who convinced me that I could do it.

Acknowledgments

As always, I thank my agent, Esther Newberg. I am indebted to Pamela and Peter Teige and Dan and Nancy Mack, who were always there with the right information whenever I needed it. To Bob Arnold, whose research efforts were enormous. To John and Virginia Hilden, who gave me Seattle. To Bruce Nitsche, M.D., and Cathy Greenawalt, R.N., who were there to handle all my medical questions. And to Susan Roth of the Author's Edge, whose input, as always, was invaluable.

June 2000

A hush settled over the fourth-floor courtroom, the kind of hush that always came at the end of a trial, before the verdict, when the frantic battle of adversaries was over, and there was nothing left to do but wait.

The San Mateo County Hall of Justice was a utilitarian building, with none of the warmth or charm or history of the Old Courthouse next door, which had been turned into a museum. The courtrooms in the new eight-story structure were functional, not grand, making the justice meted out in them seem more mechanical than traditional.

On one side of the bar in this particular courtroom, four rows of flip-down upholstered seats accommodated spectators to the show. On the other side, the bench, backed by the state seal and flanked by American and California flags, was impressive in its size, but unremarkable in its design. The jury box held twelve well-padded armchairs. Behind the bar, the floor was linoleum. In front of the bar, it was carpeted. All the walls were paneled. All the wood was mahogany. Everything else was gray.

For reasons of security or privacy or both, the room was windowless. Recessed into the ceiling was a huge bank of fluorescent lights. Two thirds of the lights had been turned off, and court personnel were quietly removing all traces of the proceeding that had just been concluded – charts, documents, photographs, pieces of

3

evidence, put into cartons and carried out. The jury box and the spectator seats had long since emptied.

Valerie O'Connor Marsh sat quietly at the defense table, a polished mahogany rectangle just inside the bar, in a simple gray dress that almost matched the color of her hair, and the color of the courtroom. It was a few minutes past three o'clock on a Thursday afternoon in early June, and there was no real reason for her to be sitting there, she knew. It could be hours, or even days, before the jury decided her fate. There was a little room just down the hall from this one, where she could wait in privacy with her attorney and her family. Or she could even go home. The court clerk would notify her attorney when the time came, and he would notify her. But it was as if the mere act of standing up was too much for her even to contemplate.

The past four days had left her drained, drained and curiously detached. Not unlike the way she had felt that night in the kitchen, almost eight months ago. A night that now seemed a lifetime away, and in many ways was, because it marked the end of the life that Valerie had lived for almost forty-four of her sixty-two years, and the beginning of the life that she would live from then on.

It wasn't the verdict that worried her, because she had no control over that. Her fate was in God's hands. Well, God and a dozen men and women she had never laid eyes on until last week. No, of far more concern to her was how she would ever be able to hold her head up in her small, coastal community . . . now that everyone knew.

Valerie had pleaded with her attorney not to go to trial, to make some deal with the district attorney, but he had been adamant, assuring her that they could win. Only, in his effort to save her, he had thrown open the door to her most private life and shone a harsh light into every corner, for everyone to see. And it had been so unbearable for her to sit there, helplessly, as every agonizing moment of her life with Jack was played out in front of strangers, that the only way she could get through it was to pretend that he was talking about some other person and some other family that had nothing to do with her.

But, of course, it did. She saw the looks she got from the people in the courtroom, read the accounts of the trial in the daily newspaper, watched the recaps on the local television channels, and her face grew hot with embarrassment. If suicide had not been a mortal sin, she knew she would have put an end to her life sooner than sit there in such anguish.

'Tell me, Mrs Marsh, had your husband ever beaten anyone to death before the night of October 26?' The prosecutor's strident voice echoed in her ears.

Valerie had held in her anger. 'Not that I know of,' she said.

'Then why did you think he was going to that night?' Valerie had not replied. She simply sat there and glared at the man. 'Your Honor, will you please instruct the witness to answer the question?'

'Mrs Marsh,' the judge said, kindly enough. 'You must answer the question.'

'I don't know, I wasn't sure,' she was forced to say, her fists clenched so tightly in her lap that her finger-nails cut little half moons into the palms of her hands. 'But my husband was a violent man, and when he was drinking, there was no way of knowing what he might do. I couldn't take the chance.'

'What chance couldn't you take, Mrs Marsh?' the prosecutor pressed. 'That you might never have had a better opportunity to do what you had been wanting to do, perhaps for years?'

Her attorney objected to that, of course, but it was too late. The damage had already been done. She could see it in the eyes of the jurors, and hear it in the gasps of the spectators. So she sat at the empty defense table in the empty courtroom, staring at nothing, with her arms wrapped tightly around her shoulders to keep herself from falling apart.

PART ONE

1955

I

Valerie O'Connor fell in love with Jack Marsh the first moment she set eyes on him. It was at her sister's North End apartment in Boston, where she had come to visit from her home in Rutland, Vermont, the summer after high school, the summer of 1955.

Marianne was Valerie's oldest sister and, if truth be known, her favorite. Marianne's husband, Tommy Santini, was a sweet and gentle bear of a man, a cook in a local Italian restaurant called Bertolli's, who had promised his wife that one day they would have a little place of their own.

'We'll call it the Irish Italian,' he would tease, 'and we'll serve corned beef and cabbage pizza.'

Tommy was deaf in one ear and always spoke in a booming voice, with exclamation points at the ends of his sentences. He had lost his hearing during a bombing raid on the MASH unit in Korea where he was a cook for two years, and he never seemed to run out of loud mess hall stories. It was on a hot night in July, right in the middle of one of Tommy's worst tales, that the door-bell rang, and when Valerie went to answer it, there was Tommy's younger brother, Joey, with his buddy, Jack Marsh, teasing and cajoling and looking for a free meal.

'These two hell-raisers were in Korea together,' Tommy said to Valerie after the introductions. 'Now they're working over at Federal Airlines. They were smart. Did their Army service in aircraft maintenance. Never got near a front line. Kept their butts nice and safe. And now all the commercial airlines are hot for their bodies.'

Valerie looked at Jack Marsh's body, at the muscles rippling beneath his thin shirt. It was hard and powerful. She felt weak.

Marianne set two more places at the dinner table. There was always enough food. Joey and his friends came around often. But Valerie barely ate a bite. She couldn't take her eyes off the young man across the table. He was as dark as she was light. His hair was black, hers blond. His eyes were strangely yellow, hers pale blue. His skin glowed like a chestnut from working outdoors, hers turned painfully pink if she were in the sun for more than ten minutes.

Valerie heard very little of the conversation that was bandied around the dinner table that evening. She caught phrases like 'the jet age,' and names like Boeing and McDonnell Douglas, and something about jet-propelled aircraft being the way of the future, and Jack seemed very excited about it all, but it meant next to nothing to her.

She didn't think he had noticed her at all. He hardly glanced in her direction, and certainly didn't have more than ten words to say to her all evening. But a week later, he called and asked her out to a movie. She was almost too nervous and excited to accept. But she did, and for the occasion, she wore a striped sundress with a halter neck and a sweater to cover her bare back. He had on jeans, a tight T-shirt, and a lightweight wind-breaker.

He put his arm casually around her during the picture, and they held hands afterward as they walked along Tremont Street to the soda fountain. They caught a reflection of themselves in a darkened shop window and made funny faces at one another, but she hardly recognized herself. She looked even smaller than she was, standing there beside his strength. It made her feel giddy. She thought he would be able to keep her safe from whatever awful things might be waiting for her out in the big world.

They saw each other almost every day after that, often going to the movies or walking the narrow little North End streets that looked and sounded like they belonged in Italy more than in America. They browsed through Paul Revere's House and the Old North Church. They strolled along the banks of the Charles River. Once, right after payday, Jack took her to dinner at the extravagantly expensive Locke-Ober Restaurant, and several times they went over to the Boston Common to hear the catchy calypso music that singers like Harry Belafonte were making popular.

One afternoon, they crossed over the Charles River to Cambridge and wandered around Harvard Yard, sticking their noses in the air and pretending they were summer session students at the university, and just as good as anyone else. Actually, Valerie didn't like Harvard very much. The buildings looked cold and unwelcoming.

Sometimes they went out with Joey, or other buddies of Jack's from work, and had a boisterous good time. But mostly, they went out alone, preferring to be quiet with each other. On occasion, when she really encouraged him, he would talk. He told her a little about his mother, who had died, and his father, who had more or less abdicated all responsibility, and she told him a lot about being in a family of nine.

'What was it like not having a mother, and not having your dad around very much?' she asked.

11

'Free,' he replied. 'What was it like having so many sisters and brothers?'

'Crowded,' she replied, and they laughed together.

He told her a little about growing up in Kansas City and she told him all about Rutland.

'Why did you join the Air Force?' she wondered.

'I spent a lot of time down at Heart Airport when I was a kid,' he answered. 'The planes always fascinated me. Or maybe it was the idea of getting on one of them and going someplace far away.'

'Where did you want to go?'

'I didn't care,' he said. 'I had this after-school job, see, at the stock pens. And one day, the manager comes over and asks me if I'd like a full-time job after high school. I had this picture of being stuck in that two-bit town for the rest of my life. So the minute I got out of school, I got on a plane and went as far away as I could get. As it turned out – it was Korea.'

'I guess I never felt that way,' she said thoughtfully.

'You like Rutland, huh?'

She had never really thought about it quite like that, but now that she did, the answer was simple. 'Rutland is home,' she told him. 'Wherever I may go in this world, whatever I may do, or wherever I may live, Rutland will always be home.'

'It must be nice to feel like that about a place,' he said slowly. 'Tell me more.'

If it was like pulling teeth to get him to talk about himself, he could talk forever about airplanes. She spent hours listening to all the finer points of wingspan and air pressure and descent rates.

He kissed her for the first time at the end of their third date. Almost, it seemed, as an afterthought. They had garlic on their breath, from the spaghetti dinner they had eaten at Bertolli's, the place where Tommy

12

worked. Garlic mixed with Chianti. She thought she had never tasted anything so good in her life. It wasn't the first kiss she had ever had, but it was the first that ever made her feel hot and cold and dizzy all at the same time, and she didn't want it to end.

Marianne and Tommy were not too sure what to make of the relationship, nor were they convinced that they should encourage it. Although he was a friend of Joey's, Jack Marsh was different somehow, older, slicker. Nice enough, maybe, but not the right man for Valerie. Marianne was secretly glad when summer ended, and Labor Day came, and her sister went home to Rutland.

But Valerie was heartbroken. In her wildest dreams, she had never imagined that anyone as attractive, or as worldly, or as wonderful as Jack Marsh clearly was could possibly have any interest in somebody as unsophisticated as she. Yet, he had.

It was true, they never actually discussed the future in terms of the two of them being together, but she was sure that he felt about her as she did about him. Why else would he have kissed her so urgently, and touched her the way he had? More than once she had struggled to control herself, and him, before they went too far. He didn't argue the issue very strenuously on those occasions, as he watched her hurry to readjust her clothing, and he always came back the next day.

They may have known each other only six weeks, but they had spent nearly all of it together. Certainly, it was time enough for him to speak of a future for them. But he didn't. He just said goodbye, and that he would write to her, maybe, or come up to see her, if he could. She was miserable. She hadn't come to Boston to find a husband, but she felt like she was going home a failure.

As autumn began to paint the Vermont foliage in brilliant gold and russet, Valerie pondered what she was

13

going to do with the rest of her life. She knew she was expected to marry and raise a family, but the Rutland boys she had grown up with seemed so young to her now, and so dull. She never said a word about Jack to anyone, but she wandered around the big house, which had been old when her mother had come to it as a bride, with a listlessness that caused her parents to worry.

Then, on a Sunday afternoon in the middle of November, after church and visiting and dinner were done with, and it was time for the family to gather in the living room on overstuffed sofas and sagging wing chairs and threadbare rugs, he appeared, out of nowhere. And when her father went to the front door in answer to his knock, he sucked up his courage and said, 'Hello, sir, my name is Jack Marsh, and I've come to marry your daughter.'

She would remember everything about that day, that moment. Who was there, where they sat, how they looked – her father dismayed, her mother delighted. She would remember every word of what they said, what they wore, what *she* wore – the pink wool dress with the lace collar she had sewn herself. And she would remember the blazing fire in the fireplace set against the brisk day, and the blazing fire inside her.

She felt just like the princess shut away in a tower who had been rescued by her prince. Except, of course, that life was no fairy tale. Her father had told her that often enough. He had taught her that it was all about hard work and disappointments and making compromises and doing the best you could, and hopefully finding a little happiness somewhere along the way. And maybe, if you didn't do it too badly, you could have the fairy tale in the next world. At least, that's what Father Joseph, her parish priest, always said anyway, and Valerie believed it.

She had been amused by the wide-eyed, dewy, dopey expressions her sisters had worn when, one by one, they fell under the spell of the 'right man,' totally oblivious to all his warts and imperfections. She thought them silly and short-sighted and she knew that she would never be so blind. Surely, she was not blind, was she? as she watched her father usher Jack Marsh into the living room.

'Do you know this man, Valerie?' he barked. 'He says he's come to marry you.'

'Yes, Daddy,' Valerie replied breathlessly. 'I know him.'

'Then suppose you tell us what this is all about.'

'I met him in Boston,' Valerie said, blushing furiously.

'We were introduced by your daughter Marianne,' Jack added. 'I'm a friend of her husband's brother, Joey.' From behind his back, he whipped a bouquet of flowers he had been clutching, and managed to pick out Valerie's mother in the crowd. 'Will you accept these, Mrs O'Connor,' he asked smoothly, 'at the very least as an apology for barging into your home like this?'

'We saw a lot of each other in Boston,' Valerie continued, after all the oohing and aahing and twittering had abated and the family's attention once again fixed on her.

'We fell in love,' Jack declared.

Valerie turned to him in surprise. 'You never said that.'

'I guess I didn't realize it until you were gone,' he replied, flashing his devastating smile. 'After that, Boston just seemed to lose all its charm.'

'We fell in love,' she said.

Jack turned to Valerie's father. 'So I've come, hoping you'll give me permission, sir, to marry your daughter.'

Martin O'Connor was a shrewd barrel of a man,

quite bald, with bristling eyebrows and piercing eyes that had scared many a suitor right down to his socks. He had recently celebrated his own thirtieth wedding anniversary and had so far married off five of his nine children. Valerie was his youngest, an uncomplicated, obedient girl, with a vulnerability that he didn't see in any of the others. 'Well, I'll just have to think awhile on that, now won't I?' he said.

A fair man, but strict and set in his ways, Martin brooked no argument from anyone in his family. His word was always final. Raised on the Bible by his father before him, he firmly believed that sparing the rod did indeed spoil the child. As a result, all nine of his children knew what the back of his hand or the snap of his belt felt like, as often as he deemed necessary.

Many a tender behind had to go to school and endure a hard wooden seat throughout the years, but no one ever talked about it. 'What goes on in this house, stays in this house,' Martin would tell them. 'That's what being a family is all about.' Of all the lessons Valerie was meant to learn about life, growing up in her parents' home, this was perhaps the one that most stuck with her.

Through diligence and hard work, Martin had turned the nearly idle granite quarry he had taken over from his father into one of the more promising businesses in Rutland, persevering even through the flood of 1947 that had devastated so many others. Over the years, he had dealt with all kinds of people and had earned himself the reputation of being tough, honest, and a good judge of both man and marble. And he wasn't so sure about the brash young man who had presented himself so candidly at the front door. It was nothing he could put his finger on, exactly. The boy was good-looking enough and charming enough and seemed smart enough and

16

smitten enough, and Valerie was certainly taken with him, no doubt about that. But there was something about Jack Marsh that bothered Martin, and his instincts had stood him in good stead now for fifty-five years.

It seemed, however, that on this particular issue, at least, he was a minority of one in his own home. His wife, Charlotte, normally a very sensible woman and in many ways just as shrewd as himself, had been swept right off her feet by the young man. She had fairly fluttered in his presence. Even his two oldest boys, Marty and Kevin, both sober and steady to a fault, had laughed broadly at Marsh's jokes and offered to take him out and show him what the town of Rutland had to offer. And Valerie, well, that poor besotted child had drifted in and out with a goofball expression on her face and never seemed able to touch a toe to solid ground.

'Whatever you say, Martin,' Charlotte said obediently, as they settled down in bed much later that night to discuss the turn of events. 'But he seems a fine young man to me. Of course, Valerie's the youngest, and it was always going to be hard for you to let her go.'

Martin considered that. He respected Charlotte's opinion. She was perceptive in ways that he was not, especially about the girls. He fell asleep examining his conscience and his heart.

But when he awoke the next morning, the misgivings were still with him. He carried them around all day, through his appointment at the bank, and his luncheon at the Knights of Columbus, and his meetings with customers. He finally left work two hours early, something he never did, just to come home and walk with Valerie through the fields behind the house, as they had often done when she was a child.

'I don't think he'll make you happy, Cornsilk,' he

17

said, using his pet name for her because that's what her long, pale hair always reminded him of. 'He's not our kind.'

But Valerie turned shining eyes and a dazzling smile on him as she replied. 'He's already made me happy, Daddy. Can't you see that?'

And of course, he could. 'But what do you know about him?' he pressed her. 'What do you know about his people?'

'There's not much to know. Jack's an only child. His mother came from a farming town in Iowa and his father came from an orphanage in St Louis and worked for a meatpacking house in Kansas City where Jack was raised. They're both dead now.'

'Still, six weeks,' Martin persisted. 'That's not a very long time.'

'Are you going to forbid me to marry him?' she asked, biting her lip nervously.

He wanted to. He knew he could. It was right there on the tip of his tongue. 'In six weeks, what could you possibly know about the kind of life he's had?' he asked instead.

'I don't think it was an easy life,' she said. 'He's been on his own for a lot of it. But what does it matter? I know that he's sincere and respectful and hardworking. Marianne and Tommy will tell you that, too. And I think he'll take good care of me.'

'I suppose that's something,' Martin conceded. 'But don't forget, marriage is for a very long time. For as long as you live. Good or bad. We're Catholic, we don't have the luxury others have of making a mistake and getting to go back and fix it.'

'Don't worry, Daddy, I'm not making a mistake,' Valerie assured him with the supreme confidence of the young and inexperienced. 'Jack may not be the man you expected me to pick, but he's the man I want to share my life with and who wants to share his life with me, whatever it may be. For better or worse, I love him, and I believe him when he says he loves me. And that's a pretty good beginning, isn't it?'

They were married right after the New Year, during Sunday morning mass at St Stephen's, the parish church where her parents had been married, and where her three sisters and two of her brothers had been married, and where she had been baptized, and christened, and had made her first communion, in front of the whole congregation that had watched her grow up.

Jack had been born to Catholic parents. Had his mother lived, he would probably have been reared in the faith, and may even have been an altar boy. As it was, he had never been inside a church and had no use for religion. But he promised to let Valerie raise their children, if they had children, however she wanted. He said it didn't matter to him, one way or the other.

So Father Joseph agreed, if somewhat reluctantly, to marry them in church. Valerie was immensely grateful. Her faith was very important to her, and being married in her church with all the sacraments meant everything. If she had had to marry Jack someplace else, she certainly would have, even if it meant finding the courage to run away from home and her father to do it. But it would not have been as perfect, and she wanted the first day of her new life to be as perfect as she could make it.

There wasn't much time for preparations, so Valerie wore her sister Cecilia's wedding gown, which she herself had helped to make, taken in two sizes. It had yards and yards of silk skirt and lace embroidery, and she fairly floated down the aisle in it. With her silky hair and radiant smile, she looked every inch a princess,

19

and Jack, looking dark and dashing in his rented tuxedo, might very easily have been taken for a prince.

And all around them, people whispered, 'It's a fairy-tale romance . . .'

'A fairy-tale wedding . . .'

'The beginning of a fairy-tale marriage . . .'

2

The new Mr and Mrs Marsh spent their wedding night at the Château du Lac, overlooking Lake Champlain, in a suite that was larger than Marianne's whole apartment in Boston. Furnished with early American antiques, including an intricate rolltop desk, a beautifully carved armoire, and a huge four-poster bed that was very like the one her parents had, Valerie could well imagine George Washington having slept there, although she knew the Château du Lac hadn't even existed when Washington was alive.

Staying there was a terrible extravagance, and a serious drain on Jack's savings, but it was the place Valerie had dreamed of spending her honeymoon all her life, and it made him feel big to give it to her. Besides, it was off-season, being the middle of winter, and the rates were almost reasonable. Then, too, it was just for one night. Early Monday, they would drive to the airport just outside of Burlington for a flight to Seattle, the home base of Federal Airlines, where Jack had been transferred to the jet maintenance school.

That was the bad part. Except for visits to Marianne in Boston, Valerie had never been more than half an hour away from home. Excited though she was to start her brand-new life, she was desolate at the thought of leaving Rutland and her family behind.

Jack, on the other hand, was delighted. The last thing

he wanted was to have a dozen other people sticking their noses into his marriage.

There were hugs and kisses and tears all around.

'I thought you were going to be in Boston, near Marianne,' her father said when he heard, more unsure than ever about his decision to let her marry someone they knew so little about.

'So did I,' Valerie said, thinking that Seattle must surely be at the other end of the world, as well as the country. 'But this is what Jack really wants, and he says it's an opportunity he can't pass up.'

Martin sighed. 'Well, I suppose you have to go where his work is,' he conceded. 'But I wish you were going to be closer.'

They reached the Château du Lac a little before ten o'clock.

'You're still in time for dinner,' the manager assured them. 'We serve until ten-thirty.'

But they were still full from the lavish reception and six-course luncheon that had followed their wedding, and declined the meal.

'As you wish,' the manager said with a polite bow.

They were shown to their suite, and then left graciously alone. A silver tray with a huge bottle of champagne in a bucket filled with ice and two exquisite cut crystal flutes waited on a little table in the sitting room. A silver-edged card propped against the bucket read, *Compliments of the Management*, and the new bride blushed furiously when she saw.

'Do you think they know?' she whispered.

Jack chuckled. 'Know what? That this is our wedding night? Of course they know. This is the honeymoon suite, isn't it? What else would we be doing here?'

But Valerie didn't think it was very funny, strangers

22

knowing what they were about to do. Now that she thought of it, had the desk clerk looked at them with a very smug expression when they checked in? Had the manager bowed just a little too politely? And had the bellhop who brought up their bags looked as though he were trying to smother a smile when Jack tipped him? She had a sudden picture of the whole staff smirking at them behind their backs, because of what they were about to do. She rushed into the bathroom, her cheeks burning.

'It could be worse, you know.' Jack's words came through the closed door. 'They might have thought we *weren't* married.'

Valerie hadn't considered that. She pictured the local sheriff bursting into the suite, summoned by the suspicious desk clerk, placing them under arrest for whatever the crime of sharing a room unmarried was called. And Jack calmly producing their marriage certificate, and demanding satisfaction for the insult to his bride. The idea made her giggle, even as she realized that from now on, whatever might happen, Jack would be there to take care of her.

There was a soft knock at the bathroom door. He was standing there, smiling expectantly when she opened the door. He had removed his coat and tie and was beginning to unbutton his shirt.

Valerie was suddenly shy. She had seen him many times without a shirt, in his bathing suit at the river, on hot August evenings on Marianne's tiny balcony, on steamy afternoons when he would work on his Chrysler. But this was different, so very different. All of a sudden, she found she couldn't look at him. Instead, she looked down at her ivory shantung traveling suit.

'Just give me a moment,' she murmured, closing the door against him. Her mouth was dry, her tongue felt thick and furry. Her fingers fumbled with the buttons on the silk jacket. It occurred to her for the very first time that the man on the other side of the door was almost a total stranger to her, someone she had met barely five months ago.

Who was he, after all? What was she doing here with him? And what was she about to do? Valerie had been so caught up in the idea of the wedding that she hadn't stopped to consider what would come next. She realized now, with a painful jolt, that despite what she may have told her father with considerable assurance, she knew very little about this man who was now her husband. For example, she didn't know what kind of music he preferred, or what books he read – or if he liked music, or if he read books. She didn't even know what he thought about most of the time, not really.

She had an almost irresistible urge to flee. Instead, she undid the buttons on her skirt and let it drop to the floor. Then she stepped out of it, picked it up, and folded it neatly with her jacket. She wasn't sure what his favorite foods were, or if he had allergies, or if he slept with the window open or closed, or if he put the cap back on the toothpaste, or if he left the lid up on the toilet seat. She wondered whether he was messy or neat. She didn't even know if he had a favorite color.

She removed her silk slip, and her stockings, and her garter belt, until she stood in her white cotton bra and panties, goose bumps popping out all over her arms and legs. And then she remembered. Her beautiful new lace peignoir set, purchased for just this occasion, lay neatly packed in her suitcase in the bedroom. She could hardly go and get it now.

She looked around the big old-fashioned bathroom. Nothing but thirsty Turkish towels hung on the bars, and wrapping herself in one of them didn't seem very sophisticated to her. Finally, she took off her bra and panties, put her slip back on, and looked in the gilt-framed mirror over the pedestal sink. Her cheeks were very pink, as though she had spent the whole day in the sun, and her eyes were luminescent.

She might not know all that much about the man who waited out there for her, but she was about to get into that beautiful four-poster bed with him and become a woman. Whatever that meant.

It wasn't that she didn't know about sex. She did. It would have been impossible for her to live her whole life as the youngest of nine children and not know something about how it worked. Moreover, her mother and her sisters had been only too happy to tell her what to expect, although none of them chose to be particularly explicit about the details.

'He may have needs that you won't always share or understand,' Charlotte said. 'But you try your best to meet them anyway, because you love him, and because it's your duty.'

'Men are easy to please,' her sister Cecilia whispered. 'They do most of it by themselves anyway. You're just sort of there. The fun part is finding out what works for you.'

'Don't let him cut the beginning too short,' her sister Elizabeth advised. 'It's not so important to men, but it can make all the difference to a woman.'

'Don't expect perfection all at once,' Marianne told her. 'It takes a lot of patience and a lot of practice. And don't worry,' she added with a twinkle in her eye, 'you won't think about how ridiculous it all looks once you're doing it.'

Valerie knew they meant well and so she listened intently. It was just that you could know something in

25

your head, but it wasn't the same as really knowing it. And that was what she was about to find out.

She took a deep breath and opened the door. Jack was already in bed. He had plumped up the pillows and half lay against them. He was not wearing a pajama top and she could see the curly black hair on his broad chest. The huge bottle of champagne was open and he had poured two glasses. He held one out to her, and as she took it, she noticed that the bottle was already almost half empty.

It made her feel a little better to think that he might be nervous, too. She looked around. His clothes were folded neatly across a chair. His bathrobe was draped carefully over one of the bedposts. She smiled to herself.

A fire glowed warm and bright in the fireplace on the far wall, and she realized it was the only light in the room. She was filled with an extraordinary sense of the romantic as she slipped between the sheets. The bed was so big that three more people could easily have fit between them. She crept toward him. He was refilling his glass, and as she reached his side he turned and clicked it against hers.

'To us,' he said. He was not wearing pajama bottoms either.

'To us,' she echoed in a suddenly squeaky voice.

He downed his champagne in one swallow, and to her dismay, she found herself gulping hers when she had meant to sip it. The bubbly liquid slithered down her throat and started a tingly path that traveled right down to the tips of her toes. He refilled his glass and added some more to hers, and this time she did sip it.

Valerie had never had more than one glass of champagne in her life, and this, on top of the several glasses she had drunk at the wedding reception, was beginning to make her feel light and carefree. They began to talk about the wedding and the reception and the weather and as many other meaningless things as they could think of, and by the time she had swallowed the last drop, he had finished the rest of the bottle. He took her glass, set it beside his on the nightstand and turned to her.

'Okay,' he said with a deep chuckle, 'let's see what I got.'

Valerie held her breath as Jack reached for her. She had been anticipating this moment ever since they had met. He began to kiss her, moist probing kisses, and she shivered deep inside. She knew what would come next, the soft nibbling and gentle caresses that would gradually build to the shattering crescendo she had heard so much about.

But she was wrong. Just as she was thinking that she could happily spend the rest of her life feeling this way, he plunged his tongue so deep into her mouth that she gagged, his hands on either side of her head holding her so tightly she couldn't move. Then when she was sure she was going to pass out, he suddenly let go and began to clutch and squeeze his way down her body, ripping her slip in the process. Whatever desire he had awakened in her vanished in a wave of nausea, and it was all she could do to keep herself from throwing up.

However, Jack didn't seem to notice, and before she quite realized what was happening, he was spreading her legs and climbing between them.

'Now,' he muttered thickly.

Valerie had never imagined that anything could hurt so much. Her mother and her sisters had told her that the first time might be a little painful, but nobody had prepared her for this. Her mother had said the discomfort would ease soon after the beginning, but it didn't.

The agony went on and on, from the moment he

plunged himself into her until the moment he withdrew. It was as though she were being ripped apart from the inside out, and she clamped her teeth over her bottom lip so hard it bled. Finally, she couldn't help it, she screamed. But Jack must have mistaken it for a cry of passion, because he began to press even harder, pumping himself to a final, convulsive thrust, before collapsing on top of her, sweating and panting, and falling asleep almost immediately.

Valerie could barely breathe beneath his weight, but she waited for what seemed hours until she was sure he was not going to awaken. Then, slowly, carefully, she squirmed out from under him, crawled from the bed, and stumbled into the bathroom, locking the door behind her with trembling fingers, and sinking to the cold tile floor like a rag doll.

She lay there, aching, numb, and shivering at the same time, while blood and sticky stuff caked her thighs and hot tears ran down her cheeks. What had seemed to her to last an eternity, from the first kiss to the last heave, had in fact taken less than five minutes. But Valerie couldn't bring herself to believe that it had had anything to do with making love. Somebody would have told her, her mother, Marianne certainly. They would not have kept such a secret from her and left her so vulnerable.

Something had to be wrong. The nausea she had felt, the revulsion, couldn't be normal. Women didn't spend their girlhoods looking forward to what she had just experienced. Sex was for the purpose of procreating, but to that end, Mother Nature had designed it to be enjoyed by both parties, that's what she had always been taught, and no one had ever given her cause to doubt it. It was only reasonable then that she had expected, well, she didn't know what she had expected. But it was certainly not what she had received. Her disappointment was overwhelming.

She wondered if the champagne had done something to her. But if so, she reasoned, wouldn't it have affected Jack the same way? He had certainly drunk a great deal more of it than she had. Physiological distinctions notwithstanding, she wondered, were men and women really so different? Common sense told her they were not. But Valerie knew that something wasn't the way it was supposed to be, and she knew she needed to figure out what it was, before it happened again. She reached up and pulled one of the towels off the rack, wrapped it around her, and began to think.

To begin with, she loved Jack, she was sure of that, and she wanted to be physically close to him. At least, the stirrings he had generated in her prior to tonight had certainly led her to believe that she did.

He had told her he was experienced, which to her meant that he knew what he was doing. Therefore, she concluded, none of this could be his fault. He had obviously expected her to be . . . well, she didn't know exactly what he had expected her to be, but it was clearly something she was not. And the fact that no one had so much as hinted at the possibility of such an ordeal confirmed that whatever was wrong must be with her.

Valerie thought about it for a long time, considering and discarding options, while her husband slept on in the big four-poster bed, and the sky over Lake Champlain turned from black to gray. Finally, by little more than process of elimination, she was left with only one possible solution. She must be frigid. One of those women she had heard whispers about who were incapable of enjoying sex. The expectations she had grown up with had obviously been based on false assumptions.

She might have had all the appropriate yearnings and all the suitable reactions, as far as they went, but clearly, they had not translated into the joys of conjugal bliss that her sisters always swooned and tittered about.

Well so be it, she decided. If that were the case, she would survive it somehow, but she would not be pitied and she would not be whispered about. She would learn how to please her husband, and not worry about herself, and no one would ever have to know the awful truth. Jack could assert his marital rights whenever he pleased, and God willing, if she couldn't learn to enjoy it, she would at least learn to bear it. But not, if she could help it, for a few more hours.

Valerie pulled herself up off the floor and ran a bath. The warmth soothed her and she soaped herself liberally, washing as much of the night before from her body as she could. Then she crept back into the bedroom, and in the faint morning light, pulled fresh clothes out of her suitcase as quietly as she could, putting them on as quickly as she could, keeping one eye on Jack and holding her breath. But she needn't have worried, he never moved. Finally, she was ready to slip on a pair of boots, grab her coat and scarf, and head for the door. At the last moment, she turned back, to find a scrap of paper, scrawl a hasty note.

'Jack, darling, just couldn't sleep anymore. Didn't want to wake you. It's such a beautiful morning. Went for a walk. See you at breakfast. Love, Val.'

A moment later, she was out the door and hurrying down the hallway. She had postponed the inevitable for a little while, at least.

Valerie walked along the snowy path by the lake until she was cold enough that the soreness inside her began to subside. Then she changed directions and wandered into the woods, listening to birdsong. A startled deer stared at her, wondering perhaps what she was up to so early in the day. She smiled and stood perfectly still until the animal was reassured that she meant no harm and trotted off.

It was a clear, crisp morning, made for laughter and lightheartedness. But Valerie's heart was heavy. She made sure she did not return to the Château du Lac until there was time for only a quick breakfast before they had to leave for the Burlington airport.

She managed to smile over the tray of fluffy omelets and croissants and hot chocolate that was brought to their suite, and she maintained her cheerfulness while she busied herself with repacking the suitcases and making sure they left nothing behind. But once she was in the big Chrysler, the sight of Jack's strong hands on the steering wheel almost made her falter. The mellow notes of 'Autumn Leaves' over the car radio saved her. It was one of her favorite songs, one she and Jack had danced to back in Boston last summer, a hundred years ago.

At that moment, Jack reached over and squeezed her hand. 'I remember that,' he said.

Valerie smiled her first genuine smile of the morning. It was such a little thing, she knew, but sometimes it was the little things that made the difference. He was so dear, and she loved him so much. She would like to have talked to him about last night, but of course she couldn't. He would be so disappointed in her, and would think her such a failure. He might even stop loving her, and she could never take that chance.

3

Jack Marsh was born in a third-floor walk-up apartment on the east side of Kansas City, Missouri, on
an unusually cold November day in 1930. He never
knew his mother. She died of a complication associ-
ated with his birth. The mid-wife couldn't stop the
bleeding.

He was raised in part by his father and in part by a
succession of cheap women who moved in and then out
of the apartment and his life, usually just after he had
grown attached to them. They were nice enough women
and Jack never minded that they were cheap because
they fed him, and dressed him, and fussed over him,
and tucked him into bed each evening with a hug and
a kiss and occasionally even a lullaby.

He rarely saw his father. Tom Marsh left for work
early in the morning and came home from the bars late
at night. Sometimes Jack was awake and would hear
him stumbling up the stairs, drunker than usual. And
sometimes he would hear the woman softly admonishing
him. Then he would cover his ears with his pillow
because he knew what came next – the shouting, the
cursing, the beating. And a day or two later, the woman
would pack up and leave, hugging Jack one last time,
crying, her nose still bloody, her cheek still swollen. And
another woman would come.

'One woman's same as another,' his father would tell
him, winking. But even as a small boy, Jack knew that

his mother had not been the same as any other, and that was the reality his father drank to forget.

From the day she had first smiled at Tom Marsh, vanquishing the misery of the orphanage he had grown up in, Ellen Marsh had been his strength, his stability, his only reason for being. Without her, his life had no purpose. It was reduced to successive blocks of time to be endured as best he could.

Jack was six years old the first time his father hit him.

He caught the boy on the way to the bathroom at two o'clock one morning and sent him sprawling in a hail of punches that split his lip, bloodied his nose, and blackened his eye, and then finished him off with a kick to the ribs once he was down.

'Why'd you have to do that?' the woman asked.

'For no reason,' Tom said, his words slurred. But even at six, Jack knew the reason. Ellen was dead because of him. He had killed his own mother, the only person his father ever loved, the only person who would ever love his father. Afterward, Tom sobbed, holding Jack tight, lamenting that the boy was the only part of Ellen he had left, promising he would never hit him again. But he did. And over the years, Jack came to hate the sobbing worse than the beating.

The woman took care of him, bathing his bruises, bandaging his cuts, and spinning magical stories to help him forget the pain.

He had few friends. Respectable families were horrified by his father's living arrangements, and he was not invited to play. The sons of other families tended to be in trouble most of the time, and Jack had no use for them. He got used to spending time by himself. It didn't bother him that much. Sometimes the woman would take him to the zoo, or to the park where he could play soldier by the Civil War cannon and sailor as he piloted his toy boat around the pond, or down to the docks where he could watch the real boats plying the waters of the Missouri River.

And for one week every summer until he was twelve, he went to stay at a farm in Iowa with his mother's parents. Dour people, who had disapproved of their daughter's marriage and resented the offspring who had taken her life, doing their Christian duty. One night toward the end of that final summer, the old man and woman died in a fire that burned their farm-house down around them while they slept. Their grandson was the only one to escape the blaze.

'What a blessing the boy was spared,' the neighbors murmured to each other, as they watched the firefighters battling the conflagration.

Jack watched, too. The fires of hell, he thought, shivering in his thin pajamas beneath the folds of a blanket someone had thoughtfully wrapped around him. It wasn't that he was glad his grandparents were dead, exactly. It was just that he was glad he wouldn't have to come to Iowa anymore.

There was never enough money. What Tom didn't drink up barely paid the rent. The woman worked sometimes and then there would be food and clothing for a while. The food was good, if plain, and the clothes were sturdy, if secondhand. But even with that, Jack was frequently cold in the winter, and more often than not, went to bed hungry.

When he was fifteen, he got an after-school job at the stockyards for minimum wage and all the scraps he could carry home with him. Within a few months, he put on twenty pounds of hard muscle, and the rich kids whose hand-me-downs he wore were no longer inclined to taunt him about it.

He was sixteen the first time he had sex. She was a whore who worked the bars of East Kansas City. He didn't care about that. She picked him up late on a slow night, and took him back to her dingy room. He had no money in his pocket, but she liked the way he looked, and she gave freebies once in a while, when business was slow.

He'd had erections before, and had figured out what to do about them, but it was so much better when somebody else did it for him. She took him to the top of the mountain, and because it amused her that she was his first, she worked him until dawn.

'Come back and see me sometime,' she said as he was leaving. He hugged her and promised he would. But he never did.

Jack was reasonably intelligent, but not particularly adept at schoolwork. He liked to build things, fix things, make things work. And he loved airplanes. He had loved them since he was ten and the woman had taken him out to the airport to watch the sleek machines take off and land. He had outgrown the park and it was another inexpensive way to entertain a boy for a whole day. After that, he spent whatever time and money he could scrape together on aeronautic magazines and model airplanes.

He wanted to quit school when he turned sixteen, but his manual arts teacher persuaded him to stay until he graduated.

'You want to be an airplane mechanic, don't you?' the teacher asked. Jack nodded. 'Well, you have to study for that,' the teacher told him. 'You have to get your diploma. Nobody will touch you until you're eighteen anyway. And then, take my word for it, the best way to learn what you want to learn is to join the Army.'

The teacher was the first person, other than the

woman, of course, who had ever taken an interest in him. Jack took his advice and received his diploma in June of 1948. Two weeks later, he enlisted in the fledgling United States Air Force. As soon as he completed basic training, he was assigned to engine maintenance technical school.

The woman packed his few belongings on the day he left, sneaking a package of home-baked goodies into the bag when she thought he wasn't looking. Then she brushed some imaginary lint off his hand-me-down jacket, and straightened his tie, and smiled up at the strapping young man with the curly black hair and the strange yellow eyes.

'Damned if you don't look just like your father,' she said, hugging him maybe a little too tightly, knowing he was never coming back. 'He's a real charmer that one, and I bet you're gonna be just like him, honey, just like him.'

The Air Force was the best thing that could ever have happened to Jack Marsh. It gave him more than a job, more than the training he wanted, more than three square meals a day where he could eat enough to fill his belly to bursting. It gave him a home. It didn't matter where you came from in the Air Force, or what your family was like, or how much money you had. Everyone was treated alike, and everyone wore the same clothes, and they were brand-new.

The war in Korea broke out before his four-year hitch was up, and after that, Jack Marsh had a mission. He was never within a hundred miles of enemy action, but he was as important to the war effort as the men who crawled along the front line with their rifles strapped to their backs. His war was in the air. He knew everything there was to know about the B-52 bomber. He could take it apart and put it back together again in his sleep, nothing to it. He could fine-tune it into a dream machine. The pilots who depended on those planes to get them where they needed to go and bring them back safely soon began asking for him by name.

Then in April of 1951, word came from the woman that his father was dying. She wrote that it had something to do with his liver going bad, and the doctors saying it was because of all the alcohol. What goes around, comes around, Jack thought. He could have gotten emergency leave. He could have gone home. Instead, he went to Tokyo for three days with a couple of buddies.

A month later, he was promoted to staff sergeant and became a crew chief. By the end of the war, he had the most efficient team of guys, and the best maintenance record, in South Korea.

Jack mustered out of the Air Force in June of 1952 with a buddy from Boston named Joey Santini who had an uncle who worked for Federal Airlines. The uncle was sure there would be a place on the maintenance crews for Joey and his friend Jack, given their experience. There was. The airline was hungry for qualified men who had been trained by the military. It was starting back at the bottom again, but Jack didn't care. He would still be working on airplanes. And Boston was as good a place to be as any.

He took a furnished room in an old brownstone on Bennet Street, not far from where Marianne and Tommy Santini lived in the North End. He hung out with members of his crew after work, and once or twice a week Joey took him over to his brother, Tommy's, place for a free meal.

The summer that Jack met Valerie O'Connor, Federal Airlines had put in its first order for the new Boeing 707 jet engine commercial airliner, and he was waiting to see if he would be one of those lucky enough to be selected for jet maintenance training in Seattle, Washington, where both Boeing and Federal were headquartered.

Valerie was a fragile little thing who looked as though she might break in a stiff wind. She hardly said a word the first time he met her, but he wasn't all that partial to talky females, and there was something kind of appealing about her. He was excited that night, juiced up about the 707s, and he really enjoyed the way she hung on his every word. She was like the kid sister he had never had, looking up to him, all wide-eyed and dewy.

It made Jack feel good to take her out, and impress her with stories about all the places he'd been. She ate it up. It didn't take long before he figured out she had flipped over him. He tried to take advantage of it a couple of times, but she wasn't having any. With all that good Catholic upbringing, she was probably holding out for the wedding ring. It didn't matter, he didn't press it. He knew where to go for what he wanted. There were places and there were women where it was a simple transaction and no strings. Just the way he liked it.

He saw her almost every day. Why not, he told himself? He had nothing better to do. But there was something about her. She was starting to grow on him. He found himself looking at his wristwatch a lot on the job, figuring how many hours it was before he could see her again. It made him uncomfortable to be so dependent on her, but he couldn't help himself, and he was glad that Labor Day was coming, when she would go back to Vermont.

That is, he was glad until she was gone. Then everywhere he went, everything he did, reminded him of her. A certain perfume, a sudden giggle, a butter pecan ice cream cone, popcorn, a haunting melody, girls with long

38

silky blond hair. He started to drink too much and stay at the bars too late. What was the point of going home? He would only be alone. When he was alone, he couldn't stop himself from thinking about her. But when he was drunk, she had no hold on him.

In the middle of November, he learned that he would be among the first group of Federal Airlines mechanics to go to Seattle. The men on his shift looked at him with new respect. Only thirty had been selected from across the entire country, thirty of the best. And the only person he wanted to tell was Valerie O'Connor.

When Jack Marsh woke up, groggy and alone, the morning after his wedding, he had no idea where he was. For the moment, he had forgotten all about his marriage and his wife. He wondered whose bed he was in. Then his head cleared and he realized he was in the suite at the Château du Lac, and the sheets beneath him were stained with blood. He looked around. Valerie was nowhere to be seen. He sat up abruptly, panicked that she had left him. Then he saw her suitcase, sitting next to his on the luggage rack at the foot of the bed, and her note propped on the nightstand beside him. He grabbed for the note, and only after reading it twice did he fall back against the pillows and yawn.

Last night hadn't been the most memorable sexual encounter of his life, but he wasn't very concerned about it. During Korea, there had been numerous wild forays into Tokyo and Hong Kong, where he had become well acquainted with the art of sex as it had been practiced on him by countless olive-skinned beauties, each expert at what she did, all well worth the paltry sums they requested in return. And since his return to the States, he had found one or two women in the seamier sections of Boston who were willing to practice the Asian ways for a few extra dollars. But he didn't love any of them.

Valerie was different. He liked to think that he loved her as his father had loved his mother. He knew she was a virgin. God, the proof was all over the bedding, and it made him feel good, somehow, to know that he had been her first.

He stretched out like a cat, climbed from the bed, and headed for the shower. The rest would come. Every girl started out as a virgin. In time, he was sure, Valerie would learn what to do, just like the rest of them did, and then everything would be fine. After all, he reasoned, women were women, and more or less the same.

4

The Federal Airlines Constellation nosed down toward Sea-Tac International Airport through a fog so thick Valerie couldn't see ten feet outside the little round window. She wondered how the pilot would see to land.

Jack laughed when she asked him. 'Radar,' he said. 'There's a system that was designed for just this kind of weather condition. The pilot doesn't have to see at all.'

But Valerie had never heard of radar, and she kept a tight hold on Jack's arm until she felt the plane's wheels come into bouncing contact with the runway. It had been an exciting flight, her very first, and Jack had told her all about how the plane worked, and had even taken her up into the cockpit where she could see for herself the huge maze of switches and lights and gauges that kept the giant engines running. Most important to her was how a big heavy thing like this could stay up in the air in the first place. She didn't understand most of his answer, but it was enough to know that he knew. She felt very secure with him beside her, and she decided that life as Mrs Jack Marsh was going to be a wonderful adventure. The night before was almost forgotten.

By the time they had deplaned and collected their luggage and found a taxicab to take them to the Olympic Hotel, where they planned to stay for a few days, it was well past four o'clock. The fog was lifting and the late afternoon sun was sinking in the western sky, turning the world pink and gold and violet in its wake. And so it was, as the cab sped them north along Route 99, past Boeing Field where Jack was going to be working, and into downtown Seattle, that Valerie had the first glimpse of her new home. Seattle itself was built up and down a series of hills and in and out of a network of water-ways. Seven hills, the cab-driver told her, just like Rome and San Francisco. Like Boston, too, she thought. Snowcapped mountains seemed to surround the city, a single high peak identified as Mount Baker in the north, the rippling Cascades along the east, and the craggy Olympics to the west, on the other side of Puget Sound.

'Look behind you, miss,' the cabbie said pleasantly. And when she turned, Valerie, who had lived her entire life at the foot of four-thousand-foot-high Mount Killington, saw the towering peak of fourteen-thousand-foot-high Mount Rainier, looking for all the world like a huge bowl of strawberry ice cream in the spectacular sunset.

'Oh, Jack,' Valerie breathed, like a little girl seeing the world for the first time, 'it's so beautiful, it's almost right out of a storybook.'

'Not a bad place to start a life together then,' he replied.

The Olympic Hotel was right in the heart of down-town Seattle. As soon as they checked into their room, Valerie wanted to go out exploring. It was growing dark, and many of the stores were getting ready to close for the night, so they settled for pressing their noses against the windows of the Frederick & Nelson department store, and then they lingered in front of several galleries that were featuring the efforts of Northwest artists.

The streets were crowded with people on their way home from work, jostling each other good-naturedly, hurrying to meet one another for drinks or dinner, running last-minute errands. It seemed to Valerie to be a bright, bustling, happy city, but it was not at all like Boston or even Rutland. The atmosphere was different. It reminded her of a frontier town, at the edge of something raw and new and exciting. And the weather was unbelievably warm.

'I almost don't need my coat,' she told Jack.

A man waiting to cross the street next to them heard her and smiled. 'Give it a few days, and you won't,' he said. He was dressed in a short-sleeved shirt and V-necked sweater.

'But it's January,' Valerie protested.

The man smiled again. 'You must be from the East.'

'Vermont,' she said.

He nodded. 'I was in New England once in January. You couldn't pay me to go again. Watch out, Seattle will spoil you.'

They went back to the hotel. It was barely six o'clock in Seattle, but they were still on Eastern Time, and they were hungry. They went to a restaurant right in the hotel called the Golden Lion, an opulent red and gold and walnut room that looked like it had just stepped out of Victorian India. And because they were on their honeymoon, they ordered the Champagne Dinner. Valerie had never had breast of guinea hen under glass before, or anything under glass for that matter. It was delicious. And this time, after the waiter had popped the cork on the bottle of bubbly, she forced herself to match Jack almost glass for glass. She thought she might get sick, drinking so much, but she got silly instead, giggling all the way back to their room. It was only once they were securely inside and she had collapsed onto the turned-down bed that the room began to spin out of orbit.

She sensed that Jack was removing her shoes and her stockings and her dress and her underwear, and then she was dimly aware that he was taking off his own clothes, too, but she made no effort to help. She made no effort to do anything. It was as though each of her arms now weighed two hundred pounds. She felt him next to her, naked and hard. She felt his tongue in her mouth and his hands on her body, going through the same motions as they had the night before, and she thought she felt him enter her, with the same invading thrust. But it was as if he were doing it all to somebody else. Somebody else was clenching her teeth and crying out, and that was just fine with her. She was asleep before he finished.

Bright and early Tuesday morning, after room service had brought them a delicious pancake breakfast, Jack went back to the airport to pick up the Chrysler that had come in overnight on a cargo flight. Valerie stayed in bed, remembering little of the night before. She had a hangover. Jack had chuckled and ordered her a Bloody Mary with breakfast, but just the name of it made her stomach rebel.

'Drink it,' he said on his way out. 'Trust me, it'll make all the difference.'

She did trust him, so after staring at it for almost an hour, she drank it, like medicine, all in one gulp. It didn't taste nearly as bad as she had feared. In fact, it was pretty good, and it did make her feel better. After another hour, she got up and went to the bathroom. Her head ached some, but the rest of her wasn't as sore as before. She decided that she had found the way to deal with the intimate part of their life together.

When Jack returned shortly after noon, he found Valerie dressed and cheerful. They had a light lunch, picked up a map of the city from the front desk, and drove out to their new home, a furnished house that Jack had rented, sight unseen, in a section of Seattle, just above Boeing Field, called Beacon Hill.

'Just like in Boston,' Valerie said, delighted.

'Only Boston's Beacon Hill is for the upper class,' Jack commented. 'This Beacon Hill is for the working class.'

It was a one-story house, about twenty-five years old, with a shingle roof and white-painted cedar siding that sat high on the side of the road, and a single-car basement garage at street level. A rockery ran up from the street to a front porch that extended the entire length of the house. A wooden swing affixed to the porch beams swayed in the slight breeze and seemed to be welcoming them.

Inside were two bedrooms flanking a bath, a sturdy brick fireplace that highlighted the living room, moss green carpeting, worn but comfortable furniture, and an old-fashioned cooler built into the north wall of the kitchen, very like the one Charlotte O'Connor used to have before Martin had modernized the farmhouse in Rutland. In the basement, they found a laundry, a built-in workbench, and an odd, out-of-date contraption that Jack said was a sawdust burner that furnished the heat for the house. Out back was a small yard with a sandbox, a hedge of rhododendron bushes, a pair of young plum trees, and a gnarled old cherry tree.

Valerie loved it. If she could have designed her very first home all by herself, it would not have looked significantly different from this one.

'Hello, there.'

Valerie spun around. A white-haired lady was smiling at her across the rhododendrons.

'Hello,' Valerie said shyly.

45

'My name's Virginia Halgren. I guess you must be the new neighbors.'

'Not until Friday,' Valerie replied, after introducing herself. 'We're staying at the Olympic Hotel for a few days.'

'Oh, what a treat.'

'Well, we're sort of on our honeymoon,' Valerie said, blushing. 'We were married on Sunday.'

'Oh, my,' Virginia said, and turned around. 'John, John, come out here,' she called. 'Come meet the new neighbors.' A tall, spare gentleman emerged from the house next door, carrying a lug wrench and a hunk of lead pipe. 'They're newly-weds.'

John Halgren nodded. 'Well, I certainly want to wish you as much happiness as Virginia and I have had,' he said with a nod. 'And we've been going strong for over forty years now.'

Jack came out then and Valerie introduced him to the Halgrens.

'Having a plumbing problem?' he asked John, nodding at the wrench and pipe.

'Yep,' John replied. 'It's a job for three hands.'

'I said I'd help you, dear,' Virginia said mildly.

'Maybe I can help,' Jack offered.

Half an hour later, they were all sitting around the Halgren table, looking at pictures of a son and daughter and grandchildren, and drinking coffee and eating Virginia's freshly baked crumb cake. It was homey and comfortable and the Halgrens reminded Valerie a little of her parents. She decided she was going to like living in Seattle.

Eight weeks later, Valerie learned she was pregnant. She fairly floated out of the doctor's office, and was so full of wonderful thoughts that she almost forgot to get off the trolley that took her home. She stopped at the liquor store and bought a bottle of French wine for dinner, ruining her food budget for the month without even noticing, and practically skipped along the street. Virginia Halgren was out weeding her rockery, and Valerie skidded to a stop when she saw her.

'I'm going to have a baby, Virginia,' she announced. 'I'm absolutely, positively pregnant.'

'Oh my,' Virginia smiled broadly, coming down to hug her, 'isn't that just wonderful.'

'I've been hoping and hoping.'

'I know you have.'

'I want to have lots and lots of babies, a dozen maybe.'

Virginia laughed. 'I had just two, and I found them more than enough.'

'But I come from such a big family,' Valerie said a shade wistfully, 'and it was so nice, sharing all the good times together.'

'How about Jack?' Virginia asked. 'Does he come from a big family?'

'No, he was an only child,' Valerie replied. 'But I'm hoping to have lots of kids, to make up to him for growing up alone.'

Valerie skipped up the stone steps into the house with only a shade less bounce. It was one thing to be so positive with Virginia, she knew, but quite another to convince Jack. Because the truth was, she knew that he didn't care about children at all. He had made that quite clear the second week they were married. Right after they'd moved into the house, in fact, and she had begun to talk of turning the second bedroom into a nursery.

'It's a sin to interfere with God's will,' she had said, openly aghast on the first night he brought rubber protection to their bed.

'Not my sin,' he had replied with a laugh. 'I'm not a practicing Catholic.'

She had drunk several glasses of champagne that night, in celebration of their first home together, and thought he must be joking, so she had let the subject drop. But in the cold sober light of morning, she raised it again.

'We can't afford to have a family now,' he said over breakfast. 'Maybe not for a long time. So what? We're fine with just the two of us, aren't we?'

But Valerie just looked at him in dismay. 'Jack, I *want* children, lots of children, as many of them as we can have.'

'Look,' he protested. 'I'm only earning a little over three bucks an hour. That barely feeds us. Maybe in a few years . . .'

'A lot of couples have less than we do, but it doesn't stop them from having children,' Valerie said reasonably.

But that made Jack angry. 'You don't know anything,' he snapped. 'We can't afford to have children unless I say we can. Now get that through your stupid little head.' And he slammed out of the house, gunned up the Chrysler, and roared off toward Boeing Field.

He had calmed down by evening, but he hadn't changed his mind, just his tactics. 'Look at your sister Marianne,' he said over supper. 'She doesn't have any kids, but that doesn't seem to be stopping her and Tommy from being happy with just each other.'

But it was the wrong tactic, because Valerie knew how anguished her sister was about being childless, and she knew that Marianne and Tommy would give anything to be parents to a whole houseful of kids.

It didn't matter, though, because the argument was moot now. Apparently, the few times Jack had bothered to use the rubber protection hadn't been effective enough to interfere with God, and whether Jack liked it or not, they were about to start their family.

Two hours later, candles lit the dining room. The table was set with the fine china and the good crystal that had come to them as wedding gifts, Valerie was wearing her best dress, the roast was carved, the potatoes were baked, the green beans were buttered, and the French wine was poured. And the time was right.

Jack Marsh stopped with his wineglass halfway to his lips. 'You're what?'

'I'm pregnant,' Valerie repeated. 'We're going to have a baby.'

The crystal slipped out of his grasp and shattered against the china plate, the red liquid spreading across the linen tablecloth like blood . . . his mother's blood.

Valerie sat with her hands in her lap, twisting her handkerchief into knots, much the same as her stomach was twisted, and looked up at Father Anthony from tear-filled eyes. 'I don't know what to do,' she cried.

'Calm yourself, my child,' the spindly parish priest said softly. 'It can't be as bad as all that.'

'He hasn't been home in three days, Father,' she sobbed, the tears spilling over once again. 'He doesn't want the baby.'

Father Anthony, little more than an arrangement of bones beneath his black cassock, leaned against the aged oak desk in his small rectory office as though needing its support to stay upright, and smiled gently at the girl before him. 'Of course he does, child. It just takes a little getting used to for some men, that's all. Women take to the idea of parenting so naturally, of course.'

'You don't understand,' Valerie whispered. 'He wanted . . . well, he didn't . . . I mean, sometimes, you know, he would use . . . something . . . so that I wouldn't get pregnant.'

Father Anthony stiffened. 'But that's a sin in the eyes of God, child.'

'He's not a practicing Catholic, Father.'

'But, before you were married, before any priest would marry you . . .'

'Oh, he agreed to raise our children as Catholics, if we were blessed with children, of course,' Valerie hurried to say. 'But I thought he meant by God's will, not his own.'

'God has His ways,' murmured the priest. 'You will have this child, Valerie, and Jack will be a good father to it. Your marriage has obstacles to overcome. As He does with all of us, the Lord has put them in your path to test you. But with the Church's guidance, you will persevere. Because, through loving Jesus, you love each other.'

'Then where has he been for three days?' Valerie cried. 'I've called everyone we know, and we don't know very many people here. He hasn't been at work. Nobody's seen him.'

'He needs time to think things through, Valerie,' Father Anthony said with genuine conviction. 'And then he'll come home. You'll see.'

Valerie sighed. 'Yes, Father,' she murmured obediently. 'I'm sure you're right. Thank you.'

She stood up and hurried out into the March afternoon, somewhat less than reassured. It had been raining since the day before yesterday, a persistent downpour that soaked deep into everything, including the bones. Jack had no warm coat with him, just the clothes he had worn home from work three days ago. She wondered if he lay dead in a ditch somewhere, the rain streaming into his staring eyes and gaping mouth, unheeded.

She hadn't really known how he would take the news about the baby. Part of her hoped he would rejoice, part of her anticipated his anger. She was totally unprepared for the heavy, hollow silence that greeted her announcement. He just sat there and stared at her for what seemed an eternity. Then, very quietly, he stood up, walked out of the house, down the rockery steps, got into his car, and drove away. There had been no word since.

Valerie hurried through the wet, anxious to get home. The awful morning sickness that seemed to linger through most of the day was threatening to erupt. She wondered what she would do if, despite Father Anthony's prediction, Jack never came back at all. It occurred to her, and not for the first time, that she lived with a man she hardly knew. She knew little of what he thought, little of how he would react. She wondered if it was that way with other married couples, and her very next thought was: If so, how did they survive?

Her various siblings had seemed quite satisfied in their unions, right from the start, and her brothers and her brothers-in-law had all professed genuine delight at the prospect of fatherhood. So, why not Jack? Parenting was peripheral to a man anyway. It was the woman whose lifework was nurturing the young. Valerie had no serious artistic ability or any great interest in business, and no ambitions for a career outside the house. She had been reared to replicate her mother. Jack might be fulfilled by his job with the airlines, but Valerie would never be fulfilled without children to raise.

The wind was whipping up, and as she turned the corner onto Hudson Street, she shut her eyes against the weather, and so missed seeing the Chrysler parked in the driveway until she was almost on top of it. She stood in the street, the rain dancing around her, wiping furiously at her eyes to make sure she wasn't dreaming.

She wasn't. The car was really there, and Jack stood on the front porch. They both began to run. Halfway up the rockery, he caught her, pulling her into his arms, and they held each other, soaked to the skin and not caring.

'I'm sorry!' they cried in the same breath.

'I needed time to think,' Jack said.

'I know,' Valerie replied.

'It just took me by surprise.'

'It'll be all right,' she said. 'I know it will.'

Jack lifted her off her feet and carried her the rest of the way up the steps and into the house.

5

John Marsh, Jr, JJ for short, was born in October of 1956, Rosemary Marsh barely a year later. Both pregnancies were problematic, and both times Valerie almost miscarried. But both babies were born perfect and healthy, and with an added side benefit. When she was able to have sex with Jack, although it still did not rank high on her list of favorite things to do, she found the tearing pain that used to accompany the act had diminished, and she no longer needed alcohol to get through it.

Valerie loved being a mother. Having children in the abstract was one thing, reality quite another. She looked forward to every moment she spent with JJ and Rosemary, whether it was to feed them, or bathe them, or hold them, or teach them. She even looked forward to changing their diapers. Raising a family was indeed what she had been born to do.

Her proudest moments were Sunday afternoons when, weather permitting, she and Jack would walk along the streets of Beacon Hill, each pushing a perambulator, and the neighbors would come out to smile and coo over her babies.

She couldn't wait until a third child came along, and sure enough, it wasn't long before she was pregnant again. Her joy was short-lived, though, because this time she did miscarry. She sank into a severe depression that lasted from early winter well into the spring. Nothing anyone said could ease her pain or her guilt as she tried to figure out what awful thing she had done to incur God's wrath. She couldn't believe her body had betrayed her for no reason at all, as Virginia assured her it had. She was listless with the children, more often than not finding it difficult even to get out of bed, and she took to sleeping for long stretches at a time. In desperation, Jack finally asked his sister-in-law Marianne to come.

'I was glad to get away,' Marianne said after Jack had collected her from the airport. 'Tommy's been driving me crazy.'

She promptly shooed him off to work, after which she inspected the house and the backyard and peeked at the two sleeping tots in the nursery. Then she went into the kitchen, fixed a tray with two bowls of hot soup and crackers, and brought it to the bedroom, rousing her sister from a deep slumber.

Valerie couldn't believe her eyes. 'How did you get here?' she cried.

'Jack arranged it,' she replied. 'Didn't he tell you?'

Valerie shook her head. 'That dear man,' she murmured. 'He never said a word.'

'I guess he wanted to surprise you,' Marianne said, smiling. She set the tray down on the night table, handed a bowl of soup to her sister, and took the other for herself.

'Tommy can't think, sleep, or breathe anything but the Irish Italian these days,' she said. 'I'm beginning to think it was a big mistake for Pop to lend him the money to buy out Mr Bertolli.'

In spite of herself, Valerie grinned. 'You mean it wasn't just a joke? He really *is* going to call the place the Irish Italian?'

'Well, it may have started out as a joke, but somewhere along the way, it stuck.' Marianne shrugged. 'The customers love it.'

The elderly owner of the restaurant where Tommy worked had made a deal with Tommy, and then he packed up his wife and moved to Florida. Tommy was ecstatic. It was a dream come true for him, to have his own place. And he was determined to make it the most popular restaurant in town.

'It's become his child,' Marianne said with a sad little sigh. 'To make up for all the ones we never had, I guess.'

Marianne and Tommy had been married for nine years, and so far, the doctors could not explain why there had been no babies. Valerie felt suddenly selfish. She thought of the two little ones sleeping peacefully in the other room, instead of the one she had just lost, and her heart went out to her sister.

'I don't know what I'd do without JJ and Rosemary,' she said softly. 'They're my whole life.'

'What about Jack?' Marianne asked.

'Jack spends more time with his friends from work than he does with us now. They go out drinking almost every night. Sometimes he doesn't get home until one or two in the morning. I guess I can't really blame him. I haven't been much of a wife to him lately, what with being pregnant most of the time, and now being so depressed over losing the baby.'

'You have to find ways, Val. You can't let go of your marriage like that.'

Valerie shifted uneasily in her bed. 'To tell you the truth, I like being pregnant.'

Marianne eyed her sister, who had never looked as pale or as frail as she did at that moment. 'From what I hear, you were pretty sick the whole nine months, both times. Not to mention losing this last one. What's to like about all that? Maybe it's time to give your body a rest, and just enjoy being with Jack for a while.'

It was exactly what the doctor had suggested to her right after the miscarriage. Valerie looked up at the ceiling. 'I couldn't stand it if it wasn't to make a baby,' she whispered.

Marianne snorted. 'Come on, Val, this is 1958, not the Dark Ages, and your health is what's important. So you think about yourself first and the Church second, for once.'

'You don't understand,' Valerie said before she thought. 'When I'm pregnant . . . Jack leaves me alone.'

For a moment, Marianne tried to tell herself she had misunderstood, but of course she hadn't. She pulled her straight-backed chair closer to the bed and eyed her youngest sister long and hard before she spoke. 'Have you talked to Jack about this?'

Valerie shook her head. 'How could I?'

'Because he's your husband, and because making love is supposed to be enjoyable for both of you,' Marianne replied, 'and obviously that's not happening here.'

'But it's not Jack's fault,' Valerie was quick to say. 'It's mine. I'm just one of those women who doesn't enjoy it very much.' She stopped short of saying that word. But even so, she was mortified. She had never intended anyone to know.

But rather than getting sympathy from her sister, Marianne burst out laughing. 'What are you saying – that you think you're frigid? Why? Did Jack tell you that?'

'No, of course not,' Valerie conceded, now totally miserable. 'It's just that I . . . well, I've known since my honeymoon that there was something wrong with me. And I've heard about women who don't . . . well, I mean, you know, who never . . . that is, can't have . . .'

'Orgasms,' Marianne said bluntly.

Valerie winced. 'Yes.'

'Would you like me to tell you about those women, Val?' her sister asked. 'Ninety percent of them aren't frigid at all, they're just ignorant. They don't have orgasms because their husbands don't know how to satisfy them. And the reason their husbands don't know how to satisfy them is because the women are too embarrassed to speak up.'

Valerie stared at her sister with eyes as round as saucers. 'How do you know that?'

'I hear things, too.'

Valerie knew there was no one else in the whole world that she would ever have been able to discuss this with, not even her doctor, and certainly not her priest. 'Did what you heard tell you why it has to hurt so much?' she asked.

'Of course,' Marianne replied. 'It hurts because you aren't ready. Women need to be aroused, much more than men, and that's why there's foreplay. And if a woman doesn't get enough foreplay, she's too dry inside, and that's why it hurts.'

'Oh.' Valerie's eyes filled with tears of relief, and Marianne reached out and took her sister's hand.

'And all this time, you've had no one to talk to about this, no one to ask, have you?' Valerie shook her head. 'Well, now you do,' Marianne said firmly. 'I'm here for three weeks.'

By the time Marianne Santini went home to Boston, Valerie was a new woman, fully recovered from her physical and emotional ordeal, and ready to face life again. She hadn't realized how lonely she had been, since her marriage, for someone she could really talk to. Virginia Halgren was a dear, always bringing by something fresh-baked, always offering to help with the children, but it wasn't the same as having someone you really knew, someone who was close to you, to confide in.

In the three weeks of her visit, Marianne and Valerie had talked about everything, about sex, money, the latest fashions, having babies, and all about living with someone you didn't really understand. Spurred to audacity by her sister, Valerie made up her mind to talk to Jack, the night after the doctor gave them the okay to resume marital relations, and he slid across to her side of the bed with obvious intentions.

'Jack, do you like making love to me?' she asked tentatively.

'Sure,' he replied as he tugged at her nightgown. 'If I didn't, I wouldn't.'

'I suppose not,' she said, pulling away ever so slightly. 'But women aren't all alike, are they? I mean, surely you've known some who were, well, better at it than I am, and maybe you—'

Jack let go of the nightgown. 'What's all this talk about other women all of a sudden?' he demanded.

'Well, it's nothing really,' Valerie began. 'I just thought—'

'Thought . . . thought what?' he snapped as his erection began to desert him. 'What could you possibly have to think about?'

Valerie was suddenly confused by his abruptness. 'What's the matter? Why are you being so defensive? I was only—'

He flung himself over to the other side of the bed. 'You were only what? Only snooping around somewhere where you didn't belong? Okay, so what did you find that was so awful? Some lipstick on my handkerchief? Some powder on my shirt?'

Valerie stiffened, her eyes widening in disbelief. This conversation wasn't going at all as she had planned. She had only meant to ask him to spend a little more time with her at the beginning of lovemaking, the way Marianne had suggested. Instead, he was as good as confessing to her that he had been with another woman.

He saw her shock. 'Look, it's not important,' he said soothingly. 'It's just something that happens when a woman gets pregnant and can't have sex, and a man can't do without, that's all. It doesn't mean anything. It's got nothing to do with us.'

She thought she might cry, but her eyes were painfully dry. 'I didn't find any lipstick,' she said around the lump in her throat.

He stared at her. 'Shit.'

She slipped quickly out of bed and fumbled for her robe.

'Where are you going?' he demanded.

She wanted to get away from him. She wanted to run from the house and stay away, as he once had. 'I'm going to check on the children,' she told him.

'Shit,' he said again.

Jack watched her leave the room, and as the door closed behind her, he picked up the heavy lamp from the table beside the bed and hurled it against the wood frame, splintering it.

She had tricked him, of course. She had known nothing, but had been able to coerce an admission from him. He was as angry with himself as he was with her, maybe even angrier. He'd meant it when he said it wasn't important. Other women meant nothing to him. It was just like he had told her, a way of relieving himself now and again when she was pregnant and he was afraid to touch her.

Valerie was always so sick when she was pregnant. It scared him and he hated being scared because it made him feel so lost, so inadequate. This last time had been the worst. She had almost died trying to carry the fetus to full term, and the doctor had told him straight out that the miscarriage had probably saved her life.

Something changed after that night. Seeing her, people thought Valerie was the same as always, but inside, safely out of sight, a part of her dried up and died, like the baby she had aborted. Trust was shattered, respect damaged. They had been married for little more than two years, and he had already been with another woman. Valerie was devastated. It didn't matter anymore that she wasn't very good in bed. She knew now that it wasn't entirely her fault, and she thought he might have been more patient with her. He should have known what the problem was. After all, he was the one who had the experience.

The thought brought tears to her eyes, tears of hurt, but also of anger. Valerie was barely twenty-one years old, and she would spend the rest of her life with this man who was her husband, but he would no longer be the hero of her story. She would wash his clothes, fix his meals, share his bed, and raise his children, but she would never again feel about him as she had felt on the day they had stood before God and pledged to love, honor, and be faithful to one another so long as they both should live.

They never spoke of it again. If Jack continued his forays into other women's beds, Valerie didn't want to know about it. When he came to her in their bed, she did not resist, and tried her best to make it pleasurable for him, but she never tried to talk to him about foreplay and mutual satisfaction. By August, she knew she was pregnant again. She waited until the middle of October to tell him.

Jack was appalled. He had insisted on using condoms.

He knew it upset her, he knew she wanted more children, but he couldn't help it. He had killed his mother and he would never forget that. He tried to convince Valerie to use a contraceptive method more reliable than the condoms proved to be, but she wouldn't hear of it.

'It's against God,' was all she said.

It didn't seem to matter to her, or God, that she was risking her life. But it damn well mattered to him. If anything were to happen to her, he knew he would not survive. She was what his mother had been to his father, his anchor, his ballast. And like his father, without her, nothing would have any meaning. He was infuriated by his need of her and his inability to get control of it. He wanted to wring her neck.

He went out and got drunk. It was past two o'clock in the morning when he came home, tripping up the rockery steps, stumbling through the front door, slamming it shut behind him. Valerie heard him clattering around. And then, a few minutes later, she heard a shattering crash. She jumped out of bed and hurried into the kitchen. Jack stood in a puddle of whiskey and broken glass.

'Bottle slipped right outta my hands,' he whined.

Valerie went for a towel. 'Go to bed, Jack,' she said wearily. 'You've had enough to drink.'

He was suddenly in a rage. 'Don't you tell me what to do,' he roared at her. 'Don't you ever tell me what to do!'

Valerie turned to him. 'You'll wake the children,' she said evenly. 'Is that what you want?'

'What I want? When did it ever make any difference to you what I want? You don't care about me. All you're interested in is babies. Babies, babies, and more babies. That's all you ever wanted from me.'

Her stomach was beginning to grind and she just

wanted to go back to bed. She began to clean up the mess. 'That's nonsense and you know it.'

He turned his back on her and fished around in the cabinets for another bottle of liquor. 'Where's the rest of the booze?'

Valerie dumped the broken glass into the trash container. 'That was all there was.'

He was livid. 'What do you mean, all there was? I want a drink.'

Valerie put her hand on his arm. 'Come to bed, Jack. It's late.'

He whirled at her touch, and lashing out, caught her full in the face with the back of his hand. She crumpled to the floor, tasting blood. Jack bent over her and pulled her up by her hair with one hand. 'I said don't-you-tell-me-what-to-do,' he roared, his other hand slashing across her face as if to punctuate each syllable. Then he began to kick her, the toe of his shoe slamming into her body.

Valerie fainted. When she regained consciousness, Jack was huddled in a corner of the kitchen, sobbing into his shirtsleeve. She pulled herself up to a sitting position. Her lip was bleeding, her cheek hurt, one eye was oozing and badly swollen, and it was difficult for her to breathe.

'I'm sorry,' he cried. 'Oh God, I'm sorry. I don't know what came over me. I must've had too much to drink. I wouldn't hurt you for the world, you know that. I love you so much. You're my whole life. I don't know how I could've . . . please, forgive me. Please, say you'll forgive me.'

Valerie dragged herself over to her husband and took him in her arms. 'It's all right,' she murmured into his hair. 'It's all right.'

They sat there in the kitchen, clinging to each other,

rocking back and forth, Jack promising, over and over, that he would never hurt her again. After a while, she managed to get him to the bedroom and into bed. Then she crept into the bathroom and threw up.

Being hit was nothing new to Valerie. She had grown up with a father who had meted out corporal punishment liberally. Valerie had always accepted that there was a reason for his action, be it an infraction of the rules, or a lesson to be learned, or a behavior to be modified. But she could think of no reason for what Jack had just done. Even if she had done something to displease him, she wasn't a child anymore, needing this kind of discipline, and it was humiliating to think that her husband might see her that way. True, he had apologized, and he had assured her that it would never happen again, but she still didn't understand.

So she lay on the bathroom floor, hugging the toilet, feeling very vulnerable, and tried to figure out what it was that had gone wrong.

The next morning, Jack was out of bed before Valerie was even awake, tending to the children, and then fixing a tray of scrambled eggs and coffee to bring into the bedroom. Valerie smiled at the gesture through the pain of her swollen lip and bruised cheek, but she couldn't eat a bite of it, she could barely even move, and sometime during the night she had begun to spot. Jack rushed her to the hospital.

Miraculously, she did not lose the baby. Three of her ribs were fractured, two badly bruised, but the fetus was uninjured, and the doctor gave her something to stop the spotting. She took it as a sign from God that everything would be all right. She told the doctor she had tripped on the rockery steps. He didn't question it. He didn't even look at Jack. He simply taped her ribs, bandaged her cheek, gave her a prescription for a mild painkiller, and told her she was to stay in bed for three weeks.

She was very quiet on the way home from the hospital. Jack glanced over at her. He had bundled her up in a blanket against the rainy autumn day so that only her face was visible. She had her eyes closed and he hoped she was asleep. But as he drove down Hudson Street and turned into their driveway, she startled him by saying in a clear, even voice, 'I've been thinking that I'd like to go home for a while, to Rutland.'

Jack felt something clutch at his heart. 'You mean you're leaving me?'

She turned to him in surprise. 'No, Jack, I'm not leaving you,' she replied. 'You're my husband. It's just that I won't be able to take care of the children by myself for a while, and it wouldn't be fair to ask Marianne to come back again so soon. And you know my parents have been wanting us to visit. This just seemed like the right time.'

'And what if I don't want you to go?' he asked petulantly.

She looked at him steadily. 'Then of course I wouldn't,' she replied.

He knew he could stop her, keep her here with him. All he had to do was say so, and she would stay. It was on the tip of his tongue to say the words, but he didn't. Because, in truth, he knew it would be a relief not to have to see her all cut and bruised and bandaged like she was, a constant reminder to him of what he had done to her.

'All right,' he said with a careless shrug, 'you can go.'

He made reservations at Federal Airlines for two days later, packed her suitcases, and drove her and the two children to the airport. He carried JJ and Rosemary onto the plane, buckled them into their seats, kissed Valerie goodbye, and joked around with the ground personnel until the plane took off. Then he went to a nearby bar where he and his buddies from Federal often hung out. It was Sunday and there wasn't much action. He struck up a conversation with one of the waitresses he knew, a tall buxom brunette about thirty-five years old, and didn't refuse when she invited him home.

Martin and Charlotte O'Connor met their daughter at the airport in Burlington late on Sunday evening. They were horrified when they saw her stitched lip and bandaged cheek and blackened eye, and alarmed when she winced from their embrace.

Valerie told them calmly about falling down the rockery steps, and they accepted her story without question. For some reason, she felt it was her responsibility to protect Jack, and it was important to her that her family continue to think well of him. Besides, it was all so far away now, it hardly seemed like such a lie. Nevertheless, she was glad when the attention finally fell on JJ and Rosemary, and she was able to sleep most of the way to Rutland.

It was like being a child again, in her old bedroom with the rosebuds that climbed up and down the walls and the featherbed of her youth, with her mother fussing over her, and her brothers and sisters pampering her, and her father watching from a distance. But, of course, Valerie would never be a child again.

She was happy to stay in bed, happy to let the baby inside of her grow quietly for a while. She slept for long periods of time. Charlotte brought her nourishing soups and healthy omelets and fresh-baked breads and home-made applesauce and stacks of pancakes smothered in maple syrup, and brushed her hair and changed the bandage on her cheek. Her sisters Cecilia and Elizabeth came to take care of JJ and Rosemary. Her brothers Marty and Kevin came to tell her bad jokes that made her laugh until her sore ribs rebelled. And her father sat in the rocking chair by the bed and read to her from *Alice in Wonderland*. It was familiar and therefore comfortable. She nestled deep into her family and felt safe.

After a few days, it was almost as though she had never left. But of course she *had* left, and in the quiet moments when she was alone, she thought about Jack and what had happened, and tried to understand.

Eventually, her lip and her cheek healed, her bruises faded, her ribs mended. The sickness that had always plagued her pregnancies began to subside. Some color came back into her cheeks. She was able to take short walks with Martin in the fields behind the house, and drive into town with Charlotte. By the middle of November, she felt strong enough to reclaim at least partial control of her children from her sisters.

'You need some new clothes,' her mother announced, when she was sure Valerie could make the trip. 'I thought we might go down to Boston for a few days, and buy out all the stores.'

'The children could use some new things,' Valerie said, 'but I really can't afford to buy anything for myself.'

'I didn't make myself clear,' Charlotte said. 'This is a treat from Dad and me.'

Valerie was delighted. She loved Boston and going there meant she would get to see Marianne.

'I hear you had a nasty accident,' her sister said as soon as Charlotte had succumbed to the exhaustion of traveling with small children and the two young women were alone together. 'Was it before or after you had your little talk?'

Valerie forced a laugh. 'You mean did I fall down the steps in the throes of passion?'

Marianne looked keenly at her youngest sister, while Valerie held her breath. Of all the sisters, their relationship had always been the closest, and Marianne had always been the hardest to deceive. The smile on Valerie's face was threatening to crack by the time her sister grinned and shrugged.

'Yeah, something like that.'

'No,' Valerie said, truthfully. 'I never got around to talking to Jack. It was never the right time, I guess.'

'And here you are, pregnant again.'

'Yes, here I am.'

Suddenly, Marianne chuckled. 'His condoms don't seem to work very well, do they?'

Valerie chuckled, too. 'No, they don't,' she said.

They stayed in Boston until the Saturday before Thanksgiving, buying out most of the shops in the city. The first big snow of the year fell on Rutland the day after they returned, well over a foot in thirty-six hours. JJ and Rosemary were delighted. They pressed their little noses to the window and watched as the big flakes flopped out of the sky and made the fields, the driveway, the front walk, and even Charlotte's vegetable garden all disappear. When the sun came out, Valerie bundled them into snowsuits borrowed from their cousins and they played all afternoon under the watchful button eyes of the roly-poly snowman their Uncle Kevin built for them. Valerie smiled from her bedroom window. She remembered all the snowmen of her childhood. They, too, had been built by Kevin. The circle of life, she thought, what a miracle it was.

The day before Thanksgiving, Valerie awakened to

the wonderful smells of pumpkin and mince and pecan pies baking in the ancient stove that Charlotte refused to part with. The woman was absolutely convinced that the modern contraption Martin wanted to buy for her would ruin her crusts.

Valerie stretched and smiled. It was such a luxury to sleep in. Later, she would help her mother make the traditional chestnut stuffing, and fresh cranberry mold, and succotash. Tomorrow, she would baste the turkey as it roasted, cut up the winter fruit salad, butter the hot muffins, and set the tables with the lace cloths and good china that were saved for special occasions. And then she would put JJ in his little blue suit and Rosemary in her pretty pink dress, and watch them enjoy their first family Thanksgiving.

Unfortunately, Marianne and Tommy would be missing. They were needed at the Irish Italian. And Valerie's middle brother, Hugh, was in the military and currently stationed in Germany. But everyone else would be there. Except, of course, for Jack.

Valerie snuggled under the covers and looked around at the room that had always surrounded her with warmth and security. She would have to go back to Seattle sooner or later, she knew. Each time Jack telephoned, his entreaties for her return grew more insistent. She was quick to tell him how much she and the children missed him, which was true, but slow to tell him exactly when he should reserve the tickets for their return flight.

'The house is so empty without you,' he said, neglecting to add that he was spending very little time there. She pleaded fatigue and a slow recuperation from her injuries. He yielded.

Valerie glanced out her window. The boughs of the pine trees that lined the drive and flanked the house drooped under their heavy blanket of snow, and glistened in the early morning sun. It would soon be December, and December in the mountains of Vermont was the most wonderful time of all. Valerie wished she could stay through Christmas, for JJ and Rosemary, as well as herself, because Christmas in Rutland was pure enchantment. In fact, she wished she could stay forever. But it was no good wishing for things that couldn't be. Seattle was her present and Rutland was her past, a past she might look in on now and again, but never really return to. The realization brought the prickle of tears to her eyes, and she wiped them away impatiently.

She and the children and the new baby she was carrying returned to Seattle a week later.

A second girl was born to the Marshes, in May of 1959, with a weak heart that was having trouble pumping enough blood to the rest of her body. The doctors at Swedish Hospital, doing everything they could think of to do, were not sure at first whether she would live. Panicked, Jack packed JJ and Rosemary off to the Halgrens, called in at work to explain the emergency, and went to the hospital.

'I want to see my daughter,' he said to the duty nurse, after he had stood beside Valerie's bed and watched her cry herself to sleep.

The nurse gave him a green gown and mask, and led him to an incubator in the corner of the nursery. Tubes and wires attached to the infant ran out of the machine and plugged into monitors that beeped and stuttered with life-sustaining regularity. Jack peered at the tiny form inside the incubator. She looked so small. She weighed only five pounds at birth, and was not gaining. He felt so helpless. He wondered whether the cracked ribs he had given Valerie had impacted the baby, after all.

'Hello there, little one,' he whispered to her through the glass. 'I'm your daddy, you know. You're having a pretty rough time of it, aren't you? But don't worry, I'm here now, and I promise not to let anything bad happen to you.'

He pulled up an empty chair, sat down, and began to wait. 'Is she going to make it?' he asked the doctors and the nurses and the technicians who came to check the monitors and adjust the tubes. 'Is my baby going to live?' The technicians shrugged, the nurses smiled, and the doctors told him that only time would tell.

Consumed with guilt, Jack kept his vigil for three days. Except for occasional visits to Valerie and the bathroom, he never left the baby's side. He dozed briefly from time to time, but mostly he spoke softly to the struggling infant through the walls of her incubator and refused, even over Valerie's anguished protests, to let a priest come near. Somehow he felt that as long as he could keep the priest and his last rites away from her, she would live.

He calmed her when she was restless, encouraged her when she seemed exhausted, and tried his best to urge life into her. When he didn't know what else to talk about, he began to tell her about himself, and about his father and the women and growing up in Kansas City. It was more, much more, than he had ever shared with Valerie. And when there was no more to say on that topic, he told her about his time in Korea, and about his love of airplanes, and finally, he shared with her all the funny, silly, weird little things that happened at work. It didn't matter to him that she couldn't understand any of it. The sound of his voice seemed to soothe her, so he kept on talking.

The nurses brought him food when he wouldn't go to the cafeteria. They murmured to one another from one shift to the next.

'Take care of him, he's neglecting himself for the child.'

'What a devoted father.'

'If that baby lives, it'll be because *he* willed it, not God.'

The doctors waited and held their breath, knowing that the first seventy-two hours were crucial, if she could hold out that long.

The baby reached the crisis point and passed it, and the doctors let out their breath and cautiously agreed that she would live. Jack staggered out of the nursery and down the hall to wake Valerie with the good news, and she saw real tears through the exhaustion in his eyes.

'They weighed her, and she's gained a whole ounce,' he said proudly.

They named the little girl Ellen. The doctors kept her at the hospital for a month, testing and monitoring, until they were certain it was safe for her to go home. Valerie went to see her every day, and Jack stopped in every evening after work.

'She'll never be as strong as JJ or Rosemary,' the doctor said on the day that Ellen was finally released from the hospital. 'She won't have their stamina or their agility, but that's all right. She's a happy baby, and she'll find her own way.'

For weeks afterward, whenever Valerie chanced to awaken during the night, Jack's side of the bed would almost always be empty. She would find him in the nursery, leaning over the crib, reassuring himself that Ellen was all right.

Five months later, Valerie suffered another miscarriage. This one happened relatively early in the pregnancy, however, and her recovery time was much shorter than before.

Virginia helped care for the children, fussing over them much the same as Charlotte had. Then one Thursday, Jack came home from work with a big smile on his face.

'I've got a couple of days off,' he announced. He had asked for the time, and was taking it without pay, but he didn't need to tell her that. 'We're going to the coast. It's all arranged.'

'But Ellen's not well enough to travel,' Valerie reminded him.

'Ellen's not going to travel,' Jack said. 'I've already talked to the Halgrens. They're going to look after the kids for us.'

Valerie opened her mouth to protest that it was too much to ask of their neighbors, and that she couldn't possibly live without her children for even a few hours, much less days, but then she closed it again, because a few days at the coast to relax and not have to worry about anything or anyone sounded like heaven.

And it was. The middle of January was off-season for the resort town of Ocean Shores, which meant that the accommodations were reasonable and the beach was nearly empty. They took a little cabin as close to the water as they could get. Although the weather was blustery and the water crashed against the sand, it rained only once during the four days they were there.

Valerie, bundled into a heavy coat, sat on the beach for hours at a time, letting the sea spray wash over her, cleansing her skin, cleansing her soul, and watching Jack feed the seabirds from bags of day-old bread he bought at the local bakery, spreading some on the sand and tossing the rest into the air, laughing as the gulls fought over who would snatch them in mid-dive.

'Why are you doing that?' she asked.

'So that the little birds get a fair shake at the crumbs on the ground,' he told her. 'The gulls are nasty birds, they'd take everything.'

When they had enough of the beach, they went to town, stopping in at quaint antique shops and trendy boutiques. In the evenings, they sampled the local restaurants, and then they would go back to their cabin and Jack would build a fire, and they would curl up on the sofa and listen to music on the radio. Sometimes, they would talk, but they didn't make love. The doctor hadn't yet given permission. Instead, they went to sleep with their arms around each other. It was almost like the summer they had met, back in Boston, when they were first getting to know each other, when they were first beginning to fall in love.

'We haven't had much time for just us, have we?' Valerie observed, 'what with the children and everything.'

'No,' Jack agreed. 'We haven't.'

They returned from the coast refreshed and renewed, promising themselves they would go back to Ocean Shores as often as they could. But a week after Ellen celebrated her first birthday, and Valerie learned that she was pregnant yet again, Jack announced that they were moving to California.

'I'm being transferred to San Francisco,' he said in explanation. 'Federal is expanding its operations down there, and I'm going to be a crew chief.'

Valerie's eyes shone with pride. 'A promotion,' she cried, hugging him. 'Oh, that's wonderful.'

'Well, don't get too excited,' he said, secretly delighted by her enthusiasm. 'There's a downside. I'll be working nights.'

'Oh, that's all right,' Valerie said brightly. 'We'll manage just fine.'

'At least it means more money, and we can sure as hell use that.'

'What's California like?' Valerie asked.

Jack, who had never been there, shrugged. 'Southern California is movie stars and wall-to-wall swimming pools. Northern California is cold water and free thinking.'

They were packed and ready to leave within a month. The landlord let them out of their lease with minimum fuss, and what few household goods they had acquired were shipped south to a five-bedroom house in a little town on the San Mateo coast, about half an hour's drive from the San Francisco airport. Jack had bought the house after a frantic two-day search and had ordered furniture from the Sears, Roebuck catalogue. He hated the idea of commuting and would have preferred being closer to the airport, but there was nothing in the vicinity that they could remotely afford, and there were very few suitable homes for rent. Martin gave them the down payment. Marianne and Tommy, who were doing well at the restaurant, insisted on helping to pay for the furniture.

Although Seattle had never exactly been home to Valerie, even after four years, it had come close, and she was sad to go. The Halgrens had been like family, the neighborhood peaceful, and the climate agreeable, despite the fact that it rained a lot.

'Now you keep in touch,' Virginia said, hugging her and the children, 'and come back and visit if you can.'

'Send pictures of the children once in a while,' John said.

'Oh, yes,' said Virginia. 'We do so want to watch them grow up.'

Valerie nodded. 'I promise.'

They drove out the way they had come in, south on

Route 99, past Boeing Field and Sea-Tac Airport. Mount Rainier, in a spring coat of snow, loomed ahead of them and then behind them. Three hours later, they crossed into Oregon.

PART TWO

1962

PART TWO

I

The April day brought little warmth to the San Mateo coastline, that strip of land nestled between ocean and mountain, home to a string of little towns that ran from Montara in the north down to Moss Beach and El Granada and finally to Half Moon Bay, the city named for the bay it sat beside.

The sun sparkled off the curve of the bay, blurring the outlines of the handful of fishing boats clustered around the dock at El Granada's Princeton Harbor, and provided the fishermen working their nets scant protection from the chill winds that whipped the water into whitecaps and set the trawlers' decks to rolling. Fishing was not a thriving industry on the Coast, even at the height of the salmon season, but a small group of stalwart souls persevered, managing to carve out meager livings before passing their boats down to sons or grandsons.

The fortunes of circumstance and transportation had all but ignored the isolated strip of land that stretched along the Pacific, some twenty miles south of San Francisco, balanced precariously as it was between the ocean and the coastal mountain range.

Dairy cows had once dotted the landscape, granite had been quarried until the pit was exhausted, and the lumber industry had prospered until a moratorium halted the wholesale slaughter of trees. Agriculture was now the predominant industry of the region. The soil was fertile, perfect for growing almost anything. Over the years, acres of potatoes and mustard had given way to the current crops of Brussels sprouts and pumpkins.

In its history, the largely inaccessible area had been a natural sanctuary for the native Costanoan Indians until Gaspar de Portolá's Spaniards came along. Then it protected the Californios, as the Mexicans who followed Portolá were called, from enterprising Europeans and land-hungry Anglo-Americans. More recently, it had represented a safe haven for rum-runners sailing up the coast from South America.

Abandoned by the railroad at the turn of the century, and all but forgotten in the land development explosion that began with the 1849 gold rush, the coastal community of 1962 was not significantly different from the small rural settlement it had been fifty, or even a hundred years before.

The fishermen were finishing their long morning's work. One by one, they jumped off their boats and headed up the weathered pier to the Gray Whale restaurant where they would wrap their cold fingers around hot mugs of coffee while waiting for lunch to be served.

Inside the Gray Whale, Valerie Marsh lay on the floor. She knew that was where she was because she could feel rough boards beneath her shoulder blades, cutting through her thin waitress's uniform, but she didn't know how she had gotten there. She opened her eyes.

The familiar restaurant surrounded her. The heavy wood ceiling beams that were draped dramatically with fishing nets holding caches of iridescent abalone shells. The gray walls that were hung with pictures of the local fishing boats and their proud, grinning owners. The solid legs of the captain's chairs that were drawn up to thick round tables. The dark quiet booths, off to the sides, that the tourists favored. The long sweep of the mirror-backed bar that she could see through the archway. And the comforting smells of fresh fish and fries, newly baked bread and beer, and bacon and coffee.

But there she was, on the floor, and all around her was broken glass, and pottery, and water. Lillian McAllister, the other waitress who worked the lunch shift, and Leo Garvey, the owner and cook, were bending over her. Some of the customers were, too, the restaurant being busy at this time of day. *Oh God*, she wondered, horrified, *what happened*?

'Honey,' Lil was saying anxiously, 'are you all right?'

Valerie considered. 'I guess so,' she said slowly. 'What did I do?'

'You just keeled over, that's what,' Leo said, barely concealing his panic. 'Scared us half to death.'

'Help her up,' someone said.

'Get her some water,' someone else said.

Valerie tried to sit up, but a sharp pain in her swollen abdomen stopped her.

'What's wrong?' Lil asked.

'I don't know,' Valerie gasped. 'It just hurt.'

'The baby?'

'It's too soon.'

'Leo, the doctor,' Lil cried. 'Get the doctor. The number's in the book by the phone.'

'I know,' Leo said. 'I know where it is.' He wrung his big hands in distress, then wiped them on his greasy apron and hurried to the telephone.

'Val,' Lil instructed, 'don't you move till Leo gets the doctor.'

But Valerie did not intend to lie there in the middle of the restaurant, making a spectacle of herself. She tried again to sit up, and this time the pain was not so bad and she was able to get to her feet with the help of Fisherman Jim and Old Billy, two of the regulars. They sat her carefully on the bench of an unoccupied back booth. Someone brought her a glass of water and she drank it gratefully.

Leo came back from the telephone. 'Doc Wheeler says we got to bring her right over to the hospital,' he said breathlessly.

'Well, I'll have to take her,' Lil said.

'Why you?' Leo asked, wanting desperately to take her himself.

But Lil was too quick for him. 'Who else is there?' she countered. 'You can't leave now – it's the middle of the lunch rush. You might be able to wait tables for me, but I sure as hell can't do the cooking for you.'

Outmaneuvered, Leo sighed and dug into his pocket. 'Okay, okay, you take her in the Chevy,' he said, handing over the keys. 'And you drive real careful, you understand?'

'Sure, Leo, sure,' Lil told him with a broad grin. 'What do you think? That I'd crack up that precious truck of yours?'

'Never mind the truck,' Leo retorted. 'It's Val I'm worried about.'

They helped Valerie out of the Gray Whale, Leo practically carrying her despite her protests, and into the shiny black Chevy pickup parked in front of the restaurant. 'You remember what I said, Lil. Watch out for the bumps.'

'I know, Leo, I know. She'll be okay.' Lil climbed up into the driver's seat and started the engine. 'You call Donna to come fill in,' she told him, referring to the third waitress who rotated shifts with them. 'Okay?'

'Okay,' Leo said. And then it occurred to him. 'Should I call Jack?'

Valerie thought for a moment. 'No,' she said finally.

'I don't want to worry him. Not unless there's some need.'

'You call me, soon as you know anything,' Leo demanded.

'We'll let you know,' Lil assured him, backing the Chevy out of its space. 'He's in love with you, you know,' she said to Valerie, as she maneuvered the truck out of the parking lot, and turned north on the Coast Highway.

Valerie smiled through the pain. 'Leo loves all his girls.'

'Yeah, maybe,' Lil conceded. 'But you most of all.'

Richard Wheeler, obstetrician and gynecologist, was waiting for them at the hospital. He put Valerie in a wheelchair and rolled her into the emergency room himself.

'Okay, let's have a look at you,' he said.

The Coast was lucky to have such a facility, the area being as isolated as it was from the rest of civilization, barely linked to San Francisco by the notorious Devil's Slide, and accessible to the more populous side of the San Mateo Peninsula only by a narrow twisting road over the mountains.

St Hilda's Hospital, a neat two-story stone structure, built around a large atrium, and perched on a hill above the ocean, had once been a cloister. It was now run by the Sisters of Hope, with as much modern equipment as their small order could afford. The gardens were maintained by the hospital auxiliary, an august body of women of no small influence in the community. Before she had died of cancer three years ago, Leo Garvey's wife had been its president.

Lil paced up and down the small waiting room. Valerie was seven months pregnant. She should not even have been working, much less carrying full plates, cleaning tables, lifting heavy trays. She had never been strong, at least not as long as Lil had known her, and it was going on two years now since the Marshes had moved to the Coast and Valerie had come to work for Leo at the Gray Whale.

There was something about the girl that touched Lil's heart and made her want to look out for her, something beyond her youth and her frailness. Lil knew that Leo felt the same way. They had both told Valerie months ago that it was time to quit. She didn't look good. She didn't look *healthy*, the way expectant mothers were supposed to look.

But Valerie had insisted that she felt fine and wanted to go on working. Besides, she said, they needed the money. Leo relented. Over the past six weeks, however, she had become paler and more haggard, and the circles under her eyes had grown bigger and darker. Now she had up and fainted, and Lil was really worried.

Inside the emergency room, Dr Wheeler was finishing up his examination. 'All right, Val, this was your last day of work,' he said, looking down at her through his rimless spectacles, his hands on his spare hips. 'And don't bother to argue with me. If you want this child, and I have every reason to expect that you do, you'll go home and go to bed and you'll stay there until you're ready to deliver.'

'But I can't,' Valerie protested. 'We need the money. If I'm not working, Jack will have to take on a second shift, and then he'll, well, he . . .' She couldn't get the words out of her mouth.

'I said bed,' Wheeler repeated firmly. 'You need rest, complete rest. You're to do absolutely nothing but sleep and eat.' He scratched his bristly blond head. 'I'll talk to Jack, if you like.'

'Oh no,' Valerie said quickly. 'Please, I'll tell him.'

She looked up at the ceiling, tears in her eyes. 'I want this baby . . .'

'Then I suggest that you do as I say and, God willing, you'll have it. And while we're on the subject,' he added, 'I want it clearly understood that this one will be your last.'

Valerie looked at him stubbornly. 'But . . .'

'Spare me your protestations,' he declared, deftly administering an injection to relieve the cramping. 'I know you're Catholic. And I know birth control is a mortal sin. But five children and two miscarriages in six years are too many. You're not strong enough for this, and another pregnancy would probably kill you. After this one's born, I'm giving you a prescription for the new birth control pills.'

'You want me to take the pill?' Valerie gasped. 'I couldn't.'

Wheeler looked at her keenly. 'If the children you already have had the choice,' he said firmly, 'I think they'd choose to have their mother around to raise them rather than to have her dead from another pregnancy. What do *you* think?'

Valerie lay back on the examining table with a heavy heart. Her last child? It wouldn't matter to Jack, she knew. He hadn't really cared much about having children in the first place. But it would matter to her. She was one of nine herself, and she had always hoped to have at least that many. But she didn't argue. She didn't have the strength.

'How will I explain it to Father Bernaldo?' was all she said, to no one in particular.

'I may work in a Catholic hospital,' Wheeler said, 'but my concern is for the health of your body. The health of your soul is between you and God.'

Valerie was silent as Lil drove her home through the

winding dirt roads of El Granada, one of a string of little towns nestled against the length of the Coast. The house on Delgada Road was a mess, as it always was when Valerie came in from work. But she was too weak to do anything about it, and too miserable to care that Lil saw.

Jack was in the kitchen, feeding the two younger children peanut butter and jelly sandwiches, so Lil took Valerie upstairs, undressed her, and put her to bed.

The bed felt delicious and Valerie sank into it, not realizing until that moment how tired she really was. In the pink nightgown with the long sleeves and high neck that Lil pulled over her head, she looked far more like a child herself than the pregnant mother of four.

Lil knew what it was like to take care of a family and hold down a job at the same time. She had two kids of her own. Her husband had died when the youngest was only two, and Lil had had to raise them by herself. But they were now a lot older than Valerie's kids were, and they could do for themselves quite nicely. Thinking about that gave her an idea.

'Val, I'm going to send you my Judy. She's sixteen now, she's been helping around the house for years, and she's pretty good at it.'

'But Lil . . .'

'No buts. I've made up my mind. Don't know why I didn't think of it months ago. She gets out of school about two-thirty, and she can be here by three. She'll pick up around the house, do the laundry, look after the kids, give them dinner, put them to bed, and still be home in time to do her homework.'

'That's awfully kind of you, Lil, really it is,' Valerie said, 'but we couldn't possibly—'

'I said no buts. And of course you can. If it's money that's worrying you, forget it. Judy wouldn't let you pay her anyway. She loves the kids and she loves you, too. She'll be happy to do it for nothing. Besides, it'll give her some practice that'll come in handy one of these days.'

'It's not right.'

'Of course it's right. And I should have thought of it sooner, but better late than never. Now it's all settled. And that's the end of it. So you just rest yourself, like the doctor said.'

Valerie smiled. She knew there was no arguing with Lillian McAllister once she'd made up her mind. She didn't have the energy to argue anyway. The bed was so nice and soft and warm. She tried to stay awake, but her eyes were too heavy.

Jack Marsh stood in the doorway, filling it up. 'What's the matter?' he asked.

'She collapsed at work,' Lil answered.

'Is she all right?'

Lil nodded. 'But Doc Wheeler says she's to stay in bed until the baby comes. No bending, no lifting, no stress.'

She looked at him sharply, but he said nothing. She wasn't sure what she had expected, but there was something about Jack Marsh that always put her a little off-balance. He was certainly good-looking enough, with that muscular body and black hair and those magnetic yellow eyes, maybe too good-looking. You could never quite trust someone that handsome. Or maybe it was the way he had of looking at you, as though he could see right through your clothes and made no bones about it. Or maybe it was something else, something lurking just below the surface, that made her so uncomfortable.

'I'm going to send my Judy over to help from now on,' Lil added. 'She'll be here by three.'

Again she waited, but there was no reaction. He

merely shrugged and walked away. Lil turned back to Valerie, and only then did she see how right Doc Wheeler had been. The girl looked more like a cadaver than an expectant mother. Whatever reserves of strength she possessed had been used up long ago. Her face was almost as white as the pillowcase and her eyes were nothing but black-ringed hollows. Lil tucked the bedcovers gently around her and quietly tiptoed out of the room. She needn't have been so careful. Valerie was already asleep.

2

Valerie awoke, all at once. It was light outside the bedroom window, behind the drawn curtains, but she had no idea what time it was. The last thing she remembered was Lil taking off her clothes and pulling a nightgown down over her head. She must have been asleep before her head touched the pillow. She twisted her neck to see the clock on the nightstand. The oversized hands read five-fifteen.

Valerie yawned and smiled. She had slept for little more than three hours and yet she felt remarkably refreshed. The house was quiet for this time in the afternoon. Usually, the children would be up from their naps by now and running about with youthful exuberance. These days, when she came home from work, she was always too busy cleaning the house, or washing and ironing the clothes, or preparing dinner to supervise calmer activities.

She sat up suddenly, finding her body unexpectedly stiff and sore. Five-fifteen! Jack went to work at three. Who was looking after the children? As if in answer to her question, the bedroom door opened a crack, and a freckle-faced teenager looked in.

'Oh good, you're awake,' Judy McAllister said brightly. 'And you must be starving. Don't move. I'll be back in a minute with a tray.'

The bedroom door closed again before Valerie could ask about the children. She vaguely remembered Lil saying something about sending her daughter over to help, and she had apparently wasted no time. Valerie lay back against the pillows. The last time a doctor had ordered her to bed was when she was pregnant with Ellen and had gone home to Rutland. She remembered how coddled she had felt then and how pleasant it was, and how much stronger, more resilient, she had been for it. She blessed Lil McAllister. It would be good to have Judy around.

Maybe Dr Wheeler was right. Maybe so many pregnancies in so short a time had been unwise. She had certainly grown weaker and more lethargic with each birth. But there wasn't one of her children that she would give up.

After her third daughter, Priscilla, was born, she had tried to discuss the situation with her spiritual adviser, short squat Father Bernaldo of the parish church in Half Moon Bay, hoping he would say that it was okay to take a break for a while. But he had only pushed his plump fingers together pontifically and reminded her of her duty.

Well, the matter was out of her hands now. Dr Wheeler would do whatever needed to be done, she knew, despite her protests. And for the rest of her married life, she would be obliged to satisfy Jack's appetites without even the promise of a reward. Valerie sighed at the thought and then shrugged. God willing, the child she carried would be born healthy, and then she would love and nurture five as she would have loved and nurtured nine or ten.

She twisted her body into a more comfortable position. In truth, she was so very tired that a respite from birthing might be welcome. She hoped Father Bernaldo would not demand too harsh a penance for that display of selfishness.

The bedroom door opened again and Judy came in, a big tray balanced on one hand. She looked, for an instant, just like her mother at work at the Gray Whale, and Valerie smiled.

'The children?' she asked as soon as the girl was all the way inside.

'Oh, don't worry about them,' Judy replied with a grin. 'I spread newspaper on the kitchen floor and tied each of them to a leg of the table and they're finger-painting each other.'

'Each other?'

'Well, actually, JJ, Rosemary, and Ellen are finger-painting Priscilla, and she's just thrilled with all the attention.'

'Finger-paint?'

'Sure. I made it with food coloring. It's perfectly harmless and it washes right off.'

Yes, Valerie thought, it would be good having Judy around.

The girl placed the tray carefully on the bed. 'We have poached eggs and sausage and home-fried potatoes and toast and orange juice and milk,' she said. 'I know it isn't exactly breakfast time, but I didn't think you'd mind.'

The food smelled wonderful and Valerie realized that she was hungry. 'No,' she said, fork already in hand, 'I don't mind at all.' She took several huge bites, washing them down with orange juice. 'Amazing, isn't it, what a little nap can do for the appetite?'

Judy laughed. 'A little nap? I guess I wouldn't call twenty-seven hours a little nap.'

Valerie blinked. 'Twenty-seven hours?' she repeated in confusion. 'What do you mean? It's not even five-thirty. I went to sleep around two.'

'That was yesterday,' Judy said.

Valerie was stunned. 'This is Tuesday?' she gasped. 'I've been asleep for a whole day?'

'You sure have,' Judy said, her hand on the door-knob. 'Mom got a little worried this morning and called Dr Wheeler. But he said to let you sleep just as long as you could.'

'I can't believe it.'

'All I can say is, you sure must have been tired,' Judy said on her way through the door.

The fork, full of poached egg and fried potato, hung suspended, two inches from Valerie's mouth. Tuesday? She had slept away a whole day? It didn't seem possible. She was always such a light sleeper, awakening when Jack came to bed at midnight and then at dawn, before the children got up. It gave her sort of a pulse of the household. Whatever happened, she was always there to know and to act, if necessary. That is, except for Monday afternoon and most of today. She felt strangely insecure. She wondered what had happened in the world while she lay oblivious. She opened her mouth to call Judy back and ask her, but then thought better of it.

'No wonder I'm hungry,' was all she said, and stuffed the fork into her mouth. The food tasted delicious. The world would wait.

Valerie had not yet decided whether she liked the sleepy coastal area that Jack had moved her and the children to. She liked the house on Delgada Road all right. From the outside, it looked like it was two separate houses, each with its own peaked roof, joined together by a flat span. Inside, it was quite roomy and had lots of windows. The big backyard was full of pine trees and reminded her of Rutland.

The first summer, Jack built a patio along the back of the house. The following spring, he put a small deck

92

off the second-floor hallway, between the two halves of the house. Then he connected the deck to the patio with a flight of redwood steps, and put a gate at the top of the steps so the children might venture out there without falling. From the deck, a sturdy redwood ladder, attached to the outside wall, led up to the flat part of the roof between the two peaks. Valerie thought it might be nice one day to have a deck on that part of the roof for sunbathing.

Not much grew in the backyard, under the pine trees, but there was pampas grass at the side of the house and wild poppies in front, and patches of eucalyptus everywhere. Valerie filled the rooms with blooming houseplants of every description, and a little herb garden struggled along on the kitchen windowsill.

The beach, an easy walk down Avenida del Oro and across the Coast Highway, was a broad strip of sand around a curve of water that had given its name to the city that had grown up at the southern edge. The children loved to play in the gentle wake of the tide, running first to meet it and then to escape it. Valerie liked to walk along the inviting stretch of sand, looking for unusual shells and interesting pieces of sea glass.

But she was lonely. True, Jack was at home most of the day, but he was often out puttering in the garage or slumped in a chair in the living room, reading technical manuals. The few neighbors she encountered were polite but not very friendly, and there was no one resembling Virginia Halgren anywhere on the street.

When they had moved in, just short of two years ago, Valerie had anticipated staying home with the children as she always had. But even with Martin's generosity, their mortgage payments were high, a fourth child was on the way, and the raise that had come with

Jack's promotion was being eaten up by a higher cost of living.

'I can work a double shift,' Jack offered when it was obvious that it would take additional income to make ends meet, 'or pick up something part-time around here.'

But Valerie shook her head. 'You're already doing your share,' she said. 'So why don't you let me get a job?'

Jack balked. 'I can support my family. I won't have anyone thinking that I have to send my wife out to work.'

'Lots of women work, Jack,' she told him. 'It's no shame. Besides, we don't know anyone here that it would matter to, do we?'

'What about your family?'

'Well now,' Valerie said thoughtfully, with a little smile, 'we don't have to tell them, if we don't want to.'

Jack relented. 'This would only be temporary, you understand, just until we get out from under.'

'Of course it would,' she agreed.

Valerie's only experience in the job world was working summers in a soda shop back in Rutland. But she was bright and attractive and willing, and she didn't think it would be too difficult finding something she could do. She canvassed the restaurants on the Coast, but none were hiring. She left her name. She spoke to retail shop owners, but their sales forces were full. She left her number. She contacted doctors, and dentists, and real estate agents, but they needed receptionists who could type sixty words a minute. She subscribed to the local newspaper and waited.

Then, at the end of July, one LouAnne Briggs up and left Half Moon Bay for marriage and a new life in Portland, Oregon. That left restaurant owner Leo Garvey one waitress short. And so Valerie came to the Gray Whale.

The restaurant became an extended family, what with Leo, Lil, Donna, the third waitress, and Miguel, the dishwasher, and of course the regular customers. It was hard work, but Valerie didn't mind. She looked forward to getting up in the mornings and getting out. She dressed the children, gave them breakfast, prepared their lunches, fed Jack, and was down at the pier by seven o'clock. She didn't tell Leo she was pregnant. She thought he wouldn't have hired her if he had known. But by the end of the first week, when he found out, he didn't care. He was already a little bit in love with her.

She worked right up to November, and when Priscilla was born, on the eleventh, Leo sent flowers and a sterling silver rattle, and Lil brought a beautiful carriage blanket she had knit herself.

'I'll bet you this was his, from when he was a baby,' Lil said, fingering the rattle. 'He and his wife never had any kids. He must have kept this, all these years, and finally found something to do with it.'

Valerie's earnings, plus the leftovers that Leo was always handing out, helped keep food on the table, and after the New Year, when she was fully recovered from the birth, she had little trouble persuading Jack to let her return to the pier. She had come to love the noisy restaurant, the clatter of crockery, the sizzle of fresh fish cooking. She listened with a smile as the regular customers complained about the abnormally high winter seas or last season's poor run of salmon, and Leo grumbled about what a mess of things the president of the United States was making.

'Take this Bay of Pigs fiasco,' he pronounced on an April Wednesday in 1961, thumping his newspaper angrily. 'Now Dick Nixon would never have gotten us in such a mess.'

'Yeah, you're right about that,' Fisherman Jim said,

forgetting the salmon for a moment. 'This Kennedy kid's a might too young and cocky to suit me.'

'Mebbe,' Old Billy said with a toothless grin, 'but he sure has got hisself a pretty wife.'

Now, almost exactly one year later, Valerie ate up her toast and drank the last of her milk, and tried to calculate the effect that Dr Wheeler's orders would have on her family for the next two months. The Gray Whale was a popular restaurant on the Coast, and while Leo paid his waitresses little more than the minimum wage, tips were good, and the food packages that accompanied her home each day were substantial. The effect would be significant.

After Judy came back and cleared away the tray, she brought the children in.

'I think there are some little people who need to know their momma's okay,' she said.

Valerie looked at them. Normally boisterous, they stood timidly at the foot of the bed, staring at her with huge round eyes. She smiled and opened her arms, beckoning them closer, and with little squeals, they fell onto the bed beside her.

'Oh my, Priscilla, what pretty colors you are,' Valerie exclaimed, while her youngest daughter beamed. 'Now let me see,' she said, looking at the hands of the others, 'I say JJ painted your arms, and Rosemary painted your face, and Ellen painted your legs. Am I right?'

The children were delighted and they laughed and tumbled around the bed together until Judy came to collect them for dinner.

'Don't worry,' the girl promised, when they proved reluctant to leave. 'After dinner, we'll play in the bathtub, and put on our jammies, and come back to say good night to Mommy, okay?'

That seemed to satisfy them and they trotted off

obediently. The moment the door closed behind them, Valerie was asleep. The first time she woke up was a little after seven o'clock, just in time to say good night to the children. The second time was much, much later, when Jack came into the room and stumbled against the steamer trunk that was kept at the foot of the bed.

'Goddam son of a bitch,' he snarled.

Valerie snapped on the lamp beside the bed with a bright smile that died on her lips. His clothes were disheveled and smelled of oil, and he had been drinking. She wished immediately that she had left the light off and pretended to be asleep. In the six years they had been married, Jack had been this drunk perhaps a dozen times, and on most of those occasions, she had asked the wrong question or said the wrong thing and paid the price. Five of those times, she had ended up in the hospital, where the doctors had silently tended to her injuries while she told them of her persistent clumsiness.

Jack always cried afterward, when he sobered up and saw the damage he had done, and promised he would never hurt her again. She wanted to believe him, but by now, she knew better. He wasn't a bad man, she reasoned, just a troubled one, sometimes, and she was his wife, for better or worse.

'Well, I see you're finally awake,' he said, peering down at her with bloodshot eyes. 'And about time, too. Some people have nothing better to do than lay around in bed all day, don't they?'

She didn't want to say anything, she just wanted to go back to sleep. 'The doctor said I need the rest, Jack.'

'Yeah, well, I need a wife, goddam it,' he shouted. He had been scared down to his soul the whole time she had slept, scared she would never wake up, scared she had found a way to leave him for good. She had looked like death when Lil brought her home Monday afternoon. A dozen times he had looked in on her in the hour before he had to leave for work. She was so still, so white. She hardly looked as though she were breathing. It was having all those damn children that was killing her. He had absolutely no doubt that one of them finally would. Just like he had killed his mother. He could have lived very nicely without children. But he couldn't live without Valerie.

When his shift ended at midnight, he was afraid to go home, afraid he would find her still unconscious, afraid of crawling into bed beside her stiff, cold body. He went to the Hangar instead, the bar just across Route 101 from the airport, where some of his co-workers hung out. About half a dozen of them were there and he drank with each of them on his way home until Scotty, the owner and bartender, turned off the lights and kicked him out. Then he, too, drove home, very carefully, because the road over the hills to the Coast was narrow and winding. And he climbed the stairs, dread building with every step, not wanting to open the bedroom door, not wanting to turn on a light, not wanting to see his wife, who was seven months pregnant and dying because of him.

She was awake. He thought she had even been about to smile. His relief was so overwhelming that his eyes began to fill with tears and he stiffened. He could never allow himself to betray such weakness in front of her. He was the head of this household, after all, and he had to be strong.

'I work eight, ten hours a day, and I come home, and maybe I want a cup of coffee or something,' he said, his words slurring, 'and you tell me you just want to rest.'

Valerie looked at him for a moment. 'All right, Jack,'

she said, 'I'll go downstairs and make you some coffee, if that's what you want.'

She struggled out of bed and slipped into her robe.

'And maybe I want to have some conversation, too.'

'Then I'll have a glass of milk with you,' she said, 'and we'll sit in the kitchen and talk.' She walked out of the bedroom and down the hall, but he caught up with her at the top of the stairs.

'Maybe I don't want to go downstairs,' he snarled. 'Maybe I want to have my coffee right up here. Maybe I want to have coffee in bed.'

'Then I'll bring it up.'

He grabbed her arm, twisting it hurtfully. 'Whatever I say, you'll do, right?'

'Yes, Jack.'

'Then how come we got a houseful of kids that are killing you? How come, when I say no more, you don't listen?'

'Jack, you don't want to talk about this here,' she said, not wanting the children to wake up and hear him. 'Come on downstairs with me.'

'I don't want to go downstairs,' he shouted. 'I want you to tell me right here.'

Valerie pulled herself free of his grasp and started down the stairs, hoping he would follow her. Neither of them saw six-year-old JJ open the door to his room and peer out into the hallway.

'Turn away from me, will you?' With a growl, Jack lunged for her. Valerie cried out. JJ screamed. Jack whirled around at the sound, and as he did, his right elbow connected with the side of Valerie's head. The blow, incidental though it was, was enough to knock her off balance, and she tumbled head over heels down the stairs, landing in a heap at the bottom.

'Mommy,' shrieked JJ.

'Val,' gasped Jack.

But Valerie couldn't hear either of them.

The lights in the main operating room at St Hilda's burned into the early hours of the morning. Dr Wheeler had brought many children into the world during his twenty-eight years of practicing family medicine on the Coast, a few, sadly, at the cost of the mother, but he was determined that would not happen this time.

Valerie briefly regained consciousness when they lifted her from Jack's car at the emergency entrance, placed her on a gurney, and hurried her into the hospital where Wheeler was waiting.

'Save my baby,' she whispered, grasping his hand with the last of her strength. 'Please save my baby.'

'I'll save you both,' Wheeler promised. 'Just hang in there.'

'She fell down the stairs,' Jack said.

The doctor sighed. Three times before, he had tended to injuries unrelated to her pregnancies, a dislocated shoulder, a broken wrist, a fractured cheekbone. He thought her brave and loyal and steadfast, not clumsy. And he knew that Catholic or not, no matter what she said, if it came to a choice, this time he was going to choose the mother.

Her injuries were significant, multiple contusions and fractures that they couldn't stop to document, and severe uterine hemorrhaging. Many times, Wheeler doubted that he would be able to keep his promise, even with an outstanding resident assistant and four of the best operating room nurses he had ever scrubbed with working diligently and tirelessly beside him. But as dawn broke on Wednesday, April 4, miraculously, both mother and fetus were still alive, and Wheeler was able to get the bleeding under control, at least for the time being, and take the baby by cesarean section. The last thing he did was to remove the ruptured uterus. There would be no need for birth control pills now. Valerie Marsh had had her last child.

The baby, a boy, weighed barely three pounds. St Hilda's had no appropriate incubator facilities, and Wheeler knew immediately that he lacked the medical expertise to treat either of them further. As soon as the surgery was completed, an ambulance sped mother and child over the coastal mountains to Stanford University Hospital in Palo Alto, where the very latest in medical technology was available.

And it was there that Jack Marsh, now sober and more frightened than he had ever been in his life, had his first conversation with God.

The doctors told him there was but a fifty-fifty chance of survival for both of them. A pediatric specialist was summoned for the premature infant and an orthopedic surgeon and a neurologist were called in to tend to Valerie. They walked around with grim expressions. Jack prowled aimlessly up and down the corridors outside the operating room. He was told surgery might last for hours. He wandered over to the nursery and looked through a glass partition at the incubator holding his son. He was told everything possible was being done.

He remembered when Ellen was born, all those wires and tubes that had been attached to her small body. But there were at least twice as many wires and tubes here, and this baby was a lot smaller than Ellen had been. He wanted to go inside, to stand vigil for his son, as he had for his daughter, but he couldn't. He didn't deserve to. He found his way to the chapel instead. There was no one else in the quiet room. Jack sat down on a bench and started to cry.

'God, help me,' he begged. 'When Ellen was born, I could tell myself it wasn't my fault, because it was so long after . . . afterward. But this time, I know. And JJ knows. And if they die, I've killed them. I've killed them both.'

Valerie lay in a coma for twelve days. In addition to the ruptured uterus, she sustained a cracked pelvis, a broken collarbone, five splintered ribs, and a fractured skull from her tumble down the stairs. It took three separate surgeries to repair all the damage.

She had taken the brunt of the fall. Amazingly, the baby was free of injury. But at seven months, his chances of survival were only fair. He was jaundiced, his lungs were filled with fluid, and he suffered from intermittent apnea. The doctors had to exchange his blood twice. Eventually, his lungs cleared and he began to breathe on his own. The nursing staff monitored his tiny heartbeat round the clock. He was put on an intravenous formula, and his incubator was kept very warm and moist.

Both mother and son survived. When Valerie opened her eyes on the afternoon of the thirteenth day, the first person she saw was Richard Wheeler. Indeed, although he had no privileges at this hospital, the doctor had been there a good deal of the time. Beside him was a tall man with short blond hair and horn-rimmed spectacles, wearing a white doctor's coat.

'Well, unless you two are angels, I must still be alive,' Valerie murmured, more as a question than a statement.

Wheeler smiled, and gestured to the man next to him. 'This is definitely an angel, but yes, you're still alive.'

'My baby?'

'The baby's alive, and so far he's doing fine,' Wheeler assured her.

'Where am I?' Valerie asked, realizing that this was not a room she recognized.

The man in the doctor's coat told her where she was. She managed to nod. But her eyelids felt heavy and her head ached. An IV was attached to her right arm. She raised her left hand to her temple and stopped. All her hair was gone, in its place, a swath of bandages.

'It'll grow back,' Wheeler assured her when he saw the shock in her eyes.

Her arm fell to the bed. 'Tell me.'

'You were brought in on April 4,' the other doctor said. 'This is April 16. You had a nasty fall and you were hemorrhaging. Your husband took you to St Hilda's, where Dr Wheeler delivered your baby prematurely. Then you were brought here, you for surgery and your baby for highly specialized neonatal care. I'm Dr Andrew Maldarone. I did your surgery, and I can discuss the details and answer all your questions when you're a little stronger. For now, I'll simply tell you that you're going to be just fine. Dr Huber, the pediatrician, tells me that your son is holding his own, too.'

'A boy?' she murmured with a smile. 'I had another boy? I'm glad. I didn't want JJ to be alone.'

With that, her eyes closed and she drifted off to sleep, the smile still on her face.

'*Will* she be all right?' Wheeler asked as the two physicians looked down at Valerie, little more than a mass of broken bones held together by translucent skin beneath the sheet.

Maldarone nodded. 'She's had a pretty bad time of it, but I suspect there's an inner strength that'll pull her through.'

Jack came early the next morning. He stood just inside the door, twisting his cap in his hands, and stared at his feet, not knowing what she would say or do, but knowing that whatever it was, he would certainly deserve it.

'I'm sorry,' he whispered. 'Oh God, I'm so sorry.'

'Never mind, Jack,' Valerie said wearily. 'I fell down the stairs, that's all.'

'I thought I'd killed you both.'

'Well, as you can see, you didn't,' she said. It was on the tip of her tongue to add *this time*, but she decided against it.

'I had a priest come,' he told her. 'He gave you both the last rites . . . well, just in case, you know.'

Jack was typically loving and thoughtful afterward. Even so, this act surprised her. 'Thank you,' she murmured.

Feeling somewhat more secure, he edged a little closer to the bed. 'Lil let Judy cut school and she stayed over for a couple of days, so the kids would be taken care of, and now Marianne's here.'

Valerie nodded. There was a pause then, and he thought she might have drifted off. But she hadn't. 'Have you seen him?' she asked.

'Yes,' he told her. 'He's awfully tiny, but they say he's a fighter.'

'I want to see him,' she said. 'I want to see my son.'

Jack scurried out of the room in search of a nurse. Only after he had gotten permission did he return with a wheelchair. Then, awkwardly but carefully, he maneuvered Valerie out of the bed and onto the seat. With one hand on the chair and the other on the portable stand that held her IV, he pushed his wife down the hall to the nursery.

The nurse draped a green gown over her and put a mask over her face. Then Jack wheeled her as close to the incubator as the maze of medical machinery would permit.

And Valerie had her first look at her second son, tiny and mottled and thrashing around as much as the tubes and wires that criss-crossed his little body would allow, with his eyes screwed up tight and his mouth wide open and his little fists punching at air.

'See?' Jack laughed from behind his mask. 'See what a fighter he is?'

Valerie smiled. She looked him over very carefully, following each tube and wire to its terminal, wondering what the flashing numbers and punctuated blips were all about. Finally, her eye caught on the little blue card attached to the foot of the incubator that read: *Baby Marsh*.

'He needs a name, Jack,' she said. 'He's two weeks old and he needs a name.'

'I know,' Jack replied. 'They wanted me to name him, but I told them no. I told them they would have to wait for you.'

'Well, then, we'll name him for two angels,' she said, with a smile her husband had no way of understanding. 'Welcome to the world, Richard Andrew Marsh.'

And almost as if he had heard her voice, the baby quieted his thrashing and turned his head inquisitively in her direction.

PART THREE

1967

I

The hot breath of the Santa Ana winds swept up from the south, dipped over the mountains, and surged along the Coast, leaving a heavy haze in its wake. October, a time of first frosts and russet leaves in other parts of the country, meant the best of summer to this part of northern California. A month of blue skies and sunbathing and the final effort to conserve water before the winter rains came to transform the dun-colored hills into green majesty, replenish the reservoirs, and turn dirt roads into mud.

Temperatures soared up into the eighties, school children played hooky, pumpkins dotted the fields, and the fetid smell of ripening Brussels sprouts filled the air. On weekends, the Coast Highway was clogged with beachgoers. Barbecues sizzled, dogs were bathed, and the locals smiled a little bit more than usual, and spent extra time out-of-doors.

'Can you believe this weather?' they would ask each other.

Valerie Marsh was spending her extra time weeding, and was out on her front lawn one morning when a woman walked casually up the driveway and stuck out her hand.

'Hello,' she said. 'I'm Connie Gilchrist. I'm going to be your neighbor.'

Valerie scrambled to her feet. 'Hello,' she returned, a shade warily. 'I'm Valerie Marsh.'

'Nice to meet you,' Connie said pleasantly, her hand still extended.

Valerie hastily wiped her dirty fingers on her shirt-tail and shook the woman's hand. 'You must be the one building the house on the corner.' There were only three houses on this block of Delgada Road, and none of them, Valerie knew, were for sale.

'The very same.'

'I guess it ought to be finished pretty soon.'

'In time for the next ice age, I expect,' the woman declared, rolling her eyes.

Valerie giggled in spite of herself. 'That's sort of what I thought, actually, but I never would have said it.'

'Would you mind if I used your telephone?' the soon-to-be-neighbor asked. 'I was supposed to meet the tile man here an hour ago, and I have to be back in the city by noon.'

'Sure,' Valerie said, abandoning her weeding and leading the woman up the steps and through the front door. The telephone sat on a small table in the hallway. Connie Gilchrist attacked it like a dog after a bone, and Valerie backed away to a distance that was safe enough for her to study the stranger in her house without being too obvious about it.

She looked to be about ten years older than Valerie, who at thirty could still pass for a schoolgirl. She was a little taller, and not quite as slender, and silver threads were beginning to streak her short brown hair. She was attractive in an effortless sort of way, wearing a gray suit and matching pumps, a pink blouse, and just the right amount of makeup. Alone, the suit would have been too severe. The blouse softened it just enough. To it she had added just the right amount of jewelry, which all together had a marvelously understated effect.

Valerie looked down at her own baggy jeans and

faded shirt, and ran a hand through her straggly pony-tail. She wondered about women who looked like Connie Gilchrist and what kind of lives they led in a world she knew nothing about.

Connie put down the telephone with an exasperated thump and turned to Valerie. 'His wife says he left over an hour ago, and he had only one itsy-bitsy little stop to make first.' She sighed. 'I'm just going to have to wait for him, I guess. That's what I get for dealing with a one-man operation.'

'You can wait here, if you like,' Valerie said before she could stop herself.

Connie smiled, and it was a warm, open, genuine smile. 'Thank you,' she said. 'I'd really appreciate that. There's no place to sit in the house, and it's too hot to wait in the car, even with the windows down.' She looked around. 'This is nice,' she said, her glance taking in the living room, the dining alcove, and what was visible of the kitchen. 'Comfortable, homey. How long have you lived here?'

'Seven years now,' Valerie replied, thinking how shabby her home must look to such a sophisticated woman. 'We keep meaning to paint and re-cover the furniture, but we never seem to get around to it.'

'I like it just the way it is,' Connie said, and she sounded so sincere that Valerie forgot about the stains on the sofa and the crayon pictures on the walls and the toys all over the floor.

'Would you like a glass of iced tea?' she asked on impulse.

'I'd love it,' Connie replied. 'That is, if I can use the bathroom first. The plumbing's not hooked up at the house yet, either.'

Valerie showed her guest to the small bathroom that was tucked inconspicuously under the stairway and then

111

hurried into the kitchen to put fresh placements on the table, slice a lemon, and pluck a just-baked banana bread from its cooling rack. She was thrilled that she had made a fresh pitcher of tea this morning, rather than wait until evening as she usually did.

'I wondered what it was that smelled so good,' Connie said, coming into the kitchen and spying the banana bread. 'Do you always do your own baking?'

'Of course,' Valerie answered, pouring the tea. 'Don't you?'

Connie laughed and sat down in the chair Valerie indicated, the only one with a reasonably intact vinyl seat. 'I wouldn't know how to bake a cake if it were the only thing standing between me and starvation.'

Valerie's eyes widened in genuine surprise. Everyone she ever knew, from her mother and her sisters to Virginia Halgren and the members of her parish church in Half Moon Bay, did their own baking. 'Going to a bakery is a real treat for me,' she said.

Connie swallowed a bite of the banana bread. 'Take it from me,' she assured her hostess, '*this* is the treat.'

'May I ask you something,' Valerie ventured.

'Sure.'

'Well, this is a pretty rural area. I mean, the people who live here are mostly laborers, farmers, blue-collar types, commuters who can't afford to live over the hill or up in San Francisco. Why would someone like you want to build a house here?'

Connie grinned. 'You mean I picked the wrong color blouse?' Valerie looked embarrassed, and Connie leaned toward her. 'Don't let my "impress the natives" getup fool you. Underneath this chic exterior, I'm a Minnesota miner's daughter with ideas above her station.'

At that, Valerie's mouth dropped open. 'My father owns a quarry in Vermont,' she said.

'That puts you a giant step above me,' Connie responded. 'My daddy never got higher than foreman of the swing shift.'

'Then how did you get to be so sophisticated?' she blurted before she could stop herself.

Connie shrugged. 'My folks wanted their kids to have a better life than they had. My father swore that none of us would ever go down the mine. I have four brothers and a sister, and I can tell you it wasn't easy. Dad worked double shifts and Mom scrubbed other people's floors and washed other people's laundry, but they saw to it that every one of us kids got a college education.'

'I'm the youngest of nine,' Valerie said. 'I have three sisters and five brothers and none of us went to college. My brothers could have gone if they'd wanted to, but my father always said that college was wasted on girls who were only going to get married and raise a family. I guess he was right. My sisters and I all got married pretty much right out of high school.'

'Well, it's never too late, you know,' Connie declared.

'Oh, my goodness, no,' Valerie said, shocked. 'I couldn't go to college at my age. I've got five children to raise. Besides, what would be the point? I'm not bright enough to be anything.' Jack had assured her of that.

Connie considered the young woman sitting across the table from her. 'I don't think I answered your question,' she said. 'I'm building a house here because I'm a real estate broker, and I think this area is due for some serious development.'

'How exciting,' Valerie exclaimed.

'My husband and I have been in business together up in San Francisco for the past fifteen years, but in two more months, he'll be my ex-husband, and he's going to be buying out my share of the company. I didn't really want to stay in the city, so I did a little survey of the surrounding area, and decided the best place to start my own firm was right here on the Coast. And the fastest way to get to know a place has always been to live in it.' Connie grinned ruefully. 'At least, I thought it was the fastest, until I hooked up with my builder.'

Valerie didn't know what to say. Except for a pediatrician in Seattle, she had never known a professional woman before, much less had a conversation with one across her kitchen table. 'I'm sorry about your marriage,' she settled on at last.

'Don't be, because I'm not,' Connie assured her. 'When two people start to hurt each other more than they help each other, they're better off being apart. Anyway, I got a terrific stepdaughter in the bargain, and that's worth a lot.'

Valerie had never known a divorcée before either.

The rains came in November. For the first few weeks, at least, everyone on the Coast was delighted. Tap water ran freely again. The seven-minute shower stretched into a luxurious twelve. Clothes no longer had to be worn several times before they were laundered. Wasting precious drops stopped being a cardinal sin. But in a climate where the year is split in half by a dry season and a wet season, it was sometimes more pleasant to anticipate the one when in the throes of the other.

By early December, reservoirs were overflowing, unpaved roads, such as Delgada and del Oro, began to run like rivers, roofs meticulously patched every spring sprang new leaks, Devil's Slide washed out, forcing commuters going north to detour east, and the geraniums Valerie had lovingly nurtured in her redwood flower boxes drowned.

'We sure do need all the rain we can get,' muffled voices in yellow slickers and rubber boots said as they sloshed past one another.

'But why do we have to get it all at once?' came the faceless reply, and everyone began to wish for the dry days of summer to return.

'I'm Dreaming of a Wet Christmas,' quipped a disc jockey on a local radio station.

The Marshes bought their tree two weeks before Christmas and left it in the garage for three days until it had dried off enough to bring into the house. Valerie had gotten used to rainy holidays, but she never stopped yearning for the old-fashioned white Christmases of Vermont. She would put the children to sleep with stories of snowball fights and sleigh rides and mugs of hot apple cider that her mother flavored with maple syrup and had ready and waiting for cold fingers to grasp.

'What's snow?' Ricky asked.

'Snow is very much like rain,' Valerie explained. 'Only the air is so cold that the raindrops freeze while they're falling out of the sky and turn white by the time they hit the ground.'

'Have I ever seen snow?' Priscilla wanted to know.

'No, you haven't,' her mother said. 'But JJ and Rosemary have. A long time ago, when they were very young, a lot younger than you are right now.'

Most of all, however, Valerie missed having her whole family gathered round her. Every year, the O'Connors begged her to come home, but Jack could never take leave from work at that time of year, and Valerie would not even consider leaving him alone over the holidays.

'Go, if you want to go,' he would tell her, thinking of some blonde or brunette in maintenance or customer services he had been making progress with. Jack rarely came home for his pleasures anymore. Since her

115

hysterectomy, after Ricky was born, Valerie had stopped pretending any interest in sex. Now that he could finally enjoy an orgasm without having to worry about the possibility of another mouth to feed, his wife had turned indifferent on him.

Not that she had ever been hot, of course, he reminded himself, but she had at least been willing to accommodate him when he edged over to her side of the bed. And when there was no one else around who aroused his interest, willing had been better than nothing. Now, it was a battle royal for him to assert his marital rights, and most of the time not worth the effort.

'We're not going to go without you,' Valerie would say firmly. 'The holidays are a time for the family to be together, not a time for you to be by yourself.'

It wasn't as though they had made any friends that might include him in their festivities, she knew. Jack had some buddies from the airline that he liked to hang out with after work, but there was no one she would call close, and he had never indicated any interest in socializing with the people that Valerie knew.

Jack was no longer working nights. He was now the day crew chief. It was not so much a promotion as the result of a cut-back. A prolonged strike in 1966 all but crippled Federal Airlines. The company was forced to lay off fifteen percent of its employees, including two thirds of Jack's night crew, and reduce its service by ten percent. Which meant that Jack was now working longer hours, with more responsibility, at a twelve percent reduction in pay.

'We think you're ready to move up, Marsh,' his boss told him.

Jack had been ready for four years. Until the strike, the company had operated on the seniority system and Tug Hurley, the former day chief, had him by seven years.

116

'This cut in pay is only temporary, Marsh,' his boss assured him when Jack hesitantly mentioned the issue of salary. 'We all have to pull the old belt in a notch or two, until the company gets back on its feet. And we will.' He slapped Jack on the back. 'We'll be right back up there before you know it, because we have top-drawer employees like you working for us.' The man shifted his feet. There was something about Jack's steady yellow-eyed stare that made him uncomfortable. Something that told him that Jack knew the pay cuts didn't extend to management. 'Besides, you're one of the lucky ones, you know,' he said, allowing a note of belligerence to creep into his voice. 'You still have a job.'

Jack smiled affably. He assured his boss that he appreciated having this challenging opportunity to serve the company, and that the raise that should have gone along with the promotion could wait. On his way home in the rain, he stopped and bought a bottle of bourbon.

'They fired Hurley because he was making top scale,' he told Valerie when he got home, dripping water on the kitchen floor, a third of the bourbon gone. 'They gave me the job because they knew they could get me cheap. Promotion? What a laugh. They just wanted someone to work for coolie wages.'

Valerie was serving dinner to the children. 'You could have been laid off,' she reminded him, putting down the last plate and coming to take his dripping raincoat.

'What do *you* know,' he snarled at her, dropping into a chair, slopping a measure of bourbon into a glass from the table, and downing it in one gulp. The children stared at him silently.

Valerie shrugged. 'I guess I don't really know anything,' she said mildly, bending to retrieve his wet shoes, 'except that you've been with Federal for such a

117

long time and they've always treated you right. Maybe now they're looking to get some of that loyalty back.'

Jack knew the airline had been good to him all these years, he just didn't like the idea of being taken advantage of. He supposed he did owe them his loyalty, but he hated it when Valerie was right. He lashed out at her, his right foot catching her in the abdomen, knocking her off her feet, sending her crashing against the refrigerator. 'I don't owe them a goddammed thing,' he roared. 'They've more than gotten their money's worth out of me.'

Eleven-year-old JJ jumped off his chair and ran to his mother.

'Leave her alone,' Jack ordered. 'She doesn't need your help.'

'I'm all right, JJ,' Valerie said between gasps. 'I just got the wind knocked out of me. Go back to the table.'

JJ stood his ground.

'I said get away from her,' Jack bellowed, rising menacingly. 'Sit down and eat your dinner.'

Valerie reached out to give JJ an urgent push, but she was too late. Jack's open hand smashed across the boy's face. 'When I tell you to do something, boy, you do it. You don't make me tell you twice.'

JJ stumbled back to the table and scrambled into his chair. Blood coming from his cut lip dripped onto his pork chop. Valerie scrambled to her feet and hurried to fetch a wet towel to press against JJ's face until the bleeding stopped. The children sat frozen.

'Eat,' Jack told them.

'I'm not hungry,' ten-year-old Rosemary said.

'I work like a dog to put food on this table and you're not going to waste a bite of it. Not if I have to force it down your throats.'

The children began to gobble their food as quickly

as they could, Jack standing over them, watching every forkful. JJ managed to stuff his peas and mashed potatoes and homemade applesauce past the big lump in his throat, but carefully avoided the bloodied pork chop.

'Everything,' his father bellowed. JJ ate his pork chop.

'Now you can go to bed,' Jack said, when the five plates were clean enough to satisfy him. The children scurried out of the kitchen as fast as their little legs would carry them.

Jack lowered himself into his chair and poured out another measure of bourbon. Valerie put his dinner in front of him and sat down across the table with her own plate and waited for the anger to vanish as suddenly as it had erupted, as it always did. She knew the signs. The fire in his eyes would fade and then his whole body would sag into itself and he would be filled with remorse. And he wouldn't even remember what had set him off. She knew he hadn't really meant to kick her or to strike JJ. It was the pressure that built up inside of him that made him lash out like that, the pressure and the liquor. She knew he would apologize to JJ later, and find a way to make it up to him.

Jack cut into his pork chop and lifted his fork to his mouth. One bite followed another, pork, potatoes, peas, applesauce, and then back again to the pork, until his plate was empty. Valerie had prepared one of his favorite meals to celebrate his promotion, but he barely tasted the food. It was something to do to cover his guilt and stave off his panic. The glass of bourbon sat untouched. He didn't need alcohol now, he needed forgiveness. He needed to know she wouldn't leave him.

'I'm sorry,' he said finally. 'I don't know what got into me.'

'I know,' she said.

'I'll make it up to you.'

'It doesn't matter.'

'Say you forgive me.'

'I forgive you.'

'Say you won't leave me.'

The routine was always the same. She knew it by heart. 'I won't leave you, Jack, you're my husband,' she recited wearily. For better or worse . . . till death do us part.

'I didn't want to hurt you.'

'It was my fault. You were upset and I shouldn't have provoked you,' Valerie said, knowing that just about everything she said or did provoked him.

'I was upset about the pay cut. I didn't have to take it out on you.'

'I'm used to it, Jack,' she told him. 'But you shouldn't take it out on the children. They didn't do anything wrong. They don't understand.'

'I know, I know,' he moaned. 'And I'll make it up to them. It's just that I don't know how we're going to make it on less money.'

'I'll talk to Leo,' Valerie said. 'Maybe he can give me some more hours.'

'You already work five days a week.'

'Just lunches now. Maybe I can pick up breakfast a couple of days a week.'

Jack started to cry. 'That job was only supposed to be temporary,' he sobbed. 'It's been seven years, and it was only supposed to be temporary.'

'I don't mind,' she said. 'I like working.'

In fact, the Gray Whale had become a second home to her, a place where she felt nourished and appreciated and safe. Leo, Lil, Donna, Miguel, and the regulars were like family. She was not unhappy that circumstances would allow her to continue waitressing there.

'What kind of a man am I if I can't even support my family?' Jack wailed and reached for the bourbon.

JJ threw up his dinner while Valerie held his head and wiped his face with a damp washcloth.

'When I get bigger,' he gasped between heaves, 'I'll protect you from him.' She hugged him, ignoring her own pain, not wanting him to see the tears in her eyes. I should be protecting *you*, she thought.

JJ was ashamed of the mess he made, but Valerie told him not to mind. She led him out of the bathroom and put him to bed with a song her mother used to sing, and sat by his side, running her fingers through his hair, until he fell asleep.

Rosemary helped her clean up. 'I think one of JJ's teeth is loose,' she told her mother.

Valerie looked up startled. 'He didn't say anything about it.'

Rosemary shrugged. 'Because he knew you'd want to take him to the dentist and there isn't any money to pay for it.'

Valerie sat down on the edge of the tub, and burying her face in the bloody towel she held, cried as she hadn't cried in years. This was all her fault. If she could only stop doing whatever it was she did to antagonize Jack, he wouldn't get so angry. All she had to do was figure out what that was. They had been married for almost twelve years, surely long enough for her to have some clue, but she didn't, not really. Because it always seemed to be something different that set him off, never the same thing twice, never something she could see coming and head off.

Jack was not a bad man, she knew, and most of the time he was very good to her and the kids. He made sure they had a roof over their heads and food in their bellies. He bought them clothes when they needed them. He remembered all their birthdays, and he made a big fuss over holidays like Christmas and Halloween and Thanksgiving and Easter.

Sometimes he would take the children out on weekends when she was working at the Gray Whale. And three years ago, when Ricky was two and she had finally recovered from her injuries and regained her strength after the circumstances of his birth, Jack had not objected to her taking the kids back to Rutland to visit her family.

Whenever he had one of his episodes, as she had come to think of them, he was always sorry afterward and would arrive home the next day with some kind of extravagant, guilt-ridden gift for her. Only the episodes seemed to be occurring more often now. Whatever stresses were building up inside of him, it took just the slightest thing she said or did to set him off. Only he wasn't just taking his anger at her out on her anymore. He was going after the kids now, too.

She couldn't control him when he was in one of his rages, and of course there was no one she could go to for help, no one she could ever tell. What went on inside the house stayed inside the house, she knew that. But somehow she had to find a way to protect her children.

Leaving him was not an option, the Church was adamant about that. Besides, what would he do if she did try to leave him? Would he just let her go? Somehow, she didn't think so. A little shiver ran through her. For right now, her only option was to put herself between her husband and her children as often as she could. It wouldn't fix the problem, she knew, but at least it was something, and it would have to do until she could think of something else.

Rosemary sat down beside her. 'Don't cry, Mama,'

the ten-year-old said earnestly. 'It'll be all right. You know it will. It always is, isn't it?'

Valerie pulled the towel away from her face and stared at her oldest daughter. Then she put her arms around Rosemary and rocked her like a baby, because she didn't want Rosemary growing up so fast, and because she didn't know what to say to her.

It took a long time to get the children settled for the night. Eight-year-old Ellen wouldn't stop praying. She knelt on the floor and resisted every effort Valerie made to coax her into bed.

'I can't go to sleep yet, Mama,' she whispered solemnly. 'I haven't finished my prayers. I haven't prayed yet for Daddy's soul.'

Ricky had a bout of the hiccups, something that had begun to occur with some frequency. The doctor had told her there was nothing wrong with his digestion, and that the condition was likely related to some kind of stress that would pass in time.

She read a bedtime story to Priscilla. 'I want to hear all about how the prince and the princess live happily ever after,' the seven-year-old said.

It was after nine o'clock before Valerie was able to go back downstairs and clean up the kitchen. Jack was nowhere to be seen, but the bottle of bourbon sitting on the table was empty. She didn't go looking for him. When the dishes were washed and put away, she decided to bake a batch of brownies to tuck into the children's lunch pails in the morning.

At midnight, she dragged herself upstairs to bed. As she had hoped, Jack was sound asleep. He was sprawled across the bed, fully clothed, snoring loudly, the last of the bourbon staining the carpet beside him where he had dropped his glass. Valerie tiptoed out of the room, and closed the door softly behind her. She stood in the

123

hallway, undecided for a moment, and then went to check on each of the children. JJ lay sideways across his bed, his covers half off. Rosemary lay on her stomach, hugging her pillow. Ellen clutched her rosary. Priscilla was curled up in a knot, the covers over her head. All of them were asleep except Ricky. His eyes were wide open when she looked into his room, and he was staring intently at the ceiling.

'What are you doing?' she whispered.

'I'm watching for Monster Man,' the five-year-old replied. 'He comes in my sleep, so if I stay awake, he won't get me.' Hiccup.

Valerie sat down beside him. 'That's what I'm here for,' she said soothingly. 'To make sure no harm comes to you in the night.'

'I think I better watch, anyway,' Ricky said after a slight pause. 'In case he's too strong for you.' Hiccup.

Valerie put her arms around him and lay back against the sturdy maple headboard. 'Okay,' she said. 'Let's watch together.'

Jack found her there the next morning when he awoke, panicked to find himself alone.

'He was afraid to close his eyes,' she said in explanation. 'I don't know why. Then I guess we both fell asleep.'

Her back was stiff from the awkward, half-sitting position she had been in, and her abdomen was sore from Jack's kick, but somehow she got the children off to school, packed a lunch for Jack, cleaned up the house, and got herself ready for work. A hot bath and three aspirin helped. Then she buttoned her raincoat over her uniform, pulled a pair of rubber boots over her white shoes, and trudged through the mud to the Gray Whale.

The restaurant hadn't changed much since she had first started working there. The photos on the walls were a little more yellowed, Leo Garvey was a little heavier, a little grayer, and the regulars came in a little earlier and stayed a little longer. But the food was the same, fresh and hearty.

'The fish you're eating here today was swimming in the ocean last night,' Leo liked to brag.

A fire burned brightly in the fireplace at the back of the restaurant when Valerie came in. That was new. The fireplace had always been there, but until last year, Leo had blocked it off with a sideboard.

'Good food and lots of it ain't enough in the restaurant business anymore,' he declared. 'Now if you want to attract the tourists, which is what you got to do to make a decent living, you got to have something called "am-bee-ants."'

The fire lent a warm and cheerful glow to the place. Leo usually saved it for the weekends when tourists flooded the area, but today it was helping to chase away what Lil McAllister called the 'damp doldrums.'

'Another dripper,' Leo grumbled as he handed Valerie a steaming mug of coffee. 'It's amazing you haven't washed down that hill by now.'

'I say a little prayer every day,' she said, taking off her boots and hanging up her coat. Leo made her sit by the fire until she finished her coffee.

'You need to warm up inside and out on a day like this,' he told her.

Valerie smiled. Inside these weathered walls, she was safe. Safe from cold, safe from hunger, safe from hurt. It was a good feeling. She finished her coffee, set her mug in the huge stainless steel sink, and pulled a clean apron off the linen shelf. Lil came out of the bathroom.

'I've got a case of the runs that just won't quit,' she whispered.

125

'Why don't you go home,' Valerie said. 'I can handle lunch.'

Lil shrugged. 'If I go home, Leo may just get to thinking he can do without me.'

Valerie laughed. 'Even if that's true, he'd never admit it.'

'That's just the point,' Lil said. 'The way business is falling off, he doesn't need three of us anymore. He just keeps us on because he's an old softy. Half the time, I think he pays us out of his own pocket.' She saw Valerie's face fall. 'What's the matter?'

'Nothing,' Valerie said, with a careless toss of her head.

'Now *that's* a lie,' Lil retorted.

'Well, actually, Jack's had to take a cut in pay for a while, you know, because of the strike, and I was going to ask Leo if I could pick up a few hours. But it isn't that important.'

'If you ask him, he'll say yes.'

'I won't ask him.' Valerie bit her lower lip. She would just have to think of something else, she decided. She would look in the local newspaper tonight.

'Before I forget,' Lil said, grabbing two menus and starting toward an elderly couple at the front of the restaurant. 'Debby has a dentist appointment this afternoon. I told her it would be all right if she dropped Ricky by here on her way.'

'Sure,' Valerie said. Debby McAllister, Lil's second daughter, had taken up where her older sister had left off. Judy McAllister was now married with a young one of her own.

Debby was eighteen, a freshman at San Francisco State University, and the first McAllister to go to college. 'I want an education before I start having babies,' she said. She was as good with the children as Judy had been, and arranged her schedule at school so that she could be back in time to pick Ricky up from kindergarten and look after him on the days that Valerie worked at the Gray Whale.

Like Judy before her, Debby refused to take any money from the Marshes. Valerie had fretted over that from the beginning, until Judy had announced her engagement. Then she knew how she could repay the girl. Valerie had not inherited her mother's skill with a needle and thread for nothing. She offered to make Judy's wedding dress.

'Just pick out the pattern,' she told her, 'and tell me what kind of material you want.'

Judy's eyes glowed, and Valerie knew this would mean more to the girl than whatever money she could have paid her. The dress was a masterpiece, yards and yards of organdy and lace, painstakingly trimmed with seed pearls, and featuring a train that floated halfway up the aisle of Our Lady of Mercy Church.

'When you get married,' she promised Debby, 'I'll make your wedding gown, too.'

Debby brought Ricky to the restaurant at one-thirty, on her way into Half Moon Bay. She took off his little yellow slicker and sat him down in an unoccupied booth in the back with his favorite coloring book and crayons. He would stay there, quite content, until Valerie was ready to leave.

'There's another note from the teacher,' Debby said, handing Valerie the neatly folded message. Valerie took it and stuffed it into her pocket. She would read it later. Doris Hesperia had had each of the Marsh children in her kindergarten class, but Ricky was the first one she had ever found it necessary to communicate about. This was the fourth note in as many months. Valerie didn't have to read it to know what it said: Your son is being uncooperative in class.

Miss Hesperia was a strict disciplinarian, and Ricky was sometimes slow to respond to her timetable. If he was involved in one project, he resented being pulled away from it to begin another. Conversely, if he was finished with a project, he resented not being able to move on to the next. Each time a note came, Valerie had talked it over with Ricky, explaining to the little boy that going to school meant learning a lot of things, doing what the teacher said being only one of them. Each time, he seemed to understand, and for a while, things would go smoothly, and then another note would come.

It must be time for another talk, she thought wearily, as she served up hearty portions of fish stew for two of the regulars. It was another hour before she thought about the note again. The restaurant was almost empty and her shift was just about over when she pulled the paper from her pocket and glanced at it. And then her face went white.

Ricky had been caught fighting, this note said. He had kicked another child in the ribs and then hit him across the face so hard that the child had to be taken to the hospital for stitches. Would either of Ricky's parents please call to discuss this totally unacceptable behavior?

Valerie walked to the back booth. Goose bumps had popped out on her arms and she was shaking so hard her teeth almost chattered. Ricky was so absorbed in the picture he was coloring, he didn't even look up.

'Do you know what this note from Miss Hesperia says?' she asked him.

'Uh-huh.'

'What?' she asked.

'It says I kicked Freddy Pruitt,' he replied. 'And then I hit him.'

'That's exactly what it says. Why on earth would you do such a thing?'

Ricky shrugged. 'Because I wanted him to give me the ball and he wouldn't.'

Valerie sank down on the seat opposite him. 'I thought Freddy was your friend.'

'Yeah, he is.'

'Well, you can't go around hurting your friends just because they don't do what you want them to.'

Ricky looked at his mother then, his father's yellow eyes bright in his little face. 'Don't worry, it'll be all right, Mama,' her five-year-old son said serenely. 'Tomorrow, I'm gonna bring Freddy a present.'

Valerie trudged along Delgada Road, holding tightly on to Ricky's hand, her heart pounding from more than the exertion of the walk. She would have to tell Jack what had happened. She would have to show him the note from Doris Hesperia. She couldn't think of any way around it, and she was pretty sure how he would react. He would be furious. He would probably take his belt to Ricky. But the boy was not to blame, that much she knew. She remembered what Rosemary had said last night and she shuddered: How else did children learn, if not from their parents?

She reached for the telephone as soon as they were inside the house. Miss Hesperia was understandably upset. 'The other boy will be all right,' the kindergarten teacher reported. 'He wasn't hurt as badly as we had first thought, but I'm afraid that doesn't minimize Ricky's behavior in any way.'

'Certainly not,' Valerie agreed. 'I'm just glad that Freddy wasn't badly hurt.'

'I don't know what could possibly have gotten into Ricky,' Miss Hesperia declared, and Valerie could almost see her wringing her fat little hands in dismay. 'He's such a beautiful little boy. Why, to look at him, he's an angel. And you'd think that being so much smaller than the rest of his classmates, he wouldn't want to get into any trouble. I just don't understand it. I really don't.'

'I'll talk to him,' Valerie assured her.

'We just can't let this kind of thing go on,' Miss Hesperia said.

'No, of course not,' Valerie agreed. 'You're absolutely right.'

'Well, you have the Christmas break to do what you can,' the teacher said. 'But I just don't know what we're going to do if this sort of violent acting out continues after the holidays.'

'I promise you it won't happen again,' Valerie replied, wondering how she was going to keep such a promise. She hung up the telephone and turned to Ricky. 'Freddy's okay,' she told him. Then she bent down and took him by the shoulders. 'I'm going to have to tell your father about this, you know, and he'll be the one to decide what your punishment will be, but first I want to tell you something from me. You must never hit anyone again, for any reason. Hitting is wrong.'

'Daddy hits,' Ricky said reasonably.

Valerie shut her eyes in pain. She reached out and touched his cheek. 'What happens in this house has nothing to do with what happens outside this house,' she said gently. 'Families sometimes treat each other differently than they treat other people. It's not always how we may want to be treated, but it's . . . forgiven, because we love one another. But it's not the way we can behave with anyone outside the family, because they wouldn't understand.'

Ricky shifted from his left foot to his right foot and

then back again, his glance wandering somewhere past her shoulder.

'Do you understand what I'm saying?' Bringing his attention back to her, the boy nodded solemnly. Valerie sighed and stood up. 'Then run along and wash your hands while I make you a snack.'

Ricky scampered up the stairs toward the bathroom and Valerie made her way into the kitchen. JJ sat at the table finishing a peanut butter and jelly sandwich and a glass of milk. He chewed very carefully around his bruised lip and loose tooth.

'Hi, honey,' she said, ruffling his hair. 'You have a dentist appointment tomorrow at three. You can ride your bike down after school.' JJ nodded. 'Where are the girls?'

'Rosemary went to play at a friend's house. Ellen and Priscilla are upstairs. I made them sandwiches.'

'Thanks, sweetheart. I guess that's what I'll give your brother.' She reached for the bread and the peanut butter. For two years now, on the days that Valerie worked, JJ had been responsible for seeing to it that his sisters got home from school.

'I heard you talking on the telephone,' JJ said. 'Was it about what Ricky did?'

Valerie nodded. 'How did you know?'

'I expect the whole Coast knows by now,' JJ replied. 'Things like that get around.'

Valerie sighed. 'I guess I'll have to call Freddy's mother and apologize.'

'Freddy Pruitt's a sissy,' JJ said. 'And so is his older brother.'

'That's no excuse,' Valerie told him sternly. But JJ only shrugged. 'I certainly hope you don't go around fighting, with sissies or anyone else.'

'No, Mama,' he said obediently.

Valerie opened her mouth to say something more, but Ricky came into the kitchen at that moment, wearing his Boston Red Sox cap. His Uncle Tommy had sent him the souvenir last Christmas and it was his most prized possession. He scrambled up onto the seat next to his brother and Valerie put his sandwich down in front of him.

'Hey, what's with the cap, squirt?' JJ asked him, pulling the rim down over the boy's eyes.

'I'm going to give it to Freddy Pruitt tomorrow,' Ricky replied with a sigh. 'I just wanted to wear it one more time.'

'I guess that's about right,' JJ agreed.

'He wouldn't give me the soccer ball,' Ricky explained.

'And I bet it was after you asked him real nice, too, at least once.'

Valerie stared at her two sons, astonished at the exchange. She poured out a glass of milk for Ricky and set it on the table.

'I kicked him pretty hard,' Ricky told JJ.

'Yeah, I heard.' The brothers smiled at each other, sharing something that did not include their mother. A five-year-old and an eleven-year-old, carrying on a conversation that would have been considered mature for two adults. Valerie was bewildered. Where had her children gone? When had two little men taken over her boys?

She decided at the last minute to make spaghetti for dinner. It was a meal everyone liked, which would relieve at least one potential pressure point for the evening. With a little luck, she could finish feeding the children before Jack came home. She set about preparing the ingredients for the meatballs, while Ricky finished his sandwich, and then, when she wasn't looking, wiped his milk mustache on the sleeve of his shirt.

'C'mon up to my room, kiddo,' JJ offered. 'I'll let you look at my baseball cards.'

'You bet,' Ricky exclaimed, bounding out of the kitchen at his big brother's heels.

Valerie smiled at their retreating backs. Bless JJ. He would keep Ricky occupied as long as he could. No need for the boy to think about what was coming until he absolutely had to.

Jack came home early. To Valerie's dismay, she heard the front door open and close and then his heavy footsteps thumping down the hall, and there he was, standing in the kitchen with a big smile on his face. He strode up to her, smothering her inside a huge bear hug and planting a wet kiss on her lips. At least he was sober, she thought, apparently passing on his usual after-work drinking with his buddies. That was a blessing. He was fairly reasonable when he was sober, even though he was acting very strangely at the moment.

'What is it?' she asked.

'Start packing,' he said.

Valerie stood there, not understanding. 'Packing what?'

'The suitcases, of course,' Jack replied. 'The Marsh family is going to spend Christmas in Vermont.'

'Vermont?' she echoed stupidly.

'San Francisco to Burlington by way of Federal Airlines Flight 386, and then Burlington to Rutland by way of an O'Connor vehicle, I hope. We leave day after tomorrow.'

Valerie couldn't believe her ears. 'We're going home for Christmas?' she whispered. The thing she had dreamed about for so many years was coming true? 'But your job – how can we?'

Jack shrugged. 'I just told the boss that if I had to take the cut in pay that went along with my promotion, the least he could do was to let me take my family home for the holidays.'

Actually, it had been his boss's idea, as a sop for the rotten deal he knew Jack had swallowed, but what difference did it make? It was a way to make Valerie happy and give JJ and the others a good time. And there she was, looking up at him like a puppy dog. If she had a tail, it would be wagging for sure. As it was, tears were running down her cheeks.

'Now don't go getting all soppy on me, for Christ's sake,' he said, but he was crowing like a rooster inside.

Valerie wiped away the tears with the back of her hand and smiled. It was over three years since she had been to Rutland, and it seemed like forever since she had been there at Christmas. Jack could be such a dear man, sometimes, that it almost . . . almost made up for the other times.

'I can't help it,' she said around the lump in her throat, reaching up to put her arms around him, hugging as hard as she could, hoping nothing would spoil the moment. 'It's just such a wonderful surprise.'

'That's the best kind,' Jack replied. 'Why don't we call the kids down and tell them?'

Like the thud of a sack of potatoes falling at her feet, Valerie remembered Ricky. She pulled away with a weighty sigh. 'Before we do,' she said, 'there's something I have to tell you.'

Even as Jack listened to the story of Freddy Pruitt, he wondered what all the fuss was about. So his kid had beat up on someone else's kid. So what? Kids were always getting into it. It was no big deal. But to look at Valerie, one would think the whole world was coming to an end.

'What am I supposed to do about it?' he asked when she finally stopped talking.

Valerie was incredulous. 'I . . . I thought you'd be mad at him.'

'Well, I'm not exactly thrilled,' he conceded, 'but I don't see as it's a major crisis. You said the Pruitt kid wasn't hurt that bad, so we're not talking about big hospital bills or anything. Seems to me, it was just a schoolyard skirmish.'

'Well, the least we should do is call the Pruitts and apologize or something, don't you think?'

Jack shrugged. 'Because our kid got the best of their bully? I say, let it alone.'

'Oh Jack, Freddy Pruitt isn't a bully, and you know it. He's just an overweight sissy.' Valerie bit her lip as the last word popped out.

'All the more reason,' Jack said, smiling to himself. A runt like Ricky, doing in a sissy twice his size, he thought. Good for the boy.

'Please,' she insisted. 'His teacher is very upset. She hinted she might even have to suspend him from school if he does it again.'

'You mean Miss Hysteria?'

Sometimes, Valerie thought, suppressing a giggle, he was worse than the children. 'We really should call the parents,' she said.

'All right, all right,' Jack agreed. 'I'll call the damn parents. I'll tell them they're fucking lucky my boy didn't beat their sissy's brains in.'

Valerie winced at his language, but she knew better than to say anything. She gave him the Pruitts' telephone number, and he stomped out into the hallway to make the call. She heard him dialing, and after a moment, she could not resist tiptoeing over to the doorway to listen.

'. . . tell you how sorry we are,' he was saying in a voice that rippled across the telephone lines as smooth and liquid as satin. 'Yes, of course, it was completely unprovoked . . . positively inexcusable . . . totally unacceptable. Of course it's not the minor injuries that matter, it's the mental anguish suffered. And you can rest assured that the punishment will fit the crime . . . oh yes, you can count on it. And thank you for your understanding and your generosity in the matter . . . absolutely . . . and you have a Merry Christmas, too.'

Valerie couldn't help it, she started to giggle. She knew she shouldn't. She knew that Ricky's behavior was disturbing, at the very least, and would have to be dealt with. But she was going home for Christmas, and serious though fighting with Freddy Pruitt might be, nothing could spoil her joy. By the time Jack sauntered back into the kitchen, grinning broadly, she was laughing outright. 'You were awful,' she cried. 'You should be ashamed of yourself.'

'Hey,' Jack countered, 'I told them exactly what they wanted to hear. What's so awful about that?'

'You didn't mean a word of it, that's what,' she replied.

They all ate dinner together and it was a happy meal. Jack regaled them with funny stories about the airplanes he worked on and the people he worked with, and the children chatted excitedly about the last day of school and the trip to Rutland. Not until the spaghetti and meatballs were eaten and the apple cobbler put on the table did Jack lean over to speak to Ricky.

'Next time you get yourself into a scrape,' he said easily, 'you make sure nobody else has to clean it up.'

The boy looked up at him with confusion in his eyes.

136

'He doesn't understand, Jack,' Valerie murmured.

'Then I'll make it plainer. The next time I have to apologize to anyone for your behavior, I'll pin your ears back. Did you get that?'

Ricky nodded vigorously and shrank back in his seat. Valerie served the cobbler.

2

They spent ten days in Rutland, and it was a magical trip for all of them, filled with mountains of snow, dozens of presents, and the embrace of a family that was now over one hundred strong.

The Marsh children knew next to nothing about winter snow and ice, and their wardrobes contained few warm clothes. Valerie was frantic, searching through closets and drawers for their warmest sweaters, thickest socks, heaviest jackets, and turtleneck shirts – anything that would help protect small bodies from the harshness of a Rutland winter.

'Don't be silly, dear,' her mother said over the telephone the next day. 'I'm sure we can find plenty of clothes to fit the children. I'll put the word out to your brothers and sisters. By morning, we'll have cartons to choose from.'

'I can't believe it, Mom,' Valerie breathed. 'After all these years, we're coming home for Christmas.'

'I can't either, darling, and I guess I won't until I see you with my very own eyes,' Charlotte replied. 'I can't wait. The children must be all grown up by now.'

They got up at four o'clock in order to get to the airport for their seven-thirty flight, and they washed and dressed in the predawn dark.

'It isn't even morning yet,' Priscilla observed when Valerie came to coax her out of bed.

'Didn't you know that all great adventures begin in the middle of the night?' her mother replied.

There was oatmeal for breakfast, but the children were too excited to eat much of it. A New England Christmas was something they had been hearing about all their lives, and they were finally about to experience it for themselves.

'Will it be as wonderful as you always make it sound?' Ellen asked.

'Even better,' Valerie promised.

They took only three suitcases with them, the biggest of which was filled with Christmas presents. Besides underwear, there was very little they had to pack. They were already wearing their warmest clothing.

The plane trip seemed interminable. They stopped twice, first in Denver and then in Chicago, so it was almost eight o'clock at night by the time they reached Burlington. JJ and Rosemary were still awake, and Ellen opened her eyes every once in a while, but the two youngest children were fast asleep. Valerie carried Priscilla off the plane, while Jack held Ricky. Ellen stumbled up the ramp yawning.

'I see Grandpa,' JJ cried, scampering past them with Rosemary in close pursuit.

'Well, hello!' Martin O'Connor called, scooping both youngsters up into his arms. 'My word, it's good to see you.' Charlotte hurried up behind him and reached out for Ellen. Then everyone was hugging everyone else and talking at once, while Martin guided them firmly in the direction of the baggage claim area.

'I declare, JJ, you've grown two feet since I last saw you,' his grandmother cried. 'And Rosemary at least one.'

'And you've grown more gray hair, Grandma,' JJ said with a grin.

The older woman laughed. 'Well, so I have,' she conceded. 'So I have.'

'Didn't I grow, too?' Ellen asked, tugging at Charlotte's sleeve.

Charlotte peered down at the tow-headed child. 'I do believe you did,' she said. 'And, I declare, you keep getting prettier and prettier all the time.'

'Me, too, Grandma?' Rosemary demanded.

'Gracious, yes, Rosemary, you, too. Why, you're as pretty as a picture.'

Priscilla and Ricky slept through it all.

'We brought the station wagon,' Charlotte announced as they collected the luggage, 'so that I could come and we'd still be sure to fit everyone in.'

'Well, we traveled light,' Valerie replied. 'I'm afraid there wasn't very much worth packing.'

'Good thing, too,' Martin said. 'Just wait till you see what's waiting for you. The house looks like a regular clothing outlet.'

Jack said little on the journey to Rutland, but Valerie was so excited she couldn't stop talking, questions about the family tumbling out of her mouth faster than Charlotte could respond. Before she knew it, they were turning in at the gate, and crunching up the icy drive between the familiar pine trees now frosted with snow and twinkling with brightly colored Christmas lights. Ahead, the house glowed, framed by more lights. A huge wreath, decorated with pinecones and holly berries and red velvet ribbon, hung on the front door, and Charlotte's slowburning spice candles flickered in the windows.

Valerie caught her breath. It was as magical as she remembered. She turned to share it with the children, but they were all sound asleep, snuggled up in the back of the wagon with the pillows and blankets her mother had thought to bring.

'They've had a long day,' Charlotte observed, reading her mind. 'Tomorrow will be soon enough.'

Valerie smiled lovingly at them, their faces so sweet in sleep. 'I didn't want them to miss a moment of it.'

'I predict we'll have more snow tonight,' Martin said. 'The kids'll like that.'

They carried all five of them into the house and put them to bed, the girls in one room, the boys in another, undressing them quickly and tucking them between sheets that Charlotte warmed with hot water bottles. They never opened their eyes.

'I've put you and Jack in your old room, of course,' Charlotte said, opening the familiar door ahead of them and slipping the last bed warmer into place. 'Would either of you like something to eat or drink?'

Valerie glanced at Jack, but he was already eyeing the bed. 'Thanks, but we're fine, Mom.'

'Are you sure?'

It was eleven o'clock in Rutland, and her parents would normally have been in bed an hour ago. Despite the long day's journey, Valerie was too excited to sleep.

'You go on to bed,' she told Charlotte. 'I guarantee you Jack will be asleep in minutes, but I may stay up just a little while longer, if you don't mind.'

'Put these on if you're going downstairs,' Charlotte said a moment later, tapping lightly on the bedroom door, handing Valerie a thick quilted robe and a pair of warm slippers. 'Can't have you catching your death your first night home.'

Valerie smiled. It had been such a long time since she had worn her mother's clothes. She slipped off her dress and wrapped the robe tightly around her. It smelled of verbena, Charlotte's scent, and it felt almost as if her mother were hugging her. She stuffed her feet into the cozy scuffs and turned around for Jack's inspection. As she had predicted, he was already in bed, one arm thrown across his eyes to block out the light. It had

141

been a hard day for him, she knew, getting them all to the airport and onto the plane, taking care of the luggage, finding ways to keep the children amused for all those hours in the air. He deserved a good night's sleep. She turned off the light on her way out and quietly closed the door.

At the other end of the house, Valerie could hear her parents getting ready for bed. They were the same reassuring sounds she had grown up with. It was so extraordinary to step back into her old life, because it was so easy – just like slipping into a warm robe. No matter what I do or how old I get, she said to herself as she held on to the banister and descended the broad wooden steps, I'll always be a child in this house. And the thought was a strangely comforting one.

She wandered through the downstairs rooms, one by one, looking, touching, remembering, and ended up in the back parlor, where boxes of clothing lined the walls. She knelt down and began to rummage through them, finding warm shirts and heavy pants and woolen skirts and thick sweaters and long underwear and snowsuits and boots enough to dress a small Arctic nation. She set to sorting out sizes, making little piles for each of the children. There was even clothing to fit her and Jack. This was what families were all about, Valerie thought with a bittersweet smile, helping, sharing, being there for one another. This was what she missed so much. With a sigh, she picked up the clothing she had set aside and carried it upstairs, tiptoeing into the bedrooms, and leaving a neat bundle beside each bed for each child to find in the morning. She looked into her room. Jack was sound asleep. She closed the door softly and padded back downstairs.

She found her way to the pantry, a sudden urge for a cup of hot chocolate directing her feet. Nothing had changed much in the big old-fashioned kitchen. Even the fixings were in the same place they had always been. She put the kettle on to boil, lifting it off the flame just before it began to whistle, mixing just the right amount of hot water with cocoa and sugar and milk in an over-sized white mug.

She held the steaming mug with both hands for a moment, letting it warm her fingers. Then she carried it into the living room, curling up in an overstuffed chair and wrapping one of Charlotte's afghans around her, to watch the candlelight dance on the windowpanes, as the house grew quiet around her. The glowing embers of a fire kept her company, snapping and sputtering now and again as a gush of cold air blew down the chimney. The grandfather clock, on the stairway landing, struck midnight.

How many memories this place held for her, of good times and hard ones. The whole of her childhood, her growing up, her launching into womanhood had been played out within these rooms. How many secrets these walls had heard, how many dreams shared, how many tears shed. Valerie smiled. This creaky, drafty, comfort-able old barn of a place, where you could hear every cough, every door closing, every toilet flush, was where all the choices she had ever made in her life had been made, after Charlotte's blessing and Martin's consent. And all in all, she didn't think she had done so badly with her choices. Except, perhaps, for one.

'*I don't think he'll make you happy, Cornsilk,*' she heard her father say across the years.

True to Martin's prediction, it snowed overnight, and a fresh blanket of white lay sparkling in the morning sunlight, hurting the children's eyes as they pressed their noses against the big window in the upstairs hallway.

'Is that snow?' asked Ellen.

'Yes, that's snow,' JJ told her.

'How do you know?' Priscilla inquired.

'Because I remember,' JJ said.

'Was it here last night?' Ricky wanted to know.

'I don't know,' JJ had to admit. 'I was asleep when we got here.'

'So was I,' Ellen said.

'So were you all,' Valerie said, coming up to hug them, hardly recognizing them in all their donated finery.

'Are these clothes really for us?' Rosemary asked her mother, pirouetting in a plaid woolen skirt and high-collared blouse and thick red sweater.

'Well, they're for you to wear while you're here,' Valerie told her. 'You wouldn't need them in California.'

'But they're so pretty.'

'Are they charity?' Ellen wanted to know.

'No, dear,' Valerie assured her. 'They belong to your cousins. We're only borrowing them.'

'Do I know my cousins?' Ricky asked.

'You know some of them,' Valerie replied. 'But I think you were probably too young to remember.'

'I remember some of them,' JJ said. 'From when we were here last.'

'Me, too,' Rosemary added.

'I don't,' Priscilla put in.

'Well, it doesn't matter,' Valerie said. 'You're going to meet them all over again very soon.'

'I guess we must have a pretty big family,' observed JJ, 'if they had all these clothes to lend us.'

'Oh my, yes,' Valerie answered. 'We have a very big family.'

'How big?' Ricky wanted to know.

'Well, let's see if we can figure it out,' Valerie suggested. 'You have five uncles and three aunts. Seven of them are married, and among them, they have thirty-two children.'

'That's forty-seven,' JJ said, counting furiously on his fingers.

'Including your grandmother and your grandfather and the seven of us, that makes fifty-six just in the immediate family. And then, by the time you add in my aunts and uncles and cousins and their children, well, we're going to have more than a hundred people here for Christmas.'

'How will everyone fit?' Ellen wondered.

Valerie laughed. 'I don't really know, but somehow they always do.'

'Gosh,' JJ said. 'More than a hundred people, all related to us.'

'I know that's hard to imagine, with us living so far away, but just wait, you'll see.'

'Which one isn't married?' Rosemary thought to ask.

'Your Uncle Patrick,' Valerie said with a proud smile.

'Why not?'

'Because he's a priest,' her mother told her. Four pairs of eyes grew very big and very round at that bit of information, Ellen's being the biggest and roundest of them all.

'Can we go out and see the snow?' Priscilla asked, her attention still on the glittering whiteness on the other side of the window.

'Of course we can, just as soon as we eat the wonderful breakfast Grandma's cooking for us,' Valerie answered. She looked at each of them. 'Isn't anyone hungry?'

'I am,' JJ said immediately.

'Me, too,' Ricky agreed.

They trooped downstairs, following their noses into the dining room. The huge table was set with pitchers of milk and orange juice and baskets of hot biscuits with several kinds of jam and pots of maple syrup. Martin and Jack were already there, seated together, drinking coffee. Dressed in a plaid flannel shirt and gray wool sweater with leather patches, Jack looked every bit a mountain man.

Valerie directed the children to their places and began pouring the milk and orange juice into the glasses in front of them. Charlotte had shooed her daughter out of the kitchen earlier, refusing her offer of help.

'There'll be time enough for that,' she said. 'Today, you're on vacation.'

Valerie knew better than to argue, but that didn't mean she was just going to sit and do nothing. She took the coffeepot from the sideboard and refilled the men's cups. Then she poured some for her mother and herself before returning the pot to its warming plate and taking her seat.

'Your dad and I have already been out,' Martin told the children.

'And I don't mind telling you, it was so cold out there, I almost froze my nose off,' Jack added.

The children giggled. They had no clear idea of what freezing cold felt like.

'Cut us down a beauty of a tree, we did,' Martin went on. 'Best one we've had in years. We'll be bringing it in this afternoon.'

'We wanted to wait until you got here,' Charlotte said, pushing through the kitchen door with two enormous platters, one of which was piled with scrambled eggs, home fried potatoes, and thick slices of fresh bacon, while the other was stacked with buttermilk pancakes and links of country sausage. 'We didn't want the children to miss anything.'

Valerie smiled. Trimming the tree was a cherished

tradition in her parents' house, an event that almost rivaled Christmas itself.

'Would anyone like some Cream of Wheat?' Charlotte asked.

The children, eyeing the huge plates of steaming food Charlotte was putting on the table, quickly shook their heads. Valerie shook her head, too, and looked at Jack and her father.

'We've already had two bowls apiece,' Martin said. 'We needed something hot sticking to our ribs before we climbed the mountain.'

Jack caught her eye with a slight wink and Valerie smothered a smile. Jack hated Cream of Wheat.

'No takers, Mom,' she said.

Charlotte sat down at her place. As though he had been waiting for just that signal, JJ started to reach for the platter of pancakes. Valerie, seated between him and Ricky, caught the movement from the corner of her eye and quickly pulled his hand down into his lap.

'Dear Lord,' Charlotte said softly, clasping her hands and closing her eyes, 'in our health, in our family, in the love we share, and in the prosperity You have bestowed upon us, we are most truly blessed. For what we are about to receive, we most humbly thank You.' Then she smiled warmly at her family and began to pass the food.

Across the table, three pairs of eyes looked at JJ in amusement. The boy blushed to the roots of his light brown hair. It was one thing to commit a blunder, it was quite another to do it in front of his sisters.

'I'm sorry, Ma,' he whispered, totally mortified. 'I forgot.'

'That's all right, darling,' Valerie murmured reassuringly. 'You'll remember next time.'

If her parents noticed the slip, it was never mentioned.

Valerie did not want them to think that she was raising a bunch of heathens, but grace was never said in the Marsh house. While Jack overlooked most of the religious trappings she brought to their marriage, he drew the line at thanking God.

'God didn't put the food on this table,' he barked once. 'I did.'

Valerie was horrified by his blasphemy, but she had never been able to change his mind. She said a silent blessing for a while, at least until the idea of eating without first giving thanks no longer seemed quite so sacrilegious.

The children ate as though they had not seen food for a week. 'It's the winter air,' Martin remarked, helping himself to a third portion of pancakes and sausage. 'The body needs more fuel to run in the cold.'

JJ seemed intrigued by that idea. 'Just like a car going up-hill,' he said.

'Cars don't eat food,' Priscilla objected.

'Sure they do,' her brother said.

'Is that true, Grandpa?' Priscilla persisted. 'Do cars eat food like people?'

Martin scratched his head. 'Well, it's the same principle, certainly,' he told her. 'A body runs on one kind of fuel, called food, while a car runs on another kind, called gasoline.'

'Can I put my milk in the gas tank?' Ricky wanted to know.

'No,' Valerie told him. 'You put your milk in your stomach.'

Before they knew it, all the platters and pitchers were empty, and their tummies were full.

'Can we go see the snow now?' Ellen asked shyly, as Martin pulled out his pipe and tobacco pouch, signaling that the meal was over.

'Oh yes, can we?' echoed Priscilla.

'Yes.' Valerie smiled. 'But first you have to get into your snowsuits.'

The children scrambled from the table and dashed upstairs to put on their outdoor clothes as quickly as they could. 'Rosemary, you help Ellen and Priscilla, and JJ, you help Ricky,' Valerie called after them. 'And don't forget your boots.'

'It's so good to have all of you here,' Charlotte said. 'Jack, I can't tell you how happy I am you were able to arrange it.'

'Well, Christmas was going to be a little thin this year, because of the strike and all,' Jack replied with a hint of apology in his voice. 'Seeing as we can fly for free, I figured this would be the best present I could give everyone.'

'I think you figured right, my boy,' Martin said heartily. Ironically, over the years, he had made his own personal peace with Valerie's husband. Jack had turned out to be reliable and hardworking, if not particularly God-fearing, and it seemed he provided well enough for his wife and children. Of course, he could have reckoned a lot better if they lived nearer.

As it was, Martin could count on one hand the number of occasions he had actually spent time with Jack in the almost twelve years the man had been married to his daughter. Twice, his son-in-law had come east on business, dropping Valerie and the kids off in Rutland on a Sunday and returning on Thursday. Once, Martin and Charlotte had flown out to California. It was that time when Valerie had fallen down the stairs and Ricky was born early, and there was such a scare that they might die. Only three times in twelve years, but each time, Jack was polite and respectful, and eventually, Martin was willing to concede that perhaps he had been too hasty in his initial judgment.

Valerie got up from her seat and began to clear the table, but this time her father stopped her. 'You two go on out with the kids,' he said. 'Soon as I finish my pipe, I'll help your mother clean up here.' Valerie's eyes popped. 'You didn't know I could wash a dish, did you?' Martin said with a chuckle. 'Well, I guess there's still a surprise or two left in me. Now you run along, before I change my mind.'

'Thanks, Daddy,' Valerie said, coming around to give him a big hug. She remembered not being well enough to go out in the snow with JJ and Rosemary that time so long ago when she had come home to mend. She didn't want to miss out again.

When the children were ready, Valerie lined them up in the front hall, checking to make sure that their snow-suits were properly fastened, and that they each had on their boots and their warm woolen caps and their water-proof mittens. She herself had put on a pair of ski pants and jacket that belonged to her sister Elizabeth and Jack had zipped himself into a down-filled parka that her oldest brother, Marty, had contributed.

'Are we ready?' Jack asked.

'We're ready,' everyone replied.

'JJ,' Jack instructed, 'to the door.' JJ scurried to the front door. 'JJ, hand on latch.' The girls giggled, and Jack glared at them with mock severity. 'JJ, open the door.' The boy pulled back the heavy door, and with a loud whoop, Jack charged over the threshold and dove headfirst into the nearest snowbank, one he had helped create earlier when he and Martin had shoveled the path. The children screamed with delight and hurried after him, jumping up and down and tugging at his legs until he emerged, staggering like Frankenstein, with his

150

teeth chattering and his eyes crossing. 'I must have taken a wrong turn,' he said.

Valerie smiled as she closed the front door behind her and then shook her head. Sometimes, it was as though she had six children instead of five. Not that she minded, necessarily, but it would be easier all around, she thought, if the oldest were a little less volatile.

She and the girls spent the morning making fascinating patterns in the new snow and watching their breath freeze on the air. Jack and the boys threw snowballs at each other. Then they all built a snowman, a towering lopsided creature, with hay for hair, prunes for eyes, a carrot for a nose, and an apple where the mouth should be. Martin contributed a corncob pipe, Charlotte produced a red stocking cap, and Jack molded two pudgy snow arms clutching a shovel instead of a broom.

'More practical, all things considered,' he declared.

The O'Connors came out to view the result. 'Kevin couldn't have done better,' Martin pronounced, and Valerie explained to Jack and the children exactly how great a compliment that was.

'If it stays as cold as it is,' Charlotte said, 'this fine fellow will still be there to greet our Christmas guests.'

The family began arriving two hours later. Valerie had barely finished cleaning up in the kitchen after lunch, having refused to let her mother dismiss her again, when Marianne and Tommy drove up in their shiny new Lincoln Continental.

'We weren't going to come at all, you know, what with the restaurant being so busy, and Tommy always liking to give most of the staff Christmas off,' Marianne admitted after she had hugged her sister and her brother-in-law and kissed all the children twice. 'Then we heard you were going to be here.'

'The restaurant must be exceptionally busy,' Valerie said, eyeing the car.

Marianne shrugged lightly. 'What else do we have to spend our money on?' she replied.

After eighteen years of marriage, the Santinis had apparently made peace with their barrenness. 'If God had wanted me to be a mother,' Marianne now said, 'He would have given me children.'

At least, Valerie thought, He had given her Tommy, and that made up for a lot. Marianne unabashedly adored her husband, and that big lug of an Italian worshipped the ground his wife walked on. Just by looking at the two of them, it was clear that they were as much in love with each other at this very moment as they had been on the day they were married. Maybe even more, Valerie thought, wistfully.

'I'm so glad you could come,' she said.

'Tommy closed the restaurant,' Marianne declared. 'First time in ten years. Gave everyone the weekend off. Said how could he expect the staff to work on the holiday if the boss wasn't going to?' She giggled. 'And then he put a sign in the window: *Gone wassailing – be back Tuesday*.'

Valerie's middle brother Hugh and his family arrived next, from Fort Bragg in North Carolina. Martin had again driven to Burlington to collect them at the airport.

'I'm an artillery instructor,' he told JJ, when the boy inquired about all the ribbons and patches on his uniform. 'I wear this salad to impress the troops and get their attention.'

'Don't you believe it, JJ,' Martin said with pride in his voice. 'Your Uncle Hugh earned every one of those honors. He was in Korea, just like your dad. Got shot up pretty bad, too. Scared your grandmother and me half to death. Then, as if that wasn't enough, they sent

152

him to Germany to fight *more* Commies. And while he was there, he single-handedly rescued hundreds of people caught behind the Berlin Wall.'

Hugh O'Connor laughed. 'Dad, if I'm ever in need of a press agent, I'll know just where to look.' He looked at his nephew. 'Don't you listen to a word of what he says,' he told the boy. 'As I recall it, most of the time I was in Germany I spent trying to persuade your Aunt Hilde to marry me.'

Hildegarde O'Connor smiled at JJ. 'Of course, that was after he rescued me from behind the Berlin Wall,' she said in a heavily accented voice.

Valerie looked at her brother. In his crisp uniform, with his sandy hair and ruddy complexion and pleasant features, he could have been the model for the soldier on the Army recruitment posters.

Last to arrive from out of town was Valerie's youngest brother, Patrick, in his neat black suit and white collar. He had been allowed to come home for the holidays from his parish in Worcester, Massachusetts, on the understanding that he would assist Father Joseph, the aging priest at St Stephen's, in any way he could. It was acknowledged that, in a couple of years, Patrick would return to Rutland to take over the parish.

Valerie had never seen her brother as a priest before. He looked taller than she remembered, and thinner, his cheekbones standing out more sharply than ever in his long face, his dark eyes deeper set. 'I'm so proud of you,' she whispered, reaching up to hug him.

The children were shy as she introduced them to Patrick, especially Ellen, who would only peer at him from behind her mother.

'Priests are still a bit bigger than life to them,' Valerie explained. 'They've never known one up close before.'

Patrick smiled down at Ellen reassuringly. 'If I

153

promise not to bite, would you give me a hug?' he asked gently.

Ellen thought for a long minute before slowly nodding, Patrick leaned down, and as the little girl put her arms tentatively around his neck, he whisked her up into his arms. 'You and I,' he whispered, 'are going to get to know each other very well.'

'Gads, I'm glad Patrick got to come home this Christmas,' Marianne said later, 'if just for a couple of days of Mom's cooking.'

There were fourteen around the dinner table that evening. The Marsh children were included in the company, but the two-year-old O'Connor twins, Hugh and Hilde's boys, were fed early and put to bed.

It was a lively meal, with everyone joking and laughing between bites and swallows. Charlotte outdid herself with a huge rib roast, and beamed from the compliments on her green bean casserole, double-whipped mashed potatoes, and secret-ingredient gravy. Martin kept the wineglasses full. From the depths of his cellar stock, he had pulled bottles of a Beaujolais that was so gentle to the palate that Valerie decided it was just like drinking fruit juice, and her glass was frequently among those that needed refilling.

Although they didn't know each other very well, Valerie and Hilde chattered on about children as if they were old friends. Martin and Tommy got into a discussion on the importance of loyal employees. Marianne teased Patrick about delaying the meal with a five-minute blessing.

'Just because you practice postponement of pleasure, my dear brother, doesn't mean we all must.'

'Marianne!' Charlotte exclaimed.

Jack and Hugh talked about Army life.

'There's a right way, a wrong way, and the Army's

way,' Hugh said wryly. 'As long as you do it the Army's way, you're taken care of womb to tomb.'

'They wanted me to stay in after Korea,' Jack said, the tenuousness of his present job and income still uppermost in his mind. 'Maybe I should have.'

'Well, you can take my word for it, it's no bed of roses,' Hugh replied.

'Hell, it's a better time than most to be a career man,' Jack declared, 'so long as you don't end up in Vietnam.'

Hugh lowered his fork and cleared his throat. 'Well, as a matter of fact . . .' he said, letting the sentence trail off.

Conversation around the table stopped. Valerie watched Hilde's fingers tighten around the stem of her wineglass.

Martin looked at his son. 'We thought you were settled at Fort Bragg.'

Hugh shrugged. 'I was, for a while. But the one thing you learn when you're in the Army is that the only thing you can count on is reassignment.'

'Aren't you too old?' Marianne demanded. 'You're thirty-five, for God's sake. You've got a wife and kids.'

'That doesn't count for career men,' Hugh replied. He looked around the table at the stricken faces of his family. 'It was only a matter of time,' he said gently.

'When?' Martin probed.

'In a month or so.'

'Will you have to be involved in actual combat?' inquired Charlotte.

'No way,' her son answered with a smile. 'I'm strictly advisory.' He decided there was no purpose in telling her that there was no such thing as strictly advisory over there. Nevertheless, he saw her lower lip begin to quiver. 'Come on, Ma,' he chided. 'You know me. I come from tough O'Connor stock. If the North Koreans

155

couldn't take me down, the North Vietnamese won't, either.'

Hilde, remembering the ragged scar that bisected her husband's abdomen, the result of Korean shrapnel, drained the wine from her glass.

'It doesn't seem fair,' Charlotte insisted. 'You've done your share.'

'It isn't fair,' Tommy said bluntly. 'If you ask me, we've got no business being over there in the first place. It's just another country's civil war we got ourselves suckered into.'

'This country stands for the principles of freedom,' Martin retorted. 'We must be willing to fight the threat of Communism wherever we find it.'

Tommy declined to respond.

'As long as I wear the uniform,' Hugh told his brother-in-law, his convictions no less firm than his father's, 'I'm obliged to do the job.'

Patrick looked across the table at his brother. 'Whatever you do, Hugh,' he said quietly, 'you'll do it well.'

'It's so nice to have the house full again,' Charlotte said, signaling the end of the conversation. She had never seen much point in arguing over things you couldn't change. Better to leave them in God's hands. 'Your father and I rattle around here so by ourselves.'

'Ma, you say that every year,' Hugh reminded her with a little chuckle.

'I know,' his mother replied brightly. 'But this year, in addition to all our other blessings, Valerie and her family are here with us.'

They gathered in the living room after dinner, as other members of the family began to drop by, and the Marsh children were reintroduced to their aunts and uncles and cousins. Marty and Kevin arrived together, stomping in from the cold with their hometown wives and teenage children. At forty-six, Marty was the image of his father, right down to the older man's bald head, while Kevin, with a thick shock of hair the same color as Valerie's, favored his mother.

'It's starting to snow again and pretty hard, too,' Marty announced, hugging Valerie, slapping Jack heartily on the back, and reaching down to pet each of the children. 'It looks like we're going to have a white Christmas for sure.'

'Just like Mama promised,' JJ said.

'I noticed a pretty impressive creature on the front lawn,' Kevin conceded. 'Looks like I've been replaced as chief snowman maker.'

The children hid their satisfied smiles behind their hands.

'God, Valerie,' her sister-in-law Betty, Kevin's wife, whispered in her ear when no one was around to notice. 'That husband of yours is the sexiest thing I've ever seen, you lucky lady. I could get hot just from looking at him. How do you ever let him out of bed?' She grinned wickedly and broke into one of the high-pitched giggles that were her trademark. Betty had always been acknowledged as the most audacious female in the family.

Valerie blushed to the roots of her pale blond hair. While on the one hand she longed to keep the image of wedded bliss intact, she knew she would choke on the answer Betty obviously expected.

'Unfortunately,' she said, hoping her voice sounded reasonably unconcerned, 'Jack's job, five children, and a house to run doesn't leave us with as much time alone as we might want.'

'Then you be sure you keep him on a tight leash,'

Betty murmured with a broad wink. 'Or one of these days he just might find himself a bed that doesn't come with encumbrances.'

Valerie's expression didn't change and she didn't say a word.

Cecilia O'Connor Paxton arrived next, with her husband and their brood. Cecilia didn't look much like either of her parents, but someone had once said she resembled a great-aunt in Milwaukee.

'Elizabeth said not to wait on them,' she announced, breezing into the living room. 'Something about the hot water heater going on the whack. They'll get here when they get here.'

'Then let's get started,' Martin said.

'Isn't Danny coming?' Valerie asked about her fifth brother.

'Bridget wasn't feeling very well,' Marty replied, referring to his brother's wife, who was pregnant with their fifth child. 'But they said they'll be here tomorrow for sure.'

'It's the first tree trimming he's missed in a dozen years,' Charlotte observed with a tinge of sadness.

'That's okay, Ma,' Valerie said lightly. 'It's the first one I've made in a dozen years.'

They started with the lights – they always started with the lights – string upon string, lacing them through the branches, Marty and Jack laboring on one side, Kevin and Tommy on the other, and everyone else giving good-natured advice.

'They're too close together, you have to spread them out more.'

'No, bring the blue one in.'

'Move the yellow one up higher, and more to the left.'

'No, it's too high, and it needs to come right.'

'Don't pull it so tight, drape it more.'

'Stretch it out, there won't be enough left for the bottom.'

Finally, it was done, and Jack went around gathering all the ends together.

'Ready?' Martin called from behind the tree.

'Ready,' Jack said.

'Wait a minute,' Marianne cried, rushing to snap off the two table lamps. 'Okay, go.'

Martin pushed the extension cord into the wall socket and a thousand flashes of color twinkled through the branches and lit up the room. The Marsh children gasped in delight. They had Christmas trees at home, of course, but never anything as grand as this.

Elizabeth O'Connor Hennessy and her family chose that moment to come bustling in. 'Oh, good timing,' she said, glancing toward the living room, 'we missed the tiresome part.'

'Let's get on with it,' Martin said, ignoring his daughter's remark.

Hugh and Patrick went down to the basement and brought up the boxes of Christmas decorations that had been collected over the years and lovingly preserved. This was the best part. As each ornament was hung, the story of where it came from and what made it special was recited. There were the hand-blown glass bells that Charlotte's grandmother had brought with her from Ireland more than a hundred years ago, and the wooden reindeer that Martin's father had carved as his ship chugged into New York Harbor and docked at Ellis Island. There was the Star of Bethlehem that Elizabeth had made in school the year she was chosen to play the cow in the nativity scene, and the set of circus animals that Kevin had painted the summer he tried to run off and join the local carnival. There was the miniature sleigh that Charlotte bought in Quebec City the time they were snowed in and had to stay three extra days, the white dove they found in a Boston antique shop when Cecilia went missing and they had to search for her, the little Hummel shepherd boy that Hugh had sent from Germany, and so many more.

When they were all hung, Martin picked up a separate carton filled with bright silver balls, one for every member of the family, with a name and date of birth engraved on it. The Marsh children were allowed to lift their own name-balls carefully out of their tissue paper nests and hang them on the tree.

Jack stood off to one side, watching. This was only his second O'Connor Christmas, his first having been the month before he and Valerie were married. He marveled now, as he had then, on the history this family shared and how close they were to one another. His own father had been an orphan, and he knew nothing of his mother's family past a bleak Iowa farm and a stoic, loveless couple. He wondered what it was like to have brothers and sisters, aunts, uncles, and cousins. He was glad his children would know. He wished these could have been his people. He wished there was a place somewhere that he could think of as home. He felt Valerie standing beside him. She smiled up at him and tucked her arm through his, almost, he thought with a start, as though she could tell what he was thinking.

When all the boxes but one were empty, they started in on a basket of bread dough ornaments that Cecilia had made, and lofted chains of cranberries and popcorn that Elizabeth had fashioned, and then they opened the packets of silver tinsel. Finally, at the very end, when every branch was bowed beneath its share of glitter and sparkle, Charlotte opened the last box. Inside was a beautiful golden angel with filigree wings and a crystal halo. Valerie's children peered into the box, their eyes widening.

'I think that must be what a real angel in heaven looks like,' Ellen breathed. The family smiled.

Elizabeth leaned toward Valerie and Jack. 'Watching them,' she whispered, 'is like seeing it all for the first time again.'

Martin had bought the prized ornament at Tiffany in New York City and given it to his wife for Christmas the week after Martin Jr was born, and each year thereafter, the youngest member of the family present placed it on the very pinnacle of the tree.

'Come on, Ricky,' Hugh exclaimed, his twins being asleep, 'up you go.' And before the little boy realized what was happening, he was balanced on his uncle's strong shoulder with the precious angel in his hands. He could feel every eye watching him as he reached out, ever so slowly, and slipped it over the topmost branch. The angel's halo barely cleared the living room ceiling.

'Just right,' Hugh proclaimed, swinging Ricky high over his head before setting him down on his feet. Everyone clapped loudly, and one by one they came up to give him a hug. The little boy had never before felt so important.

'Let's all join hands,' Charlotte said then, and the group came together while Patrick led them in the Lord's Prayer.

'Another year, another tree,' Hugh said when they finished.

The grandfather clock struck eleven.

'Good heavens,' Valerie said. 'I didn't realize the time.' She called the children over to her. 'Say your good nights now,' she told them, 'and then it's off to bed with you.'

'Not yet,' they protested.

161

'Can't we have five more minutes?'

'It's very late,' Valerie told them.

'But it's not as if we're babies anymore,' they argued.

'The babies went to sleep at seven,' their mother reminded them.

'We want to look at the tree some more.'

'The tree will still be here tomorrow.'

'We want to talk to Uncle Kevin, and Aunt Cecilia, and Cousin Billy.'

'They'll be here tomorrow, too.'

Marianne came up beside her. 'Let me,' she urged. She turned to the youngsters with a mock glare. 'Last one in the bathroom has to brush his teeth twice.'

The children bolted for the stairs.

'I can remember her doing that to us,' Patrick said with a chuckle.

'And it always worked,' Hugh added.

The ones who weren't from out of town began to leave then, with long hugs and promises of seeing everyone the next day. Those who were staying settled onto sofas and into chairs, close to the crackling fire. Then Martin brought in a huge bowl of his famous punch, setting it down on the little table next to Valerie, and ladling out a cup for everyone.

'A toast to the tree,' he said.

'To the tree,' everyone echoed, looking back over their shoulders to admire their efforts one more time.

'There's a colonel at Bragg who uses Irish Mist in his grog instead of Baileys,' Hugh told his father. 'It packs quite a wallop.'

'So I've heard,' Martin said, nodding. 'But I prefer subtlety.'

'Oh, it's subtle,' Hugh persisted. 'The wallop sneaks up on you.'

'Baileys suits me just fine,' his father replied.

'I just thought you might like to try something different one of these days,' Hugh suggested mildly.

'Folks have been praising my punch for over forty years,' his father reminded him. 'Why would I want to change now?'

Hilde gave her husband a meaningful jab in the ribs. 'My father would have said the same thing.'

'I serve Mist at the restaurant,' Tommy said. 'Some of my customers really like it.'

'I guess I'd go with the smoothness of the Cream,' Patrick put in.

Before long everyone, except Valerie, who had no particular opinion on the matter, was arguing the merits of Baileys Irish Cream versus Irish Mist.

'Irish Cream,' Marianne said, coming into the middle of the conversation, 'and let's have done with it.' She had managed to tuck the children into bed in no time, promising them an adventure in the woods the next morning if they went right to sleep.

Valerie snuggled deep into her chair, listening to the discussion, wrapping the familiar voices tight around her as she had her mother's afghan the night before, and sipped steadily at her punch. Patrick was right, she thought. The Irish Cream was indeed very smooth. So smooth in fact that, every time someone asked her to refill a cup, she refilled her own, too. Soon her face was flushed, her eyes sparkled, and she began to giggle. Her father suggested that perhaps the punch on top of all the wine she had drunk with dinner might be more than she could handle, but Valerie smiled benevolently at him. She knew better than that. For the first time in what seemed forever, she was home for Christmas, and that was far more intoxicating than any amount of liquor she might consume.

During all that time, she had thought of her life with

Jack as a form of exile. Sitting here now, warm and perhaps a bit fuzzy, she realized she was right. Somehow, she decided, she must have done something to displease God greatly, and her penance was to live on the other side of the world. An enormous sea of loneliness lapped at the edges of the cozy circle.

'"And Cain went out from the presence of the Lord, and dwelt in the land of Nod,"' she recited, not realizing she spoke aloud, not realizing that tears were now running down her cheeks.

The conversation in the room was effectively stopped as eight pairs of eyes turned in her direction. She wondered why everyone was looking at her. Did they know her sin? If she asked them what it was, would they tell her so she could repent and return to the bosom of her family?

The last thing Valerie remembered was Martin bending over her, taking the punch cup out of her hand, and peering at her intently with eyes that had always seen too much.

'Something's wrong,' he said to his wife in the privacy of their bedroom a short while later. They had said their good nights along with Jack, who had lifted Valerie from the wing chair and carried her upstairs.

'I think something's been wrong for years,' Charlotte replied, slipping between the sheets.

'Have you talked to her?' Martin asked.

Charlotte shook her head. 'I don't like to interfere.'

'Then what do we do?'

'She's a grown woman now,' Charlotte reminded him. 'She's got to make her own way, just like the rest of them.'

'Yes, but she's not like the rest of them,' Martin muttered, climbing into bed beside his wife. 'She's always been more vulnerable.'

164

'Then help her, if you can,' Charlotte said, reaching out to turn off the light.

Valerie did not awaken until after eleven, when her mother came into her room with a tomato juice tonic.

'What is it?' she asked, the simple act of speaking causing little explosions of pain behind her eyes.

'Just drink it,' Charlotte said mildly. Valerie did as she was told, wrinkling up her nose at the sour taste. 'Now, I suggest a hot bath and something to eat.'

'Where are the children?' Valerie asked.

'Oh, don't worry about them,' her mother said on her way out. 'Marianne and Tommy have had them off on a scavenger hunt through the woods all morning.'

Valerie groaned as she thrust her feet over the side of the bed and struggled to an upright position. She wondered what time Jack had gotten up, and why she had slept so long, and why she had such a headache.

She staggered into the bathroom and stepped carefully into the tub, opening the hot water faucet as far as she could stand it. The steam fogged up the mirrors, and turned her skin bright pink. Her mother was right, the bath felt wonderful. She soaked for a full half hour before climbing out and wrapping herself in a towel. There was a terrible taste in her mouth, but her head felt much better.

The idea of eating actually sounded good to Valerie by the time she had dressed in warm clothes and descended to the kitchen. She sat down at the painted wood table in the center of the room and watched Charlotte scoop a fresh portion of oatmeal into a bowl and top it with warm milk and nutmeg before putting it down in front of her.

'There's more,' she said, knowing the cereal was her daughter's favorite.

'Where is everyone?' Valerie inquired, feeling the quietness of the big house around her more than hearing it.

'The scavengers are still out and about,' Charlotte reported. 'Hugh and Hilde took the babies over to Kevin's. Patrick went down to St Stephen's. Jack is around somewhere. And your father is waiting for you in the library when you're finished.'

Valerie felt her stomach lurch. Such a summons could only mean she had done something so disgraceful last night it had earned his disapproval. Her temples began to throb as she strained to think what it could have been, but she couldn't even remember how she got to bed.

Martin was the solid rock of her childhood, his rules her guide, his discipline her reality check. Even now, the thought of having done something to displease him was enough to make her quiver, just as she had for all the years that she lived under his roof. She carried her empty cereal bowl to the sink, declining a second helping. She knew she was too old for his brand of punishment now, but there was no point in delaying the inevitable.

He answered her knock immediately. She pushed open the heavy library door and found him exactly as she expected, seated in his big leather chair by the window. For a moment, she felt an overwhelming urge to crawl up into his lap. She sat down in a small armchair directly in front of him.

'How are you feeling this morning?' he inquired kindly.

'Ashamed,' she replied, looking down at her hands twisted together in her lap.

'Ashamed of what?' he asked.

'Of . . . of whatever it was I did last night.'

'As far as I know,' her father said, 'the only thing

you did last night, aside from drinking a little too much of my Christmas punch, that is, was to quote the Bible.'

Valerie looked up then. The shrewd, steady glance fastened on her was full of concern, not displeasure. She shook her head in confusion. 'I thought you wanted to see me because you were angry. I thought I'd done something awful.'

'What would make you think that?' he asked, reaching out and covering her hands with his big paws.

'But then, why . . .?' Valerie began and stopped.

'Why did I ask to see you?' She nodded. 'Because your mother and I are worried about you, and we want to help if we can. Over the years, each time we see you, you seem to have grown thinner and more tense. I think Father Joseph would call it the outward signs of a desperate inner struggle.'

Valerie stiffened slightly, and the move was not lost on her father. 'If he really knew anything about it,' she said lightly, 'I think Father Joseph would call it raising a family.'

'Your mother isn't tense,' Martin said. 'Neither are your sisters.'

She slipped her hands from beneath his to grip the arms of her chair. 'Maybe I'm just not as good at it as they are.'

He gazed at her with troubled eyes. He and Charlotte had never pried, never tried to barge uninvited into her life. She had always come to them willingly with her problems. Now, time and distance separated them. 'Are you happy, Cornsilk?' he asked at length.

The minute she heard the words, Valerie realized she had been avoiding that question, dreading that question, preparing for that question for twelve years. She knew that all she had to do was open her mouth and let it come pouring out – Jack's violence, her failure as a wife and mother, the horror and fear of the last twelve years. If she let it out, she would be free, but she would also be damned. Because she would have broken Martin's cardinal rule, and he would never forgive her that.

So she sat up a little straighter and looked back at him, her face a smooth mask, her pale eyes unreadable. 'What a silly question,' she said brightly. 'Just look at me. I have the husband I wanted, five wonderful children, a beautiful home, enough money, my health, and my faith. Why wouldn't I be happy?'

Then she held her breath, waiting for him to challenge her, as he always had, after he had analyzed her words and found the fundamental flaw. But he just continued to gaze at her with that troubled expression in his eyes and said nothing. After a while, she knew the conversation was over. The imprints of her fingernails in the leather armrests of her chair remained long after she had left the room.

They each took something to remember back home with them, something they didn't share with the others but kept only for themselves.

Valerie basked in the special warmth of being back in the bosom of her family.

Jack realized, perhaps more painfully than ever, how empty his childhood had been, and how much he had been denied.

JJ could not forget his Uncle Hugh, a captain in the Army, standing so tall and proud in his uniform.

Rosemary thought about Cousin Billy, who pulled her into the little closet under the stairs and stuck his tongue in her mouth.

Ellen remembered the quiet serenity of her Uncle Patrick and the magnificent Christmas Eve mass at St Stephen's.

Priscilla had never had so many people who wanted to pet her and fuss over her.

And Ricky savored the proudest moment of his young life, when the attention of everyone had been focused only on him.

It was raining when they got home to Delgada Road. The house smelled musty as they hurried inside. They found three leaks in the roof that Jack would not be able to fix until the weather cleared. They set big pots out to catch the water.

Valerie returned to the Gray Whale. Leo gave her a big smile and a bear hug. 'Just look at you,' he cried. 'Your cheeks are rosy, your eyes are sparkling, and yep, I think your mother even managed to put a couple of pounds on you.'

Valerie laughed. 'She wouldn't let me leave until she did.'

'We missed you, honey,' Lil said. 'Did you have a good time?'

'I missed you, too,' Valerie answered. 'And I had a wonderful time.' She turned back to Leo. 'I really appreciated your giving me the time off, being such short notice and everything.'

'Don't worry,' Leo assured her, 'we managed okay.' Then he cleared his throat and his eyes brushed past Lil's. 'But maybe, when you got a minute, if you wouldn't mind, I could talk to you about helping out at breakfast on Saturdays and Sundays.'

Valerie looked at Lil and then back at Leo. 'Of course, I wouldn't mind,' she said slowly, 'but—'

'I know you didn't want to work so much anymore,' Leo interrupted, 'but business has really picked up on weekends, and Lil here ain't as young as she used to be.'

'Who *is*?' Lil put in.

'And Donna don't want any more hours,' Leo added.

Valerie wondered whether this was Leo's idea or whether Lil had told him about Jack's cut in pay. 'Do you really need me, Leo?' she asked him gently. 'Or has Lil been telling you my troubles?'

Leo gave her a blank look. 'What troubles could *you* have?' he replied blandly. 'Lil didn't tell me to get her some help, if that's what you mean, but I got eyes. I can see when she's doing too much.'

Valerie wanted to argue, wanted to tell Leo that he had already done enough for her, but she knew the extra money would take a lot of pressure off Jack right now, and anything that took pressure off Jack made life easier at home.

'Why don't we say that I'll pitch in as long as you need me,' she said finally.

When she told Jack, he nodded, his face set. 'Just till my raise comes through,' he said. 'Then you give it up.'

Right after the New Year, Gina Kahulani, a Federal Airlines stewardess based in Honolulu, was assigned to the San Francisco run. She had shiny black hair that fell below her waist, Polynesian eyes, and pert little breasts that didn't sag from years of nursing. She flew into SFO at eight o'clock every Tuesday night and flew out again at eight o'clock Thursday morning. As with all Federal flight personnel, she stayed at a hotel just across from the airport.

It took Jack three days to notice her, and two more days for her to notice him. By the beginning of February, he had begun to schedule regular overtime on Tuesdays and Wednesdays, leaving the terminal shortly after eight to meet Gina in the hotel lobby. They would take long baths together before they went to bed and quick showers afterward. In between, they would order room service. Around midnight, after she had brought them both off at least twice, he would put on his clothes and go home.

'It's a little extra money,' he told Valerie about the overtime, his usually direct glance sliding somewhere past her shoulder. 'We can use it.'

Valerie said nothing. If truth be told, the later he came home, the less time he spent around the children, the easier life was. And if it was late enough and he was tired enough, he generally stayed on his side of the bed. She never denied him, of course. After all, she was his wife and that gave him certain rights. But usually when he showed up after midnight, all he wanted to do was go to sleep. So she said nothing. Nor did she say anything when the shirts that smelled of strange perfume and the handkerchiefs with suspicious lipstick smears began to appear.

3

In the middle of January, Connie Gilchrist moved into her new house on the corner of Delgada and del Oro.

A huge van pulled into her driveway around noon, and stayed until well after eight that night. Valerie watched, fascinated, from her front window, as two men and a red-haired woman labored steadily. She wondered where all the sofas and chairs and tables and chests she saw being carried into the house would go, and she couldn't imagine how just one person could have filled the row after row of wardrobe containers that followed the furniture. She squinted at the red-haired woman thinking that, perhaps, Connie Gilchrist was not going to be living alone, after all.

'Oh yes, I *am* going to live alone,' Connie declared the next morning, when Valerie knocked timidly at the door with an applesauce cake fresh from the oven. 'I went from my father's house to a college dormitory room with three other girls, then back to my father's house when my mother got sick, and finally to my husband's house. I nursed my mother until she died, and then took care of my father until he remarried. After that, I raised my husband's daughter, and to tell you the truth, I raised *him* a little, too. I think I've earned the right to be all by myself for a while, don't you?'

'Oh my,' Valerie murmured. It had never occurred to her that a woman would actually live alone out of choice rather than necessity.

Connie laughed. 'Shocked you, did I? Well, come on in here, and let's have some of that cake you're about to drop. If I'm going to corrupt you, I don't intend to do it out on the front porch.'

Valerie stepped across the threshold.

The house was beautiful. It had been built on three different levels, and all at angles, with one room opening naturally into another. Huge windows took up most of the walls. What was left was painted white. Plush white carpeting covered most of the floors. Where there was no carpet, there was glazed white tile. Dusty blue and burgundy furniture seemed to float on a sea of clouds. All the wood was polished walnut. With a sigh Valerie thought of the haphazard browns and rusts and mustard yellow and mismatched oaks and maples that knocked up against one another in her own cluttered rooms.

'It's clear you don't intend any children to live here,' she said.

'No,' Connie said simply, 'I don't.'

'Won't you rattle around all by yourself?' Valerie asked. 'From the outside, I had no idea the house was this big.'

'Actually, it isn't,' Connie replied. 'It isn't even as big as yours. It's just an optical illusion. There are only six rooms, but the way they're designed to flow into one another, and the way all the windows pull the outside in, and then the way the white has been used, make it look a lot larger than it is. I get claustrophobic in small spaces.' She chuckled. 'My father didn't know it, but he never had to worry about me going down the mine.'

The main bedroom had the largest bed in it that Valerie had ever seen, and a closet that was the size of Priscilla's whole bedroom, with every hanger in it spoken for.

173

'I've never seen so many clothes in one place except in a department store,' she said in awe.

'One of my insecurities,' Connie confessed. 'The result of growing up without, I guess. As a child, I had one good dress and one plain dress. I wore the good dress to church and the plain dress to school. My mother would wash and iron it every night. And the rich kids would tease me every day. As I grew, she would add strips of material to the bottom. When I started developing breasts, she added strips of material down the front. Now, if I don't want to, I don't have to wear the same outfit twice in a year.'

They passed through the bedroom into the bathroom, which was as big as Valerie's kitchen. It had a huge step-down bath-tub as well as a stall shower, and two sinks, and all the fixtures were a dusty rose color.

'My whole family could fit in your bed,' Valerie marveled, 'and never even bump into each other in the bathroom.'

'I didn't say I was planning to live alone all the time,' Connie said with a mischievous twinkle. Valerie gasped, not sure she had heard correctly, but not for the world would she ask this sophisticated woman whether she had a lover.

Connie had turned her spare bedroom into an office, with a desk and file cabinets and a telephone. The shelves that lined two of the walls from floor to ceiling were already crammed with books. Looking at the books, Valerie was struck by a sudden thought. 'There aren't any boxes,' she said. 'You just moved in yesterday and yet everything's exactly where it belongs. How did you do that?'

'That's Rita's doing,' Connie explained with a smile. 'My housekeeper. The most organized person that ever lived. I'd be totally lost without her. She was here all day yesterday, telling everyone, including me, exactly where everything was to go.'

The red-haired woman, Valerie remembered. In her whole life, she had never known anyone who employed a housekeeper.

'Rita worked for my husband and me twice a week for ten years. She's devoted to the family. So now she works one day a week for my ex and one day for me. Aren't divorces civilized these days? You even split up the maid.'

Valerie didn't know what to say. She didn't know anything about divorce. 'You have a lot of books,' she said finally.

'Feel free to help yourself,' Connie invited.

'I used to read some, when I was growing up, but that was so long ago,' Valerie admitted. 'I haven't opened a book in ages.'

'Why not?'

'I don't know,' Valerie said. 'I guess I always seem to have too many other things to do with my time.'

Connie reached up and pulled a book off one of the shelves and handed it to Valerie. 'It's never too late to start again,' she said.

Valerie looked at the cover. *A Tale of Two Cities*, it read, written by Charles Dickens. 'Isn't this the man who wrote about Ebenezer Scrooge?' she asked.

'The very same.'

Valerie had never read *A Christmas Carol*, but she had seen the movie, and enjoyed it. She tucked the book under her arm.

They went back upstairs and into the kitchen, and Connie put a teakettle on to boil. 'Coffee or tea?' she asked.

'Coffee, please, if it isn't too much trouble,' Valerie answered.

'No trouble at all.' Connie slipped a filter into a Chemex, added a measure of coffee, and then turned to the cake. 'This looks absolutely wonderful,' she said as she began to slice the moist loaf.

'It's nothing special,' Valerie assured her. 'Just applesauce.'

Connie chuckled. 'Trust me,' she told her guest, 'for someone who lives on Sara Lee, this is special.'

Valerie blushed happily.

Connie asked about the neighborhood, and Valerie told her what she could. 'I'm sorry I can't tell you very much about the people,' she said. 'They tend to stick to themselves. But one thing for sure, get a pair of rubber boots to see you through the rest of the rainy season, or you'll likely ruin some of those pretty shoes I saw in your closet.'

'Ugh,' Connie said, making a face. 'I bought this property in the summertime. If I'd realized the place turned into Mudville six months out of the year, I might have considered another option.'

Valerie recommended Dr Wheeler, if Connie needed a physician, and Dr Albert Gold, if she was interested in a local dentist.

'Is this Dr Gold the best in Half Moon Bay?' Connie wanted to know, thinking of the dental work she was going to require soon. 'I don't do dentists well.'

'I guess you could say so,' Valerie replied. 'He's the only one in Half Moon Bay.'

Connie nodded. 'A singular recommendation,' she observed.

Valerie laughed. Her father said funny things like that, with a straight face just like Connie's. 'We have a hospital,' she offered. 'Two of my children were born there.'

'So far, I've managed to live without hospitals, thank

you very much,' Connie replied with a grimace. 'How about a supermarket? I can't live without a super-market.'

Valerie's brows furrowed thoughtfully. 'Well, there's a mom-and-pop place just a few blocks from here, and then there's a bigger mom-and-pop place down in Half Moon Bay, but I don't think either of them is exactly what you had in mind.'

Connie shrugged. 'Do they sell food?'

'Of course,' Valerie replied with a giggle.

'Then I guess that's what I had in mind.'

They discussed what other services Half Moon Bay provided, and then they talked about the weather some more, and about the beach, and about the deer who lived in the hills above them, and finally about the office Connie was about to open. Before they realized it, they had each had two cups of coffee and three slices of cake.

'I'm so sorry,' Valerie said in embarrassment when she realized. 'The cake was supposed to be for you.'

There was something about Valerie Marsh that reminded Connie Gilchrist of herself, centuries ago . . . a naïveté, perhaps, and a total unawareness of who she was and what she might have to offer. Clearly, the girl needed help.

'Look,' Connie said, 'if we're going to be friendly neighbors, you're going to have to do something about this apology thing. I don't handle guilt very well, not my own and not anyone else's.'

'I'm sorry,' Valerie said without thinking.

Connie burst out laughing. 'Say, you know, you're pretty good.'

Valerie did not correct her.

A week later, Valerie returned *A Tale of Two Cities* to Connie's bookshelf. 'It was wonderful,' she said, her eyes shining. 'I got to step into a whole other country and a whole other century, and walk around in other people's shoes. And I learned so much more about the French Revolution than I ever knew before.'

'That book made a huge impression on me, too,' Connie said. 'So, now do you think you'll be able to find time to read?'

Valerie smiled. Her neighbor might have something of a crusty exterior, but underneath, she sensed there was a good person lurking. 'Would you mind if I borrowed something else?' she asked.

Connie smiled back. 'My library is your library,' she replied.

After that, the two women saw each other often. They would have coffee in Connie's cheerful breakfast nook, or Valerie would stop by on her way to work to return one book and select another. On one occasion, they drove into Half Moon Bay together so that Valerie could introduce Connie to the local merchants, after which they checked on the contractors who were remodeling the building Connie had bought for her business.

Once, when Debby was able to come take care of the children, Connie took Valerie over to San Mateo to look for office furnishings, asking her opinion of every item before she purchased it. Then they went to the department stores in Palo Alto. Valerie couldn't afford to buy anything, but she watched as Connie tried on one glamorous outfit after another.

'What do you think of this one?' Connie asked, parading back and forth in bright blue. At first, Valerie approved of everything, but after a while, she began to notice that some styles and some colors looked better on Connie than others did.

'I like that,' she said once, surprising herself. 'Bold colors look better on you than pale ones.'

Connie gave her a big smile. 'You're learning,' she said. 'Now, tell me, what colors look best on you.'

'Gosh, I don't know,' Valerie replied. So Connie pulled a whole rack of dresses into the dressing room, and began draping different colors around Valerie's shoulders until she could see that pastels looked best with her blond hair and fair skin.

On an evening in the middle of February, when Jack was working late, Valerie volunteered to teach Connie how to bake. She left JJ in charge of the children and made her way across the vacant lot that separated her home from Connie's. 'We'll start with something simple,' she said, 'like brownies.'

Connie was all thumbs when it came to measuring out ingredients. Soon her white floor was dusted with brown, her brown hair was powdered in sugar, and Valerie was picking little pieces of eggshell out of the mixing bowl.

'Isn't there just some Betty Crocker box we can open?' Connie asked in exasperation.

'Sure,' Valerie told her. 'But you have to add eggs and oil and stuff just the same. And they don't taste nearly so good.'

On a Tuesday morning in the middle of March, Connie opened the front door to her neighbor with a lethal-looking pair of scissors in her hand. 'Today's the day,' she announced.

She maneuvered a startled Valerie into the bathroom, sat her down on a stool, and spun her around to face the mirror. What Connie couldn't do with a mixer, she could do with shears. In no time, Valerie's straggly ponytail lay on the floor, replaced by a smooth blond cap that framed her face.

'I love it,' Valerie cried, swinging her head back and forth to watch the hair ripple out and then fall neatly back into place.

Connie was studying her handiwork in the mirror. 'Not finished,' she said, as the lethal scissors began to snip-snip again, and a wisp of bangs suddenly fell forward over Valerie's brow. 'There, that's the look I want,' she declared. The shears were put down and the rouge pot was picked up. 'Now, a little color, and you'll be ready for the cover of *Vogue*.'

Valerie had never used much makeup. A pale lipstick and a light fringe of mascara for dress-up was all she ever bothered with. Connie worked over her for half an hour, brushing soft pink into her cheeks and blending pale blue with mauve above her eyes. 'I don't have anything but black mascara,' she said, applying a thin coat to Valerie's blond lashes. 'You should use brown, but this will give you the general idea.' Last, she painted Valerie's lips a pale rose. 'Okay, what do you think?' she asked finally.

Valerie stared at her reflection in the mirror in amazement, turning to catch every angle. 'I can't believe that's really me,' she whispered. She was actually a little embarrassed. Not even for her wedding had she been so made up. 'But in a million years, I'd never be able to do all that by myself.'

'Look, if I can learn to bake brownies, you can learn to put on makeup,' Connie declared.

Valerie floated through the rest of the day. Leo's eyes popped when she came into the Gray Whale. 'You look fantastic,' he blurted. 'What've you done to yourself?'

Lil gave her a big hug. 'Just look how pretty you are,' she murmured.

And some of the regulars smiled timidly at her and left extra big tips.

JJ's face lit up when she got home. 'Wow, Mom, what happened to you?' he asked.

'Your hair looks real pretty that way, Mama,' Rosemary told her.

'I don't ever remember you painting your face before,' Ellen said seriously.

'Why did you paint your face?' Priscilla wanted to know.

'You don't look like my mama,' Ricky wailed and started to hiccup.

Jack, arriving home at eight o'clock that night because Gina Kahulani's flight from Honolulu had been canceled, never even noticed.

The heavy rains subsided at the end of March. The sun came out, the mud dried up. Valerie began thinking about a good spring cleaning to rid the house of the musty smell that always built up during the rainy season. Jack began thinking about a transfer to Honolulu so he could spend five nights a week instead of two with Gina Kahulani.

He hadn't known anyone like her since Korea. She had talents that he could only describe as purely Oriental. No American woman he had ever slept with, and there had been more than a few over the years, could even come close to doing for him what she could do. While all of them had been willing, even eager, to please him at the beginning of a liaison, he had quickly learned how unskilled each was, and then boring as she began to worry more about her own satisfaction than about looking after his. The relationship wouldn't last long after that, and he would drift on to someone else.

Gina was different. Her enthusiasm increased as time went on. She was forever inventing new ways of propelling him to the pinnacle of ecstasy and postponing his payoff until she had him actually sobbing from the pain.

'God, you're good,' he would tell her.

'I come from a long line of hedonists,' she would say.

181

He didn't have any idea what that meant, but he couldn't get enough of her.

Honolulu was opening up, and Federal Airlines had acquired several new routes to the Pacific and the Far East that promised to triple the traffic through Hawaii in the next few years. The company would have to send a top-notch crew to the islands, and Jack was sure, if he asked for a transfer, he would have enough seniority to get it.

Of course, Valerie would have a fit. He had no doubt about that. California was already too far away from her precious family. But he knew the kids would like it, all that sand and surf and tropical sunshine. And in time, he felt certain Valerie would adjust, and maybe even come to like it, too. He loved his wife well enough, and he wanted her to be happy, as long as it didn't interfere with what he wanted for himself. And Gina Kahulani was what he wanted for himself.

It was a perfect setup. His wife and family would be tucked out of the way in a bungalow near the beach, and his sultry Polynesian mistress would be waiting for him after work in the high-rise apartment overlooking Diamond Head that she had told him all about.

'I've been thinking,' he said one Wednesday night, in the privacy of Gina's hotel room, when they had finally come up for air and a bucket of fried chicken, 'how great it would be if we were in Honolulu instead of here.'

'Sure, honey,' Gina said, munching on a crispy thigh.

'No, I mean it,' Jack said, tossing his drumstick at the tray and rolling over in the big bed.

'You mean your wife would be crazy enough to let you come to Hawaii solo?'

'I'm not talking about a vacation,' Jack replied. 'I'm talking about a transfer.'

The crispy thigh dropped onto the sheet, leaving a greasy spot, and the Polynesian eyes widened for an instant before crinkling into their sexy slant. 'Big joke, huh, and I fell for it.'

'It's no joke,' Jack insisted. 'I'm serious. Just think about what a sweet deal it'd be. We could have each other five nights a week instead of two.'

'I like things the way they are,' Gina told him, her voice soft, but now with a subtle edge to it that he missed. 'Two nights a week is okay with me. Isn't it okay with you?'

Jack, lying languidly against the sheets, missed the warning. 'Yeah, sure babe, two is great, but five would be sensational.'

'I'm sure it would,' she conceded in that same soft tone, 'but it's not going to happen.'

'Why not? I've got the seniority. I can get the transfer.'

Gina had her back against the headboard. Now she pulled her knees slowly up in front of her, away from him. 'Jack, I like you all right here in Frisco, but back home, I've got better things to do.'

Jack grinned. 'Other things, maybe, but not better.'

'Better,' Gina repeated.

Jack frowned. It never occurred to him that she had someone in the islands. He'd just assumed that she was his for the taking. 'Hey, I don't mind sharing for a while,' he told her, telling himself that it wouldn't be for long.

'You're missing the point,' she said.

'What point?'

'You're the guy I spend my layovers with, that's all.'

'But that's what I'm trying to tell you,' he persisted. 'That can all change now.'

'You just don't get it, do you?'

'Get what?'

Gina sighed. 'I don't want to see you in Hawaii.'

'But . . .'

She climbed off the bed. 'As a matter of fact,' she declared, 'I've just decided I don't want to see you here anymore, either.'

Jack smiled in disbelief. 'You don't mean you're cutting me loose, do you?' he teased.

'Yes,' came the reply.

The smile faded from his face. All of a sudden, he wasn't so sure he knew what was going on here. Women didn't end relationships with him. He grew tired or bored and ended relationships with *them*.

'You're just kidding, right?' he asked apprehensively.

'No, Jack, I'm not. We've had a blast, but now it's over.'

'Why? Tell me why?'

She sighed. 'Because I don't need any complications in my life.'

'And that's all I am to you, a goddam complication?' His heart was beating rapidly and he felt his face grow hot.

'You weren't a complication, you were a diversion.'

'I don't believe that. We're absolutely fantastic together.'

Gina looked straight at him. '*I* was fantastic,' she said evenly. 'You were just . . . okay.'

'What does *that* mean?' he almost shouted.

'It means that I like my sex to be a little more than a tongue in one hole and a prick in another.'

He ached to hit her, to wipe that contemptuous look from her eyes, to cut out her tongue. But he couldn't. He wanted her too much. 'And the guy in Honolulu?' he asked dully. 'Is he such a winner?'

She started to smile and her gaze slipped past his shoulder. 'He plays me like a violin,' she almost purred. 'A Stradivarius.'

He couldn't stand it. 'Please,' he pleaded, 'don't throw me out. I have to have you again.' He couldn't believe what he heard himself saying. 'Give me another chance. I won't come to Hawaii, I promise. I'll stay right here, and we can go on just like before. No, better than before. Just tell me what you want me to do, and I'll do it. Anything.'

'Go home to your wife, Jack,' Gina said, not unkindly. 'Work it out with her.'

He drove home in a daze, twice finding himself on the left-hand side of the road that wound over the hill to the Coast. He was lucky that traffic was light at that hour and that no Highway Patrol cars monitored his passage. He tuned the radio to a rock and roll station and turned the volume up as loud as it went. He didn't want to think of his last fifteen minutes with Gina, of the way he had begged, and yes, even cried, utterly debasing himself. But it was all in vain. She just stood there with her arms crossed, like stone. Finally, there was nothing left for him to do but scramble, humiliated, into his clothes and stumble out of the room. He couldn't even remember finding his car, much less making his way out of the hotel parking lot and onto the freeway.

He cursed his mention of the transfer to Honolulu. If he hadn't been so greedy, hadn't tried for such a big piece of paradise, he would still be dallying in her bed, his nerve ends shrieking, his body writhing from her touch, and not on his way home to his lump of a wife. Thinking of Valerie in conjunction with Gina actually made him groan out loud.

It was just eleven o'clock when he pulled his car into the driveway. The house was dark as he let himself in, except for the small lamp in the hallway that Valerie always left on for him. He made his way into the kitchen and found the bottle of bourbon he knew was in the cupboard. Then he sat down at the table and drank half of it all at once, not bothering with a glass. He felt the warmth spreading through him, and after a few moments, he was calm again and back in control and finally exhausted. He climbed the stairs, with leaden feet, wanting only to crawl into bed and fall into a deep, forgetful sleep.

Valerie was barely visible beneath the covers. She did not awaken as he pulled off his clothes and climbed in beside her. He burrowed under the bedding, shut his eyes, and waited for oblivion to overtake him. He waited a long time, and all the while, images of Gina, naked and gleaming, danced before him, taunting him, arousing him. He opened his eyes, straining to see familiar objects in the darkness, the straight-backed chair, the bureau, the brocade curtains covering the window. But it was no use. The Polynesian beauty was still there, perched at the foot of the bed, her body beckoning, her almond eyes mocking him.

'Stop it!' he whispered hoarsely. He clenched his fists and his teeth, while his whole frame began to shake. Gina's throaty laugh assailed his ears. He couldn't stand it. He reached for her, pulling her toward him by her hair, wondering vaguely how the long thick tresses had turned short and silky as he forced her legs apart and pushed himself into her.

Valerie was only half awake when he assaulted her. Not having the faintest idea of what was going on, she screamed.

Jack clapped his hand across her mouth, cutting off the sound, ignoring her protests. When she began to gasp for air, he took his hand away. When she begged him to stop, he slammed her across the face.

'Oh yes,' he snarled above her. 'It's your turn to beg

now, isn't it, you bitch? Well, let's see how *you* like it!' His hand closed around her neck and he thrust himself against her as hard as he could.

The more she squirmed, the deeper he plunged. 'Cunt!' he cried. 'Whore!' Again and again, in time with a rhythm of his own.

Valerie was unable to move. Jack was sprawled on top of her, snoring loudly. The whole lower half of her body was numb. Her left temple throbbed. Her nose felt swollen. Her throat was sore. The morning light, penetrating the curtains at the windows, bathed the bedroom in soft gray. She glanced toward the nightstand for perhaps the hundredth time. The clock now read just past six-thirty. She should be getting out of bed, she knew, to start breakfast and pack lunches and ready the children for school. Jack would have to get up, too. He had to be at the airport by eight.

But Valerie didn't have the strength to move Jack off her. She lay beneath him and stared up at the ceiling, trying, as she had been doing all night, to understand what had happened. But none of it made any sense. The word that kept coming into her mind was *rape*, but she knew that was absurd. A husband couldn't rape his wife. He just asserted his marital rights. Only Jack had never asserted his rights quite like that before. As though he were deliberately trying to hurt her, hitting her, choking her, calling her all those awful names.

There had been the smell of liquor on his breath, so she knew he had been drinking, but it wasn't like he was drunk. What he was like was, well, the only word she could think of was . . . *crazy*. Except, of course, she knew better than that, because there was no way she could have spent the last twelve years of her life married to a crazy man.

Every other time he had hit her, it was after he had felt provoked, usually when she had challenged him in some way, or been disrespectful enough to earn his wrath. It had never happened out of the blue like this, for no reason.

She looked at the clock. It was now ten minutes to seven. The children would be wondering where she was. She looked at Jack, sleeping soundly. Any other morning, she would simply have said his name and shaken him gently awake. But this morning, she hesitated.

Holding her breath, Valerie pulled a corner of the blanket gently loose and moved it slowly toward his face, closer and closer, until it first tickled his nose and then blocked his breathing. Jack snorted and shook his head. She waited. Then, without opening his eyes, he rolled off her onto his side of the bed.

Valerie let go of her breath and slipped out from between the sheets. Then she quietly pulled a robe over her nightgown, quickly went to the bathroom, and was in the kitchen fixing lunches when the first of the children came downstairs.

JJ stood at the kitchen door, staring at her.

'Hi, honey,' Valerie chirped. 'I'm running a little late this morning. I must've overslept. I'm afraid cold cereal will have to do for breakfast. I hope you don't mind.'

There was no response. Valerie looked up and when she saw his expression she knew at once what was wrong. She hadn't turned on the light in the bathroom when she got up, or taken the time to brush her teeth or comb her hair or look at herself in the mirror. Only now, from the expression in her son's eyes, did she realize what she must look like.

'It's nothing,' she murmured. 'Now come and eat.'

She left him at the table and hurried back to her bedroom. With relief, she saw that Jack was still asleep.

Crossing into the bathroom, she closed the door quietly behind her and turned on the light, gasping at the face that looked back at her. An angry bruise spread across her temple, her nose was twice its normal size, a bloody welt ran from the corner of her mouth, and deep red marks circled her throat. She smeared a foundation Connie had given her all over her face and neck and brushed her cheeks with a pink blusher. Then she shed her robe, took a turtleneck shirt from the hamper, and pulled it on over her nightgown.

The rest of the children were in the kitchen when she returned, huddled around the kitchen table, trying not to stare. They ate quickly, without their usual morning squabbling, Ricky stuffing spoonfuls of Cheerios into his mouth between hiccups. Valerie understood. On such a day as today, it was better to be early to school.

She packed their lunch boxes, handing one to each of them with a smile and a reassuring little hug as they darted out the door. Then she stood there, looking after them.

Ellen had her arm around Priscilla. Rosemary walked by herself. JJ held Ricky's hand. When they reached the corner of Delgada and turned down del Oro, Valerie closed the door and went upstairs to wake Jack.

'What the hell did you let me oversleep for?' he demanded when she shook him awake and he saw the clock. 'It's past seven-thirty. Thanks to you, I'm going to be late to work.'

'I tried to wake you before,' she told him, 'but I couldn't.'

'Oh, just get out of my way,' he snarled, brushing past her into the bathroom.

Confused, Valerie retreated to the children's rooms, busying herself with making beds and tidying up until she heard Jack slam the front door and gun the car engine as he roared off down Delgada. Then she began to shiver uncontrollably. She didn't understand what had happened last night, and she didn't understand why Jack wasn't remorseful this morning, as he always was after one of his episodes. But she knew that something had changed, and more than that, she knew that whatever it was that had triggered Jack's fury, it had nothing to do with anything she had said or done.

Valerie wished she could talk to someone, someone who could tell her how to be a better wife. She had tried to talk to her priest. But all Father Bernaldo had done was clasp his hands and look to the heavens.

'God tests each of us in His own way,' he had told her, 'and if you want to be worthy of His love, you have to try harder to be a good wife.'

She never discussed it with him again.

She would like to have asked Connie how to be a better wife. Connie was so smart and sophisticated, and even though she was divorced, Valerie had a feeling she would know. But of course she couldn't tell Connie what went on in her house. She could never tell anyone.

Still, last night had been different, and she needed to understand it. Because, if Jack could go off on her like he had, when she hadn't done anything to provoke him, there was no saying what could happen.

For the first time, Jack came home without a gift that evening, and without a word about the violence of the night before. However, he no longer seemed angry, just preoccupied. The children were confused. Daddy was usually very jolly after one of his episodes, and they didn't understand why this time was different. They ate their dinner in silence and escaped from the table as quickly as they could.

Valerie watched carefully for the signs she knew so

well, but none appeared. Jack ate without much conversation, sat out back by himself for a while, and went to bed early. Valerie busied herself with some mending, in no hurry to join him, and so she missed seeing that he cried himself to sleep.

His strange mood lasted into the next week. Tuesday was the worst, when he knew that Gina was back in town. He couldn't help it, he stayed at work until eight and went to the gate where she was scheduled to arrive, hiding behind a column as she came off the plane, her tight maroon uniform concealing nothing from him. She was walking with the copilot, laughing up at him in that deep, sexy laugh he knew so well. It was almost more than he could bear. He followed them through the terminal and was glad to see that she climbed into the airline shuttle bus alone, but it was a small victory. He knew Gina Kahulani wouldn't be alone for long.

His body ached so badly for her that he groaned aloud and several people passing by turned to look at him. He ducked hastily into a nearby men's room, closing himself into a cubicle, cursing himself for his weakness. Afterward, he was filled with shame and loathing for what she had reduced him to. She wasn't worth it, and there were too many other fish in the sea for him to waste his time crying over one that got away. That little blonde in Baggage Claims, for instance, with the cute Texas accent, had been giving him the eye for a while now.

He made his way out of the terminal and headed for the parking lot, locating the Pontiac he was now driving, and pressing the gas pedal to the floor when he hit the freeway. Let a cop catch him, he thought. He had tuned the Pontiac himself, he knew she was good for a hundred twenty on the open road. Let a cop chase him down and write him up, he would earn it.

But the Highway Patrol must not have wanted to take him on this night because no one came in hot pursuit. When he turned onto Route 92, headed for Half Moon Bay, he slowed to the speed limit. By the time he reached home, he was almost all right again.

'It's Ricky's birthday next week, you know,' Valerie said tentatively, as they were getting ready for bed. 'If you don't have to work late, I thought we could have a little party.'

'I don't have to work late,' he said, more than pleased that there was one person in this world, anyway, who still hung on his approval.

On impulse, Valerie asked Connie to come to the party. 'I'm afraid we make a rather shameless fuss over birthdays at our house,' she said. 'First and foremost, the children get to choose what they want for dinner. Sometimes it works out and sometimes it doesn't. This year, Ricky's picked spaghetti and hot dogs.'

'Two of my favorites,' Connie said graciously, although she had never eaten them in combination. 'I'd be delighted to come.'

Other than the Halgrens back in Seattle, this was the first time that Valerie had invited anyone other than family into her home.

Martin Luther King, Jr, was shot to death in Memphis, Tennessee, on the afternoon of Ricky's birthday. The boy came running home from kindergarten in tears.

'Martin Lukerthing Junior got dead today,' he sobbed.

'I know, sweetheart, I know,' Valerie said soothingly. 'He was a good man and the world will be a lesser place with him not in it.'

'Everybody said nobody'd want the day he died for a birthday,' Ricky sobbed.

Valerie hugged him and petted him and told him that Martin Luther King, Jr, was a fine man, and then she assured him that such a fine man wouldn't mind a bit that Ricky was born on this day.

'Nobody'd eat my cupcakes, either,' he said, choking on his tears. 'And then Miss Hesperia said a party would be in-in-in-apope-inapoperate.'

Valerie had taken chocolate cupcakes to school so the kindergarten could have the customary birthday party.

'Never mind,' she told him, drying his tears. 'After all, your real birthday party is tonight, isn't it?'

Ricky brightened somewhat at that thought. 'Is that when I get my red truck?'

Valerie smiled. 'Well, we'll see.' She took his hand and led him to the kitchen for a snack.

The birthday party was a happy affair. For the special occasion, they sat in the dining room, which Valerie had decorated with multicolored streamers and balloons. Ricky felt very important indeed, being the birthday boy, and riding to the place of honor at the head of the table on his father's shoulders. Having so many presents to open, he soon forgot his earlier upset.

His parents gave him the dump truck he had been wishing for, the bright red one with all the working parts, and it was all Valerie could do to keep him from taking it out into the sandbox the minute it was unwrapped. He was too excited to eat very much of his spaghetti and hot dog dinner, but he managed to get down two pieces of double chocolate birthday cake, after he had made his wish, of course, and blown out all his candles, with only a little help from JJ.

'If I'm only six,' he gasped, 'how come I had to blow out seven candles?'

'The seventh one was to grow on,' Valerie told him.

'Oh, good,' Ricky said. ''Cause I wished I'd grow up as big as JJ very soon.'

'You weren't supposed to tell what you wished for,' JJ whispered. 'Now it won't come true.'

Ricky looked crestfallen.

'Never you mind,' Valerie said quickly. 'God will hear you.' She smiled at him tenderly.

Dr Wheeler and numerous specialists at the Stanford University Hospital had warned her that Ricky would be undersized. The circumstances of his birth, they said. But at the time, Valerie had been so glad he was even alive, she hadn't cared about anything else. Now his sisters and brother towered over him out of all proportion to their ages, he was the smallest by far in his kindergarten class, and Jack had taken to calling him 'Runt.' He was only six years old, and already it had begun to matter to him. She would have given anything to be able to steal into his room at night and add inches to his little body.

'Don't you worry, Runt,' Jack said lightly, causing Valerie to wince. 'Just remember to take all your vitamins, and someday you'll stand eye-to-eye with the best of them, take my word for it.'

Ricky's whole face lit up at that. And Jack looked over at Connie and winked.

From her place at the end of the table nearest to him, Connie was startled by the gesture – a gesture she could not describe as anything but an attempt to seduce her. She had met Jack a few times since moving into her new home, but only in passing. Now that she had more time to look him over, she thought him handsome and charming, to be sure, if a little too egotistical for her taste. But it was his behavior throughout the evening that most fascinated her, his attempts to entice her, like a spider spinning a web, with little smiles and gestures, seemingly casual touches, and now the wink. And he wasn't being at all subtle about it, either. He was openly flirting with her, and most bizarre of all, he was doing it right in front of his wife, as though she weren't even there.

Jack shifted uneasily in his chair. He had never known a woman who made him more uncomfortable than Connie Gilchrist. He had tried every trick he knew to win her over, employing his most disarming smile, all his charm, and what he knew to be his quick wit. But her gray eyes did not reveal the interest he was accustomed to seeing in other women. It was almost as if she could see right through him, past the facade, and into his very soul. It made him feel exposed.

He knew his wife was in this woman's pocket. Every day, for what seemed forever now, although it was not yet three months, all he heard was 'Connie this' and 'Connie that,' as though she had stumbled across a goddam goddess or something.

Connie had given Valerie a new hairstyle. Connie had taught her how to apply makeup. Connie was encouraging her to think more about her appearance. Connie was showing her how to maximize her wardrobe, whatever that meant. Connie was motivating her to broaden her mind. Connie had gotten her interested in reading again. Like his wife was some sort of damn project. He wondered uneasily what else besides clothing and books they talked about when they were together. He wondered how much Connie knew about him.

As if she had read his mind, Connie looked up at him just then, with that cool gray glance of hers.

Jack signaled for a third helping of birthday cake.

Surprised, Valerie was only too happy to oblige him. Except for an occasional dish of ice cream, Jack didn't much care for sweets, and Valerie didn't flatter herself into thinking it was her baking that made this occasion different. She made the same double chocolate torte every year for all the children on their birthdays, except Ellen, who preferred white cake. She wondered if it had anything to do with Connie's being here. She could hardly help but notice how attentive he was being toward her.

The cake was sickeningly sweet and came close to turning Jack's stomach, but he ate it anyway. It gave him something to do so he didn't have to look at Connie Gilchrist. Not that she wasn't good to look at. She was hot, there was no denying it, and her off-putting attitude didn't deceive him for a moment. He knew there was fire in there, just waiting to be fanned, and he was doing everything he could think of to fan it, but he was having no success.

There weren't many women he couldn't have, just for the asking, and he was sure this one was no exception. But even as he flirted shamelessly, he kept telling himself she was too impressed with how bright and strong and independent she was, instead of knowing her place . . . which could be in her bed with him, if she played her cards right. Why not? There was no one else's bed he was sharing at the moment.

Except that she refused to play, and her indifference only made him try harder, harder than he had ever had to try before. And he was running out of ploys. He moved his leg, ever so slightly, and as if by mistake, rubbed it up against hers. There was no reaction. He tried again, but again there was no reaction. The third time, he got a reaction. With a bite of cake halfway to her mouth, Connie calmly dug the heel of her shoe into the top of Jack's foot. He pulled his leg away, doing his best to hide a grimace of pain.

He blamed Valerie, of course. If she had sat the

woman at the other end of the table, like she should have, instead of practically right on top of him, everything would have been all right. That way, Connie Gilchrist wouldn't have had the opportunity to rebuff him, and he wouldn't have had to worry that she might see his discomfort, his humiliation . . . and in spite of himself, his erection.

Connie finished her last bite of cake, and reaching for her napkin, found that it had slipped off her lap onto the floor. She bent down to retrieve it, and as she straightened back up, she caught Jack's horrified glance. He looked away immediately, but not before she saw acute embarrassment in his eyes.

In the next instant, without bothering to excuse himself, he had bolted from his chair.

4

Jack lounged against the end of the Baggage Claims counter, waiting for Marcy. The green-eyed blonde from Texas was finishing with a customer, a bald guy in a loud Hawaiian shirt, whose luggage had ended up in San Antonio instead of San Francisco. He had come in shouting, but Marcy had him purring in no time, the occasional glimpse of thigh she had provided when she bent over farther than necessary to find a form, coupled with an ingenuous smile, doing the trick.

She was a real pro, Jack thought, chuckling softly to himself. All sugar and honey. God, he thought, what a job to get stuck with. No one could ever pay him enough to trade places with her, having to deal with angry clods like that all day long. He watched as she helped Baldy fill out the forms, leaning across the counter, letting her breasts brush carelessly against his arm. Nice full breasts. Baldy's eyes bulged. So did the front of his pants. Jack almost roared.

'Thank you, Mr Hilliard,' Marcy said sweetly when the forms were finished. 'You'll have your bags back by tomorrow afternoon. And I do apologize again for the inconvenience. I know how annoying it can be not to have what you need.' She gave him her best half smile, half pout.

'Say no more, young lady,' Baldy said breathlessly. 'You've more than made up for everything. As a matter of fact, I wouldn't mind losing my bags all over again, if I could come and tell you about it.'

Marcy batted her eyelashes. 'Why, isn't that just the nicest thing you could have said, Mr Hilliard,' she drawled.

'Well, you know, I could be even nicer,' Baldy blurted boldly. 'What would you say to, uh, maybe having dinner with me?'

'I'd say,' Marcy replied, smiling sweetly and looking genuinely sorry, 'that you'd first have to ask my fella over there.' She gestured toward Jack.

Jack opened his mouth and closed it again. He was damned if he was going to play her game. Hell, they hadn't even been to bed yet. But she didn't seem to need his help. Baldy took one look in Jack's direction and beat a hasty retreat out the door.

'I'm sorry he took so long,' Marcy said, checking her wrist-watch, which read almost seven o'clock. 'And thanks for being here. Some of these guys can get a little hard to handle and it's nice to have a backup.'

'From what I saw, you played him just right,' Jack responded, a note of admiration in his voice. 'It looks to me like you can handle anything that comes your way.'

'Well,' Marcy returned with a toss of her hair, 'why don't we go and find out?'

'What about dinner?' Jack asked.

Marcy tucked her arm through his and propelled him out the door. 'First things first,' she said.

He grinned broadly. This sounded promising. He had been detouring past Baggage Claims for a couple of weeks now, checking her out, winking whenever he happened to catch her eye, and noticing that each time he did, she smiled at him. He had seen no one come to pick her up after work. Then he discovered that, on

Mondays, Tuesdays, and Fridays, she stopped in at one of the airport restaurants for dinner, sitting alone at an out-of-the-way table, and propping a book up in front of her to discourage company.

He chose a Tuesday, told Valerie that he would be working late, and followed Marcy into the restaurant, managing with a bit of pushing and shoving to arrive at her favorite table just as she did.

'What are *you* doing here?' they both asked.

'My wife's having her girlfriends over for the evening,' Jack explained.

'My roommate's a stewardess and I don't cook,' Marcy explained in turn. 'When she flies, I eat out.'

'Well,' Jack offered, 'would you like to share a table?'

'Sure,' Marcy said. 'Why not?'

It had been so simple. They began with neutral conversation about work and travel and family that became intimate conversation without either of them missing a beat. He never lied about having a wife and kids. He found it was the best way to eliminate girls who were looking for more than he was offering. He could tell by the way Marcy leaned into him when she talked which kind she was, and that he had her. She had an impish smile and a tinkling laugh and all the right peaks and valleys. Up close, he could see the fine lines around her green eyes that told him she was a lot older than she looked, but that didn't matter to him. She could have had a paper bag over her head for all he cared.

And now, here he was, three days later, following her blue Chevy Nova through the streets of San Mateo to the apartment she shared with a stewardess who was fortunately on the way to Chicago.

'So what is it with your wife?' Marcy had asked as they walked toward the parking lot. 'Does she really not mind your extracurricular activities?'

Jack shrugged. 'She's my wife, but she doesn't own me. She knows she's going to be my wife for the rest of her life, and that's all she cares about.'

'And what do *you* care about?'

Jack turned one of his special bedroom-eyed looks on her. 'Mutual pleasure,' he said, a touch of huskiness creeping into his voice.

He followed her to a small two-bedroom apartment on the ground floor of a converted house. Marcy's room was an eclectic nightmare, a hodgepodge of antiques and orange crates, a hammock chair, a western saddle, and a stuffed gorilla with flaring nostrils that left barely enough space for the brass bed covered with pink satin sheets. But Jack hardly noticed. He had half of her maroon uniform off before they even got through the door.

'Take it easy,' Marcy said mildly, taking her time in unbuttoning his shirt and loosening his belt. 'There's no hurry.'

But Jack was very much in a hurry. He stripped off her bra and panties, pushed her back onto the bed, and struggled out of his own clothes.

'You're one sexy guy, Jack Marsh, I'll sure say that for you,' Marcy cooed, looking him up and down in anticipation.

He was on top of her before the last word was out of her mouth, kissing her deeply, sliding down her body, pushing himself into her, feeling her rise up to meet him, and then spending himself immediately. He dozed off almost at once, with his head between her breasts, waking when he felt her wriggling beneath him.

'What's the matter?' he asked, his voice muffled against her.

'Now that you've had your pleasure,' she purred, 'what about me?'

'Already looking for seconds, are you?' he murmured appreciatively, drawing his five o'clock shadow across her nipples. 'I like that.'

'I wasn't talking about seconds,' she drawled. 'I was talking about firsts.'

He yawned. 'Didn't we just take care of that?'

Steady green eyes looked up at him. 'I have to go to the bathroom,' she said after a minute. He rolled off her and she slipped out of the bed, closing the adjoining door behind her. She reappeared, fifteen minutes later, wrapped in a pink silk kimono. Jack was asleep.

'Wake up, cowboy,' she said, smacking him on his uncovered butt. 'Time to hit the trail.' She picked his things up off the floor.

Jack sat up and stretched. 'It's still early,' he said. 'Why don't you fix us something to eat? And then I'm sure we can find something else to do.'

Marcy shook her head and handed him his clothes. 'I think I'll pass. I'm pretty beat.'

Jack grinned as he pulled on his pants and buttoned his shirt. 'Wore you out, huh?'

She handed him his shoes without a reply. When he was dressed, she walked him to the front door of the apartment.

'Bye, Jack,' she said.

He stepped out into the hallway. 'How about Monday?' he asked. She wasn't the best he'd ever had, but she would do for the time being.

'I don't think so.'

'Tuesday, then?'

'No, not Tuesday either. Not any day, actually.'

Jack frowned. 'What is this, a brush-off?'

'I guess you could say that,' she said evenly.

'You seeing someone else?'

'No. Not at the moment.'

'Then, what's the deal?'

Marcy shrugged. 'To be perfectly honest, it wasn't much fun, and not worth repeating.'

Jack felt a hot flush creep up around his collar. 'I didn't hear you complaining,' he said sullenly.

'You didn't give me time,' she replied. 'For that or anything else. And, frankly, I'm too old to play bathroom games.'

'What are you talking about?'

She looked at him curiously, wondering for a moment if he really was as naive as he sounded, and then deciding it didn't matter. 'Jack, you've got a great package – brains, looks, a hell of a body – but you just don't know what to do with it. It's as simple as that.'

'Wait a minute, you're not such hot stuff yourself, you know,' he retorted.

Marcy sighed. 'Gina Kahulani was right about you,' she said. It was as though she had hit him in the gut with a cannonball. He staggered back a step, unable to fend off the blow. She saw it and smiled apologetically. 'An airline is just like a fishbowl,' she told him. 'There aren't any secrets.'

'Then . . . why?' he asked, but could say no more.

She shrugged again. 'I guess I wanted to find out for myself.' There was a hint of regret in her voice that Jack misinterpreted as contempt and his face began to turn an ugly red color. Marcy didn't know what that meant, and chose not to find out. She closed the apartment door softly, but firmly, in his face, and slipped the dead bolt smoothly into place. He really was a gorgeous man, she thought. What a waste.

Jack stumbled down the street in the fading twilight. His head was throbbing, his stomach heaving. He retched into the gutter twice before he reached his car. A small community, she had said. No secrets. Her words burned into his brain. He must be the laughingstock of the airline. Gina had made sure of that, the bitch. His humiliation hadn't been enough, she wanted every female employee to snigger behind her hand when he walked by. And his buddies, who always teased him and called him King Stud, were they laughing at him behind his back now, too?

He climbed into the Pontiac and leaned his head against the steering wheel. Maybe he ought to be grateful to Marcy for telling him the score, but he could easily have wrung her neck. A long low groan escaped from the very core of him and he couldn't seem to stop his teeth from chattering. Then his shoulders began to shake. He sat there and cried the way he had as a little boy when one of the women had told him she was leaving.

There was a sharp knock on his window and Jack looked up, startled. A uniformed policeman was peering at him, shining a flashlight directly in his eyes. Jack blinked at the brightness.

'Are you all right, sir?' the cop asked.

Jack nodded.

'You sure?'

Jack brushed the tears quickly from his eyes and rolled down the window. 'I'm fine, Officer. I just wasn't feeling very good, so I thought I'd wait a few minutes before I drove home.'

'You live around here, sir?'

'No, Officer. I was visiting a friend.'

'May I see your license and registration?'

Jack fished the documents out of the glove compartment and handed them through the window. The cop shone his light on the license, checking the photograph, and then back at Jack.

'Have you been drinking, Mr Marsh?' he asked.

'No, I haven't,' Jack replied truthfully.

'Do you require medical assistance?'

'No, I don't.'

'Then as soon as you feel able,' the cop said pleasantly enough, returning Jack's documents, 'I suggest you move along.'

'Yes, sir,' Jack said.

From his side-view mirror, he watched the cop walk away and then turn to look back at the Pontiac. Jack would like to have stayed where he was a while longer, but he didn't want any problems. He turned the key in the ignition and started the engine. The cop was still watching. Jack pulled away from the curb and turned left at the first corner. He had no idea where he was and it took him some time to find a road that would lead him to the freeway, but eventually he was headed west. He drove home with exaggerated care, in no hurry to get anywhere.

Valerie was sitting in the living room, reading a book, when he came in. She looked up, but he clomped right past her and up the stairs. Maybe she would think he was drunk and stay away from him, and that was just fine with him. He couldn't face anyone right now. He fell onto the bed, without taking off his clothes, and pulled the pillow over his head.

He could steer clear of Marcy and Gina, that was easy. There was no reason for him ever to have to see either of them again, but how would he ever be able to face his buddies at work again? He shuddered at the very thought. Especially after the way he had boasted about his conquests.

'How do you do it?' they always wanted to know. 'Damned if you don't attract women like bees to honey.'

Why, he had had them begging, weak-kneed, for his discards. Had Gina gotten to them, too? Had she spread her spiteful story among his crew? Would Marcy? He groaned in misery.

The only bright spot, if there could be said to be one in this whole lousy mess, was that it was Friday. That meant he had two whole days before he had to think about going back to the airport. Two days to plot a counterstrategy, if necessary. He was sure he could come up with something, if he put his mind to it.

And then he had the answer, and it was so simple he wondered why he hadn't thought of it immediately. He would request a transfer. Not to Honolulu, of course – God, anywhere but there. Someplace back East, he thought, maybe even Boston. Valerie would like that. And it would get her away from the maddening influence of Connie Gilchrist. Joey Santini was still in Boston. The two of them could prowl around together again, like the old days. The more he thought about it, the more the idea appealed to him. He fell asleep remembering the sleazy little bar in Scully Square where they used to go to find women.

Jack ripped viciously at the shingles on the east slope of the roof. Ever since the rains had stopped, Valerie had been after him to fix the new leaks. Just to get her off his back, and out of his sight, he had dragged his toolbox and repair materials up the outside ladder immediately after breakfast.

It was a warm day in late April. The sky was a bright, clear blue, the air smelled of pine and jasmine, and blue jays squawked in the nearby trees. But Jack wasn't paying any attention to the wonders of nature. He was focusing the full force of his frustration on the stubborn wooden strips.

With every rip of his steel pry bar, he was tearing the skin off Gina Kahulani's perfect chestnut body. He was gouging the mocking green eyes out of Marcy something-or-other.

He had half awakened, just after nine o'clock, with a vague sense of dread, lying facedown on the bed, a sharp object pressing painfully into his groin. Groggy, he looked around and realized that he was still in his clothes from the night before. Digging into his pants pocket, he pulled out his bulky key ring. The pain subsided, but the dread persisted. In his state of semi-awareness, he wondered why his stomach would be churning, and why he had slept in his clothes. He wondered what time it was, what day. He noticed that the other side of the bed was empty, meaning that Valerie was already up and about.

Then he remembered. This was Saturday. Last night was Friday. The whole awful episode with Marcy came flooding back, and he came fully awake. Outside the window, he could hear the children laughing. He wondered irritably what they had to be so happy about.

He climbed out of bed and padded into the bathroom, turning the hot water in the shower on full force and letting the stinging needles massage his tight muscles. Last night, he had told himself he could easily get a transfer. In the harsh light of day, he wasn't so sure. Federal Airlines wasn't expanding its operations anywhere except in Honolulu, which meant that unless some already established city was in need of a crew chief, he was going to have to stay right where he was.

Valerie knocked on the door. 'Telephone,' she said.

'Who is it?' he called over the water.

'She didn't say,' Valerie replied.

A woman? Jack wrapped a towel quickly about his waist and went dripping out into the upstairs hallway. He had no idea what woman would be calling him at home on a Saturday morning. He picked up the extension phone.

'Sorry to call you at home, but I found your wallet on the bedroom floor,' Marcy said without introduction. 'I wanted you to know where it was when you missed it.' He hadn't. 'It must have slipped out of your pocket when you, well, you know.' He knew. 'You can pick it up at the counter on Monday morning,' she added and hung up.

He stood with the dead receiver in his hand. Just the sound of her voice was enough to turn his knees rubbery and make his stomach sick. He stumbled back into the bathroom just in time, and threw up into the toilet.

Valerie opened the door a crack. 'What's the matter?' she asked. 'Are you all right?'

'Get out,' he snapped, kicking the door shut in her face. The last thing he needed was for his wife to see him puking like a baby over some woman who'd made a fool of him. He flushed away the evidence, and staggering to his feet, leaned stiffly over the sink and brushed his teeth to wash the vile taste out of his mouth.

It was agony knowing he would have to see Marcy again. He was furious with himself for leaving his wallet behind. He was furious with her for lording it over him, forcing him to come begging for it. He was furious with her for reducing him to this slobbering clod.

It was that anger that now motivated him to triumph over the shingles. JJ had offered to help, but Jack had waved him off. It took twice as much time to do a job when you had to keep telling someone else how to do it, especially an eleven-year-old. Jack just wanted to be left alone.

Two stories below him, the cement patio he had built curved neatly around the back of the house. Ellen sat in the swing at the far end, rocking slowly back and forth, poring over the pages of a thick black book that looked suspiciously like a Bible. Rosemary was hanging out a load of wash on the clothesline he had rigged for Valerie between two spindly pine trees. Ricky was operating his bright red dump truck with single-minded concentration, transferring one payload after another from the sandbox to the cement.

Jack had been working for several hours. His sweat-soaked shirt stuck to his shoulders and the small of his back, and his damp jeans chafed the insides of his thighs. The discomfort only added to his frustration, and he cursed the heat along with the stubborn shingles.

Valerie stood at the kitchen counter, preparing lunch. It would be ready to eat by the time JJ came back from the post office. She had asked him to mail some letters for her, and he had ridden happily off on his bicycle to Half Moon Bay. She wished Jack had been a little more sensitive with JJ. Instead of dismissing him out of hand the way he had, he should have been pleased that the boy wanted to help.

Jack could be so nice when he wanted to be, taking the children to interesting places, teaching them things, making them laugh. Valerie frowned uneasily as she spread a light coat of mustard on slices of bread. Something was wrong with him again. She could hardly have missed the signs, the way he had come stomping in last night, going right to bed without a word, and then being moody this morning, not to mention throwing up. Although he had not attacked her again, his behavior was much the same as it had been on that night a month ago. As a result, there was no one more surprised than she when he announced after breakfast that he was going to repair the roof. Given his mood, she had expected almost anything but that.

'Daddy's talking to himself,' Priscilla announced coming into the kitchen.

'He's working very hard,' Valerie told her, reaching for the mayonnaise. 'And it's very hot up on the roof.'

'Maybe if we do something nice for him,' the little girl said, 'it'll put him in a better mood.'

'Why don't we,' Valerie agreed. 'What would you like to do?'

Priscilla thought. 'I know,' she answered. 'Let's make him some nice cold lemonade to drink.'

Valerie smiled. 'That's a wonderful idea. We'll make a whole pitcher and we can have the rest for lunch.' She put down the jar of mayonnaise and turned her attention to the drink.

'Can I help?' Priscilla asked.

'You certainly can.' Valerie cut the lemons in half and let Priscilla squeeze the juice into a big pitcher. Then she added sugar, water, ice cubes, and her secret ingredient, a hint of mint.

'Can I mix it?' Priscilla begged.

Valerie handed the child a long wooden spoon. 'Go ahead,' she replied as she opened the overhead cabinet where the glasses were kept.

'A tall glass for Daddy,' Priscilla directed, stirring away with all her might.

'Yes, ma'am.'

Priscilla giggled with delight as Valerie poured a measure of the frosty drink into the tallest glass she could find.

'Now, don't forget, stay on the flat part of the roof, and be careful you don't trip and fall on anything,' the mother cautioned the daughter with a hug.

Priscilla nodded solemnly and grasped the glass firmly between her two little hands. Who knew, Valerie thought, maybe doing something a little special would help Jack's mood. That is, if whatever was wrong with him was something that could be helped by a glass of lemonade.

She glanced at the clock on the kitchen wall. It was just past noon. JJ would be back any minute. Valerie sighed and went back to the mayonnaise. She wished Jack would tell her what was going on, so she could help him. She remembered, before they were married, that she had occasionally gotten him to share his worries with her. Lately, all they seemed to share was the same house. It was as if he no longer thought her important enough to discuss anything of consequence. But she knew a great deal more now than she had known at eighteen, and she didn't understand why Jack couldn't see that.

Priscilla came out onto the patio, carrying the tall glass of fresh lemonade, and started up the redwood ladder, carefully placing the glass on the rung above her at every step and then climbing up to it. It took several minutes for her to reach the top, but not a drop of the frosty drink had spilled.

Quite satisfied with herself, the seven-year-old stepped out onto the flat part of the roof where she and her brothers and sisters were sometimes allowed to play. Only her father wasn't there, he was halfway down one of the slopes.

Priscilla knew she was not allowed on that part of the roof, and her mother had just reminded her of it, but she didn't stop to think about it. She stepped over the edge and started to inch her way down the shingles.

'Mama sent you something to drink,' she said when she got to within a foot of him.

He snatched the glass from her hand without a word and drank it down almost in one gulp.

'Can I help?' Priscilla asked.

'No,' Jack replied curtly.

'If I help, you wouldn't have to work so hard,' the little girl said reasonably.

Jack thrust the empty glass at her. 'I don't need any help,' he growled. 'Now go on and get out of here before you make a mess of something.' He retrieved the pry bar he had been using and turned back to his work. He had already forgotten her.

Priscilla stood for a minute or two, and watched as her father tugged at the last layer of shingles, grunting with the effort. Every once in a while, he would reach behind him, groping for a different tool from among a selection that was strewn all over the place. The seven-year-old suddenly realized she could help her father after all. If his tools were all in one place in the toolbox, he would be able to find them better. She set the glass down beside her and went about putting the tools carefully and quietly back where they belonged. The quieter she was, she thought, the more she could surprise him.

Jack wiped the sweat out of his eyes with his arm and pulled up the last shingle. The damaged section of tarpaper beneath now had to be cut out. He reached for the X-ACTO knife he knew was right behind him, sliding his hand back and forth over the area to locate it. The knife wasn't there. He turned around irritably. Priscilla was just dropping it into its place in the toolbox.

'What the hell do you think you're doing?' he barked.

'Putting your tools back so you can find them easier,' she said proudly, reaching for the hammer.

His whole body went rigid. 'If I'd wanted them in the goddam box, I'd have left them there.'

Priscilla stared at him. 'I was only trying to help,' she whispered, her lower lip beginning to tremble.

'I told you I didn't need your help, didn't I? Now, put the hammer back where it was,' he ordered.

212

Confused, the little girl dropped the hammer into the toolbox. 'Damn it, not in there,' he roared, swiping at her.

Priscilla only meant to duck away from him, but instead, she did exactly what her mother had warned her not to do, she tripped over a pile of loose shingles, lost her footing, and toppled forward, careening head over heels past her father and down the slope of the roof. Jack lunged for her, trying to catch her, or at least break her fall, but he was too late, she was already past him. He watched, horrified, as she plunged off the roof's edge and crashed onto the cement below.

In the kitchen, Valerie was reaching for a package of bologna. Just as her hand closed around it, she heard the thud. The thing that stuck in her mind, long afterward, when she could finally bring herself to think about it at all, was that it had been such a small sound. Still, she knew somehow that it was important.

She didn't know why, but it seemed to take forever for her to reach the back door and step out onto the patio, and it seemed to take an eternity for her to turn her head and see the little girl who had just been wriggling with delight now lying so horribly still. Dimly, she heard someone screaming, a chilling, almost inhuman, wail that rose and fell and had no end. It was a lifetime before she recognized the voice as her own.

A vacant lot away, in the sunny nook off the kitchen where she was enjoying a quiet brunch on her first Saturday off in more than a year, Connie Gilchrist heard the scream. She was out the door and running up the street in a heartbeat, pushing through the bushes that overgrew the sidewalk, and darting around to the back of the Marsh house. The sight that greeted her was like a series of separate still photographs that together made up a grisly whole.

She saw Priscilla, her broken little body bent all at wrong angles, blood trickling from a gash in her forehead. She saw Valerie, standing just outside the kitchen door, the grotesque sound coming from her mouth seeming almost to be disembodied. She saw Ellen, with her lips moving as she recited something from the Bible open across her lap. She saw Rosemary, tangled in a mess of wet sheets, her eyes shut tight. She saw Jack, hanging half off the edge of the roof, frozen, staring at the motionless lump below him. And she saw Ricky, who looked so much like his father, still clutching his dump truck, and beginning to whimper and shiver as his sister's blood oozed into the pile of sand at his feet.

PART FOUR

1974

I

Ricky flattened himself against the side of the house and held his breath until the car coming up Avenida del Oro turned the corner and passed out of sight down Delgada. It was quite dark, and he was pretty sure he hadn't been seen, even in the unexpected wash of headlights, but he didn't want to take any chances. He waited for what seemed forever, shivering in the cool February night, before he was satisfied that the car was not going to come back. Then he picked up the screwdriver from the ground where he had dropped it and turned again to the sliding glass doors that led into Connie Gilchrist's bedroom.

Connie Gilchrist was not just a neighbor, she was his mother's friend, and Ricky had been wandering in and out of her house since he was six years old. He knew every turn, every angle, every piece of furniture, every hiding place. He also knew that this was Wednesday, and on Wednesday nights, Connie drove up to San Francisco to have dinner with her step-daughter, and didn't get home before midnight. It was now ten-thirty. He had plenty of time.

With a final tug of the screwdriver, the flimsy lock he had been working at gave way, and Ricky slid the heavy door back just enough to slip his small body inside.

The house was very still and very white, even in the darkness. Ricky pulled a flashlight from the pocket of his windbreaker anyway, and snapped it on. He was facing the big walk-in closet. He smiled to himself and stepped into it, moving past the bars of dresses and jackets and blouses that smelled fresh and flowery like Connie did, past the shelves of shoes and sweaters, to the wicker basket at the top of the very last row.

It was much too high for him to reach, so he searched around for the little two-step ladder he knew was there, and dragged it over in front of the shelf. Even from the top step, he had to stand on the tips of his toes, stretching his four feet five inches as far as they would go to reach the basket. It was heavier than it looked and he clutched it tightly as he backed carefully down the ladder. Ricky laid the basket on the carpeted closet floor, removed the lid, brushed away a thick layer of bright silk scarves, and lifted out the rectangular suede box that held Connie Gilchrist's jewelry.

He flipped the top open, knowing that Connie never locked the box, and shone his flashlight inside. A selection of gold bracelets and necklaces gleamed up at him, along with a number of rings with colored stones.

Ricky was two months short of twelve years old. He knew clear stones were diamonds, red and blue ones were rubies and sapphires, and green ones were emeralds, and he had seen enough movies, both in theaters and on television, to know such stones were prized, but he had no clear idea of their actual value. He didn't take it all, just enough of the splashier pieces to stuff the pockets of his windbreaker and his jeans.

Next he went to the nightstand beside Connie's bed, reaching into the top drawer, and pulling out the wad of emergency cash he had seen her tuck inside on more than one occasion. Counting it hastily, he realized he held close to a hundred dollars. A little shiver ran down his back. He had never seen so much money before in his life, much less held it in his hand. He stuffed that, too, into his pockets.

There were other places, the cookie jar in the kitchen, the little wooden box on the bookshelf in the office, the pocket of the suede jacket hanging in the closet, where he knew Connie kept other money, but he decided he had enough. Besides, it was getting late. What if, for some reason, Connie decided not to stay out until midnight this Wednesday? What if his father chose this particular evening to come home earlier than usual?

Ricky didn't press his luck. He slipped out the same sliding glass door he had entered, circled around behind the house, and scurried through the empty lot that separated Connie's home from his own.

He approached his house with caution, and again standing on tiptoe, peered through the kitchen window. Except for a pale glow of light from the foyer, the house was dark. That meant his father was not yet home. Ricky breathed a quick sigh of relief. It also meant his mother hadn't looked too closely at the mound of pillows under his covers on her way to bed. Of course, he had been pretty confident about that part when he sneaked out. His mother wasn't looking too closely into much of anything these days.

He crept up the outside steps, and let himself quietly into the second-floor hallway, making sure that he locked the door behind him. Everything was dark and silent. He waited several seconds for his eyes to adjust to the dimness. The last thing he needed to do was bump into something by mistake and wake everyone up.

Only when he could see clearly did Ricky move on down the corridor. And it was not until he gained the safety of his own room, quickly snapping on the overhead light to make sure he was alone, that he realized how dry his mouth was and how hard his heart was pounding. There was a knot in the pit of his stomach, too. He caught a glimpse of himself in the mirror mounted on top of his dresser. His face was flushed, his eyes glowed, and his lips were parted in a huge grin.

'I knew you could do it,' the boy reassured his reflection. 'Nothing to it.' He snapped his fingers to underscore his words, and did a little boxing feint at the glass. 'Piece a cake.'

He didn't dwell on the fact that he had just done something terribly wrong, since he had no intention of confessing his deed to the parish priest. It didn't matter to him how Connie would feel when she discovered the loss. All he thought about was how careful he had been, how cleverly he had planned, and how perfectly he had executed. There would be no one to tie him to the robbery. His mother would swear that he had been asleep at home at the time of the crime. Ricky giggled. It had all been so simple that he couldn't believe he had actually gotten away with it. But he had. And he felt six feet tall.

The doctors had promised him he would grow. He simply had to have a little patience. But patience was not one of Ricky's strong points. Not that he didn't gain a fraction of an inch or so every summer. The little black marks creeping up the inside of his closet door attested to that. It was just that JJ had been at least half a foot taller at Ricky's age, Rosemary and Ellen still looked down on him, and it was embarrassing to be the smallest boy in his class at school.

Each year, when Dr Wheeler gave him his checkup, thumping his chest and peering down his throat and pumping him full of booster shots, Ricky got the same message: If he stood up straight and ate all his vegetables, Mother Nature would take care of the rest.

By the time he was eight, Ricky decided it would be

prudent to have an alternate plan. He took to heart the old saying about the best defense being a strong offense and made up for being small by being tough. He staked out his territory, never backed away from a confrontation, and fought dirty, rationalizing that it made up for his lack of size and helped even the odds.

Before he had even finished elementary school, the smart kids on the Coast knew enough to steer clear of him, and the not so smart ones bore the undeniable marks of their education.

'A regular Jimmy Cagney, eh?' the principal of the intermediate school observed on the occasion of their first interaction, looking down at the sixth-grader without humor, from his more than average height.

'I was only defending myself, sir,' Ricky replied with wide-eyed innocence, wondering who Jimmy Cagney was. 'And I feel really terrible about it. You see, the other boy was so much bigger than me, I never thought I could actually hurt him.'

The principal had to admit the possibility of that. Chris Rodriguez, the other boy in question, stood a head taller than Ricky, outweighed him by at least twenty pounds, and was a known bully. Now he was faced with a clean-cut kid who stood up straight, spoke respectfully, and looked like an altar boy, with his odd yellow eyes just brimming with remorse. It was conceivable that the teacher who had witnessed the incident had somehow gotten her facts confused.

'Suppose you tell me exactly how the fight started,' the principal suggested.

'It was just a misunderstanding, sir,' Ricky replied sweetly. 'I didn't understand something he said, and when I asked him to repeat it, he didn't understand what I said, and well, it all happened so fast, after that . . .'

221

The bully had called him Pretty Boy and several other students had overheard and laughed.

'Well, it may be that Mrs Pruitt overreacted,' the principal conceded reluctantly, 'and jumped to the wrong conclusion.'

'Yes, sir,' Ricky said politely. Of course, Mrs Pruitt hadn't overreacted. Nor had she forgotten what Ricky had done to her sissy son Freddy back in kindergarten, either.

'In any case, just see to it that we don't have any more such misunderstandings.'

'No, sir,' Ricky said politely.

Chris Rodriguez took six stitches in his upper lip. Ricky apologized to him the following day and brought him an apple tart fresh from his mother's oven, making sure it was twice as large as the one he brought for himself.

'Hey, Marsh,' Chris lisped painfully around his stitches, after he had consumed the tart. 'Will you show me that move you made on me?'

'Sure,' Ricky replied, grinning.

The two boys began to hang out together. They sparred with each other in the schoolyard. They played on the same soccer team. They sat together at lunch. It wasn't long before Ricky realized that Chris never brought more than a piece of fruit to eat.

'I have a real big breakfast in the morning,' Chris explained with a casual shrug, but not quite looking Ricky in the eye. 'So I'm not real hungry at lunch.'

Ricky asked around until someone told him that Chris's dad was out of work, and that the Rodriguez family was living on his mother's income as a cleaning woman.

Ricky had never known anyone who didn't have enough to eat. He skipped dinner one night, pleading a stomachache, just to see what being really hungry would feel like. By eleven o'clock, he had crept downstairs to rummage through the refrigerator for some leftover chicken and a thick wedge of berry pie.

Despite Dr Wheeler's admonitions, Ricky was a poor eater and his mother worried over his health. When the boy suddenly started asking for double portions in his lunch bag, she was only too happy to oblige. If she ever wondered why all that extra food never seemed to put any weight on him, she never inquired.

'My mother must think I'm King Kong,' he complained to Chris one day. 'I can't eat half of this.'

Chris peered into the brown paper bag. Two thick meat loaf sandwiches, two bags of chips, a large cluster of grapes, half a dozen homemade chocolate chip cookies, and two cans of soda looked back at him.

'Wow,' he marveled.

'Look,' Ricky said, 'I know you're not so hungry, but do me a favor, will you, and help me out here. I'd feel real bad about wasting all this stuff.'

Chris hesitated as his stomach grumbled. 'Well . . .'

'Never mind,' Ricky put in. 'I'll ask Denny Henderson over there. He's a pig – he'll eat anything.'

'No, that's all right,' Chris said hastily. 'I'll help you out.'

Ricky beamed. 'Thanks, man. I owe you.'

Chris devoured one sandwich and half of the other, both bags of chips, most of the grapes, and all of the cookies. Ricky didn't mind. Half a sandwich and a soda were enough to hold him until he got home.

'I guess I was hungrier than I thought,' Chris said, grinning sheepishly as he surveyed the crumbs.

'Good thing,' Ricky told him, ''cause I wasn't.'

They were rarely seen apart after that. They shared Ricky's lunch every day, at a big round table in the middle of the room that they staked out as private. Nobody argued. They made up jokes and guffawed over them at the top of their voices. They covered for each other. They protected each other's back. With Chris's size and Ricky's quickness, they were a formidable pair.

Chris's most prized possession was a battered three-speed bicycle that his father had bought him before getting laid off, and on weekends he would pedal the four miles from his home in Half Moon Bay to Ricky's home in El Granada. Usually, he got there just in time for lunch. Afterward, the two boys would hike up into the scrubby hills behind the Marsh house, to shoot at birds and wild rabbits with Ricky's .22 caliber single-shot Sears special. Or they would go down to the pier and wait for the fishing boats to come in. If they hung around long enough, the fishermen would be sure to throw them a fish or two from their catch.

Chris took home any rabbits they were lucky enough to kill, as well as the fish.

'Half of these belong to you, you know,' he told Ricky on a day when one of the fishermen had generously thrown them four sizable snappers.

'Yuck! Everybody in my house hates fish,' Ricky lied. 'They're all yours.'

A big sigh of relief escaped from Chris's lips. In addition to his mother and father, there were three sisters at home.

They would hurry back to the Marsh house, where Ricky's mother would be sure to have a snack waiting that was almost the size of a meal. Then, when he could delay no longer, Chris would climb onto his bicycle and pedal his way back to Half Moon Bay, with Ricky waving him on until he was long out of sight.

For the first time in his life, Ricky had a friend. Not a brother or a sister or a cousin, but someone totally

224

unrelated to him who asked no questions and actually seemed to like him. His days as a loner were over.

Now the sound of a car coming along Delgada and turning in the driveway signaled Ricky into action. He snapped off the overhead light and jumped into bed, tossing aside the camouflage pillows, and burrowing under the blankets, stuffed pockets and all. He heard his father clumping up the stairs, and held his breath until the sound of feet died away down the hall without pausing. He had gotten to the light in time. His father would not come in to investigate, or have cause to wonder later on why his younger son was still awake after midnight.

Ricky shrugged out of his clothes in the dark, bundling them up and shoving them under his pillow, feeling the lumps from his night's work beneath his head. He was suddenly exhausted. He would sort out his take in the morning, he decided, before giving it to JJ.

2

Valerie never completely recovered from the death of her daughter. Part of her mind seemed to close off, and was replaced by a sort of ambiguity that drifted in and out. She would start to say something and then just stop in the middle. She would be laughing one minute and then tears would be rolling down her cheeks the next. Sometimes she forgot.

'I know I promised to bake a batch of oatmeal cookies for you for school tomorrow,' she said one evening over supper, three years after the tragic accident. They always referred to it as the tragic accident or as just the accident. 'But I won't have the time. I have to finish Priscilla's communion dress.'

The children stared at her in horror. Then JJ leaned over and put his hand on hers, patting it as though he were now the parent and she were the child. 'No, you don't, Ma,' he said gently. 'You finished it yesterday, remember?'

Valerie looked up at him uncertainly. 'Did I?' she asked. 'Are you sure?'

'Yes, Ma. You showed it to all of us. It's beautiful.'

'Oh,' she conceded vaguely. 'I guess I did then. Where did I put it?'

'It's in the closet in the pink room, Ma,' JJ told her.

Indeed, the communion dress, neatly zipped into plastic, did hang at the back of the closet in the pink bedroom that Priscilla had shared with Ellen. It wasn't finished, but that didn't matter. JJ knew his mother would never go looking for it.

'That's all right then,' she said.

Four pairs of eyes looked around the table. The same thought was in each mind: the sanitarium. Whenever Valerie seemed to lose track like that, they always attributed it to the sanitarium.

Time was what Valerie found most elusive. A whole week could go by, and she would think perhaps an hour had passed. Or an hour would pass, and she would realize it was a year later.

The O'Connors had come the day after Priscilla's death. They pieced together most of what had happened from the fragmentary things the children said, and from Jack's incoherent statements when he wasn't crying. Valerie never said a word.

Charlotte took over the household. Martin made all the arrangements for the funeral service and burial, and answered questions for the police and the local newspaper. The weather was warm and bright, flowers bloomed, birds sang, and Valerie stared into space.

The O'Connors waited just long enough for the coroner's office to declare that the death was accidental before they took their daughter and grandchildren back with them to Vermont. It was two months to the end of the school term. No one objected. Jack explained the circumstances to the people at the Gray Whale. Everybody understood. He was unable to get any time off from his job to go with them. Nobody cared.

Valerie was put to bed in her old room. If she realized where she was, she gave no indication. Ezra Carnes, the doctor who had treated the O'Connor family through three generations, came every day.

'Give her time,' he said. 'She's had a terrible shock.

Right now, this is the only way her mind can cope with it.'

The children peered at her from the doorway, but only JJ dared to venture any closer.

'Is Mama asleep?' Ellen wanted to know.

'Sort of,' Dr Carnes replied.

'How can she be asleep,' Rosemary, overhearing, whispered to JJ, 'when her eyes are wide open?'

Charlotte filled the void, keeping the children busy with games and chores, pampering them, cooking up their favorite foods. And of course, there was the rest of the family, who descended in droves with a whole inventory of diversions to occupy young minds and bodies from the time they awoke in the morning to the time they tumbled, exhausted, into bed at night.

Rosemary and Ellen were each given a room of their own, but Charlotte very wisely put Ricky in the cozy corner bedroom with JJ. Big brothers were very important to have close by in unfamiliar darkness, especially when the nightmares came.

They had started back in El Granada, two days after the accident. Ricky, who had been moved into the top bunk in JJ's room to make space for his grandparents, woke up screaming.

'I was d-d-d-drowning,' he choked, when JJ charged up the ladder. 'I was drowning in red water.'

'Open your eyes,' JJ told him. The little boy did so. 'Now, do you see any red water?'

Ricky shook his head uncertainly. 'What about under the bed?' he asked.

JJ bent down to look. 'Nope, there's no red water there.'

'What about out the window?'

JJ padded over to the window and opened it as wide as it would go. 'All I see out there is grass,' he said.

'It must've gone away,' Ricky conceded.

'It was just a dream, kiddo,' JJ assured him.

'Will it come back?'

'Well, why don't you crawl down here with me, and then, if it comes back, I'll take care of it for you.'

Ricky scurried down the ladder and climbed into the lower bunk. 'I lied,' he murmured. 'It wasn't really red water I was drowning in – it was Cilla's blood.'

'I know, don't worry, I'll take care of that, too,' JJ said.

Ricky snuggled deep under the covers and soon fell asleep. It was easy once he knew he had his big brother looking out for him. He had variations on the same dream every night for three weeks. Then the nightmares stopped and the bed-wetting began. Each time, JJ was there to take care of it.

'You won't tell anyone, will you?' Ricky begged.

'Well, Grandma has to know.' JJ replied. 'She has to wash out the sheets and your pajamas.'

'That's okay,' the little boy agreed. 'But no one else. Promise?'

'No one else,' JJ promised.

Martin spent half of one day on the telephone, shuttling from one office to another, until he got permission to enroll the children in the same schools their cousins attended. He and Charlotte both felt it would make the transition easier.

The girls adjusted quickly. Ellen was a quiet, obedient child, much like her mother had been, who followed all the rules and caused no undue attention to fall on her. Rosemary was not much of a student, but she was certainly pretty, and she delighted in being surrounded by a whole new crop of boys.

Ricky was erratic. One day, he would participate in class activities with delight. The next day, he would withdraw into a closed world and attack anyone who tried to gain access to it. He rarely paid attention, and his skill level was low. The teachers, as well as the O'Connors, made allowances, assuming his behavior was tied directly to the tragedy of seeing his sister fall dead at his feet. They were prepared to give him as much time as he needed. There was no one to tell them that this had been the pattern of his behavior since he entered kindergarten.

Of the four of them, JJ had the most significant problem. Although he had been a very good student at his middle school in Half Moon Bay, he had trouble keeping up with the sixth grade work in Rutland.

'We never studied this stuff back home,' he kept saying. Or, 'We were studying it, but we didn't get this far.'

After a month, Martin went to the school. When he came home, he had arranged for a tutor to come to the house twice a week to catch JJ up.

Martin's home was full of children again. Perhaps because they were not his to raise, but only to borrow, there was more constructive conversation than discipline. But there was discipline when it was warranted.

'Grandpa may be strict, but he's fair,' JJ said to Rosemary, rubbing his rear end after his grandfather caught him talking back to his grandmother. 'He doesn't hit for no reason.'

'And he doesn't drink first, either,' Rosemary observed.

'And there are no dumb presents,' JJ added.

'I like presents,' Ricky said, overhearing.

'So do I,' his brother told him. 'But I think it's much better when we get them for Christmas and for birthdays, just like everybody else.'

And all the while, Valerie lay in her bed and stared

up in the direction of the ceiling. Charlotte fed her and washed her and helped her to the bathroom. Every once in a while, she thought she saw a response, but it was gone so fast that she was never sure.

One afternoon in early June, Charlotte and the children came home to find Valerie gone.

'What do you mean gone?' Charlotte asked JJ, when he rushed into the kitchen with the news.

'I mean she's not in her bed or in the bedroom,' the boy replied.

'Did you look in the bathroom?'

JJ nodded. 'She's not in there, either. Honest, Grandma.'

They searched every room in the house, calmly at first, and then frantically, as room after room yielded nothing. They found her, at last, on the floor in the attic, clutching a rag doll from her childhood and rocking back and forth to the rhythm of a mindless melody.

Two weeks later, she disappeared in the middle of a thunderstorm. Martin found her, wandering aimlessly in the fields behind the house, naked.

The O'Connors called a full family conference, and everyone who could come did so. Even Marianne left Tommy at the restaurant and came up from Boston. The only one missing was Hugh, Valerie's middle brother, who was still somewhere in Vietnam.

The children were not included in the discussion, but JJ and Rosemary sneaked down the stairs to listen at the closed parlor door. JJ had no problem with that. After all, they were discussing his mother.

The family talked long into the night, arguing, crying, looking at options, seeking a solution. The next morning, Martin called Jack, waking him from a drunken sleep. Their conversation was brief. The father talked, the husband listened. Then Martin went to see Dr Carnes, and three days after that, the two men drove Valerie to a private sanitarium just south of Burlington. She stayed there for almost a year.

3

Ricky awoke with a stiff neck from sleeping on the lumpy bundle beneath his pillow. It was not quite six o'clock and still dark outside. For a brief moment, he couldn't figure out what was causing the lumps. Then he remembered. He sat up at once, snapped on a light, and began pulling his take from Connie's house out of the pockets of his rumpled jeans and windbreaker. Finished, he mounded the jewelry and cash in the middle of his bed and sat there, staring at it, trying to recapture the euphoria of the night before.

It was not the first time he had stolen. He had taken money from his mother's purse on a number of occasions when he wanted something he couldn't otherwise have had, knowing there was no risk, that she would never notice. He had ripped off a hand-knitted sweater that caught his eye from a classmate's locker. It lay in a paper bag somewhere at the bottom of his closet, because of course he could never wear it. He had helped himself to sodas and candy bars, and stuff from local shops, and was clever enough not to get caught.

But none of that amounted to anything at all when compared to what lay before him now. This wasn't penny-ante business, this was big-time. He rubbed at the back of his stiff neck and contemplated the knot of excitement in his stomach. This was something he could go to jail for.

He wondered what kind of jail they put almost-twelve-year-olds in. He didn't know, nor did he know anyone he could ask who would know. He made a mental note to find out. Not that he thought there was much chance of his ending up there, he was too smart to get himself caught, but Ricky always liked to know exactly what he was up against.

'The more you know, the better you play,' he always said.

He pulled off his T-shirt and spread it out on the bed. Then he scooped up the jewelry and most of the money, laid it in the middle of the shirt, and tied it all into a neat bundle. Satisfied, he scrambled off the bed and padded across the hall to JJ's room.

His brother was still asleep, and Ricky had to shake him awake.

'What's the matter?' JJ demanded.

'Nothing,' the boy said. 'I just wanted to give you this.' He placed the knotted T-shirt on the bed.

'What is it?'

Ricky shrugged. 'A going-away present.'

'A going-away—?' JJ eyed his brother sharply. 'What are you talking about?'

'You're taking off, aren't you?'

JJ fell back against the pillow. 'How did you know that?'

'I got eyes,' came the reply.

'Does anyone else know?'

'Nah,' Ricky said. 'Rosemary's too wrapped up in boys to notice anything else, Ellen's too wrapped up in her Bible, Ma's too wrapped up in a fog, and Pa . . . well, it's better when he doesn't notice us at all.'

'Are you going to tell?'

'If I was, I would've by now,' Ricky retorted.

JJ nodded at the T-shirt. 'So what's this?'

'Open it.'

The teenager untied the bundle and looked inside. 'What the hell?' His eyes bulged. 'Where did you get this stuff?'

'Someplace,' Ricky replied.

'What do you mean, someplace?'

'What do you care? It's enough to get you wherever you want to go, isn't it? It's enough to get you out.'

'You stole it, didn't you? Jesus, of course you stole it!'

'So what?'

'So why?'

'It's for you,' Ricky replied. 'I got it for you, so you can get away from here before he kills you.'

JJ's face darkened. 'Don't worry, he's not going to kill me.'

'Then you'll kill him.'

'Would that be so bad?'

Ricky considered that. 'Yeah,' he said finally, 'it would be. I'd rather have you gone away somewhere than in jail for the rest of your life.'

At seventeen, JJ stood as tall as his father, if not yet as broad. In the years since Priscilla's death, Jack had grown angrier and JJ had grown stronger. Varsity football and a weekend job at the local lumberyard helped. To get to the mother and the younger children now, the father had to go through the son. As a result, the son took the brunt of the punishment.

Like the occasion, barely a month ago, soon after Valerie and the children returned from a joyous Christmas in Vermont. For a week, Jack seemed glad to have them back. Then one night he came home late, and began to berate Valerie for not having dinner waiting for him. He was pushing her roughly around the kitchen when JJ walked in.

'Leave her alone, Pa,' the teenager said. 'When you weren't home by eight, she figured you weren't coming home.'

'Nobody asked you,' Jack retorted.

'You don't have to beat up on her,' JJ persisted. 'If you want something to eat, all you have to do is ask.'

Jack rounded on him. 'Don't you ever tell me what to do in my own house.' His attention temporarily diverted from Valerie, he started toward his son. 'Who the hell do you think you are?'

'I'm your son, Pa,' JJ replied calmly, slipping between his father and his mother. 'I'm just saying, if you leave her alone, she can fix you whatever you want.'

'Is this the kind of kid you raised?' Jack stormed at his wife. 'Someone who tells his father what to do?'

'He didn't mean anything, Jack,' Valerie said.

'I let you take them back to that hick town of yours, and you turn them against me, is that what's going on?'

'No, Jack, of course not,' Valerie tried to assure him.

'I'm not against you, Pa,' JJ added. 'I'm just not going to let you hurt Ma.'

'Get out of my way,' Jack shouted, trying to reach around the boy and grab hold of his wife. But JJ stood his ground. 'Did you hear me, boy? I told you to get out of the way.'

'I heard you, Pa,' JJ replied, not moving.

The rain of blows that were meant for Valerie fell over her son's head and shoulders instead. JJ didn't fight back, he didn't cry out. He just protected his mother.

Afterward, Valerie bathed his cuts and bruises, all the while begging him not to interfere. 'When you defy him like that,' she told him, 'you just make things worse.'

'How could things be worse, Ma?' he asked. 'He hardly ever comes home anymore. And when he does, it's only to beat up on us. You'd think killing Cilla

236

would've made him stop, but he's not going to stop until he kills us all.'

'JJ,' Valerie cried, 'don't you ever say that again. Priscilla's death was an accident, do you hear me? A tragic accident!'

'Okay, Ma, okay,' he said soothingly, knowing how fragile she was, even after all these years. 'Don't get upset. I'm sorry.'

'Your father was devastated by it, same as we all were,' she said through her tears. 'He just has a different way of grieving, that's all.'

'Sure, Ma,' JJ replied, but he knew it wasn't grief that drove his father. It was guilt, and that was very different.

'I know you don't understand,' Valerie tried to tell him. 'I'm not sure sometimes that I do. So just believe me when I tell you that your father loves us, in his way, and that it's his fear of losing us that makes him act the way he does. So please, for me, don't push him. It doesn't matter what he does to me. But it does matter to me what he does to you.'

No, JJ didn't understand. Maybe his mother didn't care what happened to her, but that didn't mean he didn't care, and he didn't like the idea of her being his father's punching bag. So he kept lifting those heavy loads of lumber, and he kept tackling those varsity line-backers, and every day he got a little bit stronger.

Until the night before last, when it became clear that he was strong enough.

Ever since Valerie's stay in the sanitarium, she and the children had flown back East twice each year, at Martin's insistence, for a month during the summer, and two weeks over the Christmas holidays. Although he was always included in the invitation, Jack rarely accompanied them.

He couldn't help feeling that the O'Connors somehow knew exactly what had happened up on the roof and blamed him for Priscilla's death. So he stayed home alone, drinking himself numb, blaming himself.

'I wouldn't really mind so much if Daddy came with us,' Rosemary confided to JJ once, as their airliner taxied away from the gate. 'He's a lot nicer in Vermont than he is in California.'

'He has to be nicer,' JJ told her, 'or Grandpa would punch his face out.' Martin was the only person JJ could think of who wasn't afraid of his father.

Valerie overheard. 'Don't speak against your father, JJ,' she said. 'He does the best he can.'

Each time he packed them onto the plane and waved good-bye, Jack wondered if it would be the last time, if this was the time they would not return. He was sure the day would come. With his stomach in knots, he waited for the telephone call, telling him they would not be back, telling him they were leaving him for good – like the women who had left him as a child. He didn't know what he would do when they did.

The year and a half that they had stayed in Rutland after Priscilla's death, when Valerie was in the sanitarium, was the worst time of his life. Night after night, he came home to an empty house and sat in the dark with a fifth of bourbon beside him. He didn't bother with a glass. Every couple of minutes, he would just take a swig straight from the bottle. In the dark, he didn't have to face the loneliness. He didn't have to see the accusing eyes. It was easier that way.

Five days a week, he forced himself to get up in the morning and drive to work, and the minute his shift was over, he drove back again. He began to cut corners on the job, not important ones, he told himself, just little detail stuff, because he couldn't concentrate. He no longer went out drinking with his airport buddies. He stopped chasing skirts. He just came home. The house became his prison, and he believed it was exactly what he deserved.

Sometimes he fixed himself something to eat, if he had remembered to shop, but mostly he took the bourbon into the living room and sat on the sofa, waiting for the pain to back off just far enough so that he could stumble upstairs to sleep.

Two days a week, he worked around the house. He finished repairing the roof, although the pain of going back up there was almost more than he could bear. He built a little brick wall around Valerie's vegetable garden, and tried his best to keep the plants alive. He cleaned out the garage, he rented a machine and shampooed all the furniture and carpets, he washed the windows, he painted the walls, and all the while, he wondered if his family would ever return to see it.

They did. And no sooner had they settled back into their old routine than he settled back into his. He took up with his drinking buddies again, and he found himself a waitress named Kate who worked at the airport bar. She was a widow, older than he and no beauty, but she assured him, two or three evenings a week, that he was everything she could ask for in bed.

For a while, Valerie had the children set his place at the dinner table each night, although none of them ever knew if he would be there. Most nights he wasn't.

After that, there was a grace period every time they returned from Rutland, when Jack practically walked on his knees with gratitude. Then, once he was re-assured they were back for good, things would return to normal.

It had been almost a month since his anger had erupted and he had cuffed JJ for talking back. There had been nothing in particular to trigger it, except perhaps insecurity. The waitress was still good to him, and things on the job were running smoothly.

Until Tuesday.

In addition to the prevailing winds, the takeoff and landing paths of San Francisco International Airport were governed by four main geologic features: San Bruno Mountain to the west, Mount Tamalpais to the north, Mount Diablo to the east, and San Francisco Bay to the south. Aircraft approaching from any direction avoided disaster by staying out of the triangle, turning over San Jose, and gliding above the water onto the airport's main runway.

On Tuesday, the Boeing 727 slid in from the east, well below Mount Diablo, swung wide to the south, banked sharply over San Jose, headed north, and crashed into the bay, fifty feet short of the runway.

Federal Airlines Flight 921 had taken off for Chicago at ten minutes past two in the afternoon with one hundred and thirty seven passengers and an eight-member crew on board. At a quarter past, the pilot had radioed back.

'Tower, this is Federal 921. I'm having a bit of a problem here.'

'What is the nature of your problem, 921?' the dispatcher inquired.

'Well, tell you the truth, I'm not sure,' the pilot replied. 'But something just feels funny.'

'Can you be more specific, 921?'

'Not at this time, Tower. I know that doesn't help you much, but I can't put my finger on anything specific yet. Something just doesn't feel right.'

'What do you want to do, 921?'

Captain Bill Taggart had been a pilot for Federal

240

Airlines for over twenty years. Before that, he had served in the Air Force, amassing more than a thousand hours of flying time between World War II and Korea. There wasn't much about flying airplanes that he didn't know. There wasn't anything about the 727 that he didn't know.

'Sorry, Tower,' he said reluctantly. 'I don't know what it is, but I'm coming back.'

'Roger, 921.'

The dispatcher read out a set of landing coordinates to the Boeing, and automatically began to reroute all other incoming air traffic. Then, as a matter of course, tower personnel ordered out the water rescue equipment, and alerted the emergency units. This action very likely was responsible for most of the lives that were saved.

Ninety-eight persons suffered injuries in the crash and were rushed to nearby hospitals where fully half of them were listed as serious. Thirty-three people lost their lives, among them Captain Bill Taggart.

The National Transportation Safety Board launched an immediate investigation. Federal Airlines brass were on the scene from Seattle in less than three hours. No one from the maintenance crew was allowed to leave.

By the time Jack got home, the kitchen had been cleaned, and Valerie was already in bed. A single light burned in the foyer, the rest of the downstairs was dark. The children were either asleep or in their rooms doing homework.

From his room, JJ heard the front door slam, and glanced over at the clock on his nightstand in surprise. It read twenty minutes past ten. Usually, if his father was coming home for the evening, he arrived well in time for dinner, and when he stayed out, he almost never showed up before midnight. This was something different, and JJ had learned to watch out for something different.

Sure enough, the slam was followed by angry footsteps stumbling up the stairs, and then the teenager heard the door to the master bedroom being knocked back on its hinges. He got up from his desk and moved toward his own door, opening it just a crack and peering out into the hall. Across the way, Ricky peeked out from behind his door. JJ waved him off and waited until the boy retreated before he stepped cautiously into the corridor and tiptoed toward the sound of his father's voice, putting one foot cautiously in front of the other, until he was perhaps a yard from the doorway, and then he flattened himself against the wall.

'I work my ass off for this goddam family,' Jack was shouting. 'Is it too much to ask you to have dinner on the table when I get home?'

'I'm sorry, Jack,' JJ heard his mother reply. 'When you're not here by six, it usually means you're not coming home for dinner.'

This was true. He usually spent two or three nights a week with Kate, and would have been with her tonight except for the crash. Not that it mattered. He was in no mood for her tonight anyway. After the feds had worked him over, the last thing he had on his mind was sex. He had downed half a dozen bourbons at the airport bar instead. Then he had just come home.

'Well, as you can see, I'm here now,' he retorted. 'So get up, you lazy bitch. I want a meal on the table in ten minutes. And a real meal, too, none of your open-a-can garbage.'

Valerie had been suffering from a migraine headache for a day and a half, an incessant throbbing in her temples and a darting pain behind her eyes, combined with alternating bouts of dizziness and nausea. The children had fixed the dinner tonight, and done the dishes, too. They made their mother go to bed, and brought her a tray of soup and crackers and pudding and tea. Just the thought of standing up now made the nausea rise, but she quickly judged the resurgence of her headache to be the more prudent option. With a sigh, she pushed the covers aside, and started to swing her legs to the floor.

'I'll fix you something to eat, Pa,' JJ said from the doorway.

Jack turned. 'Since when did you become a housewife?' he snarled.

'I can cook,' the teenager said evenly.

'I just bet you can,' Jack sneered. 'I bet you can sew good, too.' He turned back to Valerie. 'You got nine minutes left,' he snapped and headed for the bathroom.

'Ma's feeling sick,' JJ said. 'Let her stay in bed. I'll make you a couple of burgers and some French fries.' There were always hamburgers wrapped up in the freezer, he knew, along with boxes of crinkle-cut potatoes. He could throw it all in a frying pan and have it done in no time.

Jack squinted in his son's direction as he slowly unbuckled his belt and pulled it free of his trousers. 'You been doing a lot of talking back lately, boy, trying to tell me what I can and can't do. And I'm getting pretty damn sick of it.' He wrapped the end of the belt around his hand and advanced on JJ. 'I think it's time I taught you just who's in charge here.'

The belt snaked out and caught the teenager just beneath the armpits, the snap of it ripping clean through his cotton shirt. JJ felt the sting, as the force of the blow thrust him back against the door jamb, saw the blood spurt in a line across his chest, and caught a glimpse of his father's taunting eyes trying to focus on him. The boy never flinched, he never even blinked.

243

'I'm the boss around here, and don't you ever forget it.' The belt whipped out a second time, aimed at the abdomen. JJ didn't move a muscle.

'No one questions my authority, no one questions the quality of my work . . .' The belt was coiled again.

'Jack, stop it,' Valerie cried, struggling out of bed. 'Leave him alone. See, I'm up. I'm going down to fix your dinner right now.'

Jack whirled, his right arm lashing out, the metal buckle stinging her face. She fell back onto the bed with a cry of real pain. He loomed above her, coiling the belt yet another time.

JJ moved. In two steps he had reached his mother and stepped in front of her. Then, without stopping to think, he curled his right hand up into a tight fist and slammed it against his father's windpipe as hard as he could. Jack's eyes popped, he clutched his throat, and with a strange gagging sound, he sank to the floor and stayed there.

'Oh my God, JJ,' Valerie cried in horror, 'you've killed him.'

'No, I didn't, Ma. I just knocked the air out of him, that's all. He'll come to in a while.'

His mother sat on the edge of the bed, staring at the inert bulk of her husband. 'What have you done to us?' she wailed. 'What have you done to us?'

JJ thought quickly. 'Help me get him undressed,' he said. 'We'll put him to bed. He's drunk and maybe he won't even wake up until the morning.'

The two struggled to get Jack's clothes off, and then somehow managed to get him onto the bed. He was a lot heavier to move than a load of lumber, JJ thought, but at least he didn't resist like a linebacker. As soon as they succeeded in getting him between the sheets, Valerie threw her arms around her son, and they clung to each other as though they had just survived an earthquake.

Neither of them noticed Ricky standing in the hallway just beyond the door, or observed the spasm of hiccups that began to rack his small body.

Jack did not wake up until morning, and when he did, it was with no clear recall of what had happened the night before. The Flight 921 investigation was the only thing he could remember clearly. The NTSB, not to mention the team from Federal, were going to scrutinize that 727 from nose to tail. They were going to account for every goddam nut and bolt. They were going to take that bird apart and put her back together again as many times as it took to find out what had gone wrong.

Jack's crew had done routine maintenance on the plane. He, himself, had released it. Since the flight crew that brought her in hadn't reported anything out of the ordinary, he had skipped his normal scrutiny, and simply signed off on the checklist. He had a 707 in the shop with a fuel leak he couldn't find. It had seemed more important to stay with that. Of course, if the crash turned out to be maintenance-related, if anyone could tie it to his shop, if it came out that he had cut a corner, well, Jack knew his neck was on the line. He jumped out of bed, knowing he had to get to the airport early, to line up his guys and get their story straight.

JJ had crept out of the house during the night, shortly after his mother had sent him off into bed. He took his heavy jacket and his blanket with him and climbed up into the hills behind the Marsh property, staying there, huddled beneath a clump of eucalyptus, until he was sure his father had left for work and it was safe to return to his room. The cold and the pain from his cuts kept him awake most of the night, and he spent the time making plans.

It was clear that he and his father could no longer live under the same roof. He knew that even if they got past what had happened, sooner or later they would come to blows again, and the next time might not be when his father was sufficiently slowed by alcohol. Jack had him by forty pounds, and JJ had no illusion that it would be a fair fight.

He had one hundred and thirteen dollars stashed away from his job at the lumberyard. He had been saving up to buy a motorcycle. Plus another thirty-eight dollars they owed him from last week that he could pick up on Thursday afternoon. He didn't have a very clear idea of how far one hundred and fifty-one dollars would get him, but then he didn't yet know where he wanted to go.

Well, that wasn't entirely true. There had been a vague idea lurking around the back of his mind ever since he was eleven years old, and had first seen his Uncle Hugh in uniform. Oh, he had heard his father brag of his exploits in the Air Force during the Korean War, but it wasn't the same as actually seeing someone close up, dressed in uniform, with those little colored bars they called salad pinned to his tunic.

Of course, to JJ's friends, a soldier was only one step removed from a pig, as they now called policemen. Some of his classmates had even gone up to San Francisco last year to throw tomatoes at a group of veterans en route home from Vietnam. JJ didn't go with them. His uncle was a soldier in Vietnam, and it would have been like throwing tomatoes at *him*.

He wished he could ask Hugh about the Army, about what it was really like, and whether he thought JJ might be suited to the life, but of course he couldn't. He didn't know where Hugh was. Nor did he want anyone knowing where *he* was, either, just in case his father was looking for him.

JJ was almost a man and still a boy. He lay on his bed with tears leaking out of the corners of his eyes as he thought about what Ricky had done for him, and about leaving his mother and his brother and sisters. And they were tears of sadness and of fright. It was a big world out there, and wherever he was going, he was going to be all by himself in it.

He had planned on going to college next year. He was a good student and he had won a scholarship to the University of California at Berkeley that would have paid most of his expenses. Now he was going to have to find a way to make a life for himself, not only without a college degree, but without even a high school diploma.

He put the money Ricky had given him into his wallet, put the jewelry into a small duffel bag along with his clothes, and left a note for his mother. Then, shortly after two o'clock in the afternoon, he picked up his check from the lumberyard, cashed it at the bank, withdrew the rest of his funds, and disappeared.

Valerie stared into the open cabinet for perhaps five minutes before she reached inside and brought out the bottle of bourbon. Except for her father's Christmas concoctions, she had never drunk anything stronger than wine or champagne in her life, but today was an exception.

Her son, her firstborn, her brave young defender, was gone. The note she had carried with her since early morning was too blurred by tears now to read, but she had memorized the words.

'I think you know I can't stay here anymore, Ma. If

I do, next time, he'll kill me or I'll kill him. Don't worry about me, I'll be fine, and maybe things will be better for everyone else without me. Take care of yourself. Your loving son, JJ.'

She cried for hours, sitting on his bed, clutching at his pillow. In many ways, she felt this loss far more than she had Priscilla's. After all, Priscilla was gone from an accident, and there was nothing anyone could have done about it. But JJ had made a deliberate choice.

Not that Valerie blamed him. She didn't. She blamed herself. She blamed herself for not being strong enough to protect him the way a mother was supposed to protect her children. And she was frightened for him, so young, so alone out there in the world. She didn't know how he would get along, what would become of him.

She looked at the bottle. It was already half empty, but she was sure Jack wouldn't miss a drink or two. She twisted off the cap and poured a generous amount of the brown liquid into a glass. Her face wrinkled up at the first taste. The bourbon was sharp and sour and burned her throat going down. But it warmed her all the way to her toes, so she tried another sip, and that one wasn't nearly so bad.

She took the glass and the bottle into the living room, and sat down on the sofa. A photograph album, filled with pictures of the children, lay on the table beside her. She hefted it onto her lap and opened it to the first page. An hour later, she was at the last page, and the bottle of bourbon was empty.

Ellen, coming home from school at three-thirty that afternoon, found her lying there, unconscious, with a tear-stained picture of JJ grasped in one hand.

She vomited once when Ellen woke her up, and twice more after the girl managed to get her upstairs. Then she began to sob. Ellen took off her stained clothes and put her to bed. The girl brought a cool washcloth from the bathroom and wiped her mother's hot face. Then she sat on the edge of the bed, stroking Valerie's hair and humming her favorite spiritual until her mother's eyes closed and her sobbing ceased.

They called Ellen the shadow child, always there but never quite a part of things. Quiet, gentle, she seemed to live inside herself, and needed very little from those around her. Almost before she could walk and talk, it was Ellen who could calm a fury, soothe a pain, settle an argument. Now it was Ellen who told Jack about JJ, after piecing the story together from Valerie's tearful babbling and the few things that Ricky finally told her.

The NTSB investigation of Flight 921 was in full swing. Experts from both the company and the government were all over the place, poking their noses into every nook and cranny of Jack's operation. He had escaped the airport as soon as he could and headed for home. He was too uptight to go drinking with his buddies, and Kate worked on Thursday nights. Driving over the hill, he decided he would take Valerie to a movie. *Magnum Force* was playing and he wanted to see it. He found his wife asleep in bed.

'What's the matter with your mother this time?' he asked Ellen, coming back downstairs.

Ellen was on her hands and knees in front of the sofa, scrubbing Valerie's mess from the carpet. She had already removed the empty bottle of bourbon. 'Mama had some bad news today, Daddy.'

Jack sighed. The last thing he cared about was someone else's bad news. 'Is she getting up to fix dinner?' They would have to eat pretty damn soon if they were going to get back over the hill in time for the movie.

'JJ's gone, Daddy,' Ellen said.

Jack looked at her dumbly. 'What does that have to do with dinner?'

'He's gone – for good. He's not ever coming back. Mama's real upset.'

'What are you talking about?' He was distracted, and not really paying attention.

'I'm talking about JJ,' Ellen told him patiently. 'He's run away from home. He left Mama a note and told her not to worry about him.'

'Shit,' Jack said and Ellen winced. 'Where's a kid like that going to go?'

'He didn't tell anyone.'

'Why would he want to do a thing like that?'

Ellen shrugged and said nothing. She was an obedient girl, but not a stupid one. Ricky had told her all about Tuesday night, about what Jack had done with his belt, and what JJ had done with his fist. If her father didn't understand, she reasoned, it was not up to her to enlighten him.

Rosemary fixed dinner that night, from leftover tuna fish salad that she mixed with macaroni and vegetables to make a casserole. Valerie did not come down.

It was a grim meal. Nobody looked at anybody around the kitchen table and no one spoke. JJ's place was conspicuously empty.

As soon as the food was eaten, Rosemary escaped to a friend's house on the pretext of doing homework, and Ellen escaped to her room and her Bible. Ricky did the dishes without complaint. Jack sat where he was and stared long and hard into his empty coffee cup.

'Did you know your brother was going to go?' he asked finally.

'Nope,' Ricky lied.

'You didn't even suspect?'

'Nope.'

Jack frowned. 'Why would he do such a thing?'

Because he was sick of getting beat to a pulp, thought Ricky, *and he was going to kill you, you dumb bastard.* 'Because he wanted to, I guess.'

Valerie awoke when Jack came upstairs just after eleven o'clock. 'What time is it?' she asked, blinking in the glare of the lamp on his nightstand.

'It's late,' he replied, climbing into bed beside her. 'Go back to sleep.' If he'd had anything else in mind, one look at her would have erased it.

'I feel awful,' she said.

'You don't look so hot, either.'

'Did the children tell you?'

'Yeah.'

'What are we going to do?'

'Do?' he repeated. What did she think they could do? 'Right now, we're going to go to sleep.'

'But we have to find him,' she protested. 'He's too young to be out on his own.'

'No younger than I was,' Jack reminded her.

Valerie began to sob. 'My baby's gone. My baby's gone. Oh God, where has my baby gone?'

Jack snapped off the light and turned away from her. After an hour of listening to her wail, he drifted off.

In the morning, Valerie's head throbbed, she couldn't focus her eyes properly, and every muscle in her body ached. As soon as she got Jack off to work and the children on their way to school, she went out and bought another bottle of bourbon.

4

Rosemary sat with her hands knotted in her lap, hours early for her appointment, and watched the assortment of women that moved in and out of the frosted glass doors at the end of the waiting room. Older women, younger women, heavy, skinny, dark, light, tall, short women, each of them different, and yet all of them here for the same reason.

One of them, she noted, went in crying and came out smiling. Another went in smiling and came out crying. She counted two that went in looking panicked and came out looking relieved. But the largest number of them, four, went in looking tense and came out looking queasy.

Rosemary wondered how she, herself, looked. She knew how she felt – panicked, tense, and queasy. She was beginning to think it had been a mistake to do this alone. Of course, she could never have gone to her mother, who teetered on the edge as it was. Or Ellen, who would have been equally horrified and would have promptly started praying over her. But once Benny had been unable to come with her, she should perhaps have asked a friend.

Betsy Barth, the obvious choice, had been Rosemary's closest friend since the second grade. Betsy lived down on Avenida del Oro with her mother and half-brother. She had never seen her father or her brother's father, either, for that matter.

The two girls had gotten drunk for the first time together, smoked their first cigarettes together . . . and their first pot. They cut school on the same days, started menstruating within the same month, bought their first bras together, and went coed skinny-dipping in the bay with the skinny Dobson twins, whose things had shriveled up so much from the cold water that they all but disappeared.

Their first real sexual experience had been only days apart, when they were both barely thirteen. Their second had been shared, under a blanket in the back of a Ford pickup with, yes, the Dobson twins again. Afterward, they joked that it didn't matter that no one could tell them apart.

For the first time in the almost nine years they had known each other, Rosemary had actually managed to achieve something that Betsy had not, even if the distinction was dubious. Rosemary knew her friend would have jumped at the chance to come with her today, if only as an onlooker, but Betsy had a big mouth, and in no time it would have been all over school.

'Miss Gilchrist?'

Not that Rosemary really cared, but something told her that this was probably best kept to herself for the time being.

'Miss Gilchrist?' the nurse standing right in front of her repeated, and Rosemary looked up startled, forgetting the name she had given to the clinic receptionist on her first visit, along with a phony address.

'The doctor will see you now.'

Rosemary nodded and stood up on suddenly wooden legs. She didn't know why she had given Connie's name. It had just popped out when the woman had asked. *Catholic guilt*, she thought to herself. *If I use someone else's name, then I'm not really doing this.*

Dr Obadiyah was an amazingly thin woman with gray hair, wire-rimmed glasses, and long spiky fingers. She had examined Rosemary during her first visit, and then talked to her about options. Rosemary had pretended to listen attentively, but she already knew what she was going to do. After all, how many options did a sixteen-year-old in her situation really have?

She left her clothes and purse in the little cubbyhole that Dr Obadiyah's nurse directed her to, and put on the thin white gown she handed her. Then she climbed up onto the long table in the middle of the room, and let her feet be fit into the chrome stirrups.

'I'm going to give you something to make you drowsy,' Dr Obadiyah said pleasantly, fastening a stabilizer to Rosemary's left arm and deftly inserting an IV needle just above her wrist. 'A little Demerol. Then, when you're relaxed, I'll give you a local anesthetic called a cervical block, and that should relieve most of the discomfort.'

If it did, no one would ever be able to prove it by Rosemary. Tears of pain poured from her eyes as the doctor first dilated her so wide the girl thought she would split in half, and then began to scrape out her insides. And as if that weren't scary enough, a huge gurgling machine stood by, with a tube attached to it like a giant vacuum cleaner, waiting to suck out everything it could. Rosemary bit down hard on her bottom lip to keep from screaming.

After what seemed forever, Dr Obadiyah put down her instruments and shut off the gurgling machine. She looked down at Rosemary with a thin smile. 'That's it,' she announced.

'It's over?' Rosemary asked.

'All over,' the nurse replied, removing the Demerol IV, and helping her to sit up. 'You can get dressed now, and as soon as you have your clothes on, I'll take you down to the day ward, and you can rest there until the anesthetic wears off.'

Rosemary slid off the table, but her knees were so wobbly that she had to lean heavily against the nurse in order to negotiate the few steps to the cubbyhole and her clothes. Inside, she was hot and sore and throbbing.

The nurse waited while Rosemary slipped into her bra and panties, pulled on her skirt and blouse, and slid her feet into sandals, and then she walked the girl down the hall and into a room where a dozen cots were neatly lined up along one wall, seven of them occupied.

'Take your pick of what's left,' she whispered.

Rosemary selected an empty bed near the door. A large clock on the wall proclaimed the time as two-fifteen, and she was surprised to learn that the whole awful procedure had actually taken less than fifteen minutes.

The nurse covered her with a blanket, and Rosemary fell asleep thinking of Benny Ruiz. Benny was twenty-five years old, by far the smartest, sexiest, handsomest, and most mature man she had ever met, and she had been seeing him secretly for almost a year. She thought him dashing and dangerous, the difference in their ages only heightening her interest, and she was hopelessly in love. She had gone to him the first week of June, when her period was two months overdue, to tell him she was pregnant.

'Well, sweetcakes,' he had crooned, 'if you are, that's not a problem. You just leave it to me and I'll take care of everything.'

'You mean we're going to get married?' she asked him breathlessly.

Benny threw back his head and laughed. 'I tie myself down to you for the rest of my life just because you got a bun in the oven? That's not the way it works anymore. This is 1974. We're cool now.'

'You mean you don't want to marry me?' she said around the sudden lump in her throat.

'Sweetcakes, I don't rule anything out,' he said smoothly, because she was underage, and he knew that could cause him one hell of a problem. 'Marriage is always a possibility. But it's for when we *want* to tie the knot – not for when we *have* to.'

'I guess you're right,' she admitted, seeing his point, 'but I thought . . .'

'Well, don't think, okay? You just let me do the thinking. And afterward, I'll take you with me to Los Angeles.'

'You mean it?' she cried, brightening. 'You'll really take me with you?'

'Why not?'

'Can we go to Disneyland?' She had heard all about the magical, mystical wonders of the famous amusement park and had always dreamed of seeing it for herself.

'Sure, sure, anything you want.'

Rosemary reached over and hugged him. 'I just want to be with you,' she sighed.

Benny ran his finger down the front of her T-shirt. 'Do you, sweetcakes?' he murmured. 'Well, why don't you show me how much?'

Rosemary giggled. He never seemed to get enough. 'Do you think we should?' she asked even as he unzipped her jeans, and slipped his hand inside her panties. 'I mean, well, you know . . .'

'Seems to me the damage has already been done,' he answered, nuzzling her neck.

Benny told her what she had to do about the baby. She resisted at first, partly out of fear, and partly out of some trace of Catholic conscience, until he persuaded her it was the only solution. He gave her the address of a clinic in San Francisco and told her how to get there and what to do when she did get there.

He was sorry he couldn't get off work on the day the procedure was scheduled, but he pulled a thick roll of bills out of his pocket, peeled off five hundred dollars in twenties, and handed it to her as if it were nothing. To Rosemary, it was a fortune. 'With what's left over,' he told her, 'you go out and buy yourself something pretty to wear in L.A.'

Benny worked as a mechanic at a garage in town. While Rosemary knew mechanics could earn good money, she didn't think they earned the kind of money that Benny tossed around. When they went out, he took her to expensive places, he was always sharply dressed, and he drove a late-model Corvette.

'What else do you do?' she asked a month after they met.

'Sweetcakes, if I ever want the world to know my business,' he replied, 'I'll tell you.'

She never mentioned it again.

'Miss Gilchrist?' The nurse was shaking her gently. Rosemary opened her eyes. 'You can go home now, if you like.'

'How long was I asleep?'

'Almost two hours,' the nurse replied with a smile. 'We came in and checked your pulse and your blood pressure every ten minutes, but you never woke up. Anesthesia affects some people more than others.'

Rosemary jumped off the cot in alarm. She still felt a bit woozy, but she ignored it. She was supposed to meet Benny at the garage at five o'clock. He hated it when she was late and she was going to have to hurry to get there in time.

The receptionist gave her a bottle with a week's supply of antibiotics inside, and a sheet of instructions in case she experienced any problems. Then Rosemary hurried out into the August sunshine.

It was two minutes past five when she got to the garage. Benny was nowhere around.

'He's not here,' the owner said when he saw her.

'You mean he already left?' she asked. 'But he was supposed to meet me.'

'No, I mean he's not here anymore. He's gone. Quit.'

Rosemary shook her head, not comprehending. 'But that wasn't supposed to be for two weeks yet.'

The owner shrugged. 'I don't know anything about that. He said he had a job waiting for him in Los Angeles.'

Rosemary turned away, trying to figure it out. She and Benny had been together just last night, and he hadn't said anything about his plans being changed. But then, she reasoned, maybe he hadn't known last night, and if the plans had gotten changed this morning, then there was no way for him to have reached her.

Of course, she decided, that must be it. He wouldn't have known that she had decided to cut the whole day of school instead of just the afternoon. He had probably gone up there looking for her. Maybe he had left a message with Betsy.

'No, I didn't see Benny at school today,' Betsy told her over the telephone an hour later. 'I didn't see you, either, and that was totally weird.'

'I had a doctor's appointment,' Rosemary declared without embellishment. 'Are you sure about Benny?'

'Positive,' Betsy replied and giggled. 'He's not exactly someone I'd be likely to miss.' Rosemary was well aware that her friend was panting for a chance at Benny, and given the slightest opportunity would grab it. 'What's the matter? You two have a little spat?'

'Of course not,' Rosemary told her. 'We just got our signals crossed, that's all.' She hung up and called the rooming house where Benny stayed.

'He packed up all his belongings this morning and went,' his landlady told her. 'Paid up his last week's rent and said he wasn't coming back. No, he didn't leave any message for you.'

'Did he maybe tell you where he was going?' Rosemary persisted. 'Did he leave an address? A phone number?'

'No, he didn't.'

'I see. Well, thanks anyway.'

'Wait now,' the landlady remembered. 'He did say something about he had a friend in L.A. he was going to.'

'He did?' Rosemary asked excitedly.

'No address, though, just a name.'

'Do you remember the name? Please, it's very important.'

'Angelo,' the landlady said. 'That was it, I'm sure. Angelo.'

'Angelo?' Rosemary repeated. 'Is that a first name or a last name?'

'I don't know,' the landlady replied. '"I have to go see my friend Angelo in L.A.," he said. That's all he said.'

It wasn't much to go on, but it was all Rosemary had. She couldn't just sit around and wait for Benny to contact her. She would go crazy. No, she would surprise him. She looked in her purse. There was about two hundred dollars left from the money he had given her to pay for the doctor. She would use it to buy a bus ticket for as close to Los Angeles as it would take her, and hitchhike the rest of the way, if she had to.

Rosemary had never been to Los Angeles. She knew

absolutely nothing about the city, nor had she any clear idea of how she would go about finding Angelo. It didn't matter. She had no other choice. Life without Benny wasn't worth living.

She packed a small suitcase and waited until she thought everyone was asleep. Then she sneaked out of her room. As luck would have it, she bumped right into Ricky coming out of the bathroom.

'Shh!' she warned him, putting her finger to her lips.

The boy stood there, looking from his sister to her suitcase. 'You, too?' he whispered.

'Don't be silly,' she hissed. 'I'm just taking some things over to Betsy's. You know how Mom feels about us giving our things away before we've worn them out.'

'Sure,' Ricky said, as she turned away from him and started down the stairs. 'Good luck.'

He was the last one to see her before she rode off on a Trailways bus and was swallowed up in the streets of Los Angeles. It was five months to the day that her brother had left home.

This time, Jack didn't just shrug it off. He searched for months, using up his vacation days, talking to her friends, to the area newspapers, to the police, even to the FBI, but it was to no avail. She was gone and he had no idea where to look for her.

5

There was someplace Valerie was supposed to be. It was right there, at the edge of her mind, but she couldn't quite grab hold of it. Was it Jack's breakfast she had forgotten to make? Were the children late for school? Had she promised to go over to Connie's this morning to help her with something?

She opened her eyes, one at a time, something she had been doing every morning since Rosemary had gone. It was a way she had of protecting herself. If she didn't look at the world all at once, then the pain couldn't jump out and catch her unaware.

But it happened anyway, and Valerie sat bolt upright. This wasn't her room, this wasn't her bed. Someone had come in the middle of the night and taken her away to a strange place. She looked out the window, hoping for a clue, but all she could see was a brick wall barely six feet away. She listened for any kind of sound that would tell her where she was, but outside of an occasional car passing and the rumble of muffled voices, she could identify nothing. Her heart began to race.

Marianne Santini opened the door and peeked in. 'Oh good, you're awake,' she cried. 'The children were beginning to worry you'd sleep the whole day away.'

Valerie looked at her sister in panic. 'Where am I?' she whimpered.

Marianne caught her breath, and hurried over to the bed. 'You're perfectly safe,' she said soothingly, sitting down beside her sister and taking her hand. 'You're in our new house in Boston.'

Valerie stared at her, nothing registering.

'Tommy and I bought this big old barn of a brownstone last August,' Marianne continued. 'It's on Marlborough Street, in Back Bay. I wrote to you about it, remember? You wrote back you wanted to see it when you came East for Christmas.'

Valerie nodded vaguely.

'Mom and Dad put you and the children on the train from Rutland yesterday, and we picked you up at the station. It was New Year's Eve. We drank champagne. It's 1975 now. You and the kids are spending a couple of days with Tommy and me before you fly home to California.'

Then it all came back. 'I guess I got lost,' Valerie said in a small voice, slumping against the pillows.

Her sister smiled. 'Not to worry.'

'My medicine?'

Marianne reached for the little bottle of pills and the glass of water on the nightstand. 'Right here.' She thought it was probably the medication that kept her sister in a fog all the time. She wondered if the doctors were right to prescribe such a heavy dose.

Valerie gulped down her pills.

'There, that's better,' Marianne said. 'Do you feel like getting up?'

'Of course I'll get up,' Valerie replied. 'I can't stay in bed all day, I have too much to do. The children have to have breakfast, and Jack needs his . . .' For a moment, she couldn't remember what it was that Jack needed. Then she remembered that Jack was back home in El Granada, and she was here in Boston, and she bit her lip.

'Chores are out,' Marianne said brightly. 'Today is

262

your day of rest. Besides, Tommy's in the kitchen fixing breakfast. Well, it'll be brunch by the time we eat it. And after that, we're going to take the children ice-skating. How does that sound?'

'That sounds nice,' Valerie replied.

'The bathroom's the second door on the right as you go out into the hallway,' Marianne told her. 'Come down whenever you're ready.' She closed the door softly and went down three flights to the newly remodeled country kitchen.

The brownstone was a once elegant five-story building that, for some twenty years, had been used as a dormitory for a now defunct college. It was in appalling shape when the Santinis bought it, but Tommy had a never-ending supply of uncles and cousins in the contracting business that had swarmed all over the place for months. Even Marianne had to admit they had done an outstanding job of returning the house to a fair semblance of its former glory.

'Oh Tommy,' she cried now as she rushed into the kitchen, 'I just can't stand it. There's got to be something we can do. Valerie's just wasting away right in front of our eyes.'

'What's wrong?' Tommy replied. 'She seemed fine last night.'

'Didn't she? I couldn't understand what Mom and Dad were warning us about. I thought they must have been exaggerating. But I was just up there, and she didn't have the faintest idea where she was. I'm not even sure she knew who I was.'

'Sure she knows you, honey,' Tommy said, 'but the house is new to her. She probably just got a little disoriented or something, that's all.'

'It's those damn pills, I tell you,' Marianne retorted. 'They keep her so doped up, she doesn't know top from bottom.'

'Didn't the doctors say the medication was necessary for the depression?'

'Yes, but it's turning her into a zombie.'

'A zombie's made with rum and fruit juice,' Ricky declared from the doorway, startling them.

'And just what do you know about zombies, young man?' inquired his uncle.

Ricky grinned. 'More than I should, I bet.'

'Where's Ellen?' Marianne asked.

'I don't know,' the boy answered with a shrug. 'She's probably off somewhere praying.'

'Praying?'

'Sure. That's mostly all she does.'

Marianne sighed heavily, thinking about what was left of her sister's family. Priscilla dead, JJ and Rosemary gone, and Jack, well, Marianne had serious doubts about Jack's effectiveness, either as a husband or a father. But Ellen and Ricky were still here, and for their sake, Valerie just had to get well. Someone had to get through to her.

'I didn't realize the kitchen was so far down,' Valerie said, drifting into the room fifteen minutes later. 'Or that I was so far up.'

'Good morning, sweetheart,' Tommy boomed, giving her a bear hug. 'How about a nice cup of coffee?'

Valerie nodded. 'What are we going to do today?'

Marianne looked quickly from her sister to her husband and back to her sister. 'I think the children have ice-skating in mind,' she said. 'Of course, if you don't feel up to it, we could always—'

'I feel fine,' Valerie declared. 'I think skating is a wonderful idea.' Tommy placed a steaming mug of coffee in her hands and she smiled at him in appreciation and took a sip. 'Is today Sunday?' she asked.

'No,' Marianne told her. 'Today is Wednesday.'

'Oh.' Valerie paused for another sip of coffee. 'Why isn't Tommy at the restaurant, if it's Wednesday?'

'Ma, it's New Year's,' Ricky told her. 'It's a holiday.'

'Oh,' his mother replied vaguely. 'That's right. I forgot.'

'Food's ready,' Tommy announced. 'Ricky, go call your sister.'

Tommy had fixed a huge brunch of eggs and sausages and fried potatoes, to which Marianne added hot crisp rolls and a selection of pastries with cheese and prunes and apples.

Ricky stuffed himself to bursting. Ellen ate a polite portion. Valerie did barely more than pick at her plate.

'If you don't eat more than that,' Marianne whispered in her ear, 'you're going to hurt Tommy's feelings.'

'I don't mean to,' Valerie whispered back, and forced several bites into her mouth.

The air was crisp and cold when they started out for the river. It was just past one o'clock, and Ricky and Ellen had been ready and waiting for an hour, bundled up in their heavy coats and bright yellow hats and two pairs of socks, with their borrowed ice skates slung over their shoulders the way their Rutland cousins always carried them.

Valerie had been a good skater in her youth. As the youngest in the family, she was always on the end of the whip, and she had had to learn early how to stay on her feet.

A sizable crowd was already on hand when they reached the part of the river that was frozen solid. The children quickly laced up their skates and darted onto the ice.

'Ricky, Ellen,' Valerie called to them. 'I don't want you skating alone. Wait for us.'

'But you don't even have your skates on yet,' Ricky complained.

'I'll only be a few more minutes,' his mother said, fumbling with her laces.

'Aw, Ma!'

'That's okay,' Tommy said, standing up and clomping over to the river's edge. 'Mine are on. I'll take them.'

Valerie and Marianne watched as the big man and the small boy and girl skidded off across the ice.

'He should have had ten of his own,' Marianne said with a sigh.

The two sisters threaded their way among the skaters, arm in arm. Although Marianne was considerably taller than Valerie, they matched each other stride for stride.

'Do you remember when we used to do this as kids?' Marianne said.

'Of course,' Valerie told her. 'That's why I'm glad the children could share it, too.'

At that moment, she nearly seemed her old self again. Marianne looked at her sister. Some of the color had returned to her cheeks, her eyes almost sparkled, and she was smiling.

Ricky was growing impatient. For almost an hour, he had been plodding along with his sister and his uncle, and he was dying to strike out on his own and really work up some speed. Skating was only fun when you were going as fast as you could go, and the wind was whipping at your face and forcing its way down your throat.

His opportunity came five minutes later when a teenager involved in a game of ice tag suddenly lost control and skidded headlong into Tommy, toppling him backward onto his butt, and knocking the wind right out of him.

'Are you okay, Uncle Tommy?' Ellen asked.

'I guess so,' Tommy gasped. But as Ricky helped him up, Tommy reached for the small of his back and winced. 'Maybe I'd better get off my feet for a little while.'

'I'll go with you,' Ellen said, taking her uncle's arm and maneuvering him slowly toward the edge.

'I'll just hang out here,' Ricky said casually and waited for an objection. None came. He turned around in a full circle, scanning the ice, looking to see if his mother and aunt were anywhere in sight. They were not. It was all the encouragement he needed. He took off downriver, where he could see that the ice was less crowded, as fast as he could go.

It felt so good to stretch himself and skim along, his skates barely scratching the slippery surface. It was almost like flying. He had never skated on a river before, where he could accelerate flat out in one straight line. It was so much easier when there were no curves and turns to negotiate. He bent forward over his knees, tucked his hands behind him the way JJ used to do it, and never looked back.

A group of skaters loomed up in front of him and then they were behind him. One of them shouted something, trying to get his attention, but he didn't turn around. Ahead, the ice was clean and white and empty. No one stood in his way. He was free now and nothing could stop him.

He didn't recognize the sound at first. By the time he did, it was too late. The muted crackling became a moving, shaking, shattering rupture. A gaping hole in the whiteness appeared directly in his path and he tumbled forward into the freezing black depths of the Charles River.

Down, down, down he went, the weight of his heavy coat and skates pulling him to the very bottom. Fetid, frigid water filled his mouth, his nose, his eyes, his ears. The blade of one of his skates caught on something beneath him and held. Panicking, Ricky thrashed around in the darkness, struggling to pull himself loose. With his thick gloves still on, he yanked at the laces on the caught skate, but he couldn't get them untied. He couldn't breathe, and he was choking on the putrid water in his lungs. With every remaining bit of strength, he lashed out in one last frenzied kick.

Suddenly, he was free. He felt himself beginning to rise and he clawed feebly at the murky light above him. What was taking so long? His lungs were on fire, and his heart was pounding so hard, he expected at any moment that it would burst from his chest.

Ricky began to think that he wasn't going to make it, that he was actually going to die. He wondered what it would be like to be dead. He knew what his mother and the priest always told him about the afterlife, but he never believed any of that crap. Still, it would be nice, he thought now, if maybe some of it were true, especially the part about it being warm and safe.

A strange euphoria began to overtake him and he began to smile. He couldn't feel his legs any longer and he was losing touch with his arms, but it didn't matter. The murky light seemed to disappear, and he thought it might be nice to go to sleep.

At the instant he lost consciousness, his head, in the bright yellow cap, broke the surface of the water.

Valerie couldn't remember when she had last had such fun. The sky was so bright it almost hurt to look at it, the ice was solid beneath her skates, and all around her were laughing, happy people.

It had been such a sad year. Terrible things had happened: the horrific airplane accident at Federal that had killed so many people, the robbery at Connie's house, and two more of her babies gone. Valerie tried not to dwell on any of it, because there wasn't any point in it, really. If it were God's will that she not be happy here on earth, she would accept that. She had no choice.

The pills helped, and the alcohol. They kept the pain at bay, kept things just a little bit fuzzy, and kept the melody humming softly in her head. It was a familiar tune, a spiritual, perhaps, that she couldn't quite place. But it didn't matter, she would hear it when she needed to, whenever the pain threatened to come too close. But on a day like today, nothing bad could happen, and knowing that made her smile.

Marianne smiled, too. It was good to see Valerie happy again, even if it was only for a little while.

'Oh look,' she said, pointing past her sister. 'There's some excitement going on over there.'

Valerie looked. Sure enough, a crowd of skaters was rushing downriver. 'What is it?'

'I don't know,' Marianne replied. 'Let's go see.' The two women started off down the ice. 'Oh my,' Marianne cried, as the sisters reached the rim of spectators. 'I think someone's fallen through the ice.'

'How terrible,' Valerie said, straining for a look.

'Yes,' Marianne went on, 'that's exactly what's happened. See the ice over there, how it's broken off. Someone's definitely gone in. I'll bet it's someone who didn't know enough not to go so far downriver. That's one of the things you have to be very careful of here, the ice breaking up like that. It can be treacherous.'

But Valerie was no longer listening to her sister. She had caught a glimpse of a bright yellow hat bobbing in the water, and every maternal instinct she possessed was propelling her forward.

'That's my son,' she shrieked. 'That's my son!' She

had no idea what made her know that it was Ricky in the water and not Ellen. She just did.

The crowd quickly made a path for her. She reached the edge of the ice and would have jumped right into the frigid depths if someone hadn't stopped her.

'Take it easy, ma'am,' a man said, grasping her arm and holding tight. 'Your son's going to be all right. See, the boys out there? They've got him.'

Sure enough, with her heart in her mouth, Valerie watched as several young men pulled Ricky out of the water and quickly brought him to safety.

Apparently, somebody had thought to call the paramedics, because an ambulance appeared almost immediately, and a stretcher was wheeled right out onto the ice.

'I'm going to ride with Ricky,' Valerie told Marianne.

'Of course you are,' Marianne replied. 'I'll go find Tommy and Ellen and we'll meet you at the hospital.'

Valerie was helped up into the ambulance and seated beside Ricky. Almost immediately, the doors were shut, the engine started, and the siren wailed. She looked at her son, and her lower lip began to tremble and her eyes overflowed. He was blue.

The paramedic who was tending to him noticed. 'Don't worry, ma'am,' he said kindly. 'I think we got him in time.'

Just then, Ricky opened his eyes and recognized his mother. 'Hey, Ma,' he wheezed through chattering teeth, 'why're you crying?'

Valerie smiled at him through her tears. 'Because you gave me quite a scare.'

'What'd I do?' he asked.

'Do?' she cried. 'You fell into the river, don't you remember?'

Ricky frowned, trying to clear his head of the heavy

fog that filled it. 'I was going down,' he said, finally remembering. 'There was something holding me, and it wouldn't let go. But then it did, and something pulled me up.' The boy's eyes wandered, unfocused, around the ambulance, trying to put the pieces together. 'I think it was JJ.'

'No, darling, it wasn't JJ,' Valerie said. 'It was a group of teenagers.'

Ricky was only half awake, but he smiled at his mother. 'JJ,' he murmured as he drifted off.

'Who's JJ?' the paramedic asked.

'JJ is his older brother,' Valerie replied. 'He left home last year and we haven't heard from him. He and Ricky were very close.'

The paramedic nodded. 'Hold the thought, Ricky,' he said as the ambulance pulled up to the hospital emergency room. 'It's for sure somebody's looking out for you.'

The doors were thrown open and as several pairs of hands reached for the stretcher, Valerie reached for the little bottle of pills in her pocket. She quickly swallowed two instead of the one that had been prescribed before anyone could see, and then waited calmly for the warm, fuzzy feeling she knew would come. It was easier that way, much easier than having to think about how dangerously close she had just come to losing yet another child.

6

Ricky counted his accident as the first day of his immortality. Somehow, he had survived when by all accounts he should have died, and as far as he was concerned, that now made him invincible.

He'd spent a week in the hospital in Boston, where the doctors kept him until his lungs dried out and the bronchial infection he had developed cleared up and they were sure he wasn't going to lose any of his fingers or toes to frostbite. He kept waiting for JJ to come, but he never did. His mother tried to tell him that it was some young men who had saved his life, but Ricky knew better. Even if it had been others who plucked him out of the river just in time, JJ had sent them. He wanted to thank his brother, but he didn't know where he was. Well, not exactly, anyway.

About eight months after he had left home, JJ sent a letter to Ricky in care of Chris Rodriguez's family. There was an Alabama postmark, but no return address. In it, JJ said that the day after his eighteenth birthday he had joined the Army. He also said that he was well and happy, and he wanted Ricky to tell his mother not to worry about him.

His mother cried for a week, perhaps as much from relief that he was still alive as anything else. His father thrust out his jaw. 'Maybe the Army'll make a man of him,' was all he ever said.

Ricky talked to Chris instead, the day after he came home from Boston.

'I was done for, man,' he explained to his wide-eyed friend, embellishing freely. 'I could feel it. First my legs got numb, then my arms, then my brain. I started hallucinating, you know, just like when we drop acid. I mean, everything was warm and light, and I was in this kind of garden where the flowers were as tall as trees and the grass was real soft like velvet, and there was this sort of singing, except I didn't know the song.'

'Jeez,' his friend breathed in awe.

'Then these guys come and pull me out and crunch my ribs till I spit up all the water I swallowed, and ruin everything.'

'Sounds to me,' Chris said, 'like they saved your life.'

'Yeah, I guess so,' Ricky admitted with a grin. 'But I was dead, man. I was on my way to the hereafter. What a trip.'

'When you didn't come back to school right away, all the kids wondered,' Chris told him. 'But nobody thought of anything like that. Just wait'll they hear.'

Ricky basked in the awe of his schoolmates for almost a week. Boys who were his sworn enemies offered him free joints. Girls who had always giggled about his size batted their eyes at him. Teachers who, for the most part, found him unresponsive wanted him to tell his story in class.

Then one day at lunch, an eighth-grader asked him how he could possibly have been so stupid as to skate onto thin ice, and Ricky replied by breaking his nose. The truce was over. He was suspended from school for three days, and told to shape up.

He took to prowling the neighborhood at night. He was afraid to go to sleep because he dreamed about drowning when he did, and woke up in a wet bed, which not only embarrassed him, but totally contradicted his image of immortality.

He would wait until the house was quiet before slipping out. Nobody missed him. Between the pills and the alcohol, his mother was either oblivious or in bed by nine, and as long as his light was off, his father never bothered to check on him.

Sneaking in and out of the upstairs door became second nature to Ricky. Walking the streets until the early hours became his opiate. It also gave him a very clear picture of his neighbors and their habits. Like the Monroes on Isabella, who went out every Saturday night all dressed up like it was a coronation or something. Or the Edisons on Portola, whose house was always dark by eight o'clock. Or the Pomadas down del Oro, who both worked the night shift and took off just before ten. Or the Cooks, at the corner of Francisco, who rarely came home before dawn and usually not with each other.

The Saturday after his thirteenth birthday, Ricky jimmied the lock on the Monroes' back door and helped himself to some jewelry, a pair of silver candlesticks, a camera that looked expensive, and sixteen dollars in change that he found in a cookie jar on the kitchen counter. He stuffed everything into a pillowcase he had brought with him and swung it over his shoulder as he scurried home.

'Like a goddam Santa Claus,' he muttered with a grin.

The high he got wasn't nearly as big as the one he had gotten from robbing Connie's house last year. There had been real excitement in that and a little danger, too, wondering every minute if he would slip up somehow and get himself caught. Now he knew how easy it was. And besides, he was immortal.

Two days later, he cut school and took the candlesticks and the camera to a pawnshop over in San Mateo that Chris had told him about. His friend had gone there with his father once when one of his sisters was sick and there was no money. His father had given a man a gold ring and the man had given him enough money to pay for the medicine.

The shop was dark inside and smelled of sweat and stale cigars. Ricky approached the gray-haired, bespectacled man standing behind the counter, and put the candlesticks and camera down in front of him.

'Can you give me some money for these things, please, sir?' he asked in his most ingratiating voice. 'My mama's real sick and we have no money for medicine.'

The pawnbroker glanced shrewdly at the merchandise and grunted. 'Where's your father, kid?'

'He's . . . he's dead, sir, and there's just me to take care of my mother.'

The man peered down at Ricky. Such an angel this kid looked like, he thought, and so little to have all that responsibility. Besides, he could probably get eighty-five for the sticks, and the camera had to be good for at least a hundred and fifty.

'Well,' he said, 'seeing as your mama's in trouble, I'll give you, say, thirty-five for the lot.'

'Thank you, sir,' Ricky said earnestly.

The following week, he brought the pawnbroker the Monroe jewelry.

'Is your mother any better?' he asked.

'A little,' Ricky told him shyly. 'Thank you for asking.'

By the time the school year ended, Marvin Mandelbaum no longer asked after Ricky's mother, or wondered where all the costly items were coming from. Business had picked up considerably over the past few months and Marvin, who had two ex-wives and five children to support, was not one to look a gift horse in the mouth.

During the summer, Ricky would take the bus over to San Mateo and spend several afternoons a week with Mandelbaum. When business was slow, Marvin would take him out back and open the huge vault built into one wall of his office and show him exactly what kinds of things to look for.

'There's good stuff, and then there's *good* stuff,' he always said. 'You got to learn the difference.'

'If I do,' Ricky asked once, 'will you pay me a decent share?'

Marvin cuffed him on the ear. 'Can the smart talk, kid. First you learn, then we'll discuss partnership.'

'You got a deal,' Ricky said with a grin. 'So learn me.'

Marvin was a patient teacher, and one who had true reverence for fine jewelry and works of art. 'See this stamp on the bottom?' he would ask, pushing an item of silver under the boy's nose. 'It's called a hallmark. That and the word "sterling" or the number 925 is what you look for in silver.'

'I don't have time for detailed examinations,' Ricky protested.

'Make time,' Marvin retorted. 'And when it's real gold,' he added, dropping a bracelet into the boy's hand, 'it has to say either fourteen karat or eighteen karat on the inside. See the 14K on that?'

'What about stones?' Ricky asked.

'Stones you can't evaluate so good with a flashlight. So, don't worry about stones. As long as it's set in gold, the piece should be worth something.'

By the time Ricky was fifteen and had branched out of his neighborhood into the community at large, he knew everything Marvin Mandelbaum knew about gold

276

and silver and precious gems. And a box he kept hidden in the bottom drawer of his desk, where his mother never looked, began to bulge with five- and ten- and twenty-dollar bills.

PART FIVE

1978

I

Valerie stood on the porch of her parents' house and gazed out across the front lawn and down the tree-lined drive. It was the first week in June, and it had been a long time since she had been to Vermont in the spring. Every year for the past ten, she had come back to Rutland for two weeks at Christmas and a month in the summer, bringing the children so they could share in the joy of being part of a big family. But now it was over, and she knew she would never come here again, at any time of the year.

Five weeks ago, her father had died of a heart attack while cutting the very lawn she was now looking at. One moment he was mowing, and the next he was slumped over the machine, gone at the age of seventy-eight. Two weeks later, her mother had come down with pneumonia, lingering until the night before last, when she finally succumbed, four days shy of turning seventy-two, and ten days short of what would have been her fifty-third wedding anniversary.

'It happens that way sometimes,' the doctor said. 'When two people have been together for as long as Martin and Charlotte, they tend to go together, or not far apart.'

Valerie wondered if the same would be true for her and Jack.

There was a will. Martin had always had his affairs in order. There was a portfolio of stocks and bonds that was divided equally among the nine children. There were a few pieces of jewelry, one of them, a cameo necklace that had always been Valerie's favorite.

'And I bet you thought Ma never knew,' Marianne said with a smile when she fastened it around her sister's neck.

Martin left the quarry to Marty and Kevin. It was only fair. They had been running it for years. The house had also been left to them, which was fair, too. Although Elizabeth, Cecilia, and Danny lived in Vermont, Marty and Kevin were the only ones who had stayed in Rutland. Patrick had come back to take over for Father Joseph, but he lived in the rectory at St Stephen's, Marianne was still in Boston, and Hugh was stationed in North Carolina.

They had a family meeting, and it was decided that they would sell the house. Everyone cried, but they all knew it was for the best. The place was big and drafty and too much for any of them to keep up.

'Let someone else worry about the leaky roof and the sagging porch and that antiquated stove Ma would never let Pa replace,' Kevin said.

Thinking about that now, Valerie sighed and ran her hand along the porch railing. This house had been so much more than a roof or a porch or a stove, she thought, and it was sad to see it reduced to that. For the first eighteen years of her life, it had been her cocoon, for the last twenty-three, it had been her refuge.

She went inside and upstairs to her room, and took a little green pill.

2

Ricky sat with his back against a sand dune and watched his friend Chris riding a wave on the brand-new surfboard. A stiff breeze swirled the sand around a lot, but did little to enhance the modest swells. Half Moon Bay had never been known for superior surfing, but the sun was shining, the October temperature was in the seventies, and Chris didn't care.

The two had cut school the day after Chris turned seventeen and taken off for the beach with a six-pack of beer and a couple of boxes of cookies from the local grocery store, and a stash of grass from the local dealer. While Chris and his board headed immediately for the surf, Ricky set about rolling several joints, holding tight to the flimsy papers that fluttered in the wind, and trying to keep the Acapulco Gold as grit-free as he could.

Love of the ocean was the only thing the two teenagers didn't share. It wasn't so much that Ricky had never learned to swim as it was that ever since his dramatic rescue from the Charles River almost four years ago, he had enjoyed a healthy fear of water. And his personal image of immortality required that he not tempt fate.

Ricky glanced first to his right and then to his left, checking out the beach. Satisfied that there was no one around at this early hour, he leaned back and lit one of the joints he had rolled, pulling the acrid smoke deep into his lungs and holding it as long as he could. Not that pot ever did a whole lot more than mellow him out, it was just that it was readily available and everybody was into it.

A line of coke, on the other hand, packed a real kick. But cocaine cost real bucks and this was a very small community. If it got around that he used on a regular basis, someone would be sure to start asking the wrong questions, and Ricky didn't want anyone wondering where he had come upon that kind of money. He had not even told Chris what he did in the wee hours of the morning several times a month. As close as the two were, they had always maintained a separate space that the other never entered. What Ricky considered his personal business was between himself and no one else. Well, between himself and Marvin Mandelbaum, actually, but that was all. Ricky had saved a good part of what he had made in the past three years as legman for the pawnbroker, and as of last week, it added up to just under four thousand dollars.

The sixteen-year-old took another hit and wondered idly how far he could get on thirty-eight hundred and seventy dollars, and where exactly he would go if he went. He had no clear idea of either.

He certainly had no intention of following JJ into the Army, much as his brother raved about the life in his infrequent letters. All that patriotic crap was for fools. He might have tried to follow Rosemary, except he didn't have any idea where to look. No one had heard a word from her since she vanished into the night a few months after JJ. And the last thing it would ever occur to him to do was follow Ellen.

Chris was always talking about the ocean. Ever since his father had gotten a steady job on a fishing boat, and had taken his son along a couple of times to show him the ropes, all Chris could think about was going to sea.

'Someday,' he told Ricky, 'I'm going to get me my own boat and sail away.'

'Where you going to go?' Ricky asked, thinking about some of the Mexican ports where he had heard you could buy a ton of good marijuana for practically peanuts, and figuring he could probably unload it right here on the Coast for a small fortune.

'No particular place,' Chris said.

'Then what's the point?'

'The point is *being* there, man, not going there.'

Sailing the seven seas held no interest for Ricky, not unless there was some profit to be made from it, anyway. He had developed a keen interest in accumulating money, but not necessarily for what it could buy. What intrigued him was *getting* it, not spending it. The challenge, the risk, the high was what it was all about.

On the nights that he did not go out, Ricky loved to sit in the middle of his bed counting his take, keeping the covers folded just right so he could pull them quickly over his hoard in case someone came knocking. He would lay out the bills by denomination, and watch contentedly as, month by month, the little green piles grew higher and higher, each one representing another daring feat accomplished.

But now he had decided that three years of ripping off the neighbors was enough. The high had faded and he was bored. Besides, the pickings were getting slim. He had been reduced to going back to some of the same houses two or three times, in each case for diminishing returns. Ricky knew it was time to branch out in other directions and eliminate the need for a middleman. Almost everything he stole went through Marvin Mandelbaum, and by the time Marvin sold the stuff for less than it was worth and took his own cut, Ricky got back only a fraction of the real value. A fraction for taking all the risks.

What he needed was to stop fooling around with pearl rings and sterling silver baby spoons and just go for the serious cash. And Ricky knew exactly how to do that. He had been thinking about it for more than a month now, and tonight was the night he had decided that he would put his new plan into action.

'Wow,' Chris cried, emerging from the water with his board under his arm, 'she's a real beauty. Thanks a lot, man.'

Ricky shrugged. 'Like I told you,' he lied. 'I had no use for it.'

'But your folks must've been mad, you just giving your birthday present away like that.'

'Nah, they understood.' Ricky had bought the surfboard himself. Chris had been wanting one for almost two years now, it was almost all he could talk about, and Ricky knew that his friend's parents couldn't afford to buy it for him.

'Do you think I ought to say something to them,' Chris asked. 'You know, thank them?'

'No,' Ricky said hastily. 'I mean you don't want to do that. It would embarrass the shit out of them.'

'Okay,' Chris agreed, relieved. He didn't really know how to talk to the elder Marshes. Ricky's mother was usually, well, so unconscious most of the time that Chris sometimes wasn't sure she even heard anything that was said to her, and Ricky's father was hardly around, and sort of moved in and out like a dark shadow when he was.

'Want a hit?' Ricky inquired.

'Yeah, sure.' Chris unzipped his wet suit and dropped down onto the sand.

The wet suit had come along with the surfboard and

Chris hadn't questioned the size. Although Ricky now stood at five foot seven inches, Chris was already six feet tall.

The youngest Marsh had given up waiting for miracles. He knew he wasn't going to grow big and tall like his brother, JJ, but he had made his peace with that. At least he wasn't the shortest guy in his school anymore, and he now had a whole selection of girls he could look down on.

Chris took three big hits before passing the joint back. 'Are you going to Nancy Thaler's birthday party Saturday night?' he asked, as if reading Ricky's mind.

Ricky grinned. Nancy Thaler was one of the girls he had been looking down at a lot lately. 'You bet,' he said. 'As a matter of fact, I got me a very special invitation.'

'Way to go,' Chris chortled.

The Thalers lived up in Moss Beach, in a pretty little cottage that was practically right on the water. And along with Ricky's breathless, eyelash-batting invitation had come a whispered proposal for a private walk on a secluded stretch of sand. Just her warm breath tickling his ear had been enough to make him walk a little stiffly away from the conversation.

Nancy was one year behind him in school, but she had obviously developed early. She was pert and blond, with full lips and large breasts, and Ricky had been fantasizing about doing something with both for some months. Just thinking about the possibilities now was enough to cause him to readjust his position on the sand.

'Think you're going to get some, huh?' Chris inquired with a knowing grin.

'Maybe,' Ricky replied with a wink.

The two had done their share of experimenting

through the years, giggling over a dog-eared copy of *The Joy of Sex* that the library had tucked away on a back shelf, sharing girlie magazines in the privacy of the hills behind Ricky's house, and blatantly spying on their respective sisters. They had begun masturbating at ten, rubbing up against any girl who didn't get out of the way fast enough at eleven, and French kissing any girl who dared to come close enough at twelve. But at sixteen, neither of them had yet gone all the way with any member of the opposite sex. For Chris, it was because Theresa Hoyt, his more or less steady girlfriend, was determined not to do anything she wasn't supposed to do until a wedding band was firmly on her finger. For Ricky, it was simply a lack of opportunity.

Now there was Nancy Thaler, who had been making moves on Ricky since September, when it was clear that his summer growth spurt had been enough to overtake her in height, and come Saturday night he was going to find out if she was anything more than hot air.

'Nancy Thaler's just a tease,' Chris declared. 'Bet you get nothing but a feel or two.'

Ricky shrugged. 'With those knockers,' he observed, 'even that'd be worth my time.' But he had no intention of letting it go at that.

'I tell you every guy in school's tried her,' Chris insisted, 'and came away with zip.'

'I haven't tried yet,' Ricky said, taking the last hit off the joint.

3

Jack Marsh was now forty-eight years old. When he looked at himself in the mirror each morning, he could see that age had done nothing to diminish his good looks. The deep lines that played about his yellow eyes simply added to their intrigue, the silver streaks that darted in and out of his black hair gave him an aura of maturity, and years of manual labor and physical activity on the job had kept his body in excellent shape.

So it was with considerable embarrassment that he approached a physician, on a Monday in mid-October, about his inability to maintain an erection.

'I don't think there's anything serious to worry about,' Dr Henry Haas said at the conclusion of his examination. 'It's most likely a temporary condition that will go away of its own accord.'

'When?' Jack asked bluntly, zipping himself back into his clothes.

'Whenever the emotional or mental stress that's causing it dissipates,' the doctor replied calmly.

Jack looked at the professional man in some confusion, unable to understand what some emotional or mental stress he might be feeling had to do with his present inability to perform a bodily function that had always come as easily to him as pissing.

'Huh?' he inquired.

'Whatever the problem is,' Haas explained, 'my

examination indicates that it isn't rooted in anything physical.'

Jack squinted at the tall, spare man with round glasses whose name he had plucked from the telephone book in his need for anonymity. 'You're telling me that I can't get it up anymore because of something in my head?'

'More or less, yes.'

'Well, can you give me a pill or a shot or something to fix it?'

Henry Haas was a urologist, and had been practicing medicine for more than thirty years. It never failed to amaze, and amuse, him how many of his male patients were unable to make the natural connection between the body and the brain.

'Sit down, Mr Marsh,' he invited pleasantly.

Jack dropped heavily into the proffered chair. 'I'll take whatever medicine you got, Doc. I want to get over this thing quick.' He gave Haas a broad wink. 'It's making a real dent in my leisure time activities.'

'How long have you been experiencing impotency?' the doctor asked.

The patient squirmed in his seat. 'Uh, well, uh, off and on for maybe about a year now,' he admitted in acute discomfort. Actually, it was closer to two. 'But it didn't happen all the time, at first, just once in a while, and I kept thinking it would go away, you know, like it was some passing thing, like a virus maybe. And it did, sometimes, but then it would come back, and now it's pretty much all the time, and it doesn't go away.'

'Has there been any undue stress in your life in recent years?' Haas inquired. 'Either at work or at home?'

Undue stress? Jack considered the words. When had there not been stress in his life? He couldn't remember a time when there wasn't something or someone hassling him. For instance, it had taken over a year for the NTSB to decide, for lack of definitive evidence to the contrary, that the crash of Federal Flight 921 had most likely been caused by pilot error. Over a year before Jack and his crew were finally let off the hook. That alone was enough to cause undue stress, keeping them all dangling like that. But, of course, there was a lot more.

There was Kate, his waitress friend, who after eight uncomplicated years of satisfying most of his needs had up and moved to Denver, because her son and his family were now living there and she wanted to be closer to her grandchildren.

Then, too, there was Valerie, who was disappearing right before his eyes. The sweet country girl he had married and counted on to save him from the world couldn't even save herself. He would leave her bleary-eyed most mornings and find her stupefied most nights, no clean laundry, no dinner, the house a mess. Half the time, she never bothered to show up for her shift at the Gray Whale. And just last week, which was how he knew how serious things were, she couldn't even pull herself out of bed to go to mass on Sunday.

Jack hated coming home now. The house was so empty and so still. Even with Valerie in it, and Ricky, too, when he bothered to show up, it was as bad as that time, right after Priscilla's death, when they had all gone off to Vermont and left him alone with his guilt and his misery. Only that time, at least, they had come back.

Now, in addition to Priscilla, JJ and Rosemary were gone . . . dead, too, for all he knew. And as far as he was concerned, Ellen might just as well be. Last year, after graduating from high school, the fool girl had gone and entered a goddam convent.

'Women are getting the hell out of convents these days,' he had told her, 'not going in.'

'It's what I want to do, Daddy,' Ellen replied in that gentle, serene way she had. 'It's what I've always wanted to do.'

It was true, he knew. From the time she was barely able to read, it was hard for him to remember ever seeing her without a Bible in her hands. She had routinely been at the top of her catechism class, and he had to admit that she had always had that otherworldly sort of look about her, like she didn't really belong in this life, walking among ordinary people.

Jack wanted to stop her, but he knew he couldn't. She was of age and sound mind, and of course she had Valerie behind her, beaming through her stupor, as though the idea of her daughter slaving away for a lifetime of poverty and chastity was a blessing.

He remembered so vividly when she was born, all the problems she had had, the long vigil he had kept beside her incubator. What had all of it been for? To send her off into slavery?

He had never given much thought to his kids, but had just sort of taken for granted that they would always be around. After all, wasn't that what kids were for – to take care of parents who weren't able to take care of themselves anymore?

For the past three years, it had been Ellen who had kept the house together, looking after Valerie, getting meals on the table, making sure he had a clean shirt to wear to work every day. But now she was gone. Now four out of the five of them were gone, and he knew Ricky wouldn't be far behind. Valerie was as good as gone, and where did that leave him at almost fifty years old? More than anything else, Jack feared being abandoned.

'Yeah,' he said somewhat caustically to the doctor in front of him, 'I guess you could say there's been some undue stress in my life.'

Dr Haas scribbled something on a pad of paper, ripped off the top sheet and handed it to Jack. 'Here's the name and number of someone I think can help you,' he said.

Jack took the slip of paper. 'Is he a specialist in this sort of thing?'

'In a way,' Haas agreed. 'He's a psychiatrist.'

Jack reared up in his seat. 'A shrink? You want me to go to a shrink?'

'The days of voodoo and witch doctors are over, Mr Marsh,' the physician said mildly. 'If you want to resolve your problem, I believe this man is someone who can help you. He's one of the best in the Bay Area and I've been referring patients to him for many years now. With significant success, I might add.'

Jack stuffed the piece of paper into his pocket, mumbled his thanks, and left. Shit, it wasn't a shrink he needed, he told himself, it was the right woman. After Kate had gone, he had tried a few others, here and there, but those who attracted him were all young and spoiled and expected him to perform like some goddam circus acrobat. Which made his difficulty just that much worse.

There was always Valerie, he knew, but doing it to her was like balling a corpse. She would just lie there with her eyes closed as if to say, 'Do what you need to do.' And then, of course, he couldn't do a thing, guaranteed.

No matter, no shrink was going to go poking into his head, asking him questions he didn't want to answer, trying to get him to discuss things Jack didn't even discuss with himself. He threw the psychiatrist's name into the first trash can he came to, on his way to meeting up with a couple of his drinking buddies.

4

Ricky slid his big Harley-Davidson out of the bushes beside the house, where he had gotten into the habit of keeping it, and wheeled it down the driveway. It was just after ten-thirty. His mother was already in bed, and his father, as usual, was not yet home. Nevertheless, he walked the bike for a few blocks along Delgada before climbing on and kicking the engine into life.

Two years ago, he had told his parents that he had gotten a part-time job at a store in San Mateo, cleaning up and running errands and stuff for a Mr Mandelbaum, for pocket money that he took under the table since he was underage. It was how he explained where he went on Saturdays during the school year and on weekdays during the summer vacation, as well as some of the things he acquired, like the scarred leather bomber jacket he wore everywhere, even to mass on Sundays, when his mother was able to drag herself, and him, to church, and the secondhand motorcycle. He said he bought the motorcycle for two hundred dollars. Actually, it had cost him twelve hundred. His parents never bothered to check any of it out.

Ricky sped along Delgada and down Alhambra and turned right onto Route 1. Traffic was light at this time of night, and he cruised easily, and unnoticed, north toward Pacifica. He liked the feel of the big bike beneath him, liked having control of all that power, liked the freedom it gave him to go wherever he wanted.

He had picked out the place three weeks ago, going back at least half a dozen times to check every detail, every approach, every possible pitfall. He had even chosen the night with particular care – Monday night, because of *Monday Night Football*.

The Vistamar Bar had brought in one of those new big-screen television sets at the beginning of the season, and the place jumped on Monday nights. By the time Ricky reached Pacifica, the game would be over, the crowd dispersed, and the cash register full.

Stars twinkled all around him and a thin sliver of moon hung over his left shoulder. It wasn't especially warm or cool, but it wouldn't have mattered either way. Ricky wore his bomber jacket. In the right-hand pocket, he could feel the weight of the Browning automatic he had bought off Marvin at the pawnshop two weeks ago.

'What do you want with that?' the old man had asked when Ricky pulled it out of the showcase and plunked down the money for its purchase. 'You don't go into occupied houses.'

'You never know what can happen,' the teenager replied casually. 'I just want to be prepared.'

'Do you know how to shoot one of these things?'

Ricky shrugged. 'I know how to shoot a .22. It can't be that much different.'

The Browning didn't come with any ammunition, but Marvin promised to try and locate some. It didn't matter. Ricky had no intention of loading it or pulling the trigger. He just needed something that looked impressive to wave around when he walked into the bar.

Among his other purchases for the occasion were a pair of cowboy boots with two-inch heels that disguised his height, and a shirt with a turtleneck collar that he could pull up over a good portion of his face. He practiced with both for over a week, until he could walk in the boots without stumbling and talk through the shirt without mumbling.

When he reached Devil's Slide, that narrow strip of road that hugged the ocean and separated the coastal communities from the city of Pacifica, Ricky let the Harley's throttle all the way out and took the bike zooming around the treacherous curves as though they were straightaways.

'Hey, look at me!' he shouted to the rocky witnesses.

He rolled into the Vistamar's parking lot at ten minutes past eleven. As he had anticipated, the Monday night crowd was gone, and a quick check through the front window revealed that the bartender was alone behind the bar, washing up the last round of glasses.

Ricky left the Harley at the far end of the lot, well out of sight of anyone inside, and made his way to the door. His whole body was taut with excitement, every nerve ending on alert. He hadn't felt this good since that first time when he had ripped off Connie Gilchrist. He pushed open the door and went inside.

The big TV had been turned off and most of the place was in shadow. Only the bar was still lit, and the man behind it. Ed Costello had had a long day and he was anxious to clean up, close up, and go home. His wife was a stewardess for United Airlines, and this month she was on the Tokyo run. They hadn't spent more than two days together in the past ten. Tonight was the first night in more than a week that she would be warming his bed, and he didn't intend to miss a single moment of it. He didn't even turn around when he heard the door.

'Sorry, we're closed,' he called.

'That's okay,' came the soft reply. 'I don't want a drink.'

The hair rose suddenly on the back of Costello's neck

and he felt his heart sink into his stomach. He turned slowly around to find a very nasty-looking pistol pointing directly at him from the other side of the bar.

'Shit,' Costello muttered under his breath, because he had worked at the bar for five years now, and he had never been held up.

'Very carefully,' said the guy with the gun, 'take the bills out of the drawer and put them in this.' Ricky slid a small leather bag with a shoulder strap across the bar. 'And keep your hands and your feet where I can see them at all times.' The teenager had to smother a giggle. It was a line he had lifted off an episode of *Hawaii Five-O*.

Costello didn't argue. He began stuffing the bag with the night's take. *If I give him what he wants*, the bartender reasoned, *he'll just go away*. It had been a good night, and Costello had already done a rough estimate of the proceeds. He knew there had to be at least a thousand dollars in the cash register. The owner would throw a fit, but hell, it was only money, Costello decided, and no amount of money was worth risking his life trying to be some kind of hero. Besides, he couldn't bear the thought of never holding his wife in his arms again. He came within six inches of the alarm button, but he didn't even glance at it.

When the register was empty, Ricky took the bag and slung it across his shoulder the way he had seen women do sometimes with their purses.

'Okay,' he instructed, 'climb up on the bar and lie face-down.' Costello did as he was told. 'Now, I'm going to walk out of here, and you're not going to move, not for five minutes. Five minutes, count them. 'Cause if you do, my buddy outside is going to drill you between the eyes.' That sounded like something he had heard in a Charles Bronson movie.

The bartender didn't believe for a minute that there was a buddy outside, but he didn't move for five minutes anyway, closer to ten, actually. Half an hour later, after the Pacifica police arrived and asked him for a description of the perpetrator, all Costello could remember was the gun – big, black, and ugly.

Ricky laughed all the way home. He had watched the bills going into the leather bag, he knew there were a lot of them. When he finally finished counting them out, after separating them and stacking them in little piles in the middle of his bed, as he always did, he realized that he had taken in more in this one night than he had earned in six months of working for Marvin Mandelbaum, and he didn't have to share a dollar of it with anyone. And even better was that he had done it with an unloaded gun.

Ricky's high lasted for days. He couldn't believe he had actually pulled it off. He couldn't believe he was finally out from under Marvin Mandelbaum's thumb. Eleven hundred bucks for ten minutes' worth of work, and it was all his. At this rate, he concluded, he could be a millionaire before he hit twenty-one. He walked through the week with an imbecilic grin plastered across his face. Chris accused him of doing cocaine or something, but Ricky shook his head and just kept on grinning.

'I got it,' Chris declared on Saturday afternoon, as they sat under a eucalyptus tree on the hill above the Marsh house and munched on tuna fish sandwiches. 'It's Nancy Thaler's party tonight – the private one you're expecting on the side, that is.'

'You got it,' Ricky replied, and it wasn't a total lie.

He had been thinking a lot about Nancy Thaler lately, too. In fact, he had come in the shower this morning, thinking about Nancy Thaler. Now, as he dressed in a clean pair of jeans and T-shirt, he said a little prayer that he would know what to do when the time came. It was one thing to play cool in front of Chris, or fantasize when he was by himself, but quite another to actually pull it off with a real live girl. At the last moment, he kicked off his sneakers and slipped on the cowboy boots, figuring that a little extra height couldn't hurt, and maybe some of the confidence he had built up from Monday night might even rub off.

He got to the Thaler house at eight-thirty, an hour after the party had begun, roaring up the gravel drive on his Harley, leaving a noticeable rut.

About twenty teenagers were already there, the sounds of laughter and Led Zeppelin filling the air as Nancy opened the front door seconds after his knock. She had probably been waiting for him in the hallway, Ricky told himself.

'Hi,' she said with a bright smile. She was all dressed up in a frilly blouse and a long flowery skirt. 'I thought maybe you weren't coming,' she added. 'I'm glad you did.'

'Yeah,' he said lamely, 'me, too.' Christ, he couldn't believe he had said that. He dug the toe of one boot into the thick shag carpet, wishing he were somewhere else, and wondering where his great confidence had gone all of a sudden.

'Do you want something to drink?' Nancy asked, taking hold of his arm and drawing him toward the living room. 'We've got some beer, and Denny Henderson brought a bottle of vodka.'

Ricky tapped the pocket of his bomber jacket. 'No thanks,' he said. 'I got some grass for later.' He looked around. 'Where are your folks?'

'Over the hill,' Nancy said with a slow smile, meaning San Mateo, 'for dinner and a double feature.'

Ricky smiled broadly in return. 'That sounds promising,' he murmured, hoping he sounded more sophisticated than scared.

'Hey, man,' Chris called from across the way. 'About time you showed up.'

He had his arm around a pretty redhead. Theresa Hoyt was a junior, and she and Chris had been going together for six months now. The older girls had always looked at Chris, because he was so tall. A senior had even invited him to the prom last year. But he and Theresa were together now, Chris's arm drooping proprietarily over her shoulder, his hand occasionally brushing against her breast as though by accident.

Ricky raised an eyebrow. 'Don't look like you missed me very much,' he called back.

'Hey, Marsh,' Denny Henderson shouted, 'what are *you* doing associating with us ordinary folk?'

Denny Henderson had been large in the sixth grade, but he was enormous now as he waddled rather than walked in Ricky's direction. Except for Chris, few kids on the Coast liked Ricky, but they respected him and they knew if they stayed out of his way, he'd stay out of theirs. It was an arrangement that suited everyone.

'Every once in a while, a guy's got to check out the riffraff,' Ricky said to the obese teen.

Denny hooted, and his whole midsection began to shake like a dish of Jell-O. 'This is a first, you know,' he told Nancy. 'Marsh showing up at a party. Can't ever remember him doing that before.'

Nancy batted her eyelashes demurely. 'Then I'm honored,' she cooed, speaking to Denny but pressing up against Ricky.

He wished his bomber jacket could have been just a few inches longer so it would have hidden the sudden bulge in his tight-fitting jeans. Instead, he sort of

300

hunched over and clasped his hands in front of him in what he hoped looked like some kind of reasonably casual move.

The doorbell rang again, and Nancy scurried over to answer it. Ricky took hasty advantage of her departure, crossing the room to an unoccupied armchair where he sank into its plush depths and folded one leg over the other to conceal himself. Satisfied that he was safe, he reached down and pulled some pot out of his jacket pocket.

A senior loomed over him. 'Is that stuff you got any good, man?'

'Acapulco Gold,' Ricky replied. He lit up and took a substantial hit before passing the joint on.

'Cool,' the senior said and was gone, the reefer with him. It didn't matter. There was lots more where that had come from.

From his particular vantage point, Ricky could pretty much take in the whole party. He noted who paired up with whom, who was deliberately ignoring whom, and who was trying to get the attention of whom. As for himself, Ricky wasn't much of a social animal, far preferring to go one on one than to be stuck like this in the middle of a crowd. It wasn't that he didn't know just about everyone here, it was that he didn't have anything to say to any of them. He had come tonight for one reason only, because Nancy Thaler had as good as said that she would put out, and he was willing to go along with all the other crap to see if that actually happened.

It was already past eleven o'clock by the time she sidled up to him and suggested they might go for a walk on the beach. Ricky got up from the armchair and followed her through a pair of French doors, across a redwood deck, and down a dirt path that turned to sand as it led to the water. He had smoked three joints by this time, and his earlier jitters had all but vanished.

The stars were brighter than he had ever seen them, the waves slapping up the sand were more seductive than he had ever noticed, the Pillar Point fog horn was more melodious than he had ever heard it, and Nancy Thaler was by far the most beautiful girl in the whole world, with her blond hair and her creamy skin and her bright eyes sparkling in the moonlight.

He felt himself stirring and stiffening, and he reached out without a word and drew her to him by a hand at the back of her neck.

'What,' she said with a nervous giggle, 'no small talk first?'

'No,' he said, and fastened his lips to hers, pushing his tongue past her teeth and into the cavern of her mouth in what he hoped was true jock style. She tasted of guacamole, which was something he detested, but he sloshed his tongue around anyway.

She pulled away first, but only to entice him to follow her farther down the beach, out of sight of the house. Then she came back to him, this time pushing her tongue into his mouth.

'I guess now you can't say that you're sweet sixteen and never been kissed,' he gasped when they finally unhooked.

He saw her teeth flash in the moonlight. 'I always said if I got to be sixteen and hadn't done it yet,' she told him, 'I was damn well gonna do it, right then and there.'

'Does that mean I'm elected?' He still couldn't believe his good luck, her just handing herself to him on a platter like this, without him having to do a single little thing about it.

'You're elected,' she replied huskily. 'Unless you have a problem with that.'

'I don't got any problems at all,' he assured her. In case she had picked him because she thought he had a lot of experience or something, and knew what he was doing, he said a little prayer that it would all come out right.

She reached up and peeled off his bomber jacket. 'Kinda warm for this, isn't it?' she asked coyly.

'Yeah,' he agreed. He leaned over and tugged her frilly blouse free of her skirt and up over her head. She wasn't wearing a bra. He gulped. Her full breasts gleamed in the moonlight.

'You can touch them,' she invited, arching her back toward him.

He put his hands out cautiously, his heart beginning to pound, his mouth suddenly dry. Her breasts felt like warm mounds of alabaster, so smooth and firm they barely moved as he grasped them. The dark knobs at the ends pressed invitingly into his palms.

'Nice,' he managed to murmur.

'Nice?' she challenged. 'They're perfect.'

'Sure,' he corrected himself hastily. 'That's what I meant.'

Nancy sank her fingers into his hair and pulled his face down against her, pushing one of her nipples against his lips. Ricky felt an incredible surge in his crotch. He began to suck a little, feeling the nipple grow big and hard like a marble inside his mouth. The sensation in his crotch became pain and he sank to his knees, gasping.

'Don't stop,' she urged him, wrapping her arms around his head, so he captured the marble again and sucked on it some more.

Dimly, he felt her yanking on his T-shirt, and he disengaged long enough for her to pull it over his head. Then she put her hands at her waist and her skirt dropped. She wasn't wearing any panties, either.

Ricky couldn't stand it anymore. He pulled her down and pushed her back onto the sand and fumbled at his jeans until he got them open and his readiness sprang out for her to admire.

'Wow,' she exclaimed in a throaty voice.

With his jeans down around his cowboy boots, he rolled on top of her, groping with his hand between her legs until he found what he thought was the right place, and attempted to push himself into her.

'Not there!' she hissed beneath him.

Ricky froze. Oh shit, he thought in dismay, how many choices were there, and how could he have been so bare-assed stupid as to get the wrong one? He wished he had listened more attentively when basic anatomy had been discussed in school. Hell, he'd grown up with three sisters, hadn't he? How lame could a guy be? Now she would know he was nothing but a loser, a nerd. Worse, she would spread it all over the goddam school.

'I want to do it the regular way the first time,' Nancy was purring beneath him. 'I don't want to do any of that kinky stuff until I really know what I'm doing.'

Ricky let out his breath in relief. She was so cherry she didn't even realize that he'd blown it. Okay, he had a second chance to get it right, and he was going to take full advantage of it. He fumbled around for another possibility, and finding one, explored it first with a finger, and then waited for a reaction. Nancy moaned. Ricky grinned in the darkness, and plunged.

It was over almost before he knew it, and he cried out with wanting it to last. For one unbelievable moment, he had been in a place that was so soft and embracing and exciting that he couldn't contain himself. It was a whole lot better than coming in the shower, where he always felt a little wicked, and he was glad when he could stop manipulating himself, just in case God or his mother happened to peek into the bathroom.

He glanced down at Nancy. He had almost forgotten who she was, but he now felt a warm glow of affection for her.

She was staring up at him in consternation. 'It didn't happen,' she said.

'Whaddya mean?'

'I mean, it didn't happen. I didn't come.'

'Well, why not?' he asked.

'I don't know,' she replied. 'How should I know? Did you do everything right?'

'Of course, I did everything right,' he said, wondering what he had done wrong.

'Well then, do it again,' she said.

'I can't,' he told her, after a moment or two, now in acute embarrassment. 'I mean, not right now.'

'Why not?'

He gulped. 'I don't know why,' he said, his misery complete. 'I just can't.'

She started to cry. 'Is there something wrong with me?'

'I don't think so,' he said graciously, hoping fervently that there was. 'You felt just right to me.' He stuck his hand between her legs. She shivered. 'See, you felt that, didn't you?'

'Uh-huh.'

'Then there's nothing wrong with you.'

'Do that some more,' she suggested.

Ricky shrugged and began to rub her cautiously.

'Harder,' she instructed, spreading her thighs a bit. 'Do it harder.'

Ricky did as she requested, and after a while, she began to moan.

'Oooh! That's it,' she cried suddenly. 'That's the spot. Do it right there.'

Ricky stroked her where she indicated until she was practically writhing on the sand, and looking down, much to his surprise, he found himself able again, so he rolled on top of her and thrust himself inside and started to pump for all he was worth, wondering how absurd he would surely look to someone passing by. Almost immediately, Nancy let out a shriek, and her whole body arced and shuddered and then collapsed. He kept on pumping, as she lay limp beneath him, until he climaxed. It took longer and was even better than the first time.

'That was marvelous,' she breathed after a while. 'My hands and feet are all tingly.'

'Happy Birthday,' he muttered.

Nancy giggled. 'When's *your* birthday?' she asked coyly. 'Maybe we can do it again then.'

'In April.'

'Oh,' she said, disappointed. 'I don't want to wait that long.'

'That's good,' he mumbled, feeling warm and drowsy. He pressed his face into her fantastic breasts.

'Don't you dare go to sleep,' she chided.

He shook himself. 'I won't.'

'Do you know why I picked you?' she cooed.

He didn't have a clue. 'Because I look like Robert Redford?'

Nancy hooted. 'You don't look anything like Robert Redford, silly.'

'Then why?'

'Because I wanted my first time to be with someone who knew what he was doing.'

'Really?' Ricky managed to say, all but choking on the word.

'Uh-huh,' Nancy assured him. 'I never dug all that crap about love and two people learning about life together that my mother's always dishing out. Did you get that from your parents, too?'

'Oh, sure,' he agreed. In his whole sixteen and a half years, he had never heard the word *sex*, or anything that could even remotely be described as being connected with sex, pass his mother's lips.

'Well, I'm glad you didn't listen, either,' Nancy said with a giggle.

After a while, they did it again, now that Ricky had the hang of it, thrashing around until they were spent, and found themselves sticky with sand and sweat, and admitted to being pretty uncomfortable. So they ran down the beach and jumped into the water, able to stand the cold for only a few seconds.

'Oooh, I'm freezing,' Nancy said through chattering teeth.

'Jump up and down,' Ricky told her. They both did, Ricky noticing that her breasts barely moved, until they had warmed up and were dry, and then they put on their clothes and went back up to the Thaler house.

Ricky was fairly floating. Each time they had done it, it had gotten better. Of course, having to worry about Nancy was a pain, but he was quick enough to know that good looks and charm weren't enough in the dark. If a girl wasn't able to please herself, he was going to have to learn how to do it for her. Or he wouldn't be invited back. And now that he knew what it was really like, he definitely intended to be invited back.

It was well past midnight. Almost everyone was gone by the time they got back to the party, and her parents were halfway up the drive.

Ricky left, with a last lingering kiss and furtive grope, promising Nancy they would see each other again real soon. He gunned his motorcycle down the gravel and headed for El Granada, with the breeze cooling his face, trying to decide which had been a better high – the one he had gotten from fucking Nancy Thaler three times tonight, or the one he had gotten from holding up the Vistamar Bar in Pacifica on Monday.

Both had made him feel like a giant. He sat high in his saddle and pulled the Harley's throttle all the way out. He had almost five thousand dollars socked away for a rainy day and a girl he could have anytime he wanted her. Five thousand would do until he wanted more. Nancy Thaler would do until he wanted someone else.

Ricky grinned. He couldn't believe his good fortune. Life was just one big con, he decided. As long as you were one step smarter than the people around you, you could get away with just about anything. He was only sixteen years old and the world was his.

5

One day drifted into the next. The house was so still, the world so warm and fuzzy, that there was no reason for Valerie to distinguish one from another. Sometimes, there didn't even seem to be a reason for getting out of bed. Jack left early in the morning and came home late at night. Ricky left shortly after his father and came home whenever he felt like it. And along with Priscilla and JJ and Rosemary, Ellen was now gone.

There was no point in her cooking anymore, either. Neither Jack nor Ricky hung around for breakfast, it was rare that Jack came home for dinner, Ricky always seemed to have eaten something somewhere else, and she was never very hungry herself. The house got cleaned when she thought of it, and the laundry, which in years past used to take up half of every day, could now be done in one day . . . whenever she remembered.

When Valerie finally did drag herself out of bed, occasionally even managing to shower and dress, she would make her way downstairs to the kitchen and pull out the bottle of bourbon she kept hidden under the sink where Jack would never think to look. She would pour some into a coffee cup and sit at the table and sip at it, for hours sometimes, refilling the cup reflexively until the bottle was empty. Then she would find her handbag and walk down Avenida del Oro to the Coast Highway and take the bus to the store in Half Moon Bay to replenish her supply. She had Jack to thank for the bourbon. Without it being in the house all these years, she would never have begun to drink it, never have acquired a taste for it, never have known the blissful oblivion it could bring. She had Jack to thank for a lot of things.

Between the bourbon and the pills, life was almost bearable. Dr Wheeler had prescribed the pills for her when it was clear that she needed help to sleep. But the truth was that she also needed help to wake . . . to breathe . . . to keep from thinking . . . to get through one more day.

'The house is so terribly quiet and empty these days,' she told him. 'I keep listening for the sound of the front door telling me that JJ is home, or the sound of a cough telling me that Priscilla has the croup again. It's so strange, because I know they're both gone.'

Sometimes, she forgot all about her lunch shift at the Gray Whale. She was working only four days a week now, but one day was so much the same as another that she couldn't always remember which days she was on and which days she was off.

Leo never complained. He never even said a word. He got Donna to fill in when it was necessary. And he kept on paying Valerie, whether she showed up or not. She never knew the difference. There were only two things she could count on keeping track of – the bourbon and the pills.

If she didn't know what day it was, she often didn't know what time of the year it was, either. In northern California, one season was pretty much the same as another, and it was easy to forget. Except that she knew what today was.

It was December 18, the day she and the children

should have been on their way to Rutland, to spend the holiday with her family. Only she was here instead, and the children were all gone except for Ricky, and she didn't have the faintest idea what she would be doing on Christmas Day. She tried to think. She would have to ask Ricky if he was going to be home. She would have to ask Jack if he wanted a holiday dinner. For some reason, the idea of cooking a big meal made her head hurt.

Valerie looked in the medicine cabinet. The bottle of little green pills was almost empty.

'Good morning, Mrs Marsh,' Dennis Murphy greeted her as she entered pharmacy. 'And how is everything with you today?'

'Everything is fine, Mr Murphy,' Valerie replied with a vague smile.

'The wife and I missed seeing you in church on Sunday,' the pharmacist said. 'You're usually so regular, we were hoping there was nothing wrong.'

Valerie frowned. 'My goodness, did I miss mass?' she murmured. 'I didn't mean to. I don't remember. I guess I must not have been feeling very well.'

'Planning big things for the holidays, are you?' he inquired. 'I remember, a few months ago, you saying you were going to be here this year, for the first time in many years.'

'For the first time in ten years, Mr Murphy,' she said, hoping she sounded happy about it. 'And I'm afraid I'm a little behind on my planning. But since you ask, I have a list as long as my arm in my handbag.'

'Well, then, I expect you'll be wanting your prescription, so I'll just go on in the back and get it for you,' he declared.

'Thank you, Mr Murphy,' she murmured. He was

such a nice man, she thought, a gentle man, a kind man. Without quite understanding why, she found herself envying Dennis Murphy's wife.

6

Ricky sat easily on the Harley at the far end of the parking lot, with the collar of his bomber jacket pulled up against the cool January night, and waited and watched. It was almost eleven-thirty, but there were still a number of customers in the liquor shop. It had to be a final flurry of buying for the big day tomorrow, he decided. Tomorrow was Super Bowl Sunday. It didn't matter. He knew the store would stay open until two o'clock, and every purchase filled the cash register that much fuller.

He had picked this particular place with great care, just as he had picked the bar in Pacifica back in October, and the gas station and quick-stop shop on Highway 1 over Thanksgiving weekend. In both cases, he had come away with at least a grand. Tonight, he expected to double that.

Ricky had had his eye on the Daly City Discount Liquor Mart since before Christmas. The layout was perfect for his purpose, a small shopping center that backed onto the highway. The Chinese restaurant, the mom-and-pop grocery, the dry cleaners, the stationery store, and the beauty parlor that shared the one-story, L-shaped space were all closed up by ten o'clock. The liquor store itself was a narrow rectangle at one end, with a main entrance and rear entrance and no surprises. Only one clerk was working the Saturday night shift. Ricky had dropped in around nine, when the place had been buzzing, to make sure.

Headlights washed briefly across the front of the Harley as a police car pulled into the parking lot. Ricky tensed, slid down in his seat, and ducked his head. Two officers climbed out of the front, one tall and skeletal with a shock of light hair, the other shorter and heavyset and balding. The two stood outside for a moment stretching their back muscles before they pushed their way through the double glass doors into the brightly lit interior of the liquor store. Ricky strained over the handlebars to peer inside as the policemen came in and out of view, sauntering up one aisle and down another, finally deciding on two six-packs of beer and what looked from the distance to be a bottle of whiskey. They paid for their purchases, laughing appreciatively at something the clerk apparently said, and then they left the store with their paper sacks, got back into the police car, and drove away.

The boy on the motorcycle let out his breath. What would he have done if they had chosen to come by, say, an hour later, while he was in there, doing his thing? He rapped his knuckles smartly against the handlebar.

Marsh, you live lucky, he told himself.

He settled back to wait until the last car had pulled out of the parking lot and no new ones had appeared for half an hour.

At twelve-forty-five, he climbed off the Harley and started across the blacktop, patting the right-hand pocket of his bomber jacket where he kept the Browning and slipping the leather bag off his shoulder. When he reached the glass doors, he stopped to pull the collar of his turtleneck up over his face.

The clerk was seated behind the counter, absorbed in a paperback book. He didn't even glance up when Ricky entered.

'Good book?' Ricky inquired politely.

314

'Not very,' the clerk replied with a yawn, 'but it helps to pass the—' He looked up into the muzzle of the Browning. 'Jesus,' he breathed, the book dropping from his hands.

'Just take it easy, and no one gets hurt,' Ricky told him.

The clerk nodded.

'Slowly now, empty the cash register, bills only, please.' Ricky tossed the leather bag on the counter. 'Put them in this.'

Jose Alia was a part-time employee, working an average of twenty hours a week to pick up needed money while he was getting his degree from City College. No benefits, no vacation time, just minimum wage, but it was the best job he had been able to find. His boss was a nice guy, but routinely deducted any losses, due to breakage or pilferage, from Jose's already meager paycheck. At that rate, Jose would have to spend almost a year working for nothing to pay off what was in the cash register at this moment.

The store served a section of town that, according to Jose's calculations, was ninety-five percent blue-collar and one hundred percent alcoholic. For roughly four hours tomorrow afternoon, every TV in the neighborhood would be tuned in to the Super Bowl, and every hand would be wrapped around some kind of booze. The mart had been hopping all day, and even with discount prices, there had to be at least three grand in that box.

'Hey, man,' the clerk whined. 'You don't really want to do this, do you? It's against the law.' Jose's accent tended to grow thicker in times of stress.

Ricky brought the Browning up to eye level. 'Don't I?'

'This don't hurt the boss,' Jose persisted. 'It's coming right out of my pocket.'

'Too bad,' Ricky replied. 'Ask for a raise.'

'You make a joke, mister?'

'Does this look like it?'

Jose looked at the gun and then at the startling yellow eyes right behind it and knew this was no joke. He sighed and moved cautiously toward the cash register. He had tried to reason with the man. Now it was out of his hands. He used his right forefinger to push the release button on the register. He used his left foot to push the silent alarm button on the floor in front of him.

Jose began to count the seconds silently in his head, as he pulled the bills out of the drawers and placed them in the leather bag. Twice, to slow things down, he managed to drop some of the twenties, and had to bend down to retrieve them. Yellow Eyes never even blinked. When he had counted off one minute and fifty-five seconds, Jose stuffed the last of the money into the bag.

'Here you go, man. And I hope it's going to make you happy.'

Ricky took the bag and slung it across his shoulder. 'You have no idea,' he said with a grin. He turned toward the door and was halfway out before he saw the tall skeleton and the heavyset baldy in police uniforms waiting on the other side, faces set, guns drawn. Ricky whirled around, but Jose stood calmly behind him with a blunt-nosed revolver pointing directly at Ricky's chest.

Jose Alia shrugged. 'I tried to tell you, man,' he said softly. 'It's against the law.'

Tom Starwood leaned back in his chair, stretching its ancient wooden joints to their limit, and looked out the window of his third-floor office. He had just spent the last two hours studying the probation report on one

Ricky Marsh, and he wanted to weep. He pulled off his glasses and rubbed wearily at his pale eyes and the bridge of his nose.

A lot of reports had come across his desk in the last six years as a public defender in the juvenile justice system, and the one he had just finished was no better or worse than most, he knew. But there was something about it that had gotten to him.

'Don't ever let yourself get personally involved with these kids,' his mentor, the man he worked for, told him. 'They'll break your heart, every time.'

In six years, Ricky Marsh was the second kid to get to him, and like it or not, Tom Starwood was hooked. He looked again at the photograph attached to the report, at the slight body, the angelic face, the compelling eyes, and he felt the old familiar tug at his vitals. The boy reminded him so much of Jeremy.

Jeremy would have been twenty-three next week, but for the past six years, Tom had spent part of each February 8 beside a grave in a bleak cemetery in Colma, thinking of what might have been.

According to the police report, Jeremy Starwood died from an overdose of cocaine mixed with alcohol, but the guilt-ridden father knew that his son had really died of parental neglect.

Tom's wife had deserted them when Jeremy was five. Just up and left without warning one morning, between the breakfast dishes and the dirty laundry, with her husband off at work and her son safely in kindergarten. Tom knew why. It was because of his job – his job as a police officer. Most of their arguments had been about his being a cop, her anxiety, his indifference. Tom searched for her for months, but it was in vain. Neither he nor Jeremy ever saw her again.

Ironically, it was her leaving that made Tom finally

decide to quit the police force. He knew it was one thing for him to be selfish while his wife was there, but it was quite another for him to be a cop as a single parent. If anything were to happen to him, Jeremy would have no one. Tom had no family, and he had never known much about his wife's people.

They moved to a small apartment in a cheaper neighborhood and Tom took a job at a gas station, because it was easy work, and at the time, he had few other marketable skills. Four months later, he went back to school. He had completed two years of college before joining the force. He needed sixty more credits for his degree, and then he thought he would apply to law school.

'Why do you want to be an attorney, Mr Starwood?' the admissions officer had asked.

'Because I want to help people,' he had replied. 'I can't be a policeman anymore, I'm a single parent, with a young son to raise, and the law seems like the next best alternative.'

The school accepted him, and even scrounged up some scholarship money to help him out. Four nights a week, he fixed Jeremy a hurry-up dinner, asked a neighbor to check on him every once in a while, in case the boy got sick or something, and drove off in his battered Chevy.

It took eight long, hard years, during which Tom pumped gas seven hours a day, and studied twelve, and had little time for the boy growing up in the background. Somewhere along the way, he took a weekend job as a bartender at a hopping place over in South City, just to keep up with the bills.

Sometimes, Jeremy would help him study, holding the book open in front of him while Tom searched his mind for the answers to questions he knew would appear on one exam or another. Occasionally, father and son would go to the park together on a Sunday afternoon, and throw a baseball or two. But not very often. Most of the time, the boy was left to fend for himself.

Tom finally graduated in June of 1968, placing fifth in his class. A prestigious law firm in San Francisco hired him almost immediately, at a starting salary that was more than he had earned in the whole previous eight years, including his scholarship money. He bought himself a brand-new Oldsmobile and a three-piece suit, and began working fourteen hours a day. He did so well that, after a couple of years, his firm promoted him to senior associate and began trusting him with important, out-of-town assignments. It was well known that he was on the fast track for making partner.

Jeremy had reached his teens by then, old enough to stay by himself. At least, Tom assumed he was. It never occurred to him to ask. They moved to a nice house in the Westlake district, and for his sixteenth birthday, Tom bought Jeremy a secondhand Ford. But he never thought to question where the boy went when he drove off night after night. Kids have to be kids, he told himself. They need their space. It seemed logical. He certainly wished his parents had given him more space when he was a teenager.

Tom didn't realize how little he really knew about his son until a cold day in February when he got a telephone call from the Daly City police.

After a two-month drinking binge and a severe case of pneumonia that left him fifteen pounds lighter, Tom left the prestigious law firm, by mutual agreement, and went to work as a public defender for San Mateo County, in the Juvenile Division. He had been too busy to save his own son. Now he would dedicate his life to saving the sons of others.

There was a light tap on his door, and Tom looked up to see Mary Elizabeth Battaglia, the probation officer assigned to Ricky's case, standing there.

'Have you read the Marsh report?' she asked.

Tom nodded. 'Just finished.'

'Can't send him home. We're talking armed robbery here. It would set a very dangerous precedent.'

'Yeah,' Tom agreed. He had asked her to consider it, but he hadn't held out much hope.

'It's too bad,' she added. 'He seems like such a nice kid. He's bright, he's polite, and he looks like an angel. It makes you wonder, sometimes, doesn't it, what the world is coming to when someone like that ends up here.'

'Yeah, it makes you wonder,' Tom echoed, but he didn't really wonder. He already knew.

'I'm going to recommend continuing custody and six months in placement,' she told him. 'I'm pretty sure the judge will go for it.'

'Okay,' Tom said. 'Thanks, Mel.' It was a typical disposition for a first offense of this nature and under these circumstances, and the attorney could not have reasonably expected anything else.

'Lunch?' Mel suggested. They often shared meals. She was an attractive woman in her early forties, if a bit overweight, who favored severely cut suits and plain blouses.

'No, not today, sorry,' Tom replied. 'I've got to go talk to the kid, tell him what to expect, and then I've got to get some of this shit off my desk.' He gestured to a six-inch stack of files. 'Maybe tomorrow?'

'Sure,' Mel said easily. 'See you in court.' She ducked out of the office with a wave.

7

Connie Gilchrist pulled her front door shut, inserted the alarm key in the lock, turned it to the left, and waited for the little red light to come on. After the second robbery, she had hired a company to wire her doors and windows to a horn on the exterior wall of the house, and connected an emergency line from her telephone to the county sheriff's office. And she made sure that Ricky Marsh knew about it.

She could never prove it, of course, but Connie had a pretty good idea who the culprit was. Each one of her favorite hiding places had been ferreted out, with nothing else disturbed. It didn't take a genius to realize that the thief had known exactly where to go and exactly what to look for.

Valerie had been genuinely horrified when Connie reported the crimes to her, and given her fragile condition, Connie could never bring herself to air her suspicions. She simply protected herself as best she could and kept quiet, even when word of other burglaries began to spread throughout the neighborhood.

But then, just as suddenly as they had begun, they stopped. For several months, Connie wondered why. Then she heard on the news about the attempted robbery at the liquor store, and she understood. She picked up the telephone.

'Jack's taking care of everything,' Valerie told her

with tears in her voice. 'I'm so lucky to have Jack to take care of everything.'

Now, Connie left her house and started off on Delgada with a mission. It had taken her close to three years to figure out a plan, and then, last night, the telephone call had come and presented her with exactly what she needed.

She marched up Valerie's driveway, climbed the steps, and rang the doorbell. There was no answer. She rang again, but again there was no response. Connie frowned and glanced at her wristwatch. It was just past eight. She knew that even if Valerie were going out somewhere, it would never be this early in the morning. She usually spent her mornings doing laundry or housework. That was it. Valerie was doing housework and couldn't hear the bell.

Connie reached for the doorknob. As usual, the door was unlocked, and she pushed it open and entered the house, surprised to find Valerie in the living room, sitting on the sofa, staring at the television set, hugging a cup of coffee. On the screen, a children's cartoon was playing itself out.

'Val?' Connie said gently.

The woman looked up. 'Oh hello,' she replied dully.

'What are you doing?'

Valerie shrugged and took a long swallow of coffee. 'Waiting for my soap operas to start,' she said, her words slurring softly.

'Oh,' Connie said, knowing that there weren't any soap operas coming on for at least two hours. The real estate agent bit her lip. What had happened to the sweet, shy, pretty woman she had befriended just a few short years ago? Her beautiful blond hair had lost its sheen, her blue eyes were listless and had dark circles around them, and her face was bloated and pasty.

'Would you like some coffee?' Valerie suddenly thought to ask.

'No, thanks,' Connie answered.

Valerie giggled. 'You probably wouldn't like it anyway,' she whispered conspiratorially. 'It tastes awful, but it makes me feel so . . . good.' She turned her cup upside down. 'It's empty. I'll just go get a little more.'

Connie watched as Valerie pulled herself to her feet and shuffled into the kitchen, where she poured herself a third of a cup of fresh coffee, and topped it off from the bottle of bourbon standing on the counter. Then she shook some pills out of a vial. After stuffing them into her mouth and swallowing them with a gulp from her cup, she turned and looked in Connie's general direction.

'All I ever wanted was to have a houseful of children,' she said, her eyes welling up. 'But they're all gone. Priscilla is dead, Rosemary and JJ could be dead, too, for all I know. Even Ellen ran away, God forgive me for saying so. And now they won't let Ricky come home, and it's all my fault.'

Connie crossed the kitchen in three steps and got to Valerie just as she began to sob uncontrollably. The coffee cup slipped from her grasp and shattered against the floor.

'Oh dear, I'll have to clean it up,' Valerie cried. 'I wouldn't want anyone to see.'

'No, you don't,' Connie declared. 'There's no one to see. And right now, you're coming with me.'

She half dragged, half carried Valerie out of the kitchen, up the stairs, and into the bathroom. Reaching into the shower, she turned the cold water on full force, and pushed her friend under the icy spray. Valerie shrieked and tried to wriggle free, but Connie held her there until they were both soaked through and Valerie was shivering but no longer struggling. Then Connie turned off the water and wrapped her friend in a terry cloth robe.

'Why did you do that?' Valerie asked.

Connie shrugged. 'I don't know. It was something I saw in a movie once.'

'You don't understand,' Valerie told her. 'It's much easier when everything's . . . fuzzy.'

Connie looked at her sharply. 'Except that it takes more and more now to keep you fuzzy, doesn't it?' she asked, but it wasn't really a question. 'A year ago, you took two pills a day. Six months ago, you were taking eight. Now what is it – twelve . . . fourteen?'

'The doctor said I could have them.'

'Did he also say you could wash them down with a quart of bourbon?'

Valerie looked at Connie indignantly. 'I don't drink anything near that much.'

'Don't you?' Connie demanded. 'What would you call a few drops in your coffee, and something in your orange juice, and a couple of shots at lunch, and a few more before dinner, and then maybe one or two before bed?'

'How do you know all that?' Valerie gasped, her face coloring with embarrassment.

'How could I not know?' Connie declared.

Valerie began to cry. 'Do you think the children knew?'

'They lived in this house, Val.'

'Is that why they're all gone?'

'I don't know,' Connie answered gently. 'But how much longer do you want to go on like this? I know you've suffered some big losses in the past few years, but isn't it time to get hold of yourself?'

'You mean, stop taking my pills?' Valerie cried in alarm.

'Yes, and stop drinking.'

'But I couldn't,' Valerie replied. 'I need them to get through the day.'

'No,' Connie retorted. 'What you need is to put your life back together before you lose it completely. Kids are meant to grow up and go away, Val. Maybe some of yours went away before you were ready for them to go, but that happens sometimes. Besides, Ricky isn't going to be in that place forever, and he's going to need you to be here for him when he comes home.'

Valerie wagged her head. 'He doesn't need me anymore,' she said. 'He hasn't needed me in years.'

'Well, I don't agree, but I won't argue the point right now, because I need you, and maybe that will do.'

'What do you mean?'

'I had a telephone call last night from my step-daughter to tell me she's getting married at the end of August,' Connie announced. 'And she wants the most fabulous wedding gown that was ever created. And I told her that I knew just the woman who could make it for her.'

Valerie's mouth dropped open. 'Oh, but I haven't sewed in years,' she said.

'Then I'd say it's high time, wouldn't you?'

Valerie looked down at her trembling hands. 'I don't think I could even hold a needle.'

'It's like riding a bike,' Connie told her. 'You never forget how.'

'Well,' Valerie thought aloud, 'I suppose I could meet her and get an idea of what she wanted and then I could think about it.'

Connie smiled. 'That's a start, isn't it?'

8

It was named Hale House by the authorities. It was called Hell House by the residents. It was a three-story clapboard dwelling, painted an abominable green, in a rundown neighborhood on the outskirts of Martinez. Along with some thirty other youngsters, ranging in age from twelve to seventeen, it was the place Ricky Marsh would call home for six months.

The two cops who arrested him at the liquor store had taken him directly to the local police precinct where he was photographed and fingerprinted and put in a room by himself. He had never been so scared in his life, but by the time someone showed up to take a preliminary statement, he had made a plan.

'I needed the money,' he cried, forcing real tears from his eyes. 'My mother, you see, she's pretty sick, and she can't work or anything, and my dad can't afford to pay for her medicine and everything.'

A version of that story had worked pretty well with Marvin Mandelbaum, Ricky reasoned. It might work here, too. Of course, the truth would have worked better, that his mother was a sloppy drunk and his father was a violent one. But of course, he could never tell them that.

'My brothers and sisters are all grown up and gone away now, and there's only me left to help out. I know what I did was real bad, sir, but I was desperate.'

The officer had a sick mother of his own. He nodded

at Ricky's story, but there was nothing he could do. The next morning, Ricky was taken down to Juvenile Hall and put in a dingy little room with bars on the windows and a pimply thirteen-year-old who had murdered his stepfather.

'I stabbed him with my mother's garden shears,' the boy offered indifferently when Ricky inquired. 'I swore if the sonofabitch crawled into my bed one more night and tried to stick his dick up my ass, I'd kill him. He did, so I had no choice.'

The shock must have shown on Ricky's face because the younger boy laughed.

'Whaddya think this is, man,' he asked waving his arms around the dismal room, 'some goddam summer camp?'

On Tuesday, formal charges against Ricky were filed. On Wednesday, there was a hearing and a public defender from the Juvenile Division, some guy named Starwood, was appointed to represent him. Because of the seriousness of the offense, and the fact that he had used a gun in the commission of his crime, it was decided that he would remain at Juvenile Hall, while Mary Elizabeth Battaglia of the Probation Department proceeded with her investigation.

That was just fine with Ricky. From the look on his father's face when he saw Jack come into the courtroom in the middle of a workday, the boy knew he was safer right where he was.

Five days later, at what Tom Starwood told him was an arraignment, Ricky was instructed to plead guilty to the count of robbery in exchange for the district attorney dropping the firearm enhancement charge. It was some kind of deal that Starwood had worked out and assured him was in his best interests.

On that same Monday, his pimply cell mate was sent

to a hospital for psychiatric observation, and a dour fifteen-year-old who had been busted for possession of cocaine took his place.

'It's my third bust,' the teenager said. 'It's CYA for sure.'

'What's that?' Ricky asked.

'California Youth Authority,' the teen replied with some disdain at Ricky's ignorance. 'It's like real prison, man, and you do real time.'

On February 15, in accordance with the deal worked out by Tom Starwood, a judge ordered Ricky transferred to Hale House for the recommended period of six months.

'It's a country club compared to where I'm going,' his cell mate told him.

Hale House was far from being a country club. The secondfloor room he shared with two other boys was only a fraction larger than the one he had had all to himself at home. By the time three beds and three lockers had been positioned in it, there was barely enough space to stand, much less walk around. But there were no bars on the windows and no locks on the doors, and providing Ricky lived up to the terms of his probation agreement, and obeyed the rules of the house, he was free to come and go as he pleased.

His roommates were both seventeen, both second offenders. The dark-haired one, Eddie Melendez, had been busted for selling pot. The redhead, Patrick Clark, had been caught ripping off a gas station.

'Christ, I had it made,' Patrick elaborated on Ricky's first night. 'It was going down just like a dream, just like it was supposed to, and then a fucking cop pulls in to take a leak. Dumb luck.'

'D'you do pot?' Eddie asked.

Ricky nodded. 'Sure. Can you get any in here?'

'There are ways,' Patrick told him. 'There are always ways.'

'D'you deal?' Eddie wanted to know.

'Nah,' Ricky replied. 'I just use.'

'Too bad, man. Lots of money to be made in dealin'. I used to rip off gas stations and liquor stores, too, till I got smart. Now I got me the sweetest little setup west of Watsonville.'

'If it's so sweet,' Ricky challenged him, 'how come you're in here?'

Eddie shrugged. 'One of my pushers got a little too careless with his mouth. Punk sixth-grader. I'll take care of him when I get out.'

'What about you?' Patrick asked. 'If you know so much, how come you're here?'

'I guess I didn't know as much as I thought I did,' Ricky answered with a sudden grin. 'But next time, I'll be smarter.' Patrick and Eddie grinned back.

There was a knock on the door. 'Lights out,' the hall monitor called.

Patrick's bed was right next to the wall switch. He reached up and flicked the room into darkness. Ricky lay in the unfamiliar surroundings with the unfamiliar sounds. What he had said was true, about being smarter next time. For four years, he had led a charmed life. He had been clever and careful, never acting impulsively, always planning each job out to the last detail, no matter how small, always checking each move from every angle. The six thousand dollars stashed away in his room at home was proof of his ability, and yet he was here, shut up in this place with a bunch of losers, and he didn't understand how it had happened.

He turned into his pillow, and for the first time since the night the Daly City cops had hauled him into the police station, he let the tears come, not realizing that his heaving shoulders shook the flimsy iron bed frame beneath him. He was scared, he was alone, and he was no longer in control.

'It's all right, man,' Eddie's voice came softly out of the darkness. 'First night in is always the hardest.'

It was Eddie who showed him how to crawl out of the second-floor window, slide along the pitch of the roof, and drop down the drainpipe. It was Eddie who knew a dealer where they could score pot. It was Eddie who picked the empty houses they ripped off to get the bread they needed.

After a month, despite the enforced regimen of school and recreation and chores and counseling, Ricky decided there were a lot worse places he could have ended up.

9

In October of 1979, two months after Ricky's release from Hale House, Chris Rodriguez's father drowned, washed off the deck of the fishing boat in a freak storm that ripped up the Pacific Coast and was gone within an hour. Above his mother's protests, Chris quit school and got a job sorting fish on the docks, hoping one day to hire on as crew for one of the more prosperous boat owners.

Ricky had never cared much about school. He had gone to classes while he was at Hell House because it was the rule, but once back home, his interest waned. He was treated differently at Half Moon Bay High now. A scattering of students gazed at him, from a safe distance, with something resembling awe, but the vast majority, including all of his teachers, regarded him with barely concealed contempt. Everyone did the best they could to avoid him, except for Chris, who remained his friend in spite of everything. Nancy Thaler had been forbidden by her parents ever to speak to him again.

Bored, restless, and lonely, Ricky dropped out of school and followed Chris onto the docks. He was put to work from early morning until late at night, for practically nothing, and came home so tired he fell into his bed without even the energy to take off his stinking clothes.

The job lasted five weeks, which was as long as it took for the fishermen to discover that Ricky was selling off the rejects, cut-rate, to restaurant owners who weren't fussy. It was Leo Garvey at the Gray Whale who blew the whistle on him. The fishermen didn't bother to prosecute, they just booted Ricky off Princeton Harbor, and because they knew the two were best friends, they fired Chris as well.

'Look, man, I needed that job,' Chris exclaimed as they walked off the dock. 'More than that, it was my ticket onto one of the boats. My sisters need shoes. My mother needs a coat. I finally got myself a terrific girl – maybe I wanna buy her a Coke once in a while. Now what am I supposed to do?'

'Shit,' Ricky replied in disdain, 'that job was nothing but slave labor.'

'Maybe,' Chris shot back, 'but at least it was honest slave labor – until you had to go and fuck it up.'

Ricky shrugged. 'Anyway, why the hell would you want to be a fisherman after what happened to your dad?'

'Because I do, that's all. Whether you understand it or not.'

'Well then, you're crazy.' Despite his father's death, Chris had not lost his fascination for the sea. It bordered on an obsession that was far beyond Ricky's comprehension.

'This is it, Marsh. I stuck by you all the time you were ripping off your neighbors, and even when you started pointing guns at store clerks, because we were buddies for so long and that meant something to me, and you were only hurting yourself. But now you've hurt me and my family. So, from here on in, you're on your own.'

Ricky was stunned. The liquor store holdup had been well publicized at the time, but he had never been connected to the burglaries. 'How did you know about me ripping off the neighbors?' he demanded.

Chris wagged his head. 'The whole Coast knew, but you quit before anyone could get around to proving it.'

'Well, I'll be damned.'

'Yeah,' Chris replied. 'At the rate you're going, you probably will.' He turned his back on his longtime pal and began the four-mile trudge home.

As Ricky looked after him, a curious, hollow feeling began to steal inside. Chris had been the first and only friend he had ever had. The only person he had ever confided in, even if selectively. Chris had never been above boxing someone's ears or cutting school or doing pot or engaging in some harmless mischief now and again, but both boys had always known where he drew the line. And Ricky had crossed that line.

The seventeen-year-old veteran of the juvenile justice system tossed his head and started up the hill toward home. So be it, he told himself. He didn't need anyone, not even Chris Rodriguez. He'd make it just fine on his own, just the way he always had. But the hollow feeling persisted.

As soon as he reached the house, he locked himself into his room, dug out his cache from its hiding place, counted off five thousand dollars, which was almost all of what remained, and wrapped it into a neat package. After dinner, he rode the Harley into Half Moon Bay, leaving the bike two blocks from the Rodriguez house and walking the rest of the way. He laid the package on the front stoop, rang the bell, and darted across the street to hide behind a tree.

Mrs Rodriguez came to the door, peering out in every direction before she noticed the package at her feet and bent down to pick it up. Ricky had written Chris's name on it and he knew she would take it directly to her son.

Less than sixty seconds later, Chris came bounding through the door, the open package clutched in his hand.

Ricky flattened himself against the tree, and held his breath, but this side of the street was in deep shadow and he knew he wouldn't be seen.

Chris searched up the street and down, looking for the Harley, knowing it had to be there somewhere. He knew where the money had come from, knew how it had been earned. His conscience would tell him to return it, but the thought of his mother and sisters would remind him how badly it was needed. Ricky watched the battle play itself out across his friend's face, already knowing which side would win. After a while, Chris turned and went back into the house.

Ricky rode slowly home. Now that he had taken care of business, he could contemplate the startling information that Chris had revealed. It didn't bother him much that everyone in town knew about the neighborhood burglaries. That was past history. What bothered him was that it meant he'd been careless in some way, left some clue that had tipped people off, when he thought he was being so clever.

He would have to examine that, figure out what he had done, just as he had figured out what had gone wrong at the liquor store. Not that he planned to rip off any more neighbors, that was kid stuff, penny-ante, but just to know, to file it away in his memory bank, in case of a rainy day.

It had taken him a month at Hell House to figure out the silent alarm. Patrick had helped. 'There are security companies out there becoming regular millionaires,' the redhead had said, 'going around installing these systems in small-potato businesses like your liquor store. All they got to do is step on a button, and zap, in two minutes flat, the cops are standing on the doorstep.'

'Shit,' Ricky breathed. 'I never had a chance.'

'You got that right.'

'But there's got to be a way to get around a dumb alarm system.'

'Sure there is,' Patrick agreed. 'You look for the wires. Stuff like that is usually added after a building is built, so there got to be wires running on the outside. All you have to do is cut 'em. Of course, you got to be sure you got the right ones. If you go and cut any electrical wires by mistake, you're dead meat.'

Ricky now had two choices. The first was to go back to school and live the life of an altar boy in the community. But even the thought made his stomach turn. He had had enough of that in Hell House, conning his lawyer and his probation officer and the juvenile authorities into believing that he was truly remorseful for his crime.

Besides, living at home was barely tolerable now. His father wasn't around any more than he had ever been, but his mother had all of a sudden decided to stop drinking and doing pills. And ever since his return, she had hovered over him to the point of suffocation.

'Where are you going, honey?'

'When will you be back?'

'Where can I reach you?'

So maybe he *was* the only one left, and she wanted to make sure nothing bad happened to him, but that wasn't his fault. And living like a saint was definitely not his cup of tea.

Which left the second choice. Now that taking care of Chris had all but wiped out his little stash of cash, he had to find a way to put enough money together to get out on his own.

Ricky went to visit Marvin Mandelbaum two days after he was dismissed from the docks. His former mentor had suffered a heart attack while Ricky was interned at Hell House, and his skin looked almost as white as his hair.

'Hey, kid,' Marvin greeted him. 'Long time no see. What're you up to, these days?'

'Not much,' Ricky conceded. 'Life's pretty dull.'

The old man sighed. 'I know what you mean. Business ain't been half so good since you stopped bringing in merchandise.'

'Had to, Marvin,' Ricky said blandly. 'Got too hot.'

'Yeah. Seems I read something about you a while back.'

Ricky shrugged. 'Got a little careless.'

Marvin laughed. 'You got too big for your britches, is what you got.'

'Probably.' Ricky grinned. There was no real point in bragging about the two jobs he had pulled off successfully before getting caught.

'So what brings you around?'

'The cops nabbed the Browning,' Ricky said. 'I need a replacement.'

Marvin wagged his head back and forth. 'At the rate you're going, kid, it's likely I'll outlive you.'

Ricky selected a .38 Smith & Wesson. It was small and light, and he liked the feel of it.

'How many bullets you want?'

'Don't need bullets.'

'Look kid, let me tell you something about guns,' Marvin offered bluntly. 'They're not toys in a game. They're for real. Never point one at anybody unless you're damn well prepared to pull the trigger. And if you have to pull the trigger, you'd better have something in the chamber. And that little piece of advice may just save your life someday.'

Ricky knew better than to argue with the old man. He bought a box of shells.

The little bell over the pawn shop entrance tinkled as Ricky opened the door. 'You take care now, Marvin.

I don't want to go reading no obituary about you in the newspapers.'

'Likewise,' Marvin Mandelbaum said.

The first week in December, Ricky took on a convenience store in Woodside, where he placed himself and the Smith & Wesson solidly between the alarm button and the clerk. He resurrected his high-heeled boots and the turtleneck shirt for the occasion and it went off without a hitch. All the frightened clerk could remember, besides the gun, of course, was a pair of yellow eyes.

'Just like a cat's,' she said.

Then, two days before Christmas, Ricky knocked over a record store in San Mateo. He searched for three days for the outside wires before he realized that there was no alarm system. Unfortunately, there was an off-duty detective doing some last-minute shopping. In his confusion, Ricky's reflexes failed him. He tried to let go of the Smith & Wesson, but somehow his finger came in contact with the trigger instead. The bullet hit the policeman in the shoulder.

Despite all his efforts, Tom Starwood was unable to keep his client out of the CYA. He took Mary Elizabeth Battaglia to lunch, he took her to dinner, he even took her to bed, but she wouldn't budge.

'It's for his own good, Tom,' she told him. 'Hale House apparently didn't do anything for him. There's no point in sending him back there. Maybe a stint in CYA will straighten him out.'

'He's not a bad kid, Mel,' Starwood had implored. 'I know he's not. All he needs is someone to give him a break.'

Mary Elizabeth shook her head. 'Even if I were to agree with you, and I'm not saying I do, the DA's office would never go for it. And it's dead certain the judge won't, either. Your boy shot a cop, Tom.'

'He didn't mean to,' Starwood declared. 'He panicked and the gun just went off. He told me so and I believe him.'

'I know you do,' Mary Elizabeth said gently.

Ricky was sent to a CYA facility outside Placerville, in a special police van that seemed to inch its way out Route 50 past Sacramento, stopping finally before a pair of steel doors a foot thick set into a high concrete wall. The doors opened just wide enough to let the vehicle pass through and then swung shut again. Ricky and the two other boys who had made the four-hour journey were herded out of the van and lined up along the edge of one of the cement walks that crisscrossed a large expanse of grass.

'I'm Warden Magnuson,' said a slight, stooped man who came into view with his feet apart and his hands clasped behind him, as the van pulled out of the way. 'And so you know you've come to the right place, this is the Bolton School for Boys, a correctional institution under the auspices of the California Youth Authority. You're here because the court has ordered that you be removed from society for a specified length of time. And my job is to see to it that you get rehabilitated before you are released.'

Without moving his head more than a fraction of an inch, Ricky sneaked a look at the place he would call home for whatever length of time the state and Warden Magnuson decreed.

He had certainly been removed from society, all right. The walls around Bolton were at least twelve feet high, topped with another three feet of coiled barbed wire. A series of low buildings followed the irregular-shaped perimeter, and everywhere, uniformed guards, each with a sidearm, walked and watched.

Ricky chuckled mirthlessly to himself. Only two short months ago, he was complaining that his mother was cramping his style. Despite the broad vista of mountains he could see in the distance, claustrophobia was already making him break out in a cold sweat.

'We have rules,' the warden continued, 'which you will obey and schedules which you will follow. It isn't very complicated. Work hard, go to school, learn a trade, keep your nose clean, and you can cut your time here very easily. Cause trouble and you'll go through a lot of calendars inside these walls.'

Warden Magnuson stood not much taller than Ricky, but his cold, clipped voice bespoke the powers of a giant.

'There will be no drugs, no alcohol, and no leaving the campus unless in the scheduled company of an escort. You will be allowed to call home three times a month, collect, and visitors are permitted one weekend a month, providing you qualify.'

Ricky heard sighs from the two other boys next to him, but there was nothing the warden had said that bothered him. In the six months he spent at Hell House, his mother had been the only one to visit him. She had come exactly once, about a month after she gave up the booze, the month before he was released, and the whole time she was there, she was shaking and licking at her lips and crying.

'You will now be processed in, assigned to your dorm, and issued your clothing, all of which should be completed in plenty of time for you to make it to dinner. Good luck.'

As abruptly as he had appeared, the warden turned on his heel and departed.

Long before he had changed into the prescribed jeans and gray sweatshirt, made his bed, and stowed his few belongings in the green metal locker that separated his bunk from the next in the long rectangular dormitory, Ricky knew he would have to find a way to get out.

It took him four months, and his escape lasted thirty-seven minutes. When he was returned to Bolton, he was moved out of his dormitory and into a room by himself. The room was little more than a closet, with a cot, a locker, a sink, and a toilet that doubled as a chair. A square of glass in the door allowed a guard to peer into every corner.

'Why?' Tom Starwood implored when called to the scene.

Ricky turned wide eyes on his lawyer. 'My mom didn't come to visit me this month,' he replied with as much sincerity as he could muster. 'She said she was sick and couldn't get here, and I was worried about her. They wouldn't let me call and I had to be sure she was all right.'

Starwood nodded. 'I thought it might be something like that,' he said. 'I'll make sure that gets into your record.'

'They'll throw away the key on me now, won't they? Even though I had a good reason.'

'Not if I can help it,' the lawyer said firmly. 'Of course, that's only if you promise me you're going to play it straight from now on.'

Ricky nodded vigorously. After all, what choice did he have? They had swooped down and plucked him up before he'd barely had a chance to take a breath of free air. They would watch him like a hawk now, as if they could possibly watch anyone here any closer than they already did. He'd be lucky if he could take a leak without someone spying on him.

PART SIX

1982

I

It was two o'clock in the morning and the streets of Watsonville were deserted. Ricky turned off Route 152 and steered the Harley along back roads on his way to the converted bus in the woods that Eddie Melendez called home.

Of all the things he had missed during his six months at Hale House and then the two years he spent at the California Youth Authority facility near Placerville, it was his motorcycle. That high he got when he revved up the bike's big engine, let out the throttle, and roared down the highway, the wind whipping up his hair and burning his cheeks. Freedom.

The paved road ended abruptly. Ricky paused for a moment to get his bearings and then did as he had been instructed, turning left onto a narrow dirt path. Eddie's place was not much farther.

Ricky was released from CYA two days after his twentieth birthday. In his two years and two months at Bolton, he had had three visitors: his mother, who drove up once a month, his lawyer, who came around every couple of weeks, and Eddie Melendez, who came to see his former roommate twice during Ricky's final three months there.

'I met a guy who met a guy,' Eddie said, 'who told me you were here.'

One week to the day after his release, Ricky was on his way to Watsonville. The dirt path he was following ended at the edge of a broad thicket of eucalyptus trees, in the middle of which sat a dilapidated yellow school bus. Ricky cut the Harley's engine and swung out of the saddle just as the front door cranked open and Eddie sauntered out onto the top step.

'Hey, man, looks like you made it.'

'Sure, no sweat.'

'So how does it feel to be out?'

Ricky wondered whether Eddie was referring to the prison school or to the Marsh home, and then decided that, as far as he was concerned, there was very little difference. He sucked a gallon of air into his lungs. 'Free,' he said.

Eddie nodded. 'Solid.'

'Sometimes, you know, I thought I'd never breathe again.'

'Yeah.'

'Never thought we'd be roommates again, either.'

'Life's like that. You just never know, do you?'

'Where in hell did you get this thing?' Ricky asked, looking the yellow bus up and down.

'It was just sitting by the side of the road one day, and I figured nobody had no use for it no more, except me.'

'I'll be damned,' Ricky chuckled appreciatively. 'You stole a goddam school bus?'

'You know, the first time I ever been inside one of these things was when I drove this mother away.'

'I guess I've rode in my share,' Ricky said, 'but I'd have sure laughed myself silly if anyone had ever told me I'd end up living in one.'

'Well, what do you say?' Eddie asked, gesturing for Ricky to climb aboard. 'Ready for the big time?'

2

Valerie had just enough time to stop by the bank before opening up the shop for the day. She was carrying a check in her purse for over a thousand dollars, and she was anxious to deposit it into her account as soon as possible. Running her own business, she had discovered, was not as simple as Connie Gilchrist had led her to believe when the two had first hatched the plan eighteen months ago. Especially when receivables were late and payables were due. It required some fancy juggling, a lot of praying, and big doses of confidence. On more than one occasion, she wondered how she had ever thought she could do it.

It had taken a year for her to be able to live a day without the blissful numbness of alcohol and Elavil. A year during which Connie was there to hold her whenever the shakes took control of her, and soothe her whenever the tears overwhelmed her, and support her whenever her courage began to falter. It was often about taking two steps forward and one step back. And there were days, even weeks, when there were no steps forward, only backward.

To help boost her confidence, she got into the habit of talking to herself in the mirror, because of course she couldn't talk to anyone else.

'I think, in some way, I really wanted to die,' she told the mirror after two months. 'But I couldn't kill myself, because suicide is a mortal sin, and I would have burned in hell for all eternity.'

'I think maybe I hoped Jack would kill me, so I could be done with all the pain and guilt,' she told the mirror during the fifth month. 'But when he didn't, I thought the liquor and the pills would take care of everything.'

'I don't want to die,' she announced after eight months. 'Why not?' the mirror asked her back. 'Because I know now that I can live with what happened,' she replied. 'I thought that God had abandoned me because I couldn't protect my children. I thought He blamed me for being weak, and as punishment, He took them all away from me, one by one.' She smiled sadly at the mirror. 'But the truth is, He never blamed me – *I* blamed me. And because I was afraid to face Him, I lost Him. Now I know that it wasn't my fault, at least, not all of it was. And God was only testing me, testing my courage, testing my faith.'

'I think Jack is emotionally sick,' she told the mirror at the end of a year. 'I couldn't see it before, but I can see it very clearly now. I never should have married him. But I was immature and impulsive and positive that I knew what I was doing.' She sighed. 'I was also very much in love.'

In November of 1980, Valerie stood in front of her mirror and giggled nervously. 'I'm going into business,' she said. 'I'm going to make wedding gowns.'

It was Connie's idea, the minute she had seen the dress Valerie created for her stepdaughter. 'You can open a shop in my building,' she said. 'It's a perfect location, right in the middle of downtown Half Moon Bay. The second floor is just sitting there, waiting for you. And I'm going to defer any rent until you get on your feet.' What had started out in her mind as a diversion to get Valerie out of her depression had evolved into something far more substantial.

It took Valerie two weeks to make up her mind, two

weeks and two orders, from girls who had been bridesmaids for Connie's stepdaughter and were now engaged to be married.

'Can you believe it?' she said, giddy with excitement. 'Me, a businesswoman?'

'Of course I can,' Connie replied. 'I think it suits you perfectly. What did Jack say when you told him?'

Valerie shrugged. 'He didn't have a chance to say much of anything,' she said. 'You see, I didn't ask him if I could do it. I just told him I was going to.'

But that was not exactly the truth. When Valerie finally worked up enough courage to tell Jack about the bridal shop, he had laughed.

'What do you know about running a business?' he asked. 'You don't know anything about running a business.'

'I can learn,' she said.

'Learn?' he retorted, feeling suddenly insecure. 'If you can learn, then how come you never learned how to be a decent wife?'

Maybe if you'd been a better husband, I'd have been a better wife, she thought. But of course she didn't say it.

'I'm going into business, Mr Murphy,' Valerie announced, the next time she had occasion to go to the pharmacy.

'You are?' Dennis Murphy replied, his face lighting up at the sight of her. 'How nice. What sort of business?'

'I'm going to make wedding gowns.'

'Well, I think that's just wonderful.'

'To tell you the truth, I'm a little scared.'

Dennis looked around his shop. 'I know just how you feel,' he told her. 'If it will help to talk to someone who's been there, you just come on in anytime. And if the wife and I hear of any young ladies planning a trip down the aisle, we'll be sure to mention your name.'

By May of 1981, Valerie was paying rent.

The bank teller, a sweet, pretty girl with red hair and a face full of freckles, handed her customer a deposit receipt. 'Business must be booming, Mrs Marsh,' she said brightly.

'Well, Theresa, I must admit it's been a lot tougher than I thought it would be, running a business,' Valerie replied, 'but I think I'm finally getting there.'

'You're making Nancy Thaler's wedding dress, aren't you?'

'Yes, I am,' Valerie said with a sigh. 'Her dress and all her bridesmaids' dresses, too.'

'I know,' Theresa said. 'My cousin is one of the bridesmaids.'

Nancy Thaler had graduated from high school the previous year and had gone to work in the men's department at Nordstrom in the Stanford Mall in Palo Alto. A month later, she met a boy from Hillsborough, and with the eager support of her parents was marrying him the second week in June.

'I usually do just the bride's dress, but Nancy had her heart set on something special for her attendants that she couldn't get except to have custom-made.'

Theresa looked around hastily before leaning forward and lowering her voice. 'I don't suppose you would have any time to do the same thing for me, would you?'

'Why, Theresa, you and Chris Rodriguez?' Valerie exclaimed. The girl nodded. 'I thought he was never going to get around to popping the question.'

'Me, too,' Theresa giggled and pushed her left hand through the teller's window. A tiny round diamond, not much bigger than the head of a pin, glittered under the fluorescent lights.

'It's beautiful,' Valerie pronounced. 'Chris must be doing well at the garage.'

'He's a born mechanic,' Theresa said proudly. 'I know he'd rather be out fishing, but I'm awfully glad he isn't.'

'Have you set a date?'

'September. Labor Day Weekend.'

Valerie whipped out the appointment calendar she was now never without and flipped quickly through it. The pages told her she was booked solidly for the next sixteen months. Maybe only sixty percent of the high school graduates on the Coast went on to college, but ninety percent of them got married. She looked up at Theresa. The girl was fairly wriggling with anticipation, and Chris had been in and out of her house since he was a boy.

'Can you come for evening fittings?' she asked.

'Oh, yes, I'll come anytime you say.'

'And how many bridesmaids are you having?'

'Six. Just like Nancy.'

Valerie thought quickly. She had had to hire an extra sewer just for the Thaler job. Now she would probably have to hire another one. 'I'll need to have you all in for measurements sometime in the next two weeks.'

That was how it had been going for the last four-teen months. Someone saw one of Valerie's dresses, or knew somebody who was getting one of her dresses, and immediately wanted one, too. It seemed to be the Coast's version of keeping up with the Joneses. Except that now she was getting orders from other communities as well. Even from high-ticket places like Hillsborough, Woodside, Palo Alto, and Atherton.

'The best way to succeed in business is to find a need and fill it,' Connie had told her. 'And what's the one thing you know you can do that nobody else around here is doing?'

How right Connie had been. Over the past year, Valerie had produced dresses from patterns, from photographs, and from fantasies.

'As long as you can describe what you want,' one bride said to another, 'Mrs Marsh can make it.'

Because she was a small shop, and each of her designs was one of a kind, her prices were considerably higher than the department stores. But that didn't seem to matter to any of her customers.

'A girl plans on getting married only once,' Lil McAllister had told her on the day Valerie opened for business. 'And she'll spend whatever it takes to get the dress she wants.'

Lil had every reason to know. She had married off both of her daughters in Val Originals.

'Come work with me, Lil,' Valerie had begged at the end of her first year. 'There's too much work. The orders keep coming in, and the simple fact is, I can't do it all by myself anymore.'

Lil had fallen and broken her hip the summer before. It had taken six months to heal, and she never walked quite right afterward. She was no longer able to carry the heavy trays at the Gray Whale. Leo continued to pay her salary, and let her help out in the kitchen, but she knew he couldn't really afford it.

'What could I possibly do for you?' she had cackled. 'Lord knows, I've never been much good as a seamstress.'

'You can cut out patterns, can't you? And do some quick basting. As long as I have someone to help me with the basics, I'll be able to keep up with the finish work.'

Lil had hired on, and when the Thaler job had come

350

in, her older daughter, Judy, had come to work at the shop, too. Val couldn't pay much, but Judy didn't care. She and her husband had four kids to feed, and she was delighted to have whatever extra income she could get.

Leo Garvey had lost Valerie and now Lil, although they both came back to visit at least twice a month, to sit in a back booth, eating his famous fish and chips and chatting with all the regulars. But it wasn't the same. About the time that Judy went to work for Valerie, he decided it was time to hang up his spatula, and he put the Gray Whale up for sale.

Valerie parked her Dodge Dart behind Connie's building, and let herself into the shop through the back. That was another first for her. She had never owned her own car before, but it had become a necessity. She was paying for the used vehicle out of her profits, and if Jack had any objections, he didn't voice them.

Half a dozen dressmaker models stood patiently inside the second-floor shop, displaying the various stages of creations in progress. Valerie smiled. Coming in like this and seeing the mannequins there, waiting for her to decide whether to take a tuck here or there or change a drape or lower a neckline, never failed to excite her. She needed clear vision to sew the fine stitches and delicate beading, but she could think up designs with her eyes closed. Often, she stayed up late into the night, sketching ideas that wouldn't let her sleep.

Now that she was working all day, and many evenings as well, Jack had taken to coming home right after his shift at the airport ended.

He would sit quietly at the kitchen table while she fixed dinner, and then after the dishes were done, he would follow her into Ellen's old bedroom, which she

351

had turned into a little home office, and watch her work. On weekends, he would busy himself with any minor repairs that were required around the place, or putter in the garden, or watch whatever ball game was on television. He still drank a great deal, but there had not been a violent episode since she had announced her entry into the business world.

It was the first time in twenty-six years of marriage that he didn't appear to have a woman on the side, and it was ironic. Now that the children were all gone and she had little time for him, he had regained his interest in a home life. But to Valerie, it seemed more like the calm before the storm, and she found herself waiting, watching, knowing that the tight rope holding him in check could snap at any moment.

Five days after Ricky's return from Bolton, it did. Five days during which Valerie fussed incessantly over the boy, fixing all his favorite meals, buying him a whole new wardrobe, curtailing her hours at the shop to spend as much time with him as possible. Five days, during which Ricky slept, soaked in a hot tub, ate his way through the kitchen, helped himself to some of his father's best bourbon, and lay in the sun.

'They made you get your high school diploma in that prison school, didn't they?' Jack asked on Sunday night.

'Yeah,' Ricky replied. 'So what?'

'So, as far as I can see, all you've done since you got home is sit on your ass like some lazy good-for-nothing.'

Ricky stretched and yawned. 'I'm getting myself reacclimated,' he said, using one of Warden Magnuson's pet catchwords.

'And just how long is that supposed to take?' Jack inquired.

The twenty-year-old who had quaked in his boots in front of the police at Juvenile Hall, flouted all the rules at Hell House, and manipulated the Bolton School for Boys no longer feared his father.

'What's bugging you, Pops?' he asked. 'Can't handle the competition?'

The kitchen table was upended in one swipe, dishes shattering, spaghetti and meatballs splattering in all directions. In two steps, Jack had covered the space between them and hoisted Ricky clear off his chair by the scruff of his neck.

'What competition, punk?' he snapped. 'I'm out there in the world every day earning an honest living. Your mother's running her own business. Neither one of us ever took a dime we didn't work for, and neither one of us is going to support a sponge. So, big man, go get yourself an honest job – or get the hell out of here.'

By the time Valerie had cleaned the tomato sauce off the kitchen walls, Ricky had locked himself in his room and Jack had finished half a bottle of bourbon.

'Don't you defend him,' he warned, looming up in the bedroom doorway as Valerie silently undressed for bed. 'He's no good, and he's never been anything but no good, and you know it.'

'Whatever he is, whatever he's done,' she said, 'he's still our son.'

Jack hurled his empty glass in her direction. It smashed into the mirror over the dresser. 'It's always them, isn't it?' he shouted. 'They run off on you, hide out in goddam convents, get in trouble with the law, but it's still always about them. What about *me*? When is it *me* you're going to fuss over and care about? When does it get to be *my* turn?'

'Stop shouting, Jack,' she told him sharply. 'Do you really want the whole neighborhood to hear you?'

'What the fuck do I care? The goddam neighborhood can hear anything they like.' He stormed over to the window, and threw it open. 'Can you hear me, neighborhood?' he shouted. 'Do you want to hear all about my wonderful children and my adoring wife?'

Valerie slipped in front of him and quietly closed the window. 'That's enough, Jack,' she said. 'Come to bed.'

He grabbed her by the hair and spun her around, slamming her into the big maple armoire. 'I'll come to bed when I fucking well want to come to bed,' he roared, 'and not a minute sooner.'

There was a stabbing pain in her side, but she pulled herself up to her full height, and wrenched out of his grasp. 'If you ever lay a hand on me like that again,' she said from a place of new-found confidence, 'I'll leave you.'

Jack stopped with his hand in midair. He had been waiting for twenty-six years to hear her say that, knowing that sooner or later she would come to it, and now that she had, he felt the ground open beneath him and he began to fall, plunging head over heels into a thick, black, bottomless pit of self-loathing.

Valerie stared at the quivering lump lying at her feet that a moment ago had been a towering, raging bull. She searched her heart for all the warm feelings she had once held for him, but the only emotion she found herself able to summon was pity. She left him there, huddled on the floor, and went to bed.

The next day, Ricky packed whatever he could fit into a knapsack, kissed his mother goodbye, and saying he would keep in touch, set off on his motorcycle for a place he didn't name. Jack never said a word about his outburst, or about Ricky's departure, or about what Valerie had threatened to do, but that night, he brought home a beautiful bouquet of flowers.

It didn't matter. Valerie now knew she could support herself emotionally and spiritually, and in another few years, she would be able to support herself financially. What she didn't know was why it had had to be the death of a dream that had set her free.

She turned on the shop lights, hung up her coat, and unlocked the front door. Lil and Judy would be coming in any minute, and Nancy Thaler and her six brides-maids had a nine-thirty appointment for their final fittings. It was business as usual.

Jack didn't come home at all the night after Ricky left, and quickly resumed his habit of coming in late most other nights. He was consoling himself with a new waitress from the Hangar he had originally thought wasn't worth the effort. At fifty-two, he was still an incredibly attractive man, and had his pick of any number of available women. The waitress, Cindy some-thing, was twenty-three.

Now that Valerie knew she could live without her marriage, it didn't matter. In fact, she rather enjoyed the peace and quiet of being alone. Now that Jack knew she was strong enough to leave him, he was trying his best to stay out of her way.

3

On a Thursday evening, just three days after Ricky had moved into the school bus, Eddie Melendez was introducing him to the man, a Colombian with yellow teeth and bad breath wearing a black silk shirt and a lot of heavy gold chains around his neck. He was known as Gaucho, and he presented himself as an influential member of the South American mafia.

'So Ricky,' Gaucho said through a cigarette that hung unlit from the corner of his mouth. 'Eddie here tells me you want in on the action.'

'Yeah,' Ricky replied.

'You got a territory in mind?'

'I was thinking about the place I come from. It's up the coast a few miles, called Half Moon Bay.'

Gaucho's black eyes widened slightly. 'Say, you by any chance know a guy named Inigo Herrera in Half Moon Bay?'

'You mean the janitor over at the middle school?' Ricky replied. 'Sure, he's the local connection.'

'You ever deal with him?'

'Yeah, when I was a kid. He had the only action in town.'

A broad grin spread across Gaucho's bland features. 'Okay, Ricky, I give you Half Moon Bay. I supply you the stuff, I tell you how much I want for it, you get the difference. Eddie here shows you the ropes. And maybe what you end up doing is you put Señor Herrera out of business, *comprende*?'

'Sure,' Ricky said agreeably. The janitor was a fat slob. 'Piece a cake.'

He was already doing some rough calculations in his head and he figured, if he hustled, he could pull down at least five hundred a week, easy.

'First, you do a study,' Eddie instructed as he drove his thirdhand Z back to the bus. 'You figure out exactly what's going down, who's buying, how often, and how much. Then you start lower.'

'What do you mean?'

'If the seventh grade is buying, you start with the sixth. If the sixth grade is buying, you go down to the fifth, or the fourth, or even the third.'

'You want to go after grammar school kids?' Ricky asked, the idea making him a little queasy.

'Absolutely.'

'But they don't have that kind of bread.'

'That's why you start by giving it away. Twice maybe, three times, till you got the kid hooked. Then, you tell him the freebees are history. Trust me, he'll find a way to come up with the bread.'

'Shit, Eddie, why do we got to hit on babies?'

''Cause if we don't,' Eddie said, 'someone else will.' He turned the Z into the clearing, pulled around behind the bus, cut the engine, and clambered out. 'Want a beer?'

'Sure,' Ricky replied. 'But I got to take a leak first.'

Armed with a flashlight, Ricky walked twenty yards into the woods until he reached the primitive outhouse Eddie had fashioned out of discarded lumber. He leaned over the rough wood-framed hole, wondering why he should feel so squeamish about giving grass to babies. After all, he'd been using, himself, since he was ten.

Eddie had the small electric stove going when Ricky climbed up into the bus. Except for the driver's seat, Eddie had gutted the whole interior of the vehicle and wired it for electricity, which he ran from a generator on the roof. But there wasn't enough power for heat.

When he ran out of clean clothes, Eddie either took a load over to the Laundromat in town, or washed out his things in the lake on the other side of the outhouse.

'You really get off on living like this?' Ricky asked, through blue lips and chattering teeth, the first time he had to bathe in the frigid water and then haul a bucket to the bus for drinking.

'You think I should live better?' Eddie answered the question with a question. 'Shit, man, money don't mean that much to me. A roof that don't leak, a shirt that ain't torn, enough food to fill my belly, that's all I need. Besides, who in his right mind would believe me being driven around in a chauffeured limousine?'

'Why not?'

'My family's third-generation migrant,' Eddie told him. 'Stoop laborers, following the crops just like a dog follows its master. Illegals, picking their way up and down the valley, and then left to starve or get chased back across the border when the work runs out. Man, this place is paradise compared to some I've lived in.'

What he didn't say was that almost all of the money he made he sent down to his mother in Hermosillo.

There were worlds within worlds, Ricky realized, that he knew nothing about. Paradise or not, he never maligned the living conditions again.

'Hey, man, catch,' Eddie called, tossing a Dos Equis to his roommate as the bus's mechanical door groaned shut.

'Thanks.' Ricky dropped down in front of the stove, popped the cap, and took a long swig.

358

'Someone started a rumor once that all Mexican beer was made from piss,' Eddie said. 'But don't you believe it. Only half of it is.'

Ricky stopped in mid-gulp, sputtering beer all over his shirt, and Eddie howled. 'You got to have some trust, man, you see? Nothing works in this world without trust.'

Early Monday morning, Ricky rode the Harley back to Half Moon Bay. As luck would have it, he got to the middle school just as Inigo Herrera, armed with mop and pail, was coming out of the multipurpose room.

'Hey, amigo,' Herrera greeted him with a broad grin. 'Long time, no see.' Below his bushy mustache, there was a big gap between his front teeth.

'I was a bad boy,' Ricky explained. 'Last couple of years, I been dangling off the long arm of the law.'

'Oh, yeah?' The custodian grinned appreciatively. 'You did time?'

'Juvie time,' Ricky said with a shrug.

'So what are you doing now?' Herrera asked.

'At the moment, just looking to score some weed,' Ricky told him. 'Got any good stuff?'

Herrera lowered his voice. 'I got some Acapulco and a couple dimes of Maui.'

'Hmmm,' Ricky considered. 'Okay, I'll take a dime of Maui.'

Herrera looked around and then motioned Ricky to follow him. 'For that, we got to hit my locker.' They headed inside toward the custodian's room.

'So how's business?' Ricky inquired casually. 'Did my sudden departure louse up your quota real bad?'

Herrera laughed. 'And how! Had to find three new boys to make up for you.'

'Only three?' Ricky chuckled. 'Hell, I'd have thought I was worth at least six.'

'So did my man,' Herrera guffawed, jabbing Ricky in the ribs with his elbow.

'So you probably hooked a dozen.'

'Took me a while,' Herrera admitted, 'but things is pretty good now. In a town this small, you think not much business, but I can tell you it's a little gold mine.'

It took only two days to confirm that Herrera was still the only action in town and had both the middle school and the high school sewn up. Ricky concluded, with only a momentary twinge, that he would have to start lower. There were three elementary schools on the Coast. He began with the northernmost.

The following Thursday, he left Watsonville in time to be at the school just as the final bell rang. He never went onto school property, but hung around outside as the kids thronged past. Some of them looked at him curiously, sitting there on his bike, taking a hit now and then to keep the acrid smell swirling around him. He didn't push, he just let them come to him. Sure enough, they did.

Gaucho had fronted him a pound of grass and Ricky divided a quarter of it into nickel bags and rolled the rest into joints. Eddie told him to give it all away, but Ricky had his own ideas about that. He gave the joints away, but saved the bags. So seductive was his product that before the end of the second week, he had a dozen fifth-graders willing to break open their piggy banks or sneak into their mothers' handbags. From the nickel bags, he made a sweet three hundred dollars, and Gaucho was never the wiser.

He set up a weekly delivery schedule, taught a couple of the smarter kids how to turn their classmates on, and moved along to the next elementary school, where he had even better luck. In little more than a month, he had a lock on the preteen market. He undercut Inigo

Herrera's prices simply by shortchanging the bags a little and then adding some oregano. The ten- and eleven-year-olds didn't know the difference. They went for the four-dollar nickels and the eight-dollar dimes in droves.

Herrera cornered him one day. 'I hear you been taking care of some of my business,' he said.

Ricky shrugged. 'I ain't looking to crowd you out,' he replied with a perfectly straight face. 'But you said yourself it was a gold mine here, and I figured there was room enough for both of us.'

Herrera's beady eyes narrowed in his swarthy face. 'My man ain't going to like that.'

'Tell him I'll put him in touch with *my* man,' Ricky said shrewdly. 'And they can work it out.'

Herrera scratched his head. 'Okay, Ricky, I cut you in, but only if you tell me how you can sell your stuff for a dollar less?'

'I don't mind taking a little less profit to get things rolling,' Ricky replied.

Soon, the older siblings of his customers were coming around for the cheaper price. Without ever stepping foot in either the high school or the middle school, Ricky quietly siphoned off half of Herrera's trade. By the middle of June, Gaucho was fronting him a full four pounds a week.

'You gimme three big ones,' he told his newest protégé. 'Whatever more you can get is yours.'

By the time school let out for the summer, Ricky was clearing over a thousand dollars a week.

'I don't know why I didn't get into this sooner,' he crowed to Eddie, tossing dollar bills in the air like confetti and watching them flutter down around him. 'Piece a cake.'

'Told you, man,' Eddie replied with a chuckle. 'Didn't I tell you?'

'I should've listened harder,' Ricky giggled. 'I could've saved myself two years at Bolton.' They were sitting on their mattresses in the rear of the bus, and it reminded Ricky of the days when he used to pile his stash in the middle of his bed at home.

'Limit your exposure, minimize your risk, I always say,' Eddie said.

There was a pause. 'I got to go,' Ricky said softly.

'Yeah, I figured that,' Eddie replied.

'I got to have a place of my own up there. Besides, it's time. I've bummed off you long enough.'

'What are you going to do?'

'I got my eye on this trailer, see,' Ricky said. 'It's in El Granada, but on the other side of town from my folks. It's shit green and practically falling apart, but I figure I can fix it up some. You know, like you did here with this place.'

Eddie chuckled. 'I thought you hated this place, man.'

Ricky grinned. 'Yeah, well, I guess it kind of grew on me. Anyway, this thing's just sitting in a vacant lot, next to this guy's house, you know. And he says I can have it for two hundred a month. He's even going to run an electric wire out there and throw in a barrel of water.'

'Sounds like a deal.'

'It's pretty private, too. Not like here, of course, but far enough away from things that I can do some business if I want to.'

'You got Herrera yet?' Eddie asked.

'Soon,' Ricky replied with a confident wink. 'Trust me, by the end of the summer, he'll be history.'

A remedial session was held at the high school during July and August. The middle school hosted a day camp. A variety of recreational programs were conducted at the elementary schools, swimming lessons were given at the pool, tennis teams played on the courts, and summer soccer leagues met in combat on the ball fields. A skeleton custodial staff manned the facilities on a rotating schedule. Ricky managed to get a look at the schedule and arranged to run into Inigo Herrera the first week in July.

'I need a big favor,' he said to the beefy Mexican. 'I need to be out of town for a couple of months to do a deal. Do you think you can handle my customers for me while I'm gone?'

Herrera's beady eyes lit up. His supplier hadn't taken any too kindly to losing so much of his business, and this could be the custodian's opportunity to get some of it back.

'Yeah,' he said, a trifle too eagerly. 'I think I can handle this for you.'

Ricky smiled inwardly and pulled a slip of paper from his pocket. 'Here's all the information you'll need, okay? I made a list of how much and how often. You work out the delivery route, and I'll spread the word around.'

The Mexican's eyes bulged when he saw the exaggerated figures Ricky had written down, but Ricky pretended not to notice.

'I know this is probably chickenshit compared to your operation,' he said, 'but then, you been in business a lot longer than me.'

Herrera shrugged elaborately, not wanting to let on that this was the biggest mistake Ricky would ever make. 'I do you this favor, okay, and maybe next time, you do *me* a favor.'

'Sure,' Ricky said with a broad smile. 'After all, we're kind of like *compadres* now, aren't we? And *compadres* always watch each other's back, don't they?'

From a secure distance, Ricky had watched the

Mexican's back carefully. After a week, he felt he knew the custodian almost as well as he knew himself. He knew what route the man took to work, what he ate for lunch, how often he went to the john, where he kept his stash.

Herrera worked at the high school two days a week during the summer. If he followed Ricky's directions, and prepared the dime bags for the kids exactly as Ricky had instructed, the custodian could have as much as seven pounds of grass in his possession on the third Tuesday in July. For security reasons, he would be forced to leave the bulk of it in his battered pickup in the parking lot, and go running back and forth all day.

At precisely ten o'clock on the morning of July 20, the duty officer at the Half Moon Bay police department received an anonymous tip. When later questioned, she was unable to identify whether the caller had been a man or a woman.

In somewhat of a malapropism, the local newspapers later called it the biggest bust on the Coast. It ran the story next to a picture of a particularly well-endowed city councilwoman who had pounced on the issue and was demanding a tough anti-drug campaign in her effort to be reelected.

Ricky waited until the middle of August to visit Inigo Herrera in jail.

'Jesus Christ, man, I trusted you,' Ricky exclaimed. 'And then you go and fuck me up.'

'I don't know how it could've happened, amigo,' the Mexican whined. 'Fifteen years, and I ain't never had a problem.'

'All the way down in Mexico I heard about it.'

'You were in Mexico?'

'Yeah,' Ricky lied. 'Me and my supplier was scouting

new sources. I had to leave him flat and come chasing back up here.'

'I'm sorry, amigo.' The big man began to sob. 'I never meant to let you down.'

'Well, maybe I expected too much from you, asking you to handle such a big volume, you know, tacking my action onto yours,' Ricky conceded graciously. 'Maybe it wasn't all your fault.'

Herrera nodded eagerly. It didn't occur to him then that only a few short months ago, it had all been his action.

'Shit, everyone's gone underground, and it's going to take forever to get reorganized,' Ricky moaned. 'Maybe I should just give it all up and try my hand at TV repair work.'

'Nah, don't do that,' the ex-custodian counseled. 'You can get it all back. The action's got to go somewhere. Just give it a little time.'

'You mean, lay low till the heat blows over?'

'Yeah, that's right,' Herrera encouraged him. 'Give it a few months, then jump back in. That's all you got to do.'

'You really think I can do it?' Ricky asked with perfect guile.

The older man nodded wisely. 'You can do it, amigo. I have real faith in you.'

'If you say so,' Ricky said and then paused for an appropriate sigh of resignation, 'I guess I can hang in there for a while . . . for both of us.'

By the time September rolled around and school began, Ricky had the entire student market sewn up.

A week later, Gaucho came to pay his respects.

'You did good, kid,' he said, going for the high five. 'You did real good.'

They sat in the green trailer, drinking beer.

'I told you the kid was a winner,' Eddie chimed in from a battered sofa that doubled as Ricky's bed.

'Yeah, Eddie, you did,' Gaucho agreed. 'You told me all right.'

'There was really nothing to it, honest,' Ricky said modestly. 'The guy never knew what fell on him. It was a piece a cake.'

'Okay, kid, whatever it was, you made it happen. Which means you're moving up, right to the top. You earned it, now run with it.'

Ricky looked at the Colombian quizzically, unsure of exactly what the man had in mind. 'Run where?'

'Do you want to spend your whole life in this mistake of a place?'

'Hell, no,' Ricky replied.

'Then go after the real action. Move on up the coast, right into San Francisco itself.'

'I was planning on it,' Ricky said glibly, although the thought had never entered his mind, 'but I figured I ought to solidify my position here before I branched out.'

'It's a tough market, a lot of heavy competition,' Gaucho told him, 'and we need someone we can count on up there. So far, we haven't found the right man. Maybe you're it.'

'If you think I'm it, then I'm it.' Ricky could feel an idiotic grin spreading all over his face, but he didn't care. He was about to hit the big time.

'I got to warn you, it might be risky, but what the hell. Sometimes, to get the big returns, you got to be willing to take the big gamble.'

'You bet,' Ricky declared.

'You're a good kid, Ricky,' Gaucho said, patting him on the cheek.

They talked a little strategy after that, but Ricky was

paying only half attention. One minor success and he was going up? He couldn't believe it. Brains were obviously a premium in Gaucho's organization, which was all right with Ricky. He had enough for everyone.

'Say, Gaucho, you sure Ricky's ready to fly that high?' Eddie asked later, when he and the man were on their way back to Watsonville. 'He's still pretty green.'

'He handled Herrera just fine, didn't he?' the Latino replied.

'Herrera was an asshole.'

Gaucho shrugged. 'We'll never know what he can do until he tries. Look, Eddie, you're a smart boy. Thanks to you, we got San Jose tied up tight as a drum, but so far, we ain't even made a dent worth noticing up north. We been knocking on that door for years, and so far, all we got to show for it is four amigos in body bags and three more wasting their asses in Vacaville. We can't risk any more of our top people, but we need a piece of that market, or we ain't never going to get no respect.'

'But why Ricky?'

'Why not? Getting Herrera was a test, and the kid passed it just fine. Who knows? He's young and he's bright and he's eager. Maybe he can do something for us where it counts. If he can, he'll get his share.'

'And if he can't?'

The Colombian shrugged. 'Then he's not much use to us, is he?'

Eddie frowned in the darkened car. 'What you're saying is – he's expendable.'

'We're all expendable,' Gaucho replied.

The conversation replayed in Eddie's head long into that night and the ones that followed. He had brought Ricky into the organization, befriended him, took him into his home, and filled his head with dreams of big bucks and the easy life. Now, without a second thought, Gaucho was going to throw him to the dogs.

Eddie had no illusions about Ricky's success in San Francisco. The kid would get eaten alive. The illusions he *did* have had more to do with family and loyalty. If there was one thing he had learned, growing up the way he had, it was that nothing else mattered. He could count the number of people he had let into his life, since the gypsy days of his childhood, on the fingers of one hand. Gaucho was one of them. The Latino had scooped him up after Hell House and given him direction, security, and his first real place in the world. He was part of the team, one for all and all for one, he thought.

But, like it or not, Ricky Marsh was in Eddie's life, too. More than a teammate, more than a comrade, Ricky had become a brother, and every part of Eddie that counted cried out in the night that you didn't betray your brother.

He tossed and turned on his mattress until his head throbbed and his heart ached and the black sky of night turned gray with morning four times. In the end, it was clear what he had to do. Gaucho was the man, his savior, his mentor, his provider. But Ricky was his brother.

4

In the years since he had left the Coast, Benito Ruiz,
Benny to his friends, had grown from a two-bit pusher
into a big-time dealer, and was now the key connection
for a major South American drug cartel.

He had been back in Half Moon Bay for two weeks
before he came face-to-face with the kid who had taken
out his oldest, if most dull-witted, dealer. He couldn't
prove it, of course. The kid had set what looked like a
perfect trap, getting burned in it himself to allay suspi-
cion. But Ruiz had been around too long to fall for such
a coincidence, and he smelled a setup.

'I hear you were back in business by Labor Day,'
Benny commented when the two finally met on a
secluded cliff overhanging the ocean. 'That takes guts,
man.'

'I wasn't smart enough to know any better,' Ricky
responded with an ingenuous smile, knowing instinctively that this man in the three-piece pinstripe suit and
monogrammed silk shirt was someone to handle with
care. 'It was too risky and I should've waited longer.'

'Nah,' Ruiz told him with a careless wave of his hand.
'You strike when it's least expected. That's the way.'

'You think so?'

'Sure. You left the cops standing around, scratching
their dicks, didn't you?'

Ricky grinned. 'I guess I did.'

'You're real slick, kid, I'll say that for you. I leave

this place unattended for a couple of months, and you move right in.'

'I think it was more like dumb luck.' Ricky was nobody's fool. He didn't know exactly who or how important this guy was, but he knew enough to play it very cool.

'I could use a kid like you in my organization,' Ruiz said casually, pulling a long thin cigar from a solid gold case and lighting up. 'At the very least, you owe me a replacement for Herrera.'

'Thanks, but I already got an organization.'

'Well, sure. You'd have to have backing to muscle in on my territory as easy as you did.'

Ricky turned steady yellow eyes on the man. 'I don't think you got the story straight. Herrera and me, we were just working different sides of the street, that's all. I even asked him to mind my store for me for a while.'

'All right, kid, let's cut the crap, okay?' Ruiz said, his words slicing through the space between them with precision, drawing Ricky up short. 'You and I both know what went down here, so there's no more need for games between us. As far as I'm concerned, Herrera was an asshole, and it's probably nothing short of a miracle that he wasn't caught long ago, so I got no sympathy lost in that department.'

'I thought he was your boy,' Ricky ventured.

'He was, and I'll take care of him while he's inside, because that's how it works. But that doesn't mean I'm going to walk out of here with my fucking tail between my legs.'

'I got no quarrel with you,' Ricky said, 'but I'm doing just fine, and I ain't looking to make a change.'

'What you got is chickenshit,' Ruiz shot back, a slow smile flickering across his handsome features when he saw that he had piqued the kid's curiosity. 'What're you pulling in, five hundred bucks a week, a thousand, maybe? How'd you like to triple that for no more risk than you take right now?'

Ricky swallowed hard. Three grand a week? While his allegiance to Gaucho was solid, the idea of making a hundred and fifty big ones in a year was almost intoxicating.

'What's the angle?' he heard himself asking.

'Who you working for now, kid?'

There was no harm in telling. 'He goes by the name of Gaucho.'

'Bad teeth and breath to match?'

Ricky nodded. 'Yeah, that's him.'

Ruiz threw back his head in laughter. 'That's what I figured – the weasel.'

'Look, don't waste your time or mine down-talking him,' Ricky said defensively. 'He's been doing just fine by me.'

'Sure, kid, sure he has. And if all you want out of this world is a shit green trailer in an empty lot with no running water, you stick with him.'

'Stop calling me kid,' Ricky snapped, trying to preserve what he could of his dignity, and wondering how come this man had gone to the trouble of checking him out.

'Okay, Ricky, let's put our cards on the table,' Ruiz said. 'Herrera never could've handled what I'm going to offer you, so maybe you did us both a big favor after all. You're a bright boy, bright enough to know that grass ain't where the real money's at nowadays. My organization's been quietly moving into powder the past few years, and I think it's time for the Coast here to join the rest of the country.'

Ricky whistled through his teeth. 'You want me to push cocaine for you?' he whispered.

'Why not? Makes sense, don't it? Hook a kid on grass, and he uses a while. Hook him on coke and he's yours for life.'

'Yeah,' Ricky mused. 'Get caught dealing grass, you do a year or two. Get caught dealing coke, you go down for life.'

'You only get caught if you're stupid,' Ruiz told him. 'I been in this game since I was thirteen, and I never been inside.'

'I got to think about this,' Ricky said slowly.

'Sure.' Ruiz shrugged. 'Take all the time you want. I'm offering you the chance of a lifetime. You should have a couple of days to think it over.'

He flicked his cigar butt out into the surf and turned on his heel. He was going to be around for a few more days. He'd give the kid some space. He walked down off the cliff and got back into his car. Two men in neat dark suits were leaning against the shiny Mercedes. They jumped when they saw him coming, one of them rushing to open the back door, and the other sliding quickly behind the wheel. A moment later, they spun away in a cloud of dust.

Ricky watched the show with a hint of amusement. If it was intended to impress him, it certainly had. If it was the way the man really operated, then Ricky was even more impressed. Either way, it had achieved the desired effect. *I've made a fortune in this business*, it screamed, *and so can you*.

And Ruiz was right about what he said. Pot was something you grew out of. Coke was something you grew into. He was probably also right about a fortune being there for the taking right on the Coast.

But Gaucho had offered him San Francisco, a nut no one in the whole organization had been able to crack so far, and Ricky hadn't been able to get the challenge of that out of his head. If he could take on the big-city boys and win, the world would be his. Instead of being a grunt, he would be the fat cat who sat back and ran things.

He revved up the Harley and headed home, with his head spinning. Two opportunities, but which way should he jump? Ricky knew he needed to think everything through very carefully, because he was only going to get one shot at this, and whatever else he did, he had to be sure he made the right choice.

Eddie was coming up tonight. He had called out of the blue this morning and said he wanted to talk. They would have something to eat, smoke a couple of joints, jaw a bit, and then Ricky would ask him what he thought about Benito Ruiz and his offer.

'Take it,' Eddie said. 'Take the deal.'

'Just like that?' Ricky asked in surprise.

'Yeah, just like that.'

'I guess that's not what I expected you to say, man. I mean, don't you even want to discuss it with me first?'

'Don't have to.'

'But running out on Gaucho, him being so good to me and all, taking me in, giving me the chance to do something big?'

Eddie squirmed a little in his seat. 'Look, man, that's sort of why I came on up here tonight. To talk to you about that.'

'I'm listening.'

'You ain't nowhere near ready for Frisco, man. That's where the big boys play, not the little guys, like Gaucho, and he knows it.'

Ricky frowned. 'So why's he setting me up?'

''Cause he ain't got nothing to lose. You ain't nothing to him. If, by some fluke, you make it in some back door, shit, he's a hero.'

'And if I don't?'

'If you don't, what does it cost him? A cheap lawyer, if you're lucky. A cheap funeral, if you're not.'

'There ain't no guarantees, Eddie, I know that,' Ricky said with a lot more conviction than he felt at that moment. 'But I proved myself, didn't I? He took me in, when he didn't have to, said I was smart, that I was ready for more.'

'He took you in because he wanted to get Herrera. I didn't know it myself before, but Herrera used to be Gaucho's boy, until Benny Ruiz turned him. Gaucho never forgot that. He figured he had nothing to lose, that you could pay back Herrera for running out on him, and at the same time, hit Ruiz where it hurt.'

'Yeah, but if I jump ship, won't he come after me, too?'

'Tell Ruiz. No love lost between those two. He'll know how to square it with Gaucho.'

'What about you?' Ricky asked suddenly. 'What'll Gaucho do to you when he finds out you told me?'

Eddie shrugged. 'Kill me,' he said.

Ricky slept very little that night. Every time he drifted off, demons in silk shirts and gold chains, with yellow teeth and unlit cigarettes hanging from their mouths, were waiting to get him, and he awoke sweating and shivering, as he had so often from his nightmares as a child. Finally, he snapped on the small lamp beside his bed, chasing the demons back into the dark, and set about figuring out what to do.

All his instincts now told him that his future lay with Ruiz, not Gaucho, but he couldn't make the switch at Eddie's expense. Eddie had taken him in, connected him up, looked out for him, and been a real friend. Ricky knew he couldn't hang him out to dry. He would have to find another way. A way to get

374

Eddie out, too . . . a way that would keep them both safe from Gaucho.

The rooster in the yard three houses down had begun to crow by the time Ricky had devised his plan.

Benny Ruiz wasn't hard to find. They met at Muzzi's Café on Main Street, and with steaming mugs of coffee between them, Ricky told Ruiz what he wanted.

'You want me, then you got to take my partner Eddie in, too,' he said. 'And you got to protect both of us from Gaucho.'

'Now why would I want to do that?' Benny asked.

Ricky sat back with a little smile on his face. 'Because the Coast here is chicken feed, and you know it. Because with me and Eddie working together, we can give you all of San Mateo County. And then, with Eddie's connections, we can deliver Santa Clara County, too.'

Benny's eyes widened. 'You think he's that good, do you?'

'Eddie runs San Jose for Gaucho now. With an operation like yours behind us, me and him could go all the way to Salinas, and even Monterey, easy.'

'You got guts, I'll say that for you,' Benny said with genuine appreciation. 'So how come you don't ask me for Frisco?'

Ricky gave him a long look. 'I'm not ready for that yet,' he said softly. 'But I'll let you know when I am.'

Benny Ruiz smiled. 'You're a smart kid, Ricky,' he said. 'Let me think about it.'

'What's to think about?' Ricky challenged. 'You either want us or you don't. I ain't going to wait around for the phone to ring. So make up your mind right here and now, 'cause I got other options.'

Benny Ruiz considered himself a pretty good judge of character. 'Okay, kid,' he said. 'You and your friend got yourself a deal.'

'And you'll take care of Gaucho?'

A smile spread across the drug dealer's face. 'It'll be my pleasure,' he said.

Two weeks later, Gaucho's car careened off the Coast Highway just south of Santa Cruz, crashing into a ditch and exploding on impact. The police noted a bullet hole in one of the rear tires, and another in the gas tank, but they had no leads and didn't lose much sleep over it. After all, what did it really matter if there was one fewer drug dealer in the area?

5

Ricky had been working for Benny Ruiz for two years when Inigo Herrera got out of prison. In that time, he and Eddie had sewn up the coast from Pacifica to Santa Cruz and inland from San Jose to Salinas, just as he had promised. With Gaucho out of the picture, it had been easy.

'I hear good things about you,' the ex-janitor said.

'I been lucky,' Ricky told him. 'Benny took me on after he lost you and let me do my thing.'

'I can't find a job,' Herrera said. 'Now I got a record, nobody'll hire me. You think Benny would give me another chance?'

'I don't know,' Ricky told him honestly. 'I could ask him, next time he's up this way.'

'I got a family to feed, you know,' the man said. 'Last two years were tough on them, with me being inside. I know I messed up, but I gave Benny some good years. Maybe you could put in a word for me. I could help you out around here, you know, with any stuff you don't have time for.'

'Sure,' Ricky promised.

'I was pretty surprised when I heard you went with Benny,' Herrera said.

'Yeah? Why?'

'Well, you know, seeing as what he done to your sister and all.'

Ricky frowned. 'My sister?'

'Yeah, the pretty one. Long time ago now.'

'Rosemary?'

'Yeah, that's the one.'

The hair on the back of Ricky's neck began to rise. 'What'd Benny do to Rosemary?'

'You don't know?'

'Don't jerk me around, amigo.' Ricky's voice was soft, but Herrera heard the menace in it.

'He got her pregnant is what I heard. Then he split on her. So she followed him to LA. He didn't want her anymore, so he gave her to a friend of his, Angelo. Angelo ran a bunch of girls down there. He said your sister was born to the life.'

Ricky wanted to punch the man out, reduce him to nothing more than scattered bones and blood, but there was no point in killing the messenger. 'You sure about this?' he asked.

'Sure I'm sure,' Herrera said. 'Sorry, man. I thought you knew.'

'You know where my sister is now?'

The man shrugged. 'A few years ago, I heard she was still in the business, but I ain't heard nothing lately.'

'This Angelo,' Ricky asked casually, 'you know where to find him?'

Ricky was on an airplane the next day. Angelo Sbarga was easy to find. A tall, good-looking man in his late thirties, he cruised around the sunny streets of Los Angeles in a vintage pink Cadillac convertible.

'What kind of girl you looking for?' he asked when Ricky told him he was a friend of Benny's.

'He told me he used to have a girl named Rosemary,' Ricky said. 'He made her sound special.'

Angelo shrugged. 'If you like 'em seasoned,' he said, 'Rosemary's as good as they come.'

378

He took Ricky to a room in a shabby hotel in East Los Angeles, and told him to wait. Half an hour later, there was a discreet knock. When Ricky opened the door, he saw a woman on the other side of the threshold he wouldn't have recognized if he didn't know who she was.

'Angelo says you asked for me special,' she said, walking past him. 'So I'm going to treat you right. You tell me exactly what you want, honey, and how you want it.'

She was almost twenty-eight and looked forty. Her hair was dull and stringy and there was an unhealthy pallor to her skin. He could see it beneath the thick layer of makeup she wore. She was little more than skin and bones.

'Rosemary, don't you know me?' he asked.

She turned quickly and looked at him out of blue eyes that had once been full of life but were now dull and empty. 'Should I?'

'Yeah, actually, you should,' he said. 'I'm your brother Ricky.'

She stared at him for a moment and then broke into a laugh that was half cackle, half cough. 'Ricky? Is that really you?'

'In the flesh.'

'Well, I'll be damned, it's my little brother. What're you doing down here?'

'I came to find you,' he said.

She blinked. 'Why?'

'I don't know,' he told her. 'Maybe because you up and disappeared and we never knew what happened to you. Maybe because I just wanted to see that you were okay.'

She laughed again, that same gravelly sound. 'Well, as you can see, I'm in the pink.' She dropped down onto the bed.

'Let me look at you,' she said. 'My goodness, you're all grown up, aren't you? And you're still alive. That means the old man didn't kill you.'

'No, he didn't kill me.'

'How's Ma? Is she okay? I wanted to write or call, you know, but, well, I never really could think of anything to say.'

Ricky told her about Valerie being in business, and Jack being Jack, and Ellen being a nun, and JJ being in the Army. It was a short recitation.

'And you?' she asked.

'Me? I'm doing okay. I been working with an old friend of yours.'

'Friend of mine?'

'Yeah,' he said, watching her closely. 'Benny Ruiz.'

He saw her face darken. 'Oh, yeah?' she said. 'Well, I'm not going to tell you that's the smartest thing you could ever do.'

Ricky sat down on the bed beside her. 'What happened, Rosie?' he asked, automatically using the name they had called her as a child. 'Why did you just go off like that? Without telling anyone. At least JJ left us a note when he went.'

'I don't know,' she said with a sigh. 'It was so long ago, I can't remember.'

'I heard you got pregnant.'

'Did you?' she murmured vaguely. 'That must've been it then. I got pregnant, and had an abortion, and followed Benny because I was stupid and thought he loved me, and somehow I ended up with Angelo. Oh, well, it could've been worse.'

He wondered how it could possibly have been worse. 'Do you need anything?' he asked.

She smiled at him, like the Rosemary he remembered. 'My baby brother wants to know if I need anything?'

'Sure,' he said. 'I got money. I could take care of you.'

'You take care of yourself,' she told him, patting his cheek. 'Don't you worry about me. Angelo treats me okay.' She looked around the dingy room. 'I guess we don't have much use for this,' she said. 'Why don't we go somewhere and have a cup of coffee or something?'

'Okay,' he said and stood up.

'Ma doesn't know about me, does she?' Rosemary asked behind him. 'I wouldn't want her to know.'

'No,' he assured her. 'Ma doesn't know.'

'And you won't tell her, will you?'

'No, I won't tell her.'

'Promise?'

'Promise.'

He knew she was sick, but he didn't know how sick. When he left, he gave her his address and telephone number. 'Just in case you want to get in touch,' he said. Then he tucked several hundred-dollar bills into her hand. 'Take it,' he told her. 'Consider it a partial payment from Benny Ruiz.'

Two months later, he got a small package in the mail. It came from Angelo Sbarga and it contained Rosemary's few effects. There was a short note, telling him that Rosemary had died of pneumonia brought on by a disease called AIDS, and he had found Ricky's address among her belongings.

Ricky debated telling his mother, and decided against it. What would be the point? But he knew he was going to do something about it. He just had to figure out what.

Anna Morales came into Ricky's life by accident. Literally. He almost killed her with the Harley, coming around a corner, not seeing her crossing the street, missing her by inches, landing the motorcycle in a ditch.

'Are you okay?' he cried, picking himself up, bruised and bleeding, and hurrying to her side.

'*I* am,' she replied looking him over, 'but *you* sure aren't.'

'I didn't see you,' he explained.

'I certainly hope not,' she told him. 'Otherwise, I would have to think you almost did me in on purpose.'

She had flashing dark eyes that teased him, and were in dramatic contrast to her honey-coloured hair and olive skin. She was five years younger than he, an inch or two shorter, and thinner than he liked, but there was something about her that got to him.

As it turned out, she worked up at St Hilda's, as a nursing assistant. She insisted he go there and get checked out, accompanying him, she said, to be sure that he did. After he had been stitched up and bandaged, he took her to dinner, and then to bed. A week later, she moved into the green trailer with him.

'I know it's not much,' he told her. 'But it doesn't matter to me where I live.'

'That's okay,' Anna said. 'I like it here.' She came from a family where there was too much brutality and not enough food or love to go around. She was the fourth of seven children. Her mother had died giving birth to the seventh. Her father was a drunk who could never manage to hold a job for more than a few months at a time. The family lived in a two-room shack south of town. The children were raised mostly by the state. To Anna, the trailer was spacious.

Ricky was quite satisfied with the situation. It was wonderful to come home in the evening to a hot meal, to have clean clothes in his closet, and to wake up to the smell of fresh coffee in the morning. And as if that wasn't enough, he could have great sex anytime he wanted it.

Anna worked the day shift at the hospital, leaving

382

the trailer at seven in the morning and coming back around four. Ricky usually slept until noon, one of the few luxuries he allowed himself. Then he got up and showered and dressed and went off to do his business, returning around seven. Once or sometimes twice a week, he was gone all night.

Anna never asked Ricky where he went or what he did. She suspected it involved drugs, but it didn't matter. He was her man, and that was all she cared about. Then she got pregnant, and it did matter.

'I got to know something,' she said one night, as they were getting ready for bed.

'Yeah, what?' he asked.

'Do you use?'

'Why do you got to know that?' he demanded.

'Because we're going to have a baby,' she said, 'and I want to know if I got to be worried.'

'A baby?' Ricky could hardly get the words out of his mouth. 'You're going to have a baby?'

'No, *we* are,' she corrected him. 'I assume that's okay. It *is* okay, isn't it?'

The last thing Ricky wanted was for her to have a baby, but he thought about Rosemary and what she had done and what had happened to her. He didn't want any of that to happen to Anna.

'Sure,' he said. 'Sure, that's okay.'

'Well?' she asked. 'Do you use?'

Yellow eyes looked directly into brown ones. 'No, I don't use,' he told her. 'I used to do pot and a little coke when I was a kid, and then I did pot for a while after I got out of Bolton, but not for a couple of years now. Anything else you want to know?'

Anna shook her head. 'No,' she told him. 'I don't want to know anything else.'

* * *

'What the hell am I going to do with a kid?' Ricky complained to Eddie. 'I got things to do in this life. And anyway, I don't want to bring no kid into this fucked-up world. Shit, I don't want to be tied down to nobody.'

They were drinking Dos Equis in Eddie's new digs, a double-wide mobile home he had hauled onto the property in Watsonville when he could afford to live better than the school bus.

'You could've got rid of it,' Eddie reminded him.

'Yeah, well, I didn't want to do that.'

'So then, you got to make the best of it.'

'It's no fun going home anymore. Anna's starting to get big, she can't take care of the place most of the time, and the sex sucks.'

'Well, what did you expect, man?'

Ricky shrugged. 'I don't know. I thought me and Anna had a good thing going, and maybe we'd be together for a while. But now, I don't know. Everything's different.'

6

Anna delivered a boy on February 16, 1986, at St Hilda's Hospital. He weighed seven pounds, eleven ounces, and was declared perfectly healthy. Dr Wheeler thought how different this baby's birth was from his father's, in this very same room, almost twenty-four years ago.

Ricky wasn't there. As a matter of fact, he hadn't been there for most of the past four months. He said it was business, that now that he was going to have a family to support, he had to work harder. Anna wasn't convinced. There had always been plenty of money. She had hoped the baby would have a settling influence on him, but as the months went by, she came to realize that he wasn't going to be there for either of them.

Anna named the baby Justin, for St Justin the Martyr. She knew Ricky wouldn't care. Two weeks later, she moved out of the green trailer and back into her father's house. Valerie came to visit every chance she got, with gifts of clothes and toys and food.

'Ricky doesn't come around very much,' Anna said one afternoon. He brought money by every week or so, sometimes a lot of money, but he didn't spend any time with her, and rarely asked to see Justin.

Valerie nodded. 'I know,' she said with a sigh. 'I think he's a lot like his father. Be patient. Someday, I'm sure he'll want to know his son.'

Justin was a good baby and Anna's strength returned

quickly. She was able to go back to work after a month. She took Justin with her to the hospital. He was so beautiful and had such a sweet nature that the nurses fought over who would hold him. He had his mother's honey-coloured hair, his father's haunting eyes, and the face of an angel.

By the time Justin was a year old, Anna had given up on Ricky and started seeing a fellow who worked at a local bar. One Friday afternoon in June, she came to the shop and asked if Valerie would be willing to keep Justin for the weekend.

'What's the matter?' Valerie asked.

'Nothing,' Anna assured her. 'It's just that Dean wants to take me to Reno for the weekend. I've never been to Reno, but I don't think it's a place for kids.'

'No, I think not,' Valerie said.

She was delighted to have Justin. So much so that she left work early, hurrying to the market to buy baby food and then home to dig the crib she hadn't used since Ricky was a baby out of the basement, and the bedding that went with it out of the depths of the linen closet. She set the crib up in JJ's old room, because it was right next to her bedroom and she would be able to hear if he cried out in the night.

Anna brought Justin over at five o'clock. Valerie was all ready for him. She fed him, gave him his bath, put him in his pajamas, and then sat on the bedroom floor, playing with him. So engrossed was she in watching the boy trying to fit square blocks into round holes that she didn't notice that Jack had come home until he filled the doorway.

'What the hell is going on around here?' he growled. 'It's after seven o'clock. Where's dinner?'

Valerie was not expecting him. Indeed, this was the

first Friday in many months that he had appeared before midnight. With a sinking heart, she knew that it meant two things. He was without a woman and he had been drinking.

'I didn't realize it was that late,' she said. 'I'm afraid I lost all track of the time.' She picked Justin up from the floor. 'As you can see, we have a visitor, and the two of us have been having the best time.'

'Well, playtime is over,' Jack said. Without warning, he plucked the boy from Valerie's arms and dropped him into the crib. Justin let out a yelp.

'What do you think you're doing?' Valerie cried, scooping her grandson back up into her arms. 'If you can't treat him properly, then leave him alone.'

'I didn't hurt him,' Jack grumbled.

'Maybe not, but you certainly frightened him.'

'What's he doing here, anyway?'

'Anna's on her way to Reno for the weekend,' Valerie explained, 'and Justin is going to stay with us while she's gone.'

'Great, just what I need,' Jack snapped. 'Well, do I get any dinner around here, or do I have to find someone else to feed me?'

'I wasn't expecting you home tonight, so I wasn't planning on fixing dinner,' she told him. 'But if you like, I can make you an omelet.'

'An omelet? You'll make me an omelet? And what if I want a steak?'

'Then you'll have to go someplace else,' she said.

In one swift move, the crib was upended and the toys were scattered to the four corners of the room. 'It's bad enough you pushed me aside for your own brats,' he shouted. 'Now someone else's bastard is more important than me?'

She didn't bother to reply. She hugged Justin to her

and turned to leave the room. She hadn't gone two steps when she felt Jack's grip on her shoulder and he spun her around and flattened her against the wall. Then she saw his arm raised to strike. Justin started to cry and she held him tighter. 'Are you sure this is what you want to do, Jack?' she asked, amazed at the calmness of her voice.

It was five years since Jack's anger had last spun out of control, five years during which he had walked on eggshells around his wife and consoled himself in other women's beds. He had intended to be in another woman's bed tonight, except that, at the last moment, she had called to tell him she had met someone else and couldn't see him anymore.

He headed directly for the Hangar, and downed a few double bourbons while he waited for business to pick up. A frilly blonde came in around five-thirty. She let him buy her a drink, smiled at his bad jokes and lewd suggestions, and then politely refused when he offered to see her home.

'My boyfriend isn't into threesomes,' she said. A moment later, a guy in a pilot's uniform came through the door, and the blonde practically threw herself into his arms.

A little after six, a buxom brunette climbed onto the stool next to him. She looked to be around forty, which was usually too old for him, but she was hot and he was getting desperate. She, too, let him buy her a drink. They talked about the weather for a few minutes, she told him she was a school-teacher, he told her he was an airline pilot, and then he got right to the point.

'If you live nearby,' he whispered into her ear, 'I could show you one hell of a good time.'

'I'm sure you could,' she said, smiling sweetly. 'But if you don't mind, I think I'll hang around awhile longer, and look for someone a little closer to my age.'

She might as well have cut off his dick. He wanted to smack her from here to Oakland, but of course he couldn't. After all, he was in a public place. He paid the bill instead and stumbled out of the bar and into his car. Eight double bourbons down, he hit the road for home.

Now, he stood in JJ's bedroom, with his grandson crying, and his wife waiting for him to hit her, waiting for him to give her an excuse to leave him.

Slowly, his arm dropped to his side. Then, without a word, he walked out of the room.

Valerie soothed Justin until he stopped crying, and then she set him down on the floor with his favorite teddy bear. 'Just let me get your crib right side up again, and then we'll have a story to go to sleep on,' she said.

Half an hour later, she came downstairs. Jack was seated at the kitchen table with a bottle of bourbon beside him. But the bottle was unopened.

'Please,' he said when he saw her, 'don't leave me.'

'I can't live like this anymore,' she said. 'I won't.'

'Just tell me what you want me to do, and I'll do it,' he begged.

'You need help, Jack,' she told him.

'I'll get help,' he assured her, although he had no idea what kind of help she was talking about. 'I'll do anything. Just don't leave me.'

'Anything?' she echoed.

'Yes, anything,' he promised.

Three days later, Jack had his first appointment with Dr Roland Minter, psychiatrist.

PART SEVEN

1990

I

For Valerie, it was as though God had smiled down on her, forgiven her the sins she had committed with her own children, and bestowed upon her a miracle. A miracle named Justin. As the four-year-old sat in the sandbox behind the house, playing with his toy truck, it was as if Ricky had come back, still beautiful, still innocent, still untouched by her failure.

Anna had been a dutiful mother for the first three years of the boy's life, balancing working and parenting as best she could. Then one day, almost exactly a year ago, she had asked Valerie if she would keep Justin for a few days. It wasn't the first time she had asked, and Valerie thought nothing of it.

'Another weekend in Reno?' she asked with a smile.

'No, this time it's Las Vegas,' Anna replied. 'Dean's got a job at one of the casinos there, and he wants me to help him find a place to live. Do you mind? I don't want to leave Justin at my father's place.'

Valerie didn't mind at all. In fact, she was so delighted that it didn't occur to her to wonder why Dean would need Anna to help him find a place to live.

Justin was such a good baby, always smiling and happy, and having him all to herself, to pamper and spoil, was a real treat. Valerie took him on glorious shopping sprees to San Mateo and the Stanford Mall, and bought him whatever he asked for. She took him to San Francisco to ride the cable cars. She took him to the beach to play in the sand. And she took him to work, where Lil and Judy took every opportunity to fuss over him, as well.

'You've got a beautiful child there, Mrs Marsh,' Dennis Murphy observed when Valerie brought Justin into the pharmacy one day.

'He's my grandson,' she said proudly. 'He's staying with us for a few days.'

'He looks like an angel,' Dennis said.

'He is, Mr Murphy,' she assured him with a happy smile that abruptly faded. She remembered that Dennis Murphy had buried his wife a year ago, and that they had had no children. 'I'm sorry you never had the joy.'

'So am I,' he said with a sad little smile. 'But then, I've gotten to watch a whole generation of children grow up here on the Coast and begin families of their own. And it's helped.'

'In that case,' Valerie said on impulse, 'I'm going to bring this little one in just as often as I can.'

She thought of this time with Justin as a holiday, and delighted in every moment, wishing it could be for longer, dreading the afternoon that Anna was due to return.

Only Anna didn't return. The day and time she had specified came and went, and there was no sign of her and no word from her. Even though Valerie knew that Anna was a responsible girl, she began to worry. Then, almost a week later, when Valerie was seriously beginning to consider contacting the police, Anna finally called.

'I'm in Las Vegas, with Dean,' she announced.

'Yes, I know,' Valerie said. 'But I was getting worried. You said you would be home last week.'

'I know, but, well, you see, I've gotten a job at a hospital here, and I'm going to stay. I'm not coming back.'

'I see,' Valerie said, feeling her heart sink. She was pleased for Justin to be going back to his mother, but sad to be losing him. 'Do you want me to put him on an airplane?' She didn't want to think about not seeing the boy again for what might be a long while.

There was a pause at the other end of the line. 'No,' Anna said after a moment. 'Look, would you mind keeping him for me for a while?'

Valerie was stunned. 'Keep him?' she asked breathlessly. 'For how long?'

'I don't know yet,' the twenty-two-year-old replied. 'Dean, you see, well, he isn't exactly interested in raising someone else's kid, and Las Vegas isn't really the kind of place I'd want Justin to grow up in, anyway. And I'd rather he didn't go back to my father's house. He'd be much better off with you.'

At the age of fifty-two, Valerie had never dreamed that she would have a second chance to do it right. She went to church and thanked God for overlooking her sins and giving her this opportunity. She promised both the Almighty and herself that, this time, things would be different.

Delgada Road was as safe as Valerie could make it.

For the past three years, Jack had dutifully kept his appointments with his psychiatrist. Every Monday night after work, he drove over to Roland Minter's office in Redwood City.

He had heard about shrinks, of course, and was prepared for the kind of mind games he knew they played. But he wasn't prepared for Roland Minter. Jack had expected an equal, but the man was barely more than a midget, with thinning hair and round glasses and a smile that seemed to accept that Jack could flatten him with one punch. He expected walls filled with framed degrees and credentials and testimonials to his professional achievements, but Minter's walls were filled with framed watercolors of the California landscape. What's more, he didn't even have a couch in his office, just two comfortable chairs that faced each other across an antique mahogany coffee table.

'I'm not going to dig around in your brain any more than you want me to,' Minter said. 'We're just going to talk, about anything you like.'

At first, Jack simply sat there, slouched in his seat, glowering at the little doctor. 'I'm only here because my wife says I have to be,' he said.

'If that's the case,' the doctor responded, rubbing his chin thoughtfully, 'if you're coming here just because your wife wants you to, I probably won't be able to help very much.'

It wasn't until their third session together that Jack felt comfortable enough to look Minter in the eye.

'She said she'd leave me if I didn't come and see you,' he declared.

'Why do you think she said that?' the psychiatrist asked.

Jack shifted uneasily in his chair. 'She thinks I have a problem.'

'Do you?'

'How do I know?'

'What does she say?'

'She says I drink too much.'

'Do you?'

'No more than the next man.'

'What happens when you drink?' Minter asked during their fourth session.

'I get drunk,' Jack said.

'What happens when you get drunk?'

Jack's eyes slid away from the psychiatrist's. 'I get angry,' he mumbled.

'What do you do when you get angry?'

'. . . I take it out on her.'

Slowly, Jack came to trust the little gnome, as he had not trusted anyone but Valerie in his entire life. Slowly, he began to look at the root cause of his violence. At the end of three months, Minter wrote him a prescription for Xanax to help ease the anxiety that led to violence.

'This will ease the anxiety attacks, but you can't take it unless you stop drinking,' the doctor said.

Jack shrugged. He didn't drink because he liked alcohol. He drank because it made him feel less frightened. If the medication would do the same, he didn't need bourbon.

The medication did indeed relieve his anxiety, but it also dulled him down. 'Is this my only option?' he asked Minter. 'Either I'm a live wire or a soggy blanket.'

'In time, after you've dealt with some of your issues, you may be able to go off the medication,' the psychiatrist told him.

Jack was still working for Federal Airlines. Five years earlier, he had been promoted to aircraft maintenance supervisor. Two years ago, he had taken up weightlifting at the new health club in town, mostly because it was a good excuse to be out of the house. But it had an added benefit. At sixty, he was in better shape than many forty-year-olds.

He no longer went to the Hangar after work. He didn't need to watch his buddies drinking. But he still had his women, and three or four nights a week he would visit whatever one he was seeing at the time. The women had aged over the years, as he had, and were now more often divorcées or widows in their late forties and early fifties. As long as he took them out every once in a while, and made them feel like a million bucks, they weren't too fussy about the quality of the sex. That was another drawback of Xanax.

On other nights, he went home. Valerie actually seemed happy to see him, although he didn't know why. Mostly, they walked on eggshells around each other, moving through the house in silence, like ships passing. She wasn't interested in airplanes. He wasn't interested in wedding dresses. What was there to talk about? But as long as he wasn't drunk, as long as he wasn't angry, he was welcome.

When Justin came to stay, Jack took up with two women at the same time, a widow from Atherton and a divorcée from Cupertino, which was something he had never done before. It was often confusing, as he tried to keep the two of them straight in his head, but it assured that he would not have to be home any week-night evening before the boy was asleep.

She hadn't bothered to ask him if it would be all right to bring Justin into their home on a permanent basis. She simply told him one day that she was doing it. If she had asked him, he would have told her that the last thing he wanted at his age was another kid to raise.

Having Justin in the house was like having her children back again. Valerie could fuss over him the way she had once fussed over her own. She put Justin in Ricky's old room, and spent weeks redecorating it. She sewed the new curtains and bedspread herself, and painted the walls with ribbons and balloons, and filled the toy box to overflowing.

She took Justin to the bridal shop with her and set up a place for him in a corner of the workroom. At the appropriate times, she took him to the doctor, to the dentist, and to the barber. When he asked, Valerie told him that his mother loved him very much, but just wasn't able to take care of him for a while. He seemed to accept that. If he was troubled by the fact that she rarely called and never came to visit, he kept it to himself.

To make up for Anna's absence, Valerie devoted most of her time to the boy, to the exclusion of other things. Lil and Judy didn't mind. They gladly picked up the slack at the shop because it was so good to see Valerie smiling again. The smile was genuine. The house wasn't empty anymore.

'Grandma, why did you live in such a big house before I came here?' Justin asked one day not long after his fourth birthday.

Valerie smiled. 'Because there used to be other little boys and girls living here, just like you.'

'There did?' The four-year-old's startling yellow eyes, which were so like his father's, grew big and round. 'Who?'

'Well, there was your daddy, for one. He used to live in the very room you live in now. Then there was JJ, your uncle, who was in the room right across the hall. And then there was your Aunt Rosemary and your Aunt Ellen, who lived where the sewing room is now, and your Aunt Priscilla, who used to live in what's now the guest room.'

'Where are they all now?'

'They grew up and went their separate ways,' she told him with a pain in her heart. 'Just like all children are meant to do. Just like you will someday.'

'Oh no, Grandma,' Justin said solemnly. 'I won't do that.'

'Of course you will,' Valerie assured him. 'It's not a

bad thing to grow up and start a life of your own. It's what you're supposed to do, what everyone does.'

But the little boy shook his head. 'When I'm growed up, I want to stay right here with you,' he said.

'Now why would you want to do that?' she asked.

'So that Momma and Poppa will know where to find me,' Justin replied.

2

'Come on, Johnny, come back to bed,' the girl whined. 'It's four o'clock in the morning.'

John Marsh, Jr, who had stopped using his childhood nickname when he left home sixteen years earlier, ignored her.

It was not unusual for him to be up at this hour. Even as a boy, he had spent more time awake in the night than asleep, usually with his head buried under his pillow, trying not to cry. It wasn't much different in the Army. The first six months were pure hell, and sometimes he couldn't help but cry, and some of his fellow soldiers teased him unmercifully, calling him a sissy and a mama's boy. Then one day, he turned on the worst of them, a big strapping bully from Alabama, and broke his jaw with one punch. He spent a month in the brig for it, but no one ever teased him again. And he learned not to cry.

'Grab that energy and that anger, son,' his commanding officer had told him, 'and put it to good use.'

JJ had taken the words to heart. He put his head down, minded his business, and worked hard. He was smart and a quick learner, and he began to inch his way back up the ladder of respect. He was promoted twice in two years, due in large part to an officer he liked and admired, who had taken him under his wing and gone out of his way to show him the ropes. And he was well on his way to becoming a corporal when the officer made a pass at him in the shower one night.

Lashing out before he stopped to think, JJ slugged him.

'Oh, God, I'm sorry,' the officer exclaimed, staggering to his feet, his nose smashed and bloody. 'I thought . . . well, you always . . . you seemed . . . I guess I made a mistake.'

'Yeah, I guess you did,' JJ said.

'Please don't tell them,' the officer implored. 'The Army is my life. I've got ten years in, but I'd be out of here in an instant if anyone found out.'

JJ didn't know whether he was more angry or embarrassed, but he never said a word about what had actually happened, not even when, because of the broken nose, the incident was reported and an investigation was undertaken.

'Why would you just haul off and slug an officer?' the commanding officer asked.

'I guess I didn't like what he wanted me to do, sir,' JJ said.

'And what did he want you to do?' the officer inquired.

JJ looked him right in the eye. 'I guess he thought I was taking too much time in the shower,' he replied, making it up as he went along. 'He wanted me to scrub it down with my toothbrush.'

He was busted back to private and spent six months in the brig. It could have been worse, he knew – he could have been discharged. He was never sure why he wasn't.

He stayed out of trouble after that, mostly by doing what he was told to do, and by not getting too close to anyone. He decided it was wiser to have acquaintances rather than friends. He was stationed in Germany

402

for two years during the late 1970s. He met a girl there, a pretty thing with golden hair and green eyes, and spent most of his liberty with her and her family. But when he went back to the States, he didn't take her with him.

The only two actions that took place during his time in service was the attempt to rescue the Iranian hostages and the invasion of Grenada. Although by then, he had almost nine years in, he must have been in the wrong branch of the Army, because he wasn't a part of either operation.

'At the rate I'm going, I may never get into a war,' he wrote to his brother. 'Although the rescue attempt was a disaster and the Grenada thing didn't amount to a hill of beans, at least it was something.'

He had first written to Ricky, care of Chris Rodriguez, just after he had joined the Army. Then about a year later, he had started writing the letters on a fairly regular basis. He had no idea whether Ricky actually got any of them, but he kept on writing. It was a way for him to keep in touch. And it was a way for him to express exactly how he felt about things, without putting himself at risk.

It wasn't that JJ hungered for war, exactly, but he was just itching to know what it was like. Besides, he had been combat-trained, at great expense to his country, and while he supposed that deterrence could be a useful ploy against potential enemies, it seemed to him an enormous waste of time and effort to maintain as many as half a million troops at maximum readiness, indefinitely.

In 1989, Staff Sergeant John Marsh, Jr, was posted to Fort Hood, just outside Killeen, Texas. He promptly took up with a cute little number who worked around the fringes of the base. But after two months, she was starting to take their relationship a little too seriously, and he was starting to get restless.

'Johnny, come to bed,' she said with her most seductive giggle. 'I'm wide awake now.'

He chuckled and wasted no time in climbing under the sheets.

A week later, he and a buddy drove over to Temple, and wandered into a bar.

'What'll you have, boys?' a throaty-voiced brunette asked.

'A couple of beers,' JJ said. She looked to be five to ten years older than he was, he guessed, and she had probably been pretty once. But now she just looked as though she was doing her best to get through one more day.

Three beers later, she was looking better to him. When she brought a fourth, he asked her what she was doing after work.

'Going to sleep, soldier,' she said with a laugh.

After that, JJ came back every chance he had, by himself, and sat at one of her tables, nursing a beer, and trying to engage her in conversation whenever business was slow.

There was something about her that got to him, but he didn't know what, or why. He found out she was forty, she was divorced, and she had a boyfriend. It didn't take him long to notice that someone, he assumed the boyfriend, was taking life out on her, because several times she showed up with cuts and bruises that he could tell she had tried to cover with makeup. JJ wanted to talk to her about it, at the very least to tell her that he understood, but she never gave him the opportunity.

Then, one Saturday night, he watched as a squirrelly guy marched into the bar, grabbed her by the arm, and forced her out the back. He couldn't help himself, he followed.

They were in the alley and she was trying to tell the

guy that she wasn't holding out on him, that business had been slow and tips thin, but he wasn't listening. He was too busy whaling on her.

JJ couldn't stop himself. Before he even knew what he was doing, the guy was on the ground, his eyes bulging, his neck almost detached from his head.

'Are you crazy?' the brunette shrieked. 'What are you doing?'

'He was a punk,' JJ said. 'And he was beating up on you.'

'Yeah, so what? Who the hell do you think you are – some knight in shining armor?'

She fell down on her knees, sobbing, and tried to cradle the guy's head in her lap.

The local police showed up. The brunette told them what had happened. JJ wasn't on base, it was a civilian matter. The Army couldn't protect him. After fifteen years, his career was over. He was tried and convicted of manslaughter, just one year short of what would have been his war.

3

Ricky scrambled out of the Honda and started running as fast as his legs would carry him. He could hear the screech of tires behind him and then the shouts and the sound of feet on the pavement. At the very last moment, he ducked down a narrow alley, hugging the side of a building, making himself as invisible as he could in the hot July night.

He had left Eddie's place less than an hour ago, and although he thought he had been careful, someone had picked up his trail. The only trouble was, he didn't know if it was Benny's people after him, or the feds, and he couldn't take the chance to find out. He held his breath and waited until he heard the feet hurry past the alley without pausing. Only then did he relax.

It had taken him four years to devise and carry out his plan. Four years, during which he had become one of the top movers in Benny Ruiz's organization, and Benny had established himself as the man in the West. On his behalf, Ricky and Eddie had systematically taken over most of California. From San Diego to San Mateo, Ruiz owned the drug trade. A year ago, Ricky had approached him with an idea.

'I think we're ready to take San Francisco now,' he had told him.

Benny's eyes had widened. 'You sure, kid?'

'I'm sure,' Ricky replied, and proceeded to detail his strategy. It was simple, really, or so Ricky led him to believe. 'I've gotten in with a couple of guys up there. Ones who are in key positions with the competition and aren't too happy with the way they're being treated. Off and on, they been trying to recruit me, but I told them that I'm with an organization that treats its people right. They're interested in making a switch. It's the back door into the whole city.'

Ruiz was getting battered in San Francisco, constantly losing both men and goods to the competition. A little turnaround would be fair play. And it would give him back some respect.

'You're a smart kid, Ricky,' he said. 'And if this goes down like you say it will, you're my number one man.'

Ricky knew it would go down. He had already fixed it. It was easy. He knew exactly what to do. He went to Tom Starwood.

'I've gotten myself in a jam and I want out,' he told the attorney. 'Can you help me?'

'What are you into?' Starwood asked.

Ricky told him all about Benny, and about what he had been doing for the past six years. 'I got a kid now, and I don't want to live like this anymore,' he concluded. 'But I know Ruiz will never let me out. I'm too high in his organization. I know too much.'

The attorney scratched his chin. 'Let me make a few phone calls,' he said. 'I'll get back to you.'

Two days later, Ricky was meeting with two federal drug agents.

'In the last few years, Ruiz has become a pretty big fish in the ocean, with an organization we'd like to bust up,' one of them said. 'So we wouldn't say no to putting him out of business.'

'I got one condition,' Ricky said. 'I want Ruiz doing time. I don't want him slipping out of your grasp or skating on any smart lawyer technicalities.'

'Is this personal?' the agent asked.

'You could say that,' Ricky replied. 'He's always bragging about how he's never been inside. Well, I want to change all that for him.'

'Why?' the agent asked. 'What did he do to you?'

Ricky looked the man straight in the eye. 'He killed my sister,' he said softly.

The two agents exchanged glances. 'Okay, Ricky,' the first one said. 'We can work together on this.'

Two months later, while Ricky and the feds were still putting their plan together, two sixteen-year-old girls from Palo Alto died of an overdose of bad cocaine.

'Was this Ruiz?' the feds asked.

'Yeah, it had to be,' Ricky said, knowing it was also Eddie.

'What the hell happened?' he demanded of his friend a few hours later.

'Don't ask me,' Eddie retorted. 'I don't make the stuff. I just distribute it.'

Ricky sighed. 'We'll be lucky if we all don't go down for this,' he said. He asked Tom Starwood to talk to the feds, to get them not to prosecute. They agreed, but it made them more determined than ever to take Ruiz down.

A month later, Ricky and Benny met in a room at the St Francis Hotel with two men who passed themselves off as unhappy members of the competition. The conversation was recorded. Two weeks later, cutting Ricky out, Benny made a second, solo trip to San Francisco. But the cops were ready and waiting. With fifty pounds of cocaine and all the information Ricky had put together, Benny Ruiz went to prison for twenty years. Ricky was never indicted.

'Jeez, Benny, I feel real awful,' Ricky apologized after

the trial, after the conviction. 'I checked and double-checked. I thought these guys were solid.'

'You were had, kid,' Ruiz told him. 'And so was I.'

Ricky looked right at the drug dealer. 'I hope you don't think I set you up or anything,' he said with perfect guile. 'You're my man.'

'Sure, kid,' Benny said, a little smile playing around the corner of his mouth. 'Maybe see you around sometime.'

A week later, Ricky's green trailer mysteriously burned to the ground. It was just by chance that he happened not to be there at the time. It didn't matter. It was just a place. What mattered was that he had gotten even for Rosemary.

'You got to be crazy, man,' Eddie declared. 'We had a good thing going here. Why'd you have to go and ruin it?'

Ricky shrugged. 'Got bored, I guess.'

'They're going to come after me next,' Eddie complained. 'You know they will.'

'That's why I'm here,' Ricky said. 'To tell you to get out. Find another place.' He handed Eddie a piece of paper. 'When you're settled, go see this guy. I've set it all up. Tell him who you are, and what you've done. He'll take care of you.'

'Who is he?' Eddie asked.

'Someone a whole lot smarter than Benny Ruiz,' Ricky told him with a dry chuckle. 'Trust me, you'll be okay with him.'

'What are *you* going to do?'

'Disappear for a while.'

For almost a year, Ricky dropped out of sight. He had more than enough money stashed away. He could afford to get lost. He rented a room in a little town called

Pescadero, about twenty miles down the road from Half Moon Bay, and just for the heck of it went to work on his landlord's fishing boat. It was hard work for little pay, and much to his amazement, and amusement, he found that he liked it. His fear of water made it that much more challenging. He wondered what his old friend Chris Rodriguez would say if he knew.

Off the boat, he kept to himself, eating his meals at a local restaurant, watching a lot of television, and staying away from everyone he knew, just in case Benny's people might still be out looking for him.

When he heard that Ruiz's entire organization had been dismantled, he decided it was safe to come out. It wasn't. He hadn't shown his face in Half Moon Bay for two days before he realized someone was following him. He ditched the Harley and bought an old, nondescript Honda Accord. Then he moved inland, taking a room at a seedy motel in Redwood City.

He called the feds. They assured him that Benny's people had all been rounded up, but he knew they couldn't be certain of that. Eddie had been one of Benny's people, and they didn't have him. He asked for protection, although he knew they had no more interest in him. But he had helped them break up one of the major drug rings in the state, so they told him they'd send someone down as soon as they could.

Ricky thought about it for a while and then made a decision. He called Eddie.

'Hey, man, how've you been?' Eddie cried, delighted to hear from him again. 'Come on over. You ain't seen my new digs yet.'

Three hours later, once Ricky was certain he had ditched anyone who might be following him, he pulled into the driveway of a secluded home in the tiny town of San Martin, just north of Gilroy.

'I don't guess there was too much to worry about, after all,' Eddie said, opening the door. 'You seem to be okay, and as you can see, so am I. Benny's people have probably forgotten about us by now.'

'Probably,' Ricky said, glancing around the well-appointed house. 'It looks like business is pretty good.'

Eddie grinned. 'You could say that. That guy you sent me to was everything you said he would be. And I owe you, man, for looking out for me, and for not giving me up when the big bust went down.'

'In that case,' Ricky said, 'I need two favors.'

'Sure,' Eddie replied without hesitation.

Ricky pulled an envelope from his pocket with his mother's name written on it. 'There's a letter in here, and a key that goes to a safe deposit box at a bank in Half Moon Bay. I want my kid to have what's in it.'

'You got a relationship with your kid?' Eddie was surprised. 'You always said you didn't want nothing to do with him.'

'I don't, really,' Ricky admitted. 'Mostly because I don't want him getting caught in the crossfire, if you know what I mean. But if anything happens to me, like if you don't hear from me in the next few weeks, then I want you to get this to my mother. Will you do that?'

'Of course I will,' Eddie promised, and Ricky knew that his friend would keep his word. 'What's the second favor?'

'I need a piece, if you got one you can spare,' Ricky said. 'Strictly for protection.' He didn't tell his friend about the guys who were following him.

He had lived in a safe place for the past year. There had been no reason for him to have a gun. Eddie didn't argue. He gave him what he asked for. It was an old Colt semiautomatic. Ricky inserted the clip, cocked and locked the gun, slipped it into his pocket.

'You want back in, man?' Eddie asked. 'Just say the word and you're in.'

Ricky shook his head. The year he had spent in Pescadero had changed him in some fundamental way he wasn't sure he understood. He didn't know what he was going to do with the rest of his life, but he knew he couldn't go back to hooking babies on cocaine. He said goodbye to his friend. Less than an hour after he left Eddie's place, they found him.

He waited twenty minutes, pressed flat against the building in the alley, until he was certain they were gone. He didn't dare go back to the Honda, certain they would have it staked out, so he made his way to the highway and thumbed a ride north. He was glad he had the Colt with him. He didn't know if he would have to use it, but he knew, if he had to, he would.

Ricky was on the run for three days. When he finally made his way back to the motel in Redwood City, he found that his room had been ransacked. Quickly, he grabbed what few possessions he needed and made it out the back, barely one step ahead of two goons with bulges in their back pockets.

Without a vehicle, he moved on foot, down back roads and alleys, from Redwood City to Palo Alto, eating at fast food places, grabbing a few minutes of sleep when he thought it was safe. Twice, they almost caught up with him. Twice, he managed to elude them. He called the feds again, and again they put him off. He didn't dare call Eddie, and he didn't know anyone else he could turn to for help. He carried the loaded Colt in the pocket of his leather bomber jacket, and that gave him at least a small measure of security.

He never got a really close look at the goons who were following him, but it was close enough for him to know that one was large and dark and wearing dark clothing, while the other was of medium build and coloring and was wearing a blue shirt. He knew what to look for when they were together, but he wasn't sure he would recognize either one of them if they split up.

Around midnight, he decided it was time to find food. He had spotted a little convenience store earlier in the day, and had circled around, checking it out, waiting until he was sure it was safe. No one had gone in or out for the past half hour. He would have waited longer, but he hadn't eaten since early morning, and hunger finally took over.

A man was behind the counter. He was of average height and wore gold-rimmed spectacles and a white apron over a sizable girth. 'May I help you?' he inquired pleasantly with the soft slur of an accent Ricky couldn't place.

'What's good?' Ricky asked, the smells driving him crazy.

'Everything's good,' the man said. 'But the goulash is especially good.' He took a long spoon and began stirring something in a pan.

'What's goulash?'

'It's like a stew, and I make it with meat and onions and vegetables over noodles.'

'Yeah, okay, I'll take that,' Ricky said. 'And a Pepsi.'

The man nodded and began to dish up the food. Ricky was so preoccupied with watching him that he almost didn't hear the door open. But the instant that it did, the hair at the back of his neck stood up. Instinctively, he reached into his pocket and grasped the Colt. In the mirror behind the counter, he could see a man of medium height and coloring wearing a blue shirt.

Ricky didn't stop to think. He knew he was a dead duck from where the goon was standing. He whirled around and pulled out the gun, released the lock, took dead aim, and squeezed the trigger. The man slumped to the floor with an expression of surprise and bewilderment freezing on his face, and a bright red stream of blood staining his blue shirt.

'What the hell,' the convenience store owner exclaimed, jamming his foot hard against the silent alarm button and crouching down behind the counter. If the guy had come in here to rob him, he was sure going about it in a funny way.

'It's all right, you can get up,' Ricky called to him. 'I'm not going to hurt you.'

The man stayed where he was. 'Then what the hell is going on?'

'This guy has been after me,' Ricky replied, bending over the body, and starting to search for a weapon. 'He was trying to kill me. Don't worry, it's got nothing to do with you.'

'Trying to kill you?' the man cried. He poked his head over the counter. 'Why would Ned Hicks want to kill you?'

Ricky blinked. 'What do you mean? You know this guy?'

'Sure I know him.'

'Well, he was a drug dealer.'

The man laughed. 'A drug dealer? This guy? You're crazy. He works the swing shift over at the hospital. Comes in every night around this time for a cup of coffee.'

Ricky's heart stopped beating for two painful seconds. It had all happened so fast, and he had gotten only a quick glimpse in the mirror. It looked like one of the guys who were following him. Had he shot the wrong man?

'You sure?' he barked.

'Of course, I'm sure,' the owner said. 'He lives just a couple of blocks over. He's got a wife and two kids, for Christ's sake.'

Ricky slumped to the floor. There was nowhere to run. For some reason he could never quite explain, he didn't even try to run. Instead, he stayed by the side of the body. One clean shot to the heart had done the job, and he would have done anything to take it back. But it was too late. He reached out a finger and touched the man's cheek. It was still warm. He looked at the pool of blood that was beginning to gather, and he began to whimper and shiver much as he had as a five-year-old, staring at the body of his sister Priscilla.

He didn't react when two Palo Alto police officers entered the store with their guns drawn. He didn't resist when they put handcuffs on him and took him into custody. It didn't matter. Whatever happened to him from now on, he knew his life was already over.

Tom Starwood came to see him. 'I thought you were staying out of trouble,' the public defender said with a sigh.

'So did I,' Ricky told him dully.

'What do you want me to do?'

'I want you to tell those sonsafederalbitches that this is their fault,' Ricky said bitterly. 'If they'd sent someone, when I begged them to, this wouldn't have happened.'

'You asked for protection, and they didn't give it to you?'

Ricky nodded. 'Two of Benny's goons are after me. I been on the run for a week. I told them. They said they'd send someone.'

Starwood sighed. He had been key in helping Ricky turn in the Ruiz organization. Several times, he had acted as a go-between. Now he felt partly responsible for what had happened.

'The guy you shot. You're sure he wasn't one of them?'

'I'm sure,' Ricky replied with a groan. He turned anguished eyes on the attorney. 'It's not enough that I used to turn babies on to coke. I just shot some guy who had to work the night shift to support his family.'

Tom Starwood went into action. He began with the feds, first reaming them for not coming to Ricky's aid, assuring them that they were as responsible for an innocent man's death as Ricky was, and suggesting that if there were still some of Benny's people after Ricky, and they got to him, then the two agents involved in taking Ruiz down might be vulnerable.

'Are you threatening a federal agency?' he was asked.

'Not at all,' Starwood replied smoothly. 'I'm just telling you something you need to know.'

After that, he went to the Palo Alto police, and then to Redwood City, the county seat, calling in all the favors he had amassed in his twenty-plus years of practice. A plan was finally devised and Starwood made sure that everyone signed off on it. Then he went to Ricky.

'You're going into the Witness Protection Program,' he announced.

Ricky blinked. 'What do you mean?'

'I mean the feds are taking you in. You'll be given a new identity and relocated someplace where Ruiz's men won't be able to find you.'

'But aren't you forgetting something – I killed a guy.'

'I know, and that's unfortunate,' the attorney said. 'But it doesn't change the fact that you were an informant, and you were in fear for your life.'

'So I just get a pass?'

'What? Would you rather get a needle?'

'Hell no,' Ricky declared. 'But I don't know that I deserve to get off scot-free, either.'

'You're not,' Starwood informed him. 'Witness Protection or not, wherever you go, for the rest of your life you'll always be looking over your shoulder.'

'Alaska,' Ricky said suddenly.

'What?'

'I want them to relocate me to Alaska.'

'Why Alaska?'

Ricky shrugged. 'Because I want to go work on a fishing boat.'

A week later, Tom Starwood drove over to El Granada and knocked at the door of the house on Delgada Road. A startled Valerie let him in. They sat in the living room with cups of tea balanced on the arms of their chairs, just as though he had dropped in for a neighborly chat.

'Ricky wanted me to tell you that he's all right,' he said after he had told her as much as he could about what had really happened.

'Can't I see him?' Valerie whispered. 'Just for a moment? Just to say goodbye?'

'No,' Starwood said. 'He's already been moved.'

'Can we know where he's going?'

Starwood shook his head. 'The only way it works is if nobody knows where he is. It's for his own safety.'

'He has a son,' Valerie murmured.

Starwood nodded. 'I know. He told me. It would be better if certain people didn't know that, either.'

Valerie sighed. Ricky hadn't been much of a father to Justin when he *was* around. So she supposed it wouldn't make much of a difference now that he wasn't. She was numb. It was as if her mind was a wheel, and something had caught in the spokes to slow the turning. Ricky had killed an innocent man? Her little boy, the most vulnerable of all her children, had taken a life, and because of it, he had to disappear and she might never see him again? It didn't make any sense to her. This wasn't the way it was supposed to happen. She wished there were someplace she could go, if only in her mind, where it wouldn't hurt so much.

For the first time in a dozen years, she wanted a drink, not just one drink, but a whole lot of drinks, one right after another, so that she could bury the pain in a thick, mindless fog. The urge was so strong, she was actually licking her lips. She went and talked to her mirror instead.

Three days later, Eddie Melendez came into the bridal shop. 'I was a friend of Ricky's,' he said to Valerie. 'I wanted to tell you how sorry I am.'

'Thank you,' Valerie murmured.

True to his word, Eddie pulled the envelope with Valerie's name written on it out of his pocket. 'He told me, if I didn't hear from him for a while, I should bring this to you. He told me it's for his boy.'

Valerie blinked in surprise. 'Thank you,' she said again. 'And thank you for coming. I'm glad Ricky had a friend he could trust.'

She carried the envelope around with her until she was finished with her work. Then she opened it and removed the contents. There was a brief note. 'This key is to a safe deposit box at the bank in Half Moon Bay. I want you to use what's in it for my son. Love you, Ma, Ricky.'

She stared at the words. A safe deposit box? The bank was just a block away. She asked Lil to accompany her, and she asked Judy to watch Justin.

'My son has a safe deposit box here,' she told the teller. 'He left instructions for me to open it.'

The teller looked up the records. Ricky had indeed opened the account, and had put his mother's name on it.

'You didn't know?' the teller asked.

'No, I didn't,' Valerie replied, signing the card. The teller took her into the vault, where they inserted the keys, opened the safe, and removed the box. Then the two women were taken to a private room and left alone.

Curious and hesitant at the same time, Valerie opened the box. Inside, stacked in neat piles according to denomination, was more money than she had ever seen in one place before. With trembling hands, she started to count, stopping only after she had reached almost a quarter of a million dollars.

'Where did he get all this money?' Lil wondered, although she was fairly confident that she already knew.

'I don't know,' Valerie said. 'Do you think it's honest money?'

Lil shrugged. 'Do people have to hide honest money in a safe deposit box?' she asked.

'But it's so much,' Valerie said. 'Where could he have gotten it?'

'From being mixed up in something he shouldn't have been, I expect,' Lil replied bluntly, and then she sighed. 'I think maybe you didn't know Ricky as well as you thought you did.'

'I'm beginning to wonder if I knew him at all,' Valerie murmured.

The two women walked out of the bank in a daze. Valerie had decided to leave the money right where it was until she could figure out what to do with it.

'I'll ask Jack,' she said. 'I'm sure he'll know what to do.'

'Call that lawyer of his,' Jack suggested over dinner, the first time in over a week that he had come home at a reasonable hour. 'Maybe he can figure out a way to hide it so the government doesn't grab most of it in taxes.'

'But don't you care where it came from?' Valerie asked.

Jack shrugged. 'Not particularly. Money is money. I don't think, at this point, it makes much difference where it came from, do you?'

'Of course I do,' she replied. 'I'm sure he didn't earn it honestly.'

'Probably not,' Jack said.

Valerie thought for a moment. She could already picture her confession in church on Sunday if they decided to keep ill-gotten money. 'I don't suppose there's any way to give it back, is there?'

'I wouldn't know how,' Jack told her, a note of exasperation creeping into his voice. 'Or to who.'

Valerie sighed. 'In that case, if it is bad money, shouldn't we at least try to make it right by giving it away to charity or something?'

'Look, if Ricky'd wanted to give it away to charity, don't you think he already would have?' Jack snapped, pushing himself away from the table, ending the conversation.

Tom Starwood arranged to have the money quietly invested. 'I know someone in estate management,' he explained. 'He'll put the money into a trust fund for the boy. He'll do it in a way so that taxes can be minimized, and no one has to be the wiser.'

Valerie smiled. 'My grandson will go to college,' she said proudly. 'He'll be the first person in my family to ever go to college.'

She never told Father Bernaldo about the money. She reasoned that, wherever it had come from, it was Ricky's sin, not hers. She kept Ricky's letter. She read it over and over again, until the slip of paper threatened to fall apart. Then she pressed it between the pages of her Bible.

They were all gone now . . . Priscilla, JJ, Rosemary, Ellen, and finally Ricky. All gone. Now there was only Justin.

PART EIGHT

1999

I

At the age of thirteen, Justin Marsh was already almost six feet in height, easily the tallest boy in his seventh-grade class. More slender than strapping, he chose base-ball over football. The high school basketball coach had eyes on him, and had already approached him about switching to the indoor court, but Justin knew what he wanted, and what he wanted was one day to play short-stop for the San Francisco Giants.

He hadn't told his grandmother yet, because he knew she had her heart set on him going to college. But he figured, when the time came, she would see for herself how good he really was and how important it was to him, and then she would understand. He hadn't said anything to his mother, either. On his infrequent visits to Las Vegas, Anna always seemed much too busy with her other family, her husband and their three kids, to have any interest in him. The one person he would like to have told, who he was sure would have understood, was his father, but he didn't have any idea where Ricky was.

'Looks like you're going to take after your grandpa, for sure,' Valerie observed on the morning of his birthday when she had to raise the column of black marks climbing up his closet door by a full two inches.

'Not my dad?' Justin asked, frowning.

'No, sweetheart,' she replied with a pang of sadness that the boy had no real memory of Ricky. 'Your father isn't nearly so tall.'

'But I look like him, don't I? You've always told me I look like him.'

'That you do,' Valerie confirmed. 'Except that your hair is light and his is dark, you look very much like him.'

It was true. Justin had the same chiseled features, the same glowing eyes, the same generous smile as his father had, and the same sweet personality, too. Valerie had tried very hard to make Ricky a part of Justin's life. The boy knew from his earliest days that his father had made mistakes, but he had also been told that Ricky had paid his debt to society and was trying to turn his life around.

'Was my father a crook?' Justin asked when he was seven years old.

'Well, not exactly, dear,' Valerie told him, blurring the facts a bit. 'He was just very young and he got mixed up with the wrong people.'

'Was my father a jailbird?' he asked when he was eight.

'No,' his grandmother assured him. 'He did spend some time in a youth correctional facility, but that's very different.'

Ironically, Justin's best friend was Tony Rodriguez, Chris's son. The two boys had been inseparable since the third grade.

'Your father stole stuff,' Tony informed Justin one warm spring day when they were ten years old and had cut school to go down to the beach and share a joint that Tony had pilfered from his older brother's stash. 'My dad told me he robbed all the neighbors. Well, he robbed all those who had something worth stealing, anyway, and after that, he went and held up a liquor store in Pacifica and got caught.'

'He doesn't sound like such a great guy,' Justin said with a sigh.

'Well, he and my dad were good friends for a while,' Tony told him graciously. 'So he must've been pretty okay.'

'Yeah?'

'Yeah.'

'Then why did he do all that stuff?' Justin wondered. 'It couldn't have been for the money. My grandparents have enough.'

Tony shrugged. 'My dad said it was probably for the thrill.'

Justin contemplated that for a moment. 'Still, I wish I could know him,' he said finally.

Tony took a long drag on the joint before passing it to his friend. 'Well, you never know,' he said. 'Maybe someday you will.'

It was nine years since Valerie had last seen Ricky. Nine long years, during which had come changes. Most notable among them, other than the fact that Justin was growing like a weed, was that, in 1997, Jack had retired from Federal Airlines after forty-three years of service, with a dinner, a pension, and the heartfelt thanks of a grateful company. Discounting the terrible crash into San Francisco Bay back in 1974, he had an unblemished record.

Knowing it was coming, Valerie dreaded for months the morning that he would wake up with no place to go, and no reason to get out of bed.

'It's going to be such an enormous change, I don't have any idea what I'm going to do,' she confided to Connie. 'More to the point, I don't have any idea what *he's* going to do.'

Connie Gilchrist had retired herself. Shortly after her sixty-ninth birthday, she turned her business over to others, and began settling into a very active old age, volunteering her services to a number of worthwhile organizations, and complaining that she was a whole lot busier now than she had ever been selling real estate.

'Life as you and he know it is about to change,' she said. 'And it's likely to be a while before he adjusts.'

On the day he retired, Jack had been seeing Roland Minter once a week for exactly ten years. In the beginning, he had resented having to make the trek to Redwood City every Monday evening, but after six months had passed, he no longer minded the trip at all. And by the time five years had passed, he looked forward to it. Not that he would admit it to anyone, but Roland Minter was the first man that Jack had ever been able to talk to.

Still, when the morning came that Valerie had to get up to go to work, and Jack did not, she held her breath, and with a racing heart, tiptoed around the room, closing the bathroom door softly behind her, making as little noise as possible.

'What time is it?' he asked suddenly, startling her as she reached into a dresser drawer.

She braced herself. 'It's eight o'clock,' she told him.

'Oh,' he said and turned over and went back to sleep. Valerie heaved a silent sigh of relief, shook her head at her own silliness, and blessed Roland Minter for perhaps the millionth time.

Even after Jack had been retired for a year, Valerie was still trying to get used to having him around all the time. When she went to the bridal shop, he went to the health club. When she came home, he came home. He got into the habit of accompanying her to town when she went to the market, on the pretext of stopping in at the hardware store or the auto parts place while she shopped. He watched her cook and do the laundry, and he even carried the clean baskets upstairs for her. It was almost as though he was afraid to let her out of his sight.

'It's like having a puppy dog,' she told Connie. 'He keeps trailing after me all the time.'

'He's lost,' Connie said. 'He used to have his work, and that defined him. He used to be young and virile and *that* defined him. Now he doesn't know who he is or where he belongs.'

Jack looked at himself in the bathroom mirror and saw someone he didn't recognize . . . someone who was old and tired and used up. Someone who went to the health club almost every day because he had no other place to go, and lifted weights, just to maintain the illusion that he was still young. Only he and his trainer knew that the weights got lighter every month, and that he was lifting them with more and more difficulty.

Being retired wasn't exactly what Jack had had in mind. In his capacity as a supervisor, he felt he could have stayed on at Federal Airlines for at least another few years. He thought he had made that very clear to the brass, and he couldn't understand why they had chosen not to act on it. When they didn't, however, he rationalized that he had worked hard all his life, and deserved a respite from the daily grind. He believed that for almost a month, during which he painted the house, patched the roof, repaired the front steps, and cleaned out the garage. Then one night, feeling restless, he went to a bar up in Pacifica, and for the first time since he had begun seeing Minter, got so drunk that he didn't remember going home with the floozy from a nearby stool, not even when he woke up the next morning in a strange bed, with her all over him. His eyes were bloodshot, his head ached, he was sick to his stomach, and he felt alive again.

After that, he drove up to Pacifica two or three times a week, skipping the bar and going directly to her apartment. Valerie didn't seem to notice that he sometimes didn't come home until morning. Or maybe she noticed and just didn't care.

After a couple of years, he lost interest in the floozy. Or at least that's what he told himself when, once again, certain parts of his anatomy started not working the way they were supposed to. He thought of asking Minter for that new enhancement drug, Viagra, everyone was talking about, but he was too embarrassed, so he stopped going to Pacifica, stopped pretending that he was still young.

In January of 1999, Lil McAllister followed Jack into retirement. She had spent the past seventeen years happily doing whatever needed to be done at Val Originals, taking on additional responsibility so that Valerie could have more time to spend with Justin. But at eighty, she decided it was time to hang up her needle.

'What am I ever going to do without you?' Valerie asked.

'You'll do fine,' Lil said with a cackle. 'Probably a lot better. I was never very good at sewing, and you know it. You kept me on all these years just to have someone here who was older than you.'

So Valerie, who had enjoyed working two or three days a week during Justin's childhood, went back to working full-time.

'Jack and I seem to be going in opposite directions,' she said to Connie.

'It happens,' Connie replied.

'Actually,' Valerie admitted, 'I'm looking forward to getting back into the swing of things.'

Lil's daughter, Judy Alvarez, who had turned into a

fine seamstress, was still on hand. Along with two competent assistants, she now ran the shop, while Valerie took care of the bookings and the bookkeeping. Of course, it was still Valerie's visions that young women sought, visions that came to life, first on paper, then on mannequins, and finally on brides as they walked proudly down the aisle.

'Business is thriving, and probably will be as long as girls keep getting married,' she reported to Connie. 'We're busier now than we ever were.'

'At my age, I take great comfort in knowing that some things don't change,' Connie said. 'People will be born and people will die, taxes will be collected, and girls will keep on getting married.'

Valerie was now sixty-two. There was now far more gray than blond in her hair, she needed glasses to see, her fingers weren't as quick with the needle as they had once been, the lines around her mouth and eyes no longer completely disappeared after a smile, and the little aches and pains of life were growing more frequent, and more nagging, with each passing year. But every time she happened to glance at herself in a mirror, she was surprised by what she saw, because inside she still felt like a girl, a girl with a lot of life yet to live.

In contrast to his wife, Jack was aging quite well on the outside. At sixty-nine, his thick hair was still only partly flecked with silver. The lines around his magnificent eyes made him look more distinguished than tired, and the aches and pains of life didn't seem to be bothering him much at all. Thanks to genetics, the manual labor he had done all his life, and his daily visits to the health club, he was in excellent physical shape. It was only on the inside that he felt old and used up.

* * *

Justin had known for as long as he could remember that his grandfather didn't like him very much, but he didn't know why. His grandmother told him it had something to do with the medication his grandfather took, that it made his mind sort of fuzzy. But Justin wasn't so sure. While his grandmother, despite her full schedule, made every effort to attend his school conferences and his science fairs and his baseball games, his grandfather, with nothing but time on his hands, rarely showed the slightest bit of interest. But let Justin once forget to take out the garbage, and it was a whole other story.

'Most of the time I don't exist,' he told Tony. 'And then, all of a sudden, it's like a switch goes on in his head and he remembers I'm there and then he yells at me for some dumb reason or another. He's like schizo.'

'I never knew either of my grandfathers,' Tony said. 'Maybe that's the way they are.'

'Well, I don't know about that,' Justin declared. 'But maybe I know why my dad didn't want to stick around.'

Indeed, now that his grandfather had retired and was around the house a lot more of the time, Justin preferred not to come home until it was absolutely necessary, taking part in after-school activities or hanging out with his friends instead. He would show up just in time for dinner and then escape to his room to do his homework or play video games or listen to music on his headphones as soon after the meal ended as possible.

Other than Jack, and the lack of a good male role model in his life, Justin had few complaints. He had baseball, he had a nice house to live in – much nicer than Tony's – and he had a grandmother who doted on him. He did well enough in school to keep his teachers off his back, and he always had a little money in his pocket. He earned it for doing odd jobs for Connie Gilchrist, and it was enough for him to buy video games or a little pot now and again, and share it with Tony, who never had any money at all. The Coast was a laid-back place where crime was low, the weather was agreeable, and a kid couldn't get into much trouble, unless he wanted to.

Then, on a rainy Monday at the beginning of April, something happened to change all that.

Roland Minter's office called.

'I'm sorry, but we have to cancel your appointment for today, Mr Marsh,' the nurse said with a noticeable catch in her voice. 'In fact, we have to cancel all your appointments. You see, Dr Minter died last night.'

'What did you say?' Jack asked, certain he hadn't heard correctly.

A distinct sob came over the line. 'Dr Minter died last night,' she repeated. 'They're saying it was a heart attack, but he was only fifty-five. I'm sure you can understand that things are a bit confusing around here right now, but we can probably reschedule you with another doctor.'

There were three other psychiatrists who shared the suite of offices with Minter.

'Another doctor?' Jack echoed, as panic began to surge through him. 'Damn it, I don't want another doctor. Why would I want another doctor? Minter's my doctor. I want Minter.'

'Yes, I know,' the nurse said. 'But that won't be possible now.'

'What's the matter?' Valerie asked, coming into the kitchen and seeing the look on Jack's face as he hung up the telephone.

'Minter's dead,' he said.

Her mouth dropped open and for a long moment she couldn't think of anything to say. Although they had never once discussed it, Valerie knew what Roland

431

Minter had meant to her husband. For ten years, he had been Jack's mentor, his sounding board, his lifeline. She could not even imagine what might have happened had she not insisted that Jack see a psychiatrist. She could not imagine what might happen now.

'Are you sure there's no mistake?'

'Not according to the nurse who just canceled my appointment,' he muttered.

'Well, they have other doctors there, don't they?' she said logically. 'You can go see someone else.'

'Yeah, sure,' he said with a harsh laugh as he stomped past her and out the back door.

It had taken years for Jack to learn to trust Roland Minter. Long, hard years of prodding and poking into his most painful places before he grew comfortable with the psychiatrist. He had done it because of Valerie, who would have left him if he hadn't. But he had stuck with it because of Minter. True, he had learned a great deal about himself, his anger, and his violence along the way, but that was then and this was now. Now the shrink had upped and died on him, and left him to make it on his own. And that was exactly what Jack was going to do. He certainly had no intention of going through all that anguish and effort again with somebody else.

Of course, there was a downside to his decision, he knew. The blue oval pills he took every day to keep his anxiety at bay came by prescription only. Without Minter or another doctor to take his place, there would be no more medication. But that was all right, too, Jack reasoned, because he didn't really need the medication. He had taken it only to please Minter and to keep Valerie off his back. And surely, after all these years, he had learned enough to do without the pills, hadn't he?

* * *

It began slowly, almost imperceptibly, the slide back into hell. The mood swings that had all but disappeared during the Minter years began to reappear. The irritability increased, flares of anger countered by bouts of depression.

'Jack,' Valerie ventured at the end of two months, 'you need to see someone.'

'Who . . . a Minter clone?' he charged. 'Why? I feel fine. In fact, I can't remember a time when I felt better. All those years, all that crap I used to take, it dulled me down. I was blurry all the time. Now I'm clear.'

'No, you're not,' she said quietly. 'You're slipping back to the way you used to be. I can see it, even if you can't.'

'Yeah, so what? There wasn't anything wrong with the way I used to be, until you and Minter started messing with my head.'

One afternoon in the middle of June, Valerie came home to find him passed out across the bed, an empty bottle of bourbon beside him. After that, Jack made no effort to stay off alcohol. At any time of the day or night, he could be found sitting at the kitchen table, or in the living room, or out on the patio, drinking himself into oblivion. It was easier than having to face the fact that he was old and useless and his life was over.

Something had changed. Justin could feel it, but he didn't have any idea what it was. All he knew was that his grandmother was tense all the time and his grandfather was angry about something, increasingly angry.

He searched his memory, trying to think of something he might have done to upset them, so he could go to them and apologize, and make it all better, and get back the way things used to be. But he could think of nothing, so he went to his grandmother.

433

'Is it something I did?' he asked.

'No, of course not,' Valerie assured him. 'Your grandfather has had some bad news, that's all, and he's having a hard time dealing with it.'

Justin thought about that. It made sense, but he wondered how long it would go on. Because anything could set the old man off now, and Justin was right in his sights.

On a Tuesday afternoon at the end of July, Jack caught the boy on his way in from summer league baseball.

'I thought I told you to move those logs out of the way,' he bellowed, standing so close that Justin could smell the liquor on his breath.

Over the weekend, Jack had cut up a fallen tree, and he had instructed Justin where to stack the wood.

'Yeah, I'm sorry about that,' the boy replied. 'I meant to do it yesterday, but the game ran late. I'll do it right now.'

'Right now is too late,' Jack snapped. 'I damn near broke my neck tripping over it this morning.' His right hand shot out, cutting the boy sharply across the face, drawing blood. 'Next time I tell you to do something, you do it when I tell you, you understand?'

'Yes, sir,' Justin mumbled in surprise. His grandfather had often gotten on his case about stuff, but this was the first time he had ever hit him. He tried to get to the bathroom before his grandmother could see the blood, but he didn't make it.

'What on earth?' she cried.

'It's nothing,' he mumbled. 'I got hit by a baseball, that's all.' He hated lying, but he had the feeling that telling the truth would be worse. He cleaned himself up as best he could, but there was no hiding the cut on his lip.

Three weeks after that, it was a black eye, which he earned for tracking dirt across his grandmother's pristine kitchen floor.

'Now get down there and clean it up,' Jack instructed, pushing Justin onto his hands and knees and planting his boot on the boy's back.

At that moment, Valerie entered the kitchen. 'Jack,' she barked in a voice that Justin had never heard her use before.

But Jack had. He had heard it once before, years ago, the night he knew she was strong enough to leave him. Startled, he turned in her direction. She stood there, rigid with her own anger, her head up, her nostrils flaring, her eyes flashing. His anger abated as quickly as it had risen.

'I was only trying to teach the boy,' he whined.

'Teach him what?' Valerie asked. 'How to be afraid of you?'

Jack glared at her, but she glared right back. The enabling effect of the alcohol was gone now and he felt naked. Without another word, he slunk off.

2

On the last Saturday in September, there was a surprise telephone call from Tom Starwood. The former public defender, Ricky's staunch supporter, had resigned his job with San Mateo County, and was now in private practice, half lawyering, half counseling.

'There's been a change,' he told Valerie. 'Benny Ruiz died in prison three days ago.'

'What does that mean?' Valerie asked.

'It means that Ricky can come home.'

Valerie caught her breath. 'Did you say home?' she whispered. She had waited so long to hear those very words, and now that she had, she could hardly believe it. 'When?'

'Well, not tomorrow, I'm afraid,' Starwood replied. 'There are some things that have to be worked out first, some red tape to cut through. But I would say in a few weeks.'

'Will he be safe?'

'Reasonably so, I think, at least as far as we can tell,' the attorney replied. 'There isn't much of Ruiz's organization left, and I doubt that those who are still around would care very much about settling old scores. But the feds are checking it out. They won't let him come back if there's any question.'

'I can't believe it,' Valerie whispered. 'It's been such a long time.'

She hung up the telephone with a silly smile on her face.

436

'What?' Jack asked. He was sitting at the kitchen table, eating his lunch.

'He's coming home,' she said excitedly. 'Ricky's coming home.'

But Jack only shrugged, and poured a double measure of bourbon into a glass to wash down his sandwich.

'Your father's coming home,' she told Justin when he burst into the house, all dirty and sweaty, from an afternoon of mowing Connie's lawn and weeding her flowerbeds.

The boy's whole face lit up. For as long as he could remember, he had dreamed of the day he would meet his father again. There were so many things he wanted to say, so many questions he wanted to ask. 'Do you think he'll want to see me?'

'Of course he will,' Valerie assured him, although she was perhaps not as confident of that as she sounded. 'I'm sure he'll want to know all about you.'

'When will he get here?'

'Well, I don't know the exact answer to that,' Valerie said. 'There's some stuff that he'll have to go through first. But I would say sometime within the next several weeks.'

'Will he want his room back?' Above almost anything else, Justin loved his room, which he had decorated almost as a shrine to all his favorite Giants. 'He can have it if he wants it.'

'No, I think we'll put him in the guest room,' Valerie said. The guest room was the one down the hall that for far too brief a time had belonged to Priscilla. 'I think that will suit him just fine.'

Justin ran to the telephone. 'My dad's coming home,' he told Tony. 'It's going to happen. I'm finally going to get to meet him.'

* * *

Justin began counting the days.

Every afternoon, when he came home from school or the video arcade in town, or Tony's house, his first question to his grandmother was: 'Have you heard anything?'

'Not yet,' she would tell him, every bit as anxious as he was.

He didn't know why it was so important to him that he meet his father. He didn't know why it would matter what kind of man he was. He didn't know what difference it would make to know him. He just knew there was a hole in his heart that ached to be filled.

The more excited Justin and Valerie got, the more morose Jack got, drinking more, swearing more, yelling more. Between her business and her grandson, his wife paid little enough attention to him as it was. Having Ricky home was only going to make it worse. He had never liked the kid much, anyway. He had never been any good. Or was it that, every time he looked at him, Jack was reminded of the circumstances of his birth?

Four long weeks later, Tom Starwood finally called again. And when Justin bounded into the house that evening, his grandmother had a different answer to his question.

'Your father is coming home next week,' she told him.

After that, Justin began counting the hours.

The Boeing 727 banked over San Jose and turned north onto the approach path for San Francisco International Airport. Ricky Marsh peered out the window, looking for familiar landmarks. To the west, he could see the mountains slipping down toward the coast, and he could just make out the edge of the water. He knew Half

Moon Bay and El Granada were over there somewhere, hidden by fog.

Ricky smiled faintly. He had once thought those mountains tall and grand, and now they looked like little more than mole-hills. Living in Alaska certainly changed one's perspective. He wondered what else had changed in nine years.

He knew he had. It had taken a long time for him to come to terms with his life and the things he had done. Even now, there weren't many nights that he didn't wake, sweating, to see the face of an ordinary man who had worked the swing shift to support his family. It tormented him, even more than the thought of one of Benny Ruiz's henchmen finding him and exacting revenge. In those first lonely years, he lived more in fear of God than of man.

He found employment on a fishing boat out of Kodiak, and that helped. It was hard work, manning the nets, hauling and sorting the catch, and it took all his concentration not to get washed overboard. He was never tall, but he soon muscled up, and the skin on his face and hands and neck grew leathery from sun and wind. The crew on board the boat were a rugged lot, each with a story to tell. They accepted him without question, taught him what he needed to know, and pretty much left him to himself. They all had nightmares of their own.

The real healing didn't begin until two years later, when Carolyn Wick hired on as a waitress at a place down near the pier. The food wasn't as good as some, but whenever his boat was in, Ricky found himself going back there. Kodiak wasn't a big town, word got around, and he knew the story of Carolyn's husband going down with his boat in a sudden storm. There hadn't been much in the way of insurance left after the debts were settled, and she had two young sons to support.

There was something about her, something that was strong and at the same time vulnerable. She was almost as tall as Ricky was, with a sweet, generous nature and a smile that lit up a room when she walked in, and, too, she had straight blond hair and blue eyes that reminded him of his mother.

Their relationship began with conversations over the Blue Plate Special, progressed to handholding over coffee after her shift, and ended up with him moving into her neat little cottage at the edge of town.

'My husband was a good man, but he was hard on the boys,' Carolyn said. 'He was under enormous pressure, depending on how the salmon was running, and sometimes, he hit them.'

'Did he hit you, too?' Ricky asked.

She shrugged. 'It didn't matter about me so much. But it mattered about my sons. They're good kids.'

'Don't worry,' he said. 'I grew up with a man who hit. I know what it's like to live like that. I'll never hurt you or the boys.'

The first night that he lay in her soft, warm bed, with her arms around him, he couldn't help himself, the whole, awful story came out, and he cried himself to sleep. When he woke up, shivering and sweating from his nightmare, and realized that her arms were still around him, he knew he had found a home.

Perhaps the thing that most surprised him was how easily he took to fatherhood. Many of his happiest moments were spent in the company of Carolyn's two sons. He took them hiking and camping, and once, with the permission of his captain, he took them out on the boat. When, after three years, and the vigorous encouragement of half the town, he and Carolyn finally got around to getting married, Ricky insisted on legally adopting the boys.

'I'm not just marrying your mother,' he told them. 'I'm marrying the two of you, too, so we'll always be family.'

Now, as his plane touched down in San Francisco, Ricky's first thought was to find a telephone so he could call home and tell everyone that he had arrived safely.

His second thought was to find Tom Starwood.

'You're sure it's safe?' he asked the moment he found the attorney.

'Yes,' Starwood assured him, 'It's safe. The feds wouldn't have given the okay otherwise.'

Ricky nodded. 'It's just that I've got a family, and I don't want anyone coming after them.'

'There's no one left to come after them.'

'Good.'

'Are you headed over to the Coast now?' Starwood asked.

'In a while,' Ricky replied, his glance sliding past the attorney's shoulder. 'I have a few things to do first.'

'I told your mother it was today,' Starwood said.

'Yeah, don't worry, I'm going,' Ricky replied, a bit defensively. Because he had a new life now, and he didn't like the idea of getting sucked back up into the old.

Starwood gave him a shrewd look. 'You weren't talking about your family in El Granada, were you?' he asked softly. 'You're not here to stay.'

Ricky shook his head. 'No,' he confirmed. 'This is strictly a visit.'

The Coast had grown some in the past nine years, but the house didn't look very different, a little older, perhaps, but substantially the same. Ricky drove down Delgada Road several times in his rented Ford before finally turning into the driveway, turning off the engine, and climbing out.

441

He didn't get two feet up the front path before his mother came flying out of the house, a tall, gangly kid hanging behind her.

'We thought you'd never get here,' Valerie cried, throwing her arms around her son.

'Hi, Ma,' Ricky said, hugging back as best he could. Her cheeks were wet with tears, and he had forgotten how frail she was. She was older, too, her hair gray, her skin almost translucent.

'Oh, my goodness, just let me look at you,' she cried, leaning back, holding him at arm's length. 'I do believe you've gained some weight, and it looks like you've been working out-of-doors.'

'As a matter of fact,' he said, 'I work on a fishing boat.'

'A fishing boat?' she echoed. 'I'd never have guessed that.' He had left nine years ago, still a child. Now at thirty-seven, he was a man.

He smiled. 'Sometimes, life is just full of surprises.'

Suddenly, Valerie gasped. 'Good heavens, speaking of surprises, I almost forgot.' She turned around and gestured to the gangly boy behind her. 'There's somebody here who's been waiting a very long time to meet you.'

Justin was unexpectedly shy as he gazed at the man who had been the main fantasy of his young life.

Ricky frowned. 'No, this can't be,' he said, shaking his head. 'This can't be Justin. This can't be my boy. My boy's barely knee-high to a cornstalk. Who is this grown-up person?'

'It most certainly is Justin,' Valerie cooed.

'Well, I'll be damned,' Ricky murmured. Then a big smile spread across his face, and he opened his arms. 'Well, are you going to stay all the way over there, or are you going to come on over here and give your dad a big hug?'

Justin didn't need to be asked twice. He covered the space between them in an instant and threw his arms around his father, almost knocking him off his feet. Valerie looked on, choking back her tears.

'Well, you sure didn't take after me, now did you?' Ricky said with a chuckle, looking up at his son.

'Oh, yes, I did,' Justin assured him fervently. 'I bet I'm exactly like you, just maybe a little taller.'

'Well, let's hope not exactly,' Ricky murmured, more to himself than the boy. 'Now tell me, what are you doing home at this hour?' he asked. 'Shouldn't you be in school or something?'

'They let me out of class early today, because you were coming home,' Justin replied happily. Valerie had arranged it.

'School sure is different than I remember,' Ricky observed with a chuckle.

'Grandma's put you in the guest room,' Justin rattled on. 'But you can have your old room back, if you want it.'

'Doesn't matter where I sleep,' his father said. 'What matters is that you and I have a chance to catch up on the past nine years.'

'There's a science fair on Saturday, and my project might win an award,' the boy said in a rush. 'Can you come?'

Saturday was four days away, and Ricky had planned to be long gone back to Alaska by then. 'I wouldn't miss it,' he said. 'Will your mother be there?'

'I guess not. She lives in Las Vegas.'

'In Las Vegas?'

'Yeah.'

For some totally illogical reason, considering his own position, Ricky felt a surge of anger at Anna. 'She lives there and you live here?'

'I go visit her sometimes, but she has another family now and it's not so much fun,' Justin said. 'I like it better here.'

Ricky looked at his mother. 'I didn't realize,' he said.

'It's been okay,' Valerie assured him. 'At least, until recently.'

'What does that mean?'

Valerie shrugged. 'Your father retired two years ago, way before he wanted to. Then a couple of months ago, a psychiatrist who'd been helping him died. He hasn't been handling either very well.'

Ricky shook his head. 'And you're still making excuses for him.'

'We're none of us perfect,' she reminded him.

'All right, where is he?' Ricky asked. 'Might as well get it over with.'

'He's in the house.'

'And can't wait to see me, I bet.'

'I'm sure he's looking forward to seeing you,' she told him.

Justin was already poking around in the trunk of the rental car. 'Where's all your stuff?' he asked, a single suitcase in his grasp.

'What you see is what we've got,' Ricky told him. 'I travel light.' Then he saw the look in the boy's eyes, of anticipation becoming confusion and then slowly dissolving into comprehension.

'You're not staying, are you?'

'Sure I am,' Ricky declared before he realized that he had spoken. 'For a while, anyway. How about until you get sick of me and throw me out?'

Justin grinned. 'Oh, not until then, huh?' he said.

They went up the front path and into the house. The inside didn't look much different than it had nine years ago, either, Ricky noted.

'Jack,' Valerie called brightly. 'Jack, come see who's here!'

There was no response.

Valerie smiled nervously. 'He must be out in the backyard and just didn't hear me,' she said. 'Why don't we get you settled upstairs first, and then we'll go find him?'

Justin was already halfway up the steps with Ricky's suitcase, and he carried it to the room at the far end of the hall. Ricky followed him, stopping in the doorway, thinking how strange it was to be a guest in his old home.

'We'll leave you alone now,' Valerie said, propelling Justin out the door. 'You come down whenever you're ready.'

Whenever he was ready, Ricky thought as the door closed softly behind them. If it were up to him, that could be a very long time. He was beginning to think he had made a terrible mistake, coming back at all. He didn't belong here anymore, if he ever had, where everyone had expectations and relationships were too complicated. Life was so simple and straightforward up in Kodiak. With a shake of his head, he began to wish that he were there instead of here.

Half an hour later, he forced himself to go downstairs. Justin and his mother were nowhere to be seen, but Jack was in the living room.

'Aha,' the old man said, raising the glass in his hand. 'The prodigal son returns.' He didn't know what the phrase meant, but he had heard it somewhere, years before, and it had stuck in his mind. It was three o'clock in the afternoon, and he was drunk.

'Hello, Pa,' Ricky said. 'Nice to see you, too.'

'Nice to see me? Is that what you say after all these years? What's wrong with "How're you doing, Pa? Whatcha been up to?"'

Some things never changed, Ricky thought, swallowing his irritation. 'How are you doing, Pa? What've you been up to?'

'Well, I'm doing just great, as long as you're asking,' Jack snapped. 'I'm sitting here on my butt like a fucking useless clod. Thrown away, that's what I was. Too old, they said. Too old? Too old for what, I want to know. I could do that job in my sleep, and they knew it! Know how I spend my days now? Cleaning up after your mother and your pissant son, that's how! That's what happens when you get old – you get to clean up after women and kids. When you get old, that's all anyone thinks you're good for.'

'You're not old, Pa,' Ricky said, because he didn't know what else to say. 'You still got plenty of life left in you.'

'Yeah, well, don't you go telling me what I am and what I ain't. You don't know nothing, you hear me?'

Ricky sighed again, this time audibly. 'You're right, Pa,' he said, 'I don't know nothing.'

Before Jack could say anything more, Ricky ducked out of the living room and headed down the hall toward the kitchen.

Valerie was coming in the back door with her arms full of freshly cut flowers. 'Are you all unpacked?' she asked with a bright smile, laying the blooms on the counter, and preparing to arrange them in a vase.

'Almost,' Ricky replied, although he had yet to remove a thing from his suitcase.

She beamed at him. 'It's so good to have you home again.'

'I saw Pa in the living room,' he told her. 'He was thrilled to see me. At least, he would have been if he could see straight.'

Valerie's face fell. She had so hoped that Jack would

446

be at least reasonably sober for Ricky's arrival. 'I'm sorry,' she said.

'Is that all he does all day – sit around and drink?'

'He doesn't drink all the time. He goes to the health club sometimes, but not as often as he used to. He helps with things around the house, and he takes care of all the repairs.'

'And when he *does* drink?'

Valerie knew what he was asking, and her glance slid away from his. 'He does the best he can,' she murmured.

The hair on the back of Ricky's neck rose. 'Has he laid a hand on Justin?'

'He really cares about the boy,' she assured him. 'He's just strict with him, that's all.'

'Don't give me that crap, Ma. I grew up in this house, remember?'

'It's all right,' Justin said, coming into the kitchen and catching the tail end of the conversation. 'I'm tough. He doesn't bother me.'

Ricky looked at his son, barely into his teens. He thought of his boys up in Kodiak, now free from abuse and growing up happy. He knew he would have to do something.

'This is my most favorite place,' Justin told his father an hour later, when they had climbed the hill behind the house and sat themselves down on a little ridge of earth beneath a canopy of trees. Below them, they could see the rooftops of El Granada, and beyond, the sweeping curve of Half Moon Bay.

Ricky smiled, a rather sad smile. In his own youth, he had escaped to this very spot whenever things at the house grew too hot. 'It was mine, too,' he said.

Justin's eyes widened in disbelief. 'You came up here, too?'

'Sure did. A lot.'

'It's so weird, you know,' Justin said happily. 'Not to know you, and then to finally meet you, and realize how much I'm like you.'

'I hope not as much as you think,' Ricky told him. 'I hope you're better than that. I thought I was so smart when I was your age, but I was stupid. I did a lot of dumb things. Things that didn't just hurt me, but hurt other people, good people, who never did me any harm.'

'But you turned out all right, didn't you?'

Ricky sighed. 'I'm still working at it,' he said.

They were silent together for a while before Justin spoke again. 'Grandpa gets awful angry about things,' he confided. 'I think it's me. I don't think he likes me very much.'

'Your grandfather's been angry his whole life,' Ricky told the boy. 'It has nothing to do with you.' He paused for a moment and then turned to the boy. 'Justin, I'm going to talk to your grandmother. I'm going to tell her that we need to find another place for you to live.'

'I can't leave Grandma,' Justin said. 'She needs me.'

'You can't stay here, not with your grandfather acting like he is,' Ricky told him.

'But it'll be all right, now that you're here,' Justin assured him. 'Between the two of us, we'll be able to handle him.'

Ricky took a deep breath. 'I live in Alaska now,' he said gently. 'I came here because I wanted to see you and your grandmother, and spend some time with you, but then I'm going to go back there.'

Justin wanted to understand, but he didn't. 'I thought you were gone away from us because you had to be, not because you wanted to be.'

'In the beginning, that was true. But I've spent nine years in Alaska, making a life for myself, because I didn't

448

think I'd ever be able to come back here. It's home now. It's where I want to be.'

'Is Alaska nicer than here?' Justin asked.

'It's . . . less complicated,' his father told him.

'Would Grandma like it there?'

'Your grandmother will never leave your grandfather,' Ricky said. 'But I'm hoping you'll come to visit soon. There are a couple of people in Kodiak who I think would like to meet you and get to know you.'

Outside of baseball, Justin had clung to one idea, one dream in his life. That one day his father would come home and live with them.

'You mean you have another family, too,' he said dully.

'I have a wife,' Ricky informed him. 'And I have two boys.'

'So does my mother,' Justin said, trying his best to hold back the tears. 'Are they more important than me, too?'

To be honest, Ricky had never dreamed that Anna would abandon the boy. He had pictured her married to a great guy who would be a great father to Justin, and he was dismayed to learn that it had been nothing but a fantasy on his part. The last thing he had expected was for Anna to take off and leave the boy with his parents.

'No,' he said, putting his arm around the boy's shoulder, 'not more important.'

They ate dinner promptly at six-thirty. Valerie had prepared a huge meal, including all of Ricky's favorite dishes.

'No one makes chicken pot pie as good as you do, Ma,' he said appreciatively, between his second and third helpings.

449

'It's *my* favorite, too,' Justin said, beaming.

They were doing their best to ignore Jack, who did little more than sit sullenly at the table and push the food around his plate.

After the pot pie came a freshly baked apple cobbler. Much as he loved Carolyn, Ricky thought with a smile, her cooking couldn't hold a candle to his mother's. But with the ice cream beginning to melt in his dish, Jack abruptly pushed himself away from the table, pulled a fresh bottle of bourbon from the cupboard, and stomped out of the kitchen.

'Is it like this every night?' Ricky asked.

'No,' Valerie assured him, although it happened more nights than not. 'I know he was looking forward to your coming home, in his way, but he just doesn't know how to deal with it.'

'What'll he do?'

'He'll drink some, and then he'll go to sleep,' she told him.

'She means, he'll get loaded and then pass out,' Justin clarified. 'She's just too polite to say it.'

'Justin,' Valerie said reprovingly.

'Ma, this is no good,' Ricky said. 'Maybe you've lived your whole life like this, but it's not right for Justin, and you know it. What do you do – walk around, waiting for the next shoe to drop?'

'He's had to face some adversity, and he's having a hard time adjusting,' Valerie said. 'But I'm sure things will get better.'

'And meanwhile?'

'Meanwhile, we don't dwell on it.'

Together, Ricky and Justin did the dinner dishes, and then Justin went off to his room to do his homework.

'Ma,' Ricky said as soon as he was gone, 'this is no

450

place for Justin to be living, and you know it. I had no idea that Anna would bail, and that he'd end up here with Pa.'

'I was thinking that the two of you should find a place together,' Valerie told him. 'I'll miss having him here, but maybe it's for the best.'

'I'm not here to stay, Ma,' he said. 'I've got a place in Alaska, and a family. I'm just here to visit.'

'You have a family?' Valerie asked, wondering why she should be surprised.

'I have a wife and she has two boys,' he replied. 'I adopted them a while back. They're teenagers now. The older one is heading for college in the fall.'

'How nice for you,' Valerie exclaimed, genuinely pleased. 'But in a way, how sad for Justin.'

'Not at all,' Ricky said. 'Obviously, I have to talk to Carolyn first, but I think he should be in Kodiak, with me. I'm thinking maybe we could start with a visit, you know, maybe over the summer.'

'I think he'd like that,' Valerie said. She opened her mouth to say something else, but at that moment, the telephone rang. It was Connie. 'Yes, he's right here and he looks just wonderful and he's all grown up and he's got a family of his own,' she told her neighbor in one breath. 'Oh dear, how did it happen?' she replied in response to something Connie said. 'Where are you?'

'What?' Ricky asked.

Valerie put her hand over the phone. 'Connie fell in the bathroom,' she whispered. 'She may have hurt herself. Would you mind if I ran over there and gave her a hand?'

'No, go,' Ricky said. 'If you need help, call me.'

'Are you sure?'

'I'm sure, Ma. I'll be fine. I want to call home anyway, and then I want hang out with Justin for a while.' He smiled. 'Don't worry. I'll still be here when you get back.'

'Well, if you're sure it's all right.'

'I'm sure. Go.'

'All right, Connie,' she said into the receiver. 'I'll be right over.' She hung up and turned to Ricky. 'I'll only be a few minutes,' she said. 'I just want to make sure she's okay. If you get hungry, there's fruit in the refrigerator and fresh brownies in the breadbox.'

'Thanks, Ma, but I think I ate enough dinner to keep me for quite a while,' he said. 'A couple of hours, anyway.'

She gave him a kiss on the cheek and hurried out the back door.

Ricky pulled a chair up to the kitchen counter, sat down with the same corded telephone that had been installed in the house almost forty years ago, and called Kodiak, collect. Carolyn answered on the first ring.

'I thought it would be you,' she said. 'How is it going?'

'Not like I expected,' he told her. 'Jeez, not anything like I expected.'

They spoke for about ten minutes, and would probably have spoken longer had not Jack come stumbling into the room.

'What're you doing?' he growled, 'running up the phone bill your first night home?'

'No, Pa,' Ricky said calmly, saying his goodbyes and hanging up. 'I called collect.'

'Collect? You're here less than a day, and you're already calling somewhere else collect?'

'I just called home, Pa, that's all. It was no big deal.'

'Where's your mother?' Jack barked, losing interest in the issue of the telephone. 'I'm hungry. I want some dinner. Where is she?'

'We had dinner, an hour ago,' Ricky reminded him. 'Ma's gone out for a while.'

'Gone out? Whaddaya mean, gone out? She's supposed to be here for me, so I can have something to eat when I want it.'

'What do you want, Pa?' Ricky inquired. 'I'll fix it for you.'

'Oh, so you're a cook now? Is that what you do up in Alaska? Woman's work? I bet you look real pretty in an apron, too.'

'No, Pa, I work on a fishing boat up in Alaska, but I can cook well enough to fix something for you. What do you want?'

'I want my wife, goddam it, that's what I want!' he bellowed. 'I want the care of a good woman. I don't want no sissy doing for me.'

'I'm your son, Pa,' Ricky said with mild sarcasm. 'How could I be a sissy?'

'Nah, you were never my son,' Jack snarled. 'JJ, now he was my son. He went into the Army and made us proud. You were always a momma's boy. That's why you turned out so bad. And you got a son growing up just like you.'

'What exactly about JJ made you proud, Pa?' Ricky asked with a barely concealed edge. 'Was it the fellow soldier he beat up for no particular reason? Or was it the officer he assaulted? Or was it the civilian he killed for making mincemeat of his girlfriend?' The letters from JJ had continued to come to the Rodriguez house, where Chris's mother still lived. For the past ten years, however, they had come from a prison near Gatesville, Texas. Chris dutifully sent the letters on to Tom Starwood, who passed them along to a federal agent, who forwarded them to a post office box in Kodiak, Alaska, that was registered to one James Hayes. 'Is that why he's your

453

son, Pa? Because, when it was all said and done, he turned out to be just like you?'

'How do you know all that?' Jack demanded. 'You don't know anything. You just made all that up!'

Justin and Valerie had been wrong. After Jack got loaded, he didn't pass out, he got nasty. Ricky wondered what else they hadn't told him. 'Well, if you don't want something to eat,' he said, 'I'll just head on up to my room.'

But suddenly, there was Jack, barring the way. 'You think you're going to slink out of here without paying up?' he demanded. 'Well, you can just forget it. You been slinking out of places your whole life, boy. It's time you paid the piper.'

'What are you talking about, Pa?' Ricky asked, making every effort to hold his temper. 'I don't know what you're talking about.'

'Like hell you don't,' his father snarled. 'You break your mother's heart without a second thought, shaming us like you did. Then you have a kid and you run out on him. You leave him behind like so much garbage for someone else to clean up. There you are, living the high life up in Alaska, courtesy of the United States government and my tax dollars, while we struggle to feed your kid and make ends meet.'

'I left my son well provided for,' Ricky said evenly. 'There was more than enough money to see to it that ends got met.'

'Yeah, except that your mother stashed it away,' Jack informed him. 'And I been supporting the bastard ever since.'

'You've been supporting him?' Ricky snapped, finally losing the battle with his temper. 'You son of a bitch, what do you support him on – your pitiful pension that, from the looks of it, is spent on booze?'

454

It was the wrong thing to say. Ricky knew it the minute the words were out of his mouth, but it was too late to take them back. He saw Jack's face engorge with fury, and he knew what was coming. However, his father was a lot slower than he used to be, and Ricky had no trouble ducking away from the right hook. It was the left jab he didn't see, and it caught him full in the stomach, knocking the breath out of him and sending him crashing against the kitchen table, the chairs skittering in all directions. Even at sixty-nine, the old man still packed quite a wallop.

'Not so old I can't give you exactly what you deserve, you punk!' Jack cried.

Ricky knew he had two choices. He could stay and let his father have it, or he could leave. It was an easy choice to make. He figured the old man would calm down once he was out of there. 'Forget it, Pa,' he said. 'I'm not your punching bag anymore. And since you don't seem to want me here, I'll leave.'

Before Jack could react, Ricky pulled himself up and left the room.

'You're not just a punk, you're a coward, too!' his father yelled after him.

Ricky didn't respond. He left through the front door, got into his rental car, and drove off down Delgada to Avenida del Oro and out onto the Coast Highway.

There was no one he was interested in seeing, and no place he particularly wanted to go, so he just drove around for a while. Finally, he pulled into the parking lot in front of the Gray Whale, and made his way out onto the Princeton Landing. It hadn't changed much since he had last seen it, twenty years ago. A few fishing boats were tied up for the night, bobbing gently in the light breeze, water slapping against hulls, fenders rubbing against wood. Ricky knew that sound well. It reminded him of Kodiak. It reminded him of home.

He sat down, with his back against the dock house, pulled his knees up to his chest the way he had done as a boy, and sucked the sea air deep into his lungs.

Justin finished his homework and went downstairs in search of his father. He found his grandfather instead. Jack was seated at the kitchen table, all the chairs but the one he was occupying were askew, and he was drinking straight out of a bottle of bourbon. Justin knew what that meant, and he turned to get out of there as quickly as possible. But Jack was up from his chair before Justin could get out the door, and he spun the boy around by the scruff of his neck.

'I told you it was time to pay the piper,' he snarled, punctuating his words with a sharp blow to the side of Justin's head.

The boy, unable to see anything but stars for a moment, shook his head to clear it. 'I don't know what you're talking about, Grandpa,' he said.

'I'll teach you to turn your back on me!' Jack growled.

'I didn't mean to do that,' Justin tried to explain, but the words were barely out of his mouth before his grandfather was all over him, punching, kicking, yelling.

'You're just plain no good,' he roared. 'You never were any good. You'll never be any good, no matter where you live!'

Justin didn't understand what his grandfather was talking about. Or what he was so mad about. On the floor, his hands raised to fend off the hail of blows, Justin tried to tell the old man that he wasn't going anywhere.

Neither of them saw Valerie in the doorway, coming back from Connie's. Neither of them heard her gasp.

'Jack!' she barked in that voice that brooked no argument. But he was either totally out of control, or never heard her. She didn't wait to find out which. She picked up the first thing at hand, a heavy cast iron skillet from the stove, and swung it with all her might, again and again, until Jack's skull fractured and blood began to spurt from his nose and mouth. He buckled at the knees and collapsed.

Valerie stood, looking down at her husband, for what seemed an eternity before she turned to her grandson. 'I thought he was going to kill you,' she said.

'He was drunk, and saying all kinds of stuff that didn't make any sense,' Justin sobbed, scrambling to his feet. His face showed some cuts and bruises, but most of the blood on him was his grandfather's. He stared at the body. 'Do you think he'll be all right?'

Before Valerie could reply, Ricky was there, stopping short when he saw Jack on the floor. 'What the hell . . . ?'

'He was going to kill Justin,' Valerie told her son.

'You hit him?' Ricky asked in disbelief.

His mother glanced at the skillet lying at her feet. 'I . . . I guess I must have,' she replied.

'I think you should take a look at him,' Justin said. 'He's not moving.'

But Ricky didn't have to look. 'He's not going to move,' he told the boy.

'Jeez,' Justin exclaimed, backing away. 'Now what do we do?'

'I think we have to call the police,' Valerie said. 'I think that's what we have to do.'

'Not until we think this through,' Ricky said quickly. His mother was right, of course, they would have to call the police, but what were they going to say? 'Before we do anything, I want you to tell me exactly what happened.'

Between them, Justin and Valerie did so, as best they could, neither of them being too clear about the details.

'I remember coming back from Connie's and seeing Jack,' she said with a sudden shiver. 'He had Justin on the floor and he was hitting him. I think I tried to stop him. Dear God, I must have hit him with the frying pan.' She frowned. 'But how could I? I'm not that strong. And I certainly couldn't have hit him that hard . . . could I?'

Just to make sure, Ricky stepped carefully over the body and pressed his fingers to Jack's neck, and found himself looking at his father's brain. 'It was hard enough,' he said.

'Jeez,' Justin breathed.

Ricky supposed they could tell the police that the old man slipped and fell and hit his head. Except that, these days, the cops had sophisticated ways of finding out what really happened. No, they would have to tell the truth. It was something like self-defense, anyway, and he supposed they might get away with it. Of course, it would mean dragging his mother through the system, and depending on how nasty the authorities wanted to be, it could ruin the rest of her life. He sighed. 'Look, I think I should tell the police that I was the one who hit him,' he said.

'Don't be silly, dear,' Valerie said, actually smiling at her son. 'You weren't even here . . . were you? No, of course you weren't, which means that I must be responsible, and that's exactly what we'll tell the police.'

'Ma, you're in shock, you don't know what you're saying,' Ricky told her. 'Believe me, it's better if I take the blame.'

Valerie was suddenly, frighteningly, very calm. 'Nonsense,' she told him. 'We're not going to lie to the police. That would be a terrible thing to do.'

Her husband was dead, and apparently she had killed

458

him. What was there to talk about? She crossed to the telephone and picked it up. How appropriate that Jack should meet his end here in the kitchen, she thought as she dialed 911, the scene of so much violence. She said a little prayer for his soul.

'I'm sorry, Grandma,' Justin said. 'It's all my fault.'

'No,' she replied. 'If it's anyone's fault, it's mine. You see, I never should have married him. My father tried to warn me, but I was just too young, too foolish, too headstrong to listen.'

3

Two police cars and an ambulance responded to Valerie's call, their sirens wailing, their lights flashing down the quiet neighborhood street. It was just past eight, not very late for a weeknight, but even so, she wondered what the neighbors would think.

All three of them had stayed in the kitchen the whole time, standing a macabre vigil over the body, saying nothing, touching nothing, moving nothing, not even the kitchen chairs that were overturned.

Once, when both Valerie and Justin went to the bathroom at the same time, Ricky walked over and knelt beside his father. 'What goes around comes around, old man,' he murmured to the oozing lump on the floor that could no longer hear him. He was not particularly sorry that his father was dead, he was just sorry that his mother had beaten him to it.

When they heard the front doorbell, Valerie squared her shoulders, Justin bit his lip, and Ricky went to let in the police.

Half a dozen people crowded into the kitchen, snapping photographs, examining the body, asking questions, viewing the scene from every angle, collecting bits and pieces of a family's history.

'My father could be a violent man when he was drinking, and he had been drinking,' Ricky explained, having carefully rehearsed what he would say. 'We've never gotten along, and we got into an argument. I left the house, thinking that he would cool down, but apparently he didn't, and he went after my son. My mother came in on them, and when she couldn't get him to stop, she had no choice.'

'Were you a witness?' they wanted to know.

'No, I came in right afterward.'

The policemen turned to Valerie. 'What happened?'

'I don't know . . . I think I hit him,' she told them.

'You think?' they asked.

'I don't really remember,' she said. 'But he's dead, isn't he? So I must have.'

'How many times did you hit him?'

'I don't remember.'

'Did you feel that you and your grandson were in imminent danger?'

'I must have.'

They looked at Justin. His bruises were numerous, but superficial. They looked at Valerie. There wasn't a scratch on her.

'Did you intend to kill him?'

'Of course not. I just didn't want him to kill my grandson.'

A little after nine-thirty, they moved the body onto a gurney and took it away. An hour and a half later, they finished their examination of the scene and were ready to leave.

'We may have more questions,' they said politely. 'Will you be available?'

'Of course,' Ricky assured them. 'We're not going anywhere.'

They were halfway out the door when they turned back, as if in afterthought. 'Do you have an attorney, Mrs Marsh?' they asked.

Valerie was startled. 'Am I going to need one?'

461

They shrugged. 'You never know.'

'My mother has an attorney,' Ricky told them.

'I do?' Valerie asked.

'Yes, you do,' Ricky said.

No sooner had the police driven off than Connie, who had badly bruised her kneecap in her bathroom fall, came limping up the front path. 'What happened?' she cried.

'It's Pa,' Ricky said.

'I saw the ambulance, and I thought someone must be sick,' Connie said. 'Then I saw the police, and I didn't know what to think.'

'Would you do me a favor and take Ma upstairs,' Ricky asked. 'I'm pretty sure she's in shock. She may need a doctor. I don't want her to be alone.'

'Of course,' Connie said. Without another word, she took Valerie by the elbow and led her toward the steps.

'Ricky frets too much,' Valerie said when they reached the second floor landing and started down the hall. 'You shouldn't be walking on that knee. You certainly shouldn't be climbing stairs. You should be at home, and you should have an ice pack on it. Don't listen to Ricky. As you can see, I'm perfectly all right. I'm not in shock. Why should I be in shock? All I did was kill my husband.'

Connie blinked. 'You did – what?'

'I cracked his skull with a frying pan,' Valerie replied, breaking into an uncontrollable wave of giggles. 'Can you imagine that?'

'No, I can't,' Connie replied, wondering what on earth had gone on here tonight. They reached the bedroom. 'Why don't we get you undressed and into bed? And I'll sit here with you for a while.'

The giggles were subsiding and Valerie nodded. She was suddenly very tired. But just as she was reaching up to unbutton her blouse, she began to retch. She got to the bathroom just in time. When she emerged, ten minutes later, her blouse was stained, her face was white, and she was shivering from head to toe.

Connie sat her down on the bed, somehow managed to get her clothes off, and get her under the covers. But the shivering didn't stop. 'I'll be right back,' she whispered, hurrying out of the room and down the stairs, as fast as her knee would let her, to tell Ricky that it would be a very good idea to call the doctor.

The local newspaper printed a brief obituary, but nothing more. The police were not releasing the details. Ricky told anyone who asked that Jack had fallen and died from a fractured skull. It was almost true.

A funeral was quickly arranged, but it wasn't publicized. In the forty years he had lived on the Coast, Jack had never stepped foot inside Our Lady of Mercy Church, but because of Valerie, and the fact that Jack had been born Catholic, Father Bernaldo agreed to make an exception.

Only a handful of people attended. But by afternoon, friends and neighbors began to arrive at the house on Delgada Road, along with those members of the congregation who hadn't been able to attend the service, a surprising number of Valerie's customers, and even some of Justin's friends. It was the first time in over two decades that Chris Rodriguez had been to the house.

Ellen came from her convent, looking thin and pale in her black habit. She petted her mother, and spoke softly to everyone, and as she always had, even as a child, quietly took over.

Marianne came from Boston. She was now in her late seventies and had been widowed for almost a decade. She stayed as close to Valerie as she could, wanting to help her sister deal with the grief she was sure would come.

Throughout the afternoon and into the evening, people continued to arrive, bringing casseroles and fruit salads and Bundt cakes, and offering their condolences. Leo Garvey brought a huge pot of shrimp cioppino he had made at home.

'I figured there'd be a crowd,' he said, hugging her.

Valerie hugged him back.

Dennis Murphy, the pharmacist, brought soda bread. 'It was my wife's recipe,' he told Valerie with some embarrassment. 'I'm not sure it came out right.'

How very sweet he was, she thought.

The house was full. But it was clear that the people who filled it weren't there to celebrate Jack's life or mourn his passing. They barely knew him. They were there for Valerie.

Tom Starwood sat in the living room a week after the funeral. 'I have to be honest with you,' he told both Valerie and Ricky, 'I don't know which way the district attorney's office will jump on this.'

'The sonofabitch was violent,' Ricky insisted. 'He used my mother like a punching bag. He killed my little sister. It's a miracle he didn't kill all of us. What do they want?'

'Ricky!' Valerie cried.

'Ma, he's got to know. He's your lawyer.'

'The problem we have here,' Starwood told her, 'is that the officers who were on the scene that night didn't find any evidence that either you or Justin was in any imminent danger.'

'I see,' Valerie said.

'They're saying that what you might have done was simply to take advantage of an opportunity to rid yourself of an undesirable husband.'

464

'But she was defending my son,' Ricky insisted, 'clear and simple.'

Starwood shrugged. 'Unfortunately, the DA doesn't see it that way.'

'You mean, they don't think Jack was trying to kill Justin?' Valerie asked.

'The officers reported that Justin's injuries were minor, you had no injuries, and the only weapon on the scene was the frying pan, which you've already admitted you wielded,' Starwood replied.

'What charges are we looking at?' Ricky asked.

'More than likely, they'll try to go for murder two,' Starwood replied.

Ricky was stunned. 'Why?'

The attorney shrugged. 'That's how they see it.'

'What does that mean?' Valerie asked, looking from one to the other.

'They're saying you meant to kill him,' Ricky told her. 'And if you get convicted, you go to prison, maybe for a very long time.'

'The district attorney thinks Jack wasn't trying to kill Justin, so I had no reason to hit him with the frying pan,' Valerie said slowly. 'But how do they know that? They weren't there. They didn't see.'

'And that's why I wouldn't worry about being convicted of anything just now,' Starwood said. 'Even if this does go to trial, we have an excellent defense.'

'What?' Valerie wanted to know.

'Battered wife syndrome.'

'Battered wife syndrome?' Valerie repeated. 'You want to defend me by telling everyone that my husband beat me?'

'Essentially, yes,' Starwood replied. 'You and the children. The point being that whether Jack was going to kill Justin or not, based on past history, you had every right to think he was.'

Valerie shook her head vehemently. 'No.'

Starwood blinked. 'What do you mean – no?'

'I mean I'm not going to let you save me from going to prison by dragging my family through the mud. It's none of anyone's business what went on in my home.'

'Ma, listen to him,' Ricky said. 'He knows what he's doing.'

'No, he doesn't,' Valerie said, stiffening. 'Not if his way of saving me is to sacrifice what's left of this family.'

'What family? There's only Justin and me left, and Ellen in the convent,' Ricky argued, not bothering to mention JJ and where he was. 'For God's sake, if we don't care anymore, why should you?'

'Don't take the Lord's name in vain,' Valerie admonished automatically. But in the end, she relented. She had to. Ellen and Marianne both agreed with Ricky.

'I lived in that house,' Ellen declared with far more spirit than the nun usually displayed. 'If I have to, I'll get up on the witness stand and tell.'

'You have to think about yourself now,' Marianne said. 'What's past is past. It can't hurt you anymore. So why let it ruin the rest of your life?'

PART NINE

2000

I

The jury was made up of four men and eight women. Tom Starwood had tried his best to choose older women who might better understand a middle-aged victim of abuse. And he had looked for married men who he thought would never tolerate violence against their wives or children. He believed he had been reasonably successful.

The trial began on Monday, June 5, with Stuart Matheny, the assistant district attorney for the county of San Mateo, telling the jury that on or around eight-thirty on the evening of Tuesday, October 26, 1999, Valerie O'Connor Marsh did murder her husband.

'You will hear testimony presented by the defense,' he said in his opening statement, 'that will suggest that Jack Marsh was a violent man. We won't dispute that. You will hear testimony that his wife was long-suffering, and we won't dispute that, either. You will also hear testimony that Valerie Marsh was acting in defense of her grandson when she picked up a cast iron frying pan and hit her husband in the head, and that we *will* dispute.

'Was Jack Marsh beating up on his grandson when the defendant came upon them that night? Yes, he probably was. But we will show that the boy's injuries were minor, and that there is no indication that his life was ever in danger. Further, we will show that the defendant stayed with her husband long after her children were gone, long after she was financially independent, long after she could have left him. And we will show that, although she knew her husband was abusive, it didn't stop her from bringing her grandson into her home, and putting him at risk.

'Ladies and gentlemen, the evidence will show, beyond all reasonable doubt, I believe, that Valerie Marsh was not in fear for her grandson's life that night. She had simply had enough of her violent marriage, and she took advantage of an opportunity to get out of it.'

Valerie sat at the defense table with her hands folded in her lap and no expression on her face. She looked at the witnesses and listened to their testimony as though none of it had anything to do with her, as though it was all nothing more than a mildly interesting television show.

'Jack Marsh died of a massive skull fracture,' the medical examiner testified, using charts and photographs to illustrate his findings.

'And did you conclude, with any degree of certainty,' Stuart Matheny asked, 'how a woman of Valerie Marsh's age and build could fracture her husband's skull with a frying pan?'

'To do the kind of damage that was done,' the doctor replied, 'I'd say there was a lot of luck and forty years of anger behind that pan.'

'Did you just say that as a medical certainty, Doctor?' Tom Starwood inquired.

'No,' the pathologist conceded. 'It was an opinion.'

'Then please tell us, in your opinion,' the defense attorney pressed, 'what kind of results would we have gotten from forty years of fear?'

'She didn't seem particularly remorseful,' one of the police officers who had been to the scene on the night

470

of the murder testified. 'She didn't seem upset, and she didn't seem very concerned about her husband at all. In fact, all I recall, she was quite matter-of-fact about the whole thing.'

'Are you familiar with the effects of shock?' Tom Starwood asked the witness.

'I know what it is,' the officer replied.

'Can you describe it for the jury?'

As it happened, the officer had taken several psychology courses at a local college. If the lawyer thought he was going to make him look like a fool, he had another thought coming.

'People in shock can become catatonic, a condition that's characterized by muscle rigidity and mental stupor, or great excitement alternating with confusion,' the policeman recited. 'Or they can experience a complete emotional breakdown, and lose touch with what's going on around them. Or they can develop a true psychosis, where they lose touch with reality altogether.'

'I see,' Starwood said thoughtfully, because he knew all about the psychology courses. 'Now tell us, doesn't any of what you've just described exactly describe the way Valerie Marsh was behaving on the night her husband died?'

'I've been studying spousal murder and the battered wife syndrome for a number of years now,' the state's psychiatrist testified. 'And there is no doubt in my mind that when Valerie Marsh swung that skillet, it wasn't to stop her husband from abusing her grandson. She intended to kill him.'

'How much time did you spend with my client before coming to this conclusion, Doctor?' Tom Starwood asked.

'Roughly an hour and a half. But my reports are usually based on my extensive research of the subject.'

'Well, I assume my client had some impact on your conclusion, so will you share with the jury what she might have said, during that time, that so convinced you that she intended to kill her husband?'

'Nothing,' the psychiatrist declared, shifting a little in his seat. 'She never said a word.'

When it was her turn to testify, Valerie did exactly as Tom Starwood had told her to do. She answered all the questions as straightforwardly as she could, and she looked at the jury, fixing on each juror in turn, although she could not say afterward that she would have recognized any of them outside the courthouse.

After all the testimony was over and Stuart Matheny had told the jury that the evidence proved beyond a reasonable doubt that Valerie had not been defending her grandson, but had indeed intended to kill her husband, Tom Starwood got up.

'The prosecutor here has told you a story about what he thinks happened in the Marsh kitchen on the evening of October 26,' he said to begin his closing argument. 'But that's all it is – a story. Because Mr Matheny wasn't *in* the Marsh kitchen on the evening of October 26, and he doesn't really know what happened, he's just guessing, spinning a scenario to fit his version of the facts. But there are two people who *were* in that kitchen and who *do* know what happened. And you heard from both of them. Justin Marsh told you that his grandfather had been drinking all day, and had worked himself into a towering rage over something that night. And he further told you that the man was kicking him and punching him when his grandmother came into the kitchen. He also told you that his grandmother shouted

472

at her husband to stop, but that her husband ignored her. And he told you that he didn't know whether his grandfather was going to kill him or not, but he was frightened enough to think he might. Ladies and gentlemen, if *he* didn't know, how could his grandmother? How could Mr Matheny?'

Starwood took a few steps toward the jury.

'Valerie Marsh told you that, in her mind, she believed her husband was going to kill Justin,' he continued. 'Given the history of this family, is that so unreasonable? For over forty years, Valerie lived with Jack Marsh's abuse. She stood by, in helpless horror, while his actions caused the death of one child and drove away all the others. She promised herself she would never let that happen to Justin. She made her husband go to a psychiatrist, and for years, things were all right. But then the psychiatrist died, and then things weren't all right. And when she came into the kitchen on the night of October 26, and saw her husband kicking and punching and threatening her grandson, she had every reason to believe that he was going to kill the boy. She has told you that when she picked up that frying pan she wasn't thinking about murdering Jack Marsh, she was thinking about saving Justin. And there hasn't been a shred of evidence presented at any time during this trial to tell you that it happened any other way.'

The attorney walked slowly along the length of the jury box, looking each juror in the eye.

'Soon, you're going to go into the jury room to begin your deliberations. Now, I'm not going to ask you to put yourselves in Valerie Marsh's shoes and walk around in her life for a while, because I'm not sure it's possible for anyone to do that who hasn't lived with the kind of violence that she has. I'm simply going to ask you to think about Valerie Marsh's life, as she knew it, a life filled with violence and secrecy and fear. And I'm going to ask you to think about who Valerie Marsh really is . . . a person who was brought up in a faith and a generation where girls were raised to be obedient, and where wives were taught to be subservient to their husbands, to support them, and to keep their families together, no matter what. For more than forty years, Valerie tried to do that. She tried her best. Should the fact that she failed now be held against her?'

Starwood suddenly stopped his pacing and turned to face the jury as a whole.

'So what do we do with her?' he asked them all with an elaborate shrug of his shoulders. 'Do we send her to prison for the rest of her life because she was too weak to save her children . . . or because her religion prevented her from divorcing a violent husband . . . or because she was raised to believe that it was not only her place but her duty to take his abuse without complaint or criticism? Do we want to send her to prison for the rest of her life because we know, without any doubt, that *we* would have handled things differently?'

He paused for a moment to look each of the jurors in the eye. 'Or do we send her home,' he concluded, his voice suddenly soft, 'because on that night, at that moment, she had every reason to believe that her husband was going to kill her grandson, and after forty-three years, she was finally strong enough to stop him?'

2

The jury was out for two hours. When word came, at five minutes past five in the evening, that there was a verdict, no one was more startled than Tom Starwood.

'It's too soon,' he murmured to Ricky. 'Much too soon.'

'What does that mean?' With permission from his boss and Carolyn's blessing, Ricky had flown down from Kodiak the day before the trial had begun. It was his third trip to the Bay Area since October.

'It means I didn't think the case was that open-and-shut. I thought it would take them more time to go over all the evidence and to think everything through. I hoped they would at least try to understand what your mother's journey has been like. I hoped they would consider the circumstances.'

'The fact that it's so quick – is that good or bad for us?' Marianne asked. She, too, had been shuttling back and forth since October.

The attorney wagged his head. 'I don't know,' he said.

Marianne had been horrified by what she heard during the trial. She remembered the times she had come to the Marsh home, after the miscarriage, after Ricky was born, and she remembered the year that Valerie had spent in the sanitarium after Priscilla had died. But Jack had always seemed so solicitous, and Valerie had always pleaded such clumsiness that she had never put it together.

'Was it as bad as the lawyer made it sound?' she asked Ricky.

'It was worse,' he said.

'Wasn't there anyone she could go to for help?'

'She had her priest,' Ellen said. 'But I don't think she ever told him. I don't think she ever told anybody.'

Marianne sat with her sister for hours each day after court, holding her hand. 'If we had only known, Tommy would have killed him for you,' she said.

Valerie hadn't moved. She was still in the same place at the defense table that she had been in two hours earlier. Tom Starwood had come in several times, as had Ricky and Justin and Marianne and Ellen, to ask if she wanted anything, to see that she was all right. She didn't. She was. She smiled at them gently.

'Don't worry about me,' she said. 'I'm fine.' But of course she wasn't fine, and they knew it, even if she didn't.

In the quiet before the storm broke, Valerie sat in the darkened, empty courtroom and wondered, when all was said and done, who really knew what was in her heart and mind that night, at that moment. Because that's what this trial had been all about, knowing . . . or guessing.

The lawyers who had argued the case certainly didn't know, nor did the judge or the jury, nor her family or her friends. She was the only one who knew the truth of it, and that's what made this whole proceeding seem so surreal. Because it wasn't about what had actually happened that night, it was about what could or couldn't be proven had happened, about what the jury saw when they looked at her, and about what they thought when they looked at the evidence. And none of that, she knew, really had anything to do with what she had been thinking when she picked up that frying pan and swung it at her husband.

She had had a lot of time to consider what she had done, eight long months, during which she rarely left the house, and seldom spoke to anyone outside the family. Then, during the trial, when the circumstances of Jack's death began to leak out, she saw shock on the faces of her neighbors and the people she came in contact with on the one afternoon that she stopped at the market.

'Did this mild-mannered woman we thought we'd known for so many years murder her husband?' they seemed to be wondering.

And she knew that the moment her back was turned, the whispers would begin. Of course, no one outside the family knew the whole ugly story, for which she was most grateful, but there was enough in the fact that a wife had killed her husband to keep the tongues wagging.

It was impossible to work. As the news got around, her business dropped off, and she had to let one of her assistants go. It was a difficult time, but she didn't blame anyone.

For some reason, the one person who seemed totally undisturbed by the revelations that were being meted out on an almost daily basis in the local newspaper was Dennis Murphy. On the few occasions that Valerie had to go to the pharmacy, he was always unfailingly kind, and although he never spoke of it directly, and had no way of knowing all the facts, he treated her almost as though he understood and even in some way approved of what she had done and why she had done it.

'It's so good to see you, Mrs Marsh,' he would say, giving her a warm smile. 'And how is everything going with you?'

'I'm taking it one day at a time, Mr Murphy,' she would reply, trying to smile back.

'That's as much as we can hope for.'

'I suppose so.'

One day, before the trial began, he had come out from behind the counter, and looking at her almost shyly, had cleared his throat. 'I want you to know,' he had said, 'that if there's ever anything I can do for you, anything at all, I would consider it an honor.'

Valerie was a little embarrassed by his kindness, but knowing that there was someone outside her immediate circle who was not judging her too harshly, and finding her wanting, really went a long way toward making up for the others.

The courtroom was quietly filling back up. Court personnel were taking their places, the clerks at their tables below the bench, the bailiff by the door. Spectators were slipping back into their seats, their voices muffled. Tom Starwood took his chair at the defense table beside Valerie. Stuart Matheny and his assistant returned to their positions on the prosecution side. Only after everyone was assembled did the judge come through the door to the left of the bench and lower himself into his seat.

'Let's have the jury,' he said.

The bailiff crossed to the door to the right of the bench and opened it. Everyone watched as the eight women and four men filed into the jury box and sat in their assigned armchairs.

Perhaps Tom Starwood stared at them the hardest, trying to read an expression here, a body movement there, anything that would indicate which way they were going to go. Two of the jurors looked at Valerie. The rest did not. His heart sank.

'Members of the jury,' the judge said, 'I am told that you have reached a verdict in this matter.'

A woman in her late fifties stood up. 'Yes, Your Honor,' he replied.

The clerk took the jury form from her and handed it up to the judge. He glanced at it and passed it back. The clerk then returned it to the jury foreperson. There wasn't a sound in the courtroom.

'Will the defendant please rise?'

Valerie tried to stand, but her legs had suddenly turned to jelly, and Starwood had to physically lift her to her feet and hold her upright with his arm around her waist.

'All right, Ms Foreperson,' the judge inquired, 'how does the jury find?'

Starwood held his breath.

The woman opened the paper and cleared her throat. 'On the charge of murder in the second degree,' she said in a soft but clear voice, 'we the jury find the defendant, Valerie Marsh . . . not guilty.'

There was a collective gasp in the courtroom. Starwood, still holding his breath, tightened his grip around Valerie's waist, because they were only halfway there. The jury might have rejected the idea that Jack's death was premeditated, but they could still conclude that it was intentional.

'On the charge of manslaughter in the first degree,' the jury foreperson continued as soon as everyone had quieted down, 'we find the defendant . . . not guilty.'

Justin let out a hoot. Ricky punched his left hand with his right fist. Ellen said a quick prayer. Marianne smiled and nodded. Connie Gilchrist and Lil McAllister hugged each other. Stuart Matheny sagged in his seat. Tom Starwood let out his breath and let go of Valerie, who promptly fell back into her chair, so numb that he wasn't even sure she had heard the verdict.

'It's over,' he whispered to her.

She looked up at him and he saw tears in her eyes. 'No, it's not,' she said. She looked at the jury. 'It's over for them, and it's over for you, but I still have to answer to God for what I've done.'

3

Valerie turned over and glanced at the clock on the table beside her bed. It was after eight, long past time for her to have been up. She had heard Justin moving around an hour ago, and told herself that he needed breakfast, but she hadn't moved, and now the house was quiet, which meant he had already left for school.

She pulled the covers up over her head. It was so much easier to hide, and she had been doing so for the past four days, ever since the verdict that had set her free had come down. For the four days before that, while her whole life was being exposed to the world, in the most horrific way possible, she didn't know how she would ever be able to walk into the bank or the market or the pharmacy again. The last thing she wanted was to talk about it, and she knew it was all anyone else would *want* to talk about. And if they couldn't talk about it to her face, then they would most surely talk about it behind her back. She shuddered under the covers.

It had been hard enough to talk to Connie, who had been in the courtroom the whole time, and had heard firsthand every gruesome detail.

'I never intended anyone to know,' she said when she couldn't avoid it any longer. 'I was raised to believe that private things were meant to be kept private.'

'I think on some level I knew, anyway,' Connie

replied. 'Probably for the very reason that you never talked about what went on in your life, like most people do. But I don't think I ever understood how bad it really was. Or maybe I just didn't want to know.'

'And now everyone knows,' Valerie said sadly. 'Now absolutely anyone can peer into my life and judge me for what I did or didn't do, whether they understand it or not. I think maybe that's the part that hurts the most.'

'The jury came down on your side,' Connie reminded her.

'Yes, but they made a legal judgment, not a moral one.'

'It doesn't matter,' Connie said firmly. 'You can't hide here forever. Among other things, you have a business to run.'

'What business?' Valerie retorted. 'Last time I looked, customers were deserting in droves.'

'Well, according to Judy, you had three calls in just the last week.'

Valerie blinked. 'Really?'

'Really.'

Thinking on it now, Valerie knew that Connie was right. She couldn't hide in the house forever. Sooner or later, she was going to have to go out in the world and take whatever was coming to her. The clock now read eight-thirty. With a groan, she threw off the covers and got out of bed.

'Oh, you just have no idea how glad I am to see you!' Judy exclaimed when Valerie came through the door of the bridal shop at nine-thirty. 'I've got two sick kids at home, the phone is ringing off the hook, and Nicole Deavers has been in absolute tears over her neckline.'

Valerie smiled. Nicole's wedding was in August. One of the few clients not to jump ship, she had changed her mind twice already, first wanting a high neckline, and then wanting a low neckline. And now there was no telling what she had in mind. 'I'll call her,' Valerie said.

'And I know I told Connie we had three new customers,' Judy went on. 'But now there are four.'

It was almost five before she could get away from the shop, with several errands yet to run. Or maybe she had delayed on purpose. She managed to get to the bank just before closing, making her deposit by autoteller rather than going inside. Next, she picked up a few things at the market, keeping her head down, and trying not to notice the stares that followed her. Finally, she headed for the pharmacy, the little bell over the door tinkling gaily as she opened it.

'Oh, how nice it is to see you out and about, Mrs Marsh,' Dennis Murphy said, his face lighting up with the warm, genuine smile he always reserved for her. 'And what can I do for you today?'

'Justin needs his acne prescription refilled, Mr Murphy,' she replied.

'I'll get that for you right away,' he told her. He went into the back room and came out a few moments later with the medication and a single red rose. 'Something for Justin, and something for you, if you'll allow me,' he said shyly. 'It's my first bloom of the season, you see, and I brought it in today, thinking I just might like to give it to someone.'

'Why, Mr Murphy, thank you,' Valerie murmured, actually blushing. She remembered the bouquets that Jack used to bring her, and what they had signified, and she looked up at the pharmacist and smiled. 'It's a beautiful rose,' she said.

He really was a very sweet man. He was also very

attractive, and Valerie found herself wondering idly why he had never remarried.

Connie had seen Valerie drive off this morning, and had waited, in truth, somewhat impatiently for her return, hurrying across the vacant lot the minute she saw Valerie turning into her driveway. 'So, how horrible was it?' she asked.

'It wasn't as horrible as I thought it would be,' Valerie had to admit. 'Most everyone was very nice.' Her eyes twinkled. 'Especially Mr Murphy.'

'You mean the Coast's most eligible widower?' Connie asked.

'Yes. He even gave me a rose. He said it was the first from his garden.'

'Well, well, well,' Connie crowed. 'Now that should be good for a paragraph or two in the local rag.'

'What's in the local rag?' Justin asked, coming into the conversation. He was as happy as he had ever been. In two weeks, he would be out of school for the year, and two days after that, he would be on an airplane, on his way to Alaska, to spend the summer with his father.

'Mr Murphy down at the pharmacy gave your grandmother a rose,' Connie told him.

'A rose?' Justin echoed. 'Gee Grandma, that must mean he's sweet on you.'

'Oh stop it, both of you.' Valerie was embarrassed. She busied herself at the kitchen counter, making tea, so they wouldn't see that her cheeks were flushed.

'I told you it would be all right,' Connie asserted. 'I told you nobody would fault you for the awful things that Jack did. You only thought they would.'

'She's right, Grandma,' Justin confirmed. 'Nobody cares.' In fact, many of his classmates and most of his teachers had made a special point of coming up to him at school to tell him how happy they were about the verdict, and how sorry they were that his family had endured such sorrow, and how glad they were that it was finally over.

'I suppose you're both right,' Valerie conceded.

'Of course we are,' Connie declared with a derisive chuckle. 'After all, who in his right mind would ever think you would kill your husband on purpose?'

Pulling teacups out of the cabinet, Valerie's back was turned, and so it was that neither of them saw the little smile that stole silently across her face.

AN ISOLATED INCIDENT

Susan R. Sloan

'A good place to visit – a great place to raise a family'

The motto that welcomes travellers to Seward Island, a lovely, quiet community off the coast of Washington State. But Seward has suffered an inexplicable tragedy. A fifteen-year-old girl from the island's most prominent family has been found brutally slain.

For Ginger, a young earnest detective, and for Ruben Martinez, the battle-weary Mexican-born chief of police, the murder is baffling. While building the case against their Jewish suspect, Ginger begins a relationship with Ruben that is at once forbidden and exhilarating. As her personal life collides with her job as a detective, she begins to have serious doubts about the work she is doing.

Is she the heroine of Seward Island – or part of a terrible rush to judgement? What is more important: to be a good police officer, or to obey the dictates of her conscience?

'A well-built and very powerful piece of fiction'
COSMOPOLITAN